Praise for Kerrigan Byrne and her captivating novels

"The dark, violent side of the Victorian era blazes to life as a caring, competent heroine living under the radar is abducted by a notorious crime lord with wonderfully gratifying results in this exceptional and compelling vengeance-driven romantic adventure."
—*Library Journal* (starred review) on *The Highwayman*

"The romance is raw, edgy, and explosive . . . the path they take through adversity makes the triumph of love deeply satisfying." —*Publishers Weekly* on *The Highwayman*

"A truly mesmerizing series that highlights dangerous heroes who flout the law and the women who love them."
—*Library Journal* (starred review) on *The Hunter*

"Dramatic, romantic, and utterly lovely." —*BookPage*

"Byrne is a force in the genre."
—*RT Book Reviews* (Top Pick!) on *The Highwayman*

"Romantic, lush, and suspenseful."
—Suzanne Enoch, *New York Times* bestselling author

"A passionate, lyrical romance that takes your breath away."
—Elizabeth Boyle, *New York Times* bestselling author

"Beautifully written, intensely suspenseful, and deliciously sensual." —Amelia Grey, *New York Times* bestselling author

The
DUKE

KERRIGAN BYRNE

St. Martin's Paperbacks

THE DUKE

Copyright © 2017 by Kerrigan Byrne.

All rights reserved.

For information address St. Martin's Press, 175 Fifth Avenue, New York, NY 10010.

ISBN: 978-1-250-11824-0

Our books may be purchased in bulk for promotional, educational, or business use. Please contact your local bookseller or the Macmillan Corporate and Premium Sales Department at 1-800-221-7945, ext. 5442, or by e-mail at MacmillanSpecialMarkets@macmillan.com.

Printed in the United States of America

St. Martin's Paperbacks edition / February 2017

St. Martin's Paperbacks are published by St. Martin's Press, 175 Fifth Avenue, New York, NY 10010.

10 9 8 7 6 5 4 3 2 1

For Monique
Who can see the forest for the trees.
And knows where to put them.

CHAPTER ONE

Imogen Pritchard shuddered as the fine hairs on her body prickled with alarm. The usually oppressive atmosphere of the Bare Kitten Gin and Dance Hall turned electric with danger, charging every nerve in her body with the awareness of an advancing predator. After placing her armful of empty ale and gin glasses on the sideboard, she palmed a knife from the utensil bin, concealing it in the folds of her skirts as she turned to face the threat.

A cadre of scarlet-clad soldiers filed through the door, their lean, young bodies taut with masculine restlessness. Their eyes gleaming with feral hunger. They reminded Imogen of a roving pack of wolves, licking their chops and smiling their sharp-fanged smiles in anticipation of a macabre feast.

Since she'd been forced to work at the Bare Kitten, Imogen's instinct for peril had been honed as sharp as the sabers hanging from the soldier's waists. And these men, these young wolves, were on the hunt for trouble, only waiting—*straining*—to be unleashed by one affirmative gesture from their alpha.

As dangerous as they might prove to be, she knew at once that the young soldiers, now fanning into an arc, hadn't been the source of her internal alarm.

Their *leader* had.

He was a point of disturbing quietude in their chaotic energy. He rose head and shoulders above them, looking down upon all in his path by the sheer necessity of his towering height. *His* was the iron fist that held them in check. *His* was the will upon which they lived or died. *His* was the command they executed without question.

And well he knew it.

Imogen couldn't remember glimpsing such a haughty brow before, nor such astonishingly handsome features. The structure of his face would have been ideal fodder for the Greek sculptors. They'd have used their most precise tools to carve the aristocratic features, almost perfect in their symmetry, from only the best stone. Her fingers tightened around the knife, though they itched for her paintbrushes. She'd paint his long body in great, rigid strokes and broad, bold lines.

A stab of recognition pierced her. She'd seen him somewhere before, surely. Normally, a unique color palette such as his would have clung to her memory. It was as though God had sculpted him out of precious metals. His skin was brushed with a golden hue, his hair shone with a darker, more phosphorous accumulation of bronze, and his eyes, too luminous to be brown, gleamed in the dim lantern light like two smoldering copper ingots as they surveyed every shadow and nook of the great room.

That gaze landed on her and didn't waver for an uncomfortably long time. His expression never changed from stony and assessing. Though something about the strain between his eyebrows, and the slack in what must have been a normally rigid jaw painted the hint of an emotion that bewildered her.

Was he . . . exhausted? Or sad?

As Imogen struggled to breathe, she became *quite* certain they'd never met before. She'd have remembered sharing the same room with him, let alone being introduced. And yet, she'd had a chance to admire the sharp, patrician nose. She'd traced the barbaric cheekbones and wide, square jaw that created the perfect frame for the acerbic slash of his hard lips.

But where?

Beneath the weight of his unrelenting stare, she found herself identifying with the deer chosen by the alpha to cull from the herd and take to ground. Retreating, she turned on her heel and almost ran into Devina Rosa.

"*Mierda,* but it's going to be a long night," she complained, tossing her sable curls and knocking back someone's half-finished gin. Imogen had never been certain if Devina was her real name, or merely what the Spanish harlot called herself.

"Aye, it is at that." Heather, a freckled buxom Scotswoman, agreed while adjusting the line of her bodice to reveal more of her generous breasts. "I know men with their marching orders when I see them. They'll try to fuck their fear into us tonight."

"I'll fetch extra oils." Devina sighed.

"And *I'll* get them drunk," Imogen offered.

"See that ye do, Ginny." Heather called her by the moniker she used while working in this house of ill repute. "Make yourself at least *somewhat* useful."

Imogen barely registered the bitterness in her words

anymore. She knew many of the girls didn't at all like the understanding she'd forged with their proprietor, stipulating that she didn't have to spread her legs as they did.

"If we're lucky, a few of them will be afflicted with the Irish curse and we can still get our money off of 'em," Heather mused.

"You mean del Toro will get our money." Devina spat and cast a mutinous look at her pimp, and the owner of the Bare Kitten, who had to turn sideways to avoid knocking over chairs and patrons in his exuberance to welcome the newcomers.

The women only dared to make soft murmurs of displeasure, lest he overhear.

"What's the Irish curse?" Imogen whispered her query to Devina, who barked out a very indelicate chortle.

"It's a dead-drunk cock, ye daft cow," Heather answered for Devina with a melodramatic roll of her eyes. "It's when they've had too much so trying to tup them is like trying to stab someone with a rope, ye ken?"

"Yes," Imogen muttered, blushing furiously. "Your explanation is *quite* sufficient, thank you." She dared a glance at the soldiers, who followed Ezio del Toro's corpulent frame to the corner reserved for only their most important guests. Frowning, Imogen wondered what for. An Italian immigrant, del Toro had no fondness for men in any kind of uniform, nor was he particularly patriotic.

Why then the special treatment?

Del Toro plucked Flora Latimer as she sashayed by, proudly advertising the abundant flesh she had on display. Her eyes widened in astonished increments as he breathed orders into her ears. By the time he'd finished and shoved her toward the sideboard where Imogen and the others lingered, she resembled a big, blue-eyed owl.

"You'll never guess 'ew just walked in," she tittered, flushed with excitement. "Though what 'e's doing in Soho, I couldn't begin to imagine. Don't get much of 'is like 'ere."

"Spit it out, ye crooked whore, we're not about to be guessing," Heather demanded.

"See that one there?" Flora pointed at the officer who folded his long frame into a chair at the head of the table. "The tall one wot looks like a fallen angel?"

They all nodded, not wanting to interrupt her long enough to point out that a man such as he was impossible to miss.

"Well, your eyes be feasting on Collin *sodding* Talmage, fresh from the funeral of his father and brother. Del Toro tells me 'e's leaving at dawn for his final service to the crown before 'e returns to take 'is seat as the Duke of Trenwyth."

Of course. That was why he'd been so familiar. His story was inescapably sensational. His father, the late Duke of Trenwyth, his mother, the duchess, and their heir apparent, Robert, had all been killed when a locomotive derailed near the French Alps, leaving behind their second child, Harriet, and their youngest, Collin. His likeness had been on the front page of every paper and periodical for a week. Lord, but they'd never done him justice, hadn't been able to capture the potent masculinity that draped like a royal mantle from his wide shoulders.

And a royal he nearly was. Some distant Hanoverian mixed in with an ancient family from Cornwall, directly related to their own dear Queen Victoria. It certainly made sense that he'd descended from those fierce Germanic barbarian hordes that kept Rome at bay so long ago. She could see it in his bone structure, in the way he surveyed his surroundings, as though he'd already conquered them.

He'd looked at *her* like that.

Furthermore, she'd been right. It was sadness she'd glimpsed on his features. A sadness he valiantly concealed.

"No time to dawdle." Flora bustled them in the direction of the table. "Del Toro said it's all hands on deck tonight, and that every man at that table must leave 'ere feeling like it's 'is birthday. Especially His Grace, as 'e's footing the entire bill."

Simultaneously, the women turned and checked their reflections in the gilded mirror above the sideboard. Even Imogen adjusted her dark wig and made certain her lip rouge was fresh and even. It didn't really matter what she looked like, so long as she kept the drinks coming. She wasn't a prostitute, only part of the serving staff, someone to look at, someone to sneer at and grope, but never anything beyond that.

Such was the deal she'd struck with del Toro, that she work at night in the Bare Kitten for as long as it took her to pay off her late father's gambling debts. She toiled here, even handing over her gratuities to the loathsome man, and then kept her mother and younger sister, Isobel, housed and fed with her job as a nurse at St. Margaret's Royal Hospital.

"Ye heard her." Heather dug her elbow into Imogen's side hard enough to cause her to stumble forward. "Stop yer lollygagging, and get them ready for us."

Imogen snatched an empty tray from the sideboard and clutched it to her middle, feeling the need for whatever scant protection it would provide.

She wound her way to the bar, where Jeremy Carson already had one pitcher of ale waiting, and was filling the next. At twenty or so, he was only younger than her by a few years, so Imogen felt guilty that she always thought of Jeremy as a boy rather than a man. His face, while clean, achingly young, and earnest, didn't at all match his scouse accent, which hailed from the Liverpool docks. "Looks to be a night to remember, in'nt Ginny? A duke in here and all."

"I can't believe it, myself." She placed the pitchers he provided and a stack of clean glasses on her tray. If she appreciated one thing, it was Jeremy's cleanliness and attention to the needs of her customers.

"What do you suppose a man like him orders to drink?" the barkeep speculated, flashing a conspiratorial smile full of crooked teeth that made him seem even younger.

Even on the worst day at the Bare Kitten, Imogen found it impossible not to return one of Jeremy Carson's smiles. "I'm about to go discover that very thing."

"Well, you take care around them tonight, Ginny," he warned with uncharacteristic gravity. "They say soldiers are to be feared and respected, even among those they protect."

Imogen didn't know who'd said that, as she'd never heard the saying before, but as she threaded through the sparsely occupied tables toward the duke and his rowdy compatriots on legs made of lead, she knew the truth of it.

Trenwyth adopted an expression of sardonic amusement, but rarely participated in the masculine conversation. Though she approached from his periphery, he glanced over at her the moment she moved, and didn't look away. His intense regard turned the innocuous walk from one side of the hall to the other into a perilous, heart pounding journey.

She only stumbled the once before she reached them,

almost upsetting her tray. Cheeks burning with mortification, she placed herself between Trenwyth and a black-haired Scotsman who would have been handsome but for the cruel gleam in his marble-black eyes. She meticulously poured the ale, avoiding the awareness of the duke as he watched her in complete silence.

That accomplished, she opened her mouth to address them—*him*—and froze, her mind seizing in panicked fits and groping for her memory. Anyone in service worth the starch in their skirts knew to address the person with the highest rank and work their way down the line. But just *what* title should she use for Trenwyth? A duke was the highest peer of the realm not in the direct line of the royal family. They were generally addressed as *Your Grace*. When in uniform, a soldier's rank often superseded any other title, but Trenwyth's uniform frock coat was like none she'd ever seen before. The dominant color black, rather than the traditional scarlet, and red only adorned the sleeves and high collar. He had no hat with him to help her to guess. The stitched braiding about his cuffs and shoulders was intricate and fine and utterly foreign to her. He could have been anything from a captain to a colonel and she had no *sodding* idea which.

"Better ye close yer mouth, love, unless ye're advertising yer services," the dark Scot drawled. "In that case, we appreciate yer eagerness, but we'd like to drink first, if it's all the same to ye."

Imogen snapped her mouth shut so hard she worried that she'd cracked a tooth as the dozen men surrounding the table guffawed at her expense. A tremor of misery clutched at her, and she chased it away with the brightest smile she could possibly muster and aimed it at Trenwyth. *He,* at least, wasn't laughing.

"What—what would you like?" was all she could manage.

"What are you offering?" His question landed in her belly like hot coals tumbling out of the hearth. His mouth didn't move much when he spoke, his voice barely above a murmur, but the register was of such depth and resonance that it vibrated through her, spearing her chest with the duplicitous meaning.

Again she found herself without words or breath.

"No punch, sherry, brandy, or port at the Bare Kitten," the Scot answered for her. "Only the best ale brewed this side of the Thames, gin, absinthe, and whisky. A place for a *real* man, not a *gentle*man. But what they lack in their variety of alcohol, they *more* than make up for in their assortment of other vices. Is that not so, lass?" A sharp pinch of her backside brought a gasp and the prick of tears behind her eyes.

Imogen turned and placed her tray in between herself and the Scot, baring her clenched teeth at him in what she hoped del Toro interpreted as a smile. "It is *indeed*, sir," she said stiffly, eyeing her astute employer as he glared daggers at her in a warning to behave.

This was turning into a disaster, she could feel it.

"Ye can call me Major Mackenzie, and that's not just a title, it's a promise." He cupped himself lewdly as the table erupted with hilarity. "One that will be verified later when ye are unable to walk."

Imogen's breath whooshed out of her in a great gasp when she was abruptly seized around the waist. She lost her feet from beneath her and fell backward, panicking as she was pulled down onto Trenwyth's knee, landing in a heap he controlled with his immense strength.

This seemed to greatly entertain everyone at the table

except, of course, for Major Mackenzie, whose features tightened with mutiny.

Instantly she became rigid, preparing to spring back to her feet and retreat to the safety of the bar. She'd done it before, and used a limp, boneless sort of squirming to avoid the grapple of many a drunkard.

But none as big as this, none so intensely solid and unyielding.

"Don't. Move." The hard command froze Imogen in place, and she brought her chin to her shoulder, looking up in slack-jawed astonishment to assess just how much danger she was in from Trenwyth.

His eyes lit with perilous fire, the copper glowing in the forge of his temper, but he didn't spare her a glance, nor did he speak another word. His unflinching stare captured and held that of Major Mackenzie's with silent dominance. The air thickened, threatening to smother her in masculine challenge. Muscles tensed beneath her, around her, until she feared if he flexed any further, she might be crushed. Imogen held absolutely still, careful not to draw the notice of these two wolves, lest they rip her in half.

Major Mackenzie was the one to break eye contact, glancing down at the table.

Trenwyth's arm about her waist relaxed, but he didn't release her. "I'll have whisky."

"A whole case ought to do it," a young lieutenant with a dark but sparse mustache chuckled. "It'll at least whet our appetites for other pleasures the night may provide."

Imogen nodded and hurried to stand, finding herself pulled tighter against the duke. Her legs were braced on either side of his knee, her back ramrod straight, straining to keep her body away from his torso.

"In order for me to fetch your drinks," she began gently, "you'll have to let me up."

After a silent pause, he made a derisive sound from behind her, and the sweet-apple smell of brandy drifted to her from his breath.

He'd already been drinking.

Instead of letting her go, he gestured to del Toro who hovered at a discreet distance and hurried over as fast as his short legs could heft the rest of him.

"We'll have your finest whisky. As many bottles as it takes." This elicited hearty delight from his men.

Imogen could see del Toro counting his profits in his head. "We've just received a case of Ravencroft's famous Scotch."

"Make mine gin," Major Mackenzie snarled. "I'd rather drink fetid water from the Thames than another drop of Ravencroft Scotch."

"I say, Hamish, old boy." The mustached lieutenant addressed the major. "Isn't Ravencroft a Mackenzie?"

The major said nothing, though his knuckles turned white with strain.

"That's right, Thompson," another soldier heckled. "Marquess Ravencroft, the Demon Highlander, himself, is Hamish's *younger* brother."

"Younger brother?" Thompson lifted his eyebrows in surprise. "That would mean you're—"

"A bastard," Hamish finished darkly. "Want to find out just how much of a bastard I can be?"

"Enough," Trenwyth clipped quietly, the command effectively ending all conversation. "Scotch for the table, and a gin for my friend the major."

Hamish threw a grateful, if brooding, glance at Trenwyth from beneath his dark brows. The tension dissipated as Imogen was forgotten by the surly, middle-aged Hamish Mackenzie.

"We can only afford the younger Scotch, mind you, but it's yours for the taking, as is anything *else* my establishment can offer you." Del Toro gestured at the women posing across the bar with far more practiced and inviting smiles than hers aimed at the men.

"Excellent." Trenwyth's brusque way of speaking appealed to Imogen, though she couldn't say why. "It seems the lads are eager for companionship."

Murmurs of enthusiastic agreement passed around the table as the famous "kittens" of Lower St. James's Street wound their way to the table with audible purrs. To Imogen's surprise, Heather gave Major Mackenzie a wide berth and look of reluctance, choosing to lean across a young man on the opposite side of the table. Imogen couldn't think of a time she'd truly seen the bawdy woman afraid before. Major Mackenzie had spoken of the place as though he'd been here often, though Imogen couldn't say she recognized him. Perhaps Heather did. Perhaps she'd even had a negative experience with him. Imogen's own intuition jangled uncomfortably in his presence, alerting her that he was a man capable of the most terrible things.

And yet, so was Trenwyth, of that she was certain.

"You heard him, Ginny," del Toro said tightly, breaking into her thoughts. "Fetch the drinks."

Imogen nodded, eager to comply, but remained trapped by the iron grip of Trenwyth's arm about her waist.

"She stays where she is." Trenwyth's statement, delivered pleasantly enough, brooked no argument. Though his accent was that of the noblest of men, a cold note of steel threaded through the highborn gentility. He was a man who needn't raise his voice to be obeyed. "*She* serves no one but me tonight."

Imogen could feel her eyes widen and her lips compress in alarm as Trenwyth tugged the serving tray out of her talonlike grasp and idly handed it to del Toro.

"As you wish, Your Grace." Her employer bowed over his large belly and snapped his fingers at the staff. He turned away without giving Imogen a second look.

She hadn't been aware of her trembling until Trenwyth leaned forward, pressing his lips very close to her ear.

"Ginny." The word rumbled all the way down her spine and skittered along her skin until every hair rose to vibrating attention. "That is your name?"

"Yes, Your Grace." She whispered the lie. It was her "kitten" name. It was who she became at night in this dim, overwrought, and garish place frequented by poor bohemians, soldiers, and wealthy merchants alike. But rarely nobility. His sort had places like Madame Regina's and other such pleasure palaces that certainly didn't reek of absinthe and stale tobacco.

"Don't let's use formalities, Ginny." He exhaled against her ear again, and she had to bite down on her lip against the strange and shivery sensations he'd elicited. "Don't call me Your Grace again tonight, everyone else has agreed not to."

She lowered her chin in what was supposed to be a nod. "What should I call you then?" she queried, instinctively turning her head toward him, not realizing how close it brought their lips to one another's until they almost met.

"Those closest to me call me Cole," he informed her mouth.

"But . . . I am not close to you."

Tightening his arm around her once more, he grasped her hip with his other hand, and pulled her up his startlingly long and muscled thigh with a slow, languid move, until she straddled him as high as his leg would allow. Even through her skirts and petticoats, the movement created an unfamiliar friction against her sex that elicited an alarming but not unpleasant pressure. He didn't stop until the curve of her bottom settled against his lap. She was aware of a surprisingly insistent cylindrical shape pressed against her. She'd worked at the Bare Kitten long enough to know *exactly* what it was.

"Far be it from me to contradict a lady, but I beg to differ. You and I are very close, indeed."

Imogen hadn't been aware how tense and inflexible she'd remained until the aching tremble of her muscles became unbearable. "I am not a lady." She'd meant it as a statement of fact, but it escaped as a lament.

"That is precisely why I've picked you." Gently, he brushed the curls of her raven wig to the side, and dropped a casual kiss on her bare shoulder as a bottle of Scotch and a couple of pristine glasses were placed in front of them.

Imogen felt that kiss with every part of her body.

"Your job tonight is to make certain I don't see the bottom of that glass and to *disagree* with everything I say, can you do that, Ginny?" The good-humored manner in which he delivered his orders was underscored with something else. Something desperate and dismal.

"Disagree with you?"

"Yes," he murmured, his eyes again arrested by her lips. "It'll be quite novel for someone not to do everything I tell them to."

"Of course, Your—" She caught herself in time. "Of course . . . Cole." Saying his name lent even more intimacy to the moment, so she turned away and poured him a healthy glass of whisky.

"There's a good girl," the lieutenant called to her. "Get him soused enough to tell us where he's off to."

"Knowing would be your peril, not mine," Trenwyth quipped, tossing back his drink with one great swallow. "All I can say is that Major Mackenzie is going with me."

The lieutenant laughed. "You're a spy, admit it," he cried good-naturedly. "Secret missions, the matchless uniform, and they're not letting you stay home despite . . ." The man seemed to catch himself before he brought up the funeral. "Despite the circumstances. I mean, you're a duke now, dash it all."

"I thought we weren't discussing that." Once again Trenwyth's tone was deceptively mild, but the lieutenant blanched. "Besides," the duke continued wryly. "They're not secret missions if everyone apparently knows about them."

"We find out after the fact," another officer stated. "You're gone, and then we catch wind of the assassination of a tribal warlord in the desert and you return looking quite brown claiming to have been on holiday."

"And don't forget!" The lieutenant was back in the conversation, encouraged by Trenwyth's enigmatic smirk. "That time you left and the frightening business in the Alps suddenly resolved. I was told by a friend at the military hospital in Switzerland that you were treated there for frostbite just then." He made noises as though he'd won some sort of athletic competition, receiving congratulations from his compatriots.

"I heard the Demon Highlander, himself, claim that you were just as deadly as he was and twice as skilled," someone else jibed.

"He was being kind," Trenwyth said modestly.

"Have ye met my brother?" Hamish asked around a tittering Devina, who'd draped herself across his lap. "He's never kind."

Trenwyth let out a sound that could have been mirth or bitterness, it was impossible to tell. When he leaned forward to have his glass refilled, Imogen had the bottle at the ready. "You don't believe them, do you?" he whispered to her as though they shared a private joke while she poured him another.

"Not a word," she replied, granting him the first genuine smile she'd given all night.

"I knew you were clever." She didn't tense half so much as he again brushed his lips across her shoulder, this time closer to her neck.

Over the course of the next hour or so, Imogen's back relaxed by incremental degrees Eventually, she allowed her shoulders to lean against him as the men turned guessing his next assignment into a drinking game. The large buttons of his coat dug into her back, so she straightened again. Shifting her effortlessly, he unfastened the buttons with one hand and divested himself of his coat, settling her back into the circle of his arms as though she'd often been there. The movement increased her body's awareness of him a thousandfold. Also, she noted, most men of her acquaintance weren't half so thoughtful, and her opinion of him rose incrementally.

Against her back, his wide chest was hard as iron and warm; with every movement she could feel naught but honed muscle bunch and flex beneath her. She even caught herself enjoying the way he smelled, like the cedar chest where he, no doubt, stored his dress uniform and good sharp whisky, underscored by something she couldn't at all place. Something that couldn't strictly be identified nor reproduced, like the scent of a rainstorm or a perfectly ripe berry.

The men settled on Afghanistan as his next target, due to the trouble erupting there between Russia, Britain, and the Ottomans, and the drinking games dissolved into drunken stories, then into an abnormal amount of toasts. They toasted the queen, of course, and fallen comrades, living comrades, battles they won, battles they lost, ships they'd sailed on, and, most vehemently, women they'd loved. Imogen found it strange that they didn't toast the new Duke of Trenwyth, or his recently deceased family. Though, she supposed, he seemed to very much want to avoid the subject altogether.

Of course, it was not her place to say anything, but she found herself sneaking surreptitious glances over her shoulder at him. He didn't join the toasts, but he certainly drank to all of them. He didn't tell any stories, but he made the appropriate noises. He seemed pensive. Withdrawn. But his stunningly handsome features were always kind when he looked at her, and his touch was more casually sensual than demanding or tawdry.

That in itself was a pleasant change. Most men tended to become heavy-handed when they drank, pinching, slapping, or squeezing bits of her until she wished she had nothing feminine with which to draw their attentions. But Trenwyth's hands, while uncommonly large, were caressing as they occasionally tested her curves. He'd rest them in her skirts on her thighs, or slide them up her waist causing her heart to trill in her chest, though he'd stop just shy of her breasts, his fingertips barely grazing beneath them.

Still, it set her teeth, but not with disgust. With . . . something else altogether.

By now, half the men had disappeared through the curtain adjacent to the bar, behind which a long hallway with many doors stretched the length of the building. Those who went through those doors with one of the kittens paid del Toro first.

When Trenwyth adjusted his position, his leg rubbed against her so intimately, a stab of sensation caused her to gasp and clench her feminine muscles.

His thigh instantly tensed beneath her and, for a moment, Imogen was terrified that she'd offended him.

Until he did it again.

She had to reach out a hand to the table to steady herself against an assault of wicked pleasure.

His sex hardened against her backside once more, and he leaned up to gather her close. "I have a distinct feeling that you're quick tinder to set ablaze, aren't you?" His words slurred a little, but his movements were steady as one hand drifted down her waist and the other up her thigh, angling to meet in the middle.

Imogen caught his wrists, and he allowed her to hold him as though she had the strength to do so. "I'm compelled by your earlier directive to disagree," she said solicitously, mostly because she had no idea what he'd meant. His mouth quested behind her ear, down her neck, until he nibbled the slight rise of her muscle as it angled south down the column of her back.

Delicious shivers again erupted over her entire body, and she was unable to control the clenching of her thighs as a concerning rush of warmth pooled between her legs.

"It makes no matter to me." His voice was deeper than before, rougher, and her nipples tightened in response. "You could take as long as you like."

CHAPTER TWO

Swallowing around a tongue gone suddenly dry, Imogen tried with everything she had not to pant, though her lungs felt heavy. "Would you . . . like another drink?" Failing that, she handed him the half-full glass he'd set on the table, hoping to distract him.

He paused and pulled back, as though pondering the question.

"No." He answered with the careful diction of a man aware of his own inebriation.

"Then . . . is there aught else you need?" she queried. "I really should be getting back to my . . . to my duties."

"I've kept you for quite a while without recompense for your time," he said ponderously. "That must be why your . . . employer keeps glaring."

"Not at all," Imogen rushed to soothe him. Del Toro had been sending her warning looks, reminding her not to cock this up or it would be her hide.

Trenwyth's strength astounded her once more as he

lifted her bodily and settled her on the bench beside him as though rearranging a sack of potatoes. "Excuse me," he muttered, then stood and made his unsteady way toward del Toro.

Imogen was surprised he could walk at all, as he'd imbibed enough Scotch to drown an elephant. Every tense moment he and del Toro conversed was an eternity, but they seemed to come to an understanding that pleased them both. Trenwyth paid, and disappeared behind the curtain without a backward glance.

Imogen didn't take the time to wonder why a pang of disappointment deflated her before she rose and made her way toward the sideboard, meaning to pick up a tray and a cloth with which to start cleaning up.

Del Toro intercepted her, and the gleam in his eyes sent her heart plummeting into her stomach with a suspicion he quickly confirmed.

She cut him off at the pass. "You gave your *word* that I'd never have to—"

"That was before he gave me a twenty-pound note," del Toro marveled.

"Twenty pounds?" Imogen's legs gave out, and she plopped heavily into an unoccupied chair. "Surely you mean *two* pounds." Even *that* sum was an unheard-of price for a place like this. Only those at Covent Garden or Madame Regina's could charge two pounds a night.

Scratching at his thinning hair, del Toro produced the note, but wouldn't let her touch it. "I'd sell my own daughter for twenty pounds," he said without a modicum of shame. "Just think, this pays close to a third of what your father owes me."

Imogen glanced at the men playing the gambling tables, seized in the grip of a desperate hope. Twenty pounds was more than half a year's wages at the hospital. It would take her more than a year to earn that here. She had seventy and four pounds left of her father's debt to remunerate. It would save her a year of her life working in this miserable place. Leaving her sentence, as she'd come to see it, only two years rather than three.

It would only cost her virginity.

Though Trenwyth was ridiculously handsome and desirable, Imogen shook her head before she'd quite made the decision to refuse. By now, she'd given up all her childhood dreams of Continental travel and artistic exploration to care for her family, but she hadn't lost *all* hope of being able to live a normal life, eventually. She wanted to marry someday. Though he was an obsessive gambler, her father had once been a wealthy and respectable textile merchant. Her family still had many of his contacts, and she'd always thought that perhaps she'd marry a banker or a doctor, someone respectable.

But if she was no longer a virgin . . .

"I *can't*."

"*You will*." Del Toro was generally a soft-spoken man, but once his temper flared, he showed a dark and violent side that illustrated just how little he cared for the women in his employ. He beat them sometimes, if they fell out of line, and Imogen had lived in fear of the day he ever raised his hand to her.

"You don't understand, if I find myself . . . in trouble I'll lose my other position, and thereby my way of supporting my family." Supporting a child at this point was completely out of the question.

Del Toro shrugged, his chins wobbling with a disgusting ripple. "My kittens will teach you a few *new* positions, and you can work here." He chuckled at his own terrible pun before sneering at her with derision. "Oh, I forget, you are too good for us, too reputable to be seen with us during the day."

"That isn't what I—"

"I wonder if Isobel would think herself too good for this place. I could send Bartolomeo and Giorgio to fetch her to me, just like I did you." Del Toro slid the bill beneath his nose, testing the scent of so much money.

"She's only just fifteen," Imogen gasped, a desperate fear winching the breath from her lungs. "You said you wouldn't bring her into this, that she and my mother would never know—"

"I've employed girls as young as thirteen before. And I made you that promise before I was handed twenty pounds." He shrugged. "What does your family think you do all night? Are they so stupid they don't *already* suspect that you are a whore?"

"I told them I work extra shifts at the hospital and give the money to you."

"It's *you* or your sister." His voice and color began to rise, heralding his dangerous temper. "You are getting old to be of much use to me for long, perhaps I will not need you for the two years it would take to work here, but *Isobel* is young and supple . . . It would be easy for me to turn her out, and there would be *nothing* you could do."

A sick weight landed upon her shoulders, compounding the exhaustion caused by working and living under such stress. At three and twenty, she was indeed beginning to age out of the profession. Not only that, she was dangerously close to becoming a permanent spinster.

Reaching down, del Toro grabbed her arm and yanked her to her feet, his fingers digging into her flesh with a painful pinch. "Get back there," he snarled, shoving her toward the curtain. "You do whatever he wants, and if he doesn't leave the most satisfied customer ever to pass through this door, I'll have my men ugly your face after they teach you some humility, so you'll be of no use to anyone."

Woodenly, Imgoen turned toward the curtain; its crimson and black arabesque design was faded and dingy from so many men tossing it aside on their way back to the bedrooms.

"Room seventeen," del Toro called after her.

Of course it was room 17. Only the best for the Duke of Trenwyth.

Room 17 was one of the very few suites abovestairs in the narrow, long building that housed the Bare Kitten. Climbing those stairs felt like scaling Kilimanjaro to Imogen, who was out of breath by the time she reached the top. Not because she was unused to stairs, but because her corset, combined with the band of fear squeezing her lungs, didn't allow her to properly inhale. Room 17 might as well have been the gallows. It wasn't that the man within didn't appeal to her his beauty was unparalleled— but it would mean that she'd truly become what she'd never imagined herself to be.

A prostitute.

Reaching for the latch, Imogen paused, placing a hand low on her belly where it seemed an entire flock of birds flapped and churned their wings in equal measure to the violent trepidation she felt.

She closed her eyes and sent a prayer for strength to a God who would condemn her for what she was about to do. Then she stepped inside, shutting the door on her innocence.

Trenwyth was already naked.

Her shock had her flattened against the door as she gaped at him with blatant stupefaction. As a nurse, Imogen had been privy to the nude male form before, and again as an artist. But *nothing* in her extensive experience had prepared her for the pure splendor of Collin Talmage. Not even when she'd been held against him did she comprehend the raw, corded strength he wielded. With his back to her, she was able to somewhat adjust to the sight of all that perfect bare flesh.

Before she was compelled to touch it.

One lantern sputtered dimly on the bedside table where he set a drink next to a ready decanter, completely unabashed by his own nudity. The shadows cast by the lone flame into the grooves of his long, taut muscles were just as tantalizing as the illumination.

"Would you like a drink?" He gestured to the golden liquid he'd abandoned. "I believe I've had quite enough."

He turned around, and Imogen couldn't have swallowed had liquid been poured straight into her gaping mouth. Somehow, she knew that Collin Talmage, the Duke of Trenwyth, had never in his *life* been afflicted with the Irish curse. His sex stood proudly erect from the sinewy definition of his lean hips. He glanced down, rather sheepishly, and flicked her a look full of pure, sinful invitation.

Surely he didn't mean to put that . . . *that* . . . inside of her. It wouldn't, *couldn't* possibly fit. Her mind recoiled, but her body . . . her *body* responded. She suddenly felt like a rosebud about to bloom, trembling with the instinct to open. To bare herself. The impulse frightened her enough that she wrapped her arms around her middle in a foolish attempt to hold together.

Glancing at the chair where he'd discarded his uniform, she noted the gleam of a veritable arsenal of weapons.

Two pistols, *seven* knives of alternating sizes, the saber, a strange-looking vambrace that must have been beneath his shirtsleeves, and . . . good Lord, was that a syringe? Just where had he stashed all those on his person?

Imogen glanced back at the duke with wide-eyed suspicion. What if he really *was* a spy?

He returned her wild gaze with a steady one. Carefully, without breaking eye contact, he lowered himself to the bed, his knees falling open slightly as he lounged. A lion at rest.

"Come to me," he said, holding his hand out to her.

Imogen could barely feel the legs that carried her to him, but somehow she traversed the shadows of the crimson room, until she stood before him as still as stone.

This close, she found it difficult not to become overwhelmed by his beauty. His relaxed posture was deceptive, she realized, as his muscles were coiled as tightly as a predator ready to spring. Though his expression remained inscrutable, a distinctive sense of leashed violence wove through the air between them, though his placid, enigmatic features never revealed it.

He released a breath he'd been holding too long, his eyes becoming heavy-lidded as his tongue snaked out to moisten lips gone dry.

He reached for her, and then seemed to change his mind. "Take that off," he commanded softly.

Struck by a shy uncertainty, she didn't believe that her fingers would be capable of the task.

"You could . . ." she offered hesitantly. "You could undress me, if you like."

"*You* wouldn't like that," he warned, shifting his position to angle slightly away from her.

"I—I don't mind. I'm to do whatever you ask."

"If I touch that dress, I'll shred it," he said tightly. "And I don't believe you're ready for that." How a man could manage to appear savage, bleak, and seductive at the same time was beyond her. But, in the end, it was the soul-haunting sorrow beneath the naked desire in his eyes that brought her fingers to the buttons of her scandalously low bodice.

His feral gaze latched onto the movements of her unsteady hands, and Imogen groped for something to say as she peeled her dress down her arms.

"Twenty pounds?" Her eyes closed in mortification. How vulgar and stupid it was to bring up money when you were being paid for fantasy.

"I didn't like Mackenzie's hands on you." His own hands curled as her dress slid in a heap to the floor, leaving her only in her corset, drawers, stockings, and slippers. "Then I realized it was because I wanted to put my hands on you. Only *my* hands. I could feel how warm you were all night against my thigh."

The memory apparently proved too much for him.

He sprang and she started, but the arms that pulled Imogen down to him were careful, if not gentle. Trenwyth was a man aware of his own strength. Used to tempering it, controlling it, and only unleashing it upon the deserving.

He split her thighs over his lap and, true to his word, he rent her undergarments with his big hands and tossed them to the floor. She was too astounded to make a sound, to do anything but kneel above him and hope her trembling bare thighs didn't give out. Without thinking, her hand gripped the unyielding flesh of his shoulders to steady herself.

Their eyes met and clung, her face only inches from

his. She didn't dare look down, couldn't think of the chill of the air against the heat of her most intimate flesh. Flesh she'd bared to no one before this night. Didn't want to see how close it was to the aroused column of his sex.

Dear God, she thought in a rush of panic, how could she bring herself to do this?

His hands gripped the span of her hips to steady her. Her muscles trembled and quivered beneath them, and he ran his thumb over the protuberance of her hip bone in a soothing gesture.

"Of all the torments I've experienced, and they've been many, the heat of your slit against my leg had to be the *most* pleasant torture yet." The unfettered depravity of his increasingly garbled words elicited a startled sound from her, one that he covered with a kiss.

Her mouth felt uncommonly soft beneath his hard lips. Her flesh and bones even more delicate against a body so hard and lean.

He reminded her how breakable she was and yet . . . she felt nothing but protected.

Desired.

His questing tongue tested the seam of her lips, and instinct drove her to let him inside. Crushing her against him, corset and all, he released a growl as his tongue conducted a wet exploration of her mouth. The sound vibrated up between their bodies, and somehow lent the night an even darker hue. Had she heard a sound like that elsewhere she'd have run from it, screaming for help. But now, like this, it thrilled through her, causing another of those unsettling spasms deep inside her as her sex clenched around its own emptiness.

Imogen thought she'd been kissed before, but she'd been utterly mistaken. His siege of her mouth went on and on until she lost her breath and didn't care. Her thoughts scattered like a flock of panicked birds chased out of their roost. Even inebriated, his skill with his mouth pushed her beyond her wits. He tasted of Scotch and sin, and Imogen wondered if intoxication was as contagious as a fever, because she felt quite funny.

Just when she thought there was no other place for him to lick, he would begin to suck and nip. To sample and savor. First her bottom lip, then the top before gently capturing her tongue. She thought she'd go mad from the busy sensations.

Eventually he relented, pulling his tongue away and dragging his mouth across hers in great, gentle sweeps, letting some of his evening stubble rasp at her tender lips.

His hands didn't remain idle. They tested the garters securing her stockings to her thighs. They spanned her hips again, apparently enjoying that particular part of her anatomy, and then molded to the curve of her bottom before reaching beneath and—

Imogen surged away and tried unsuccessfully to clamp her thighs shut as questing fingers found a wellspring of moisture between her legs.

"Hold still," he breathed out on a shudder.

Scandalized and overstimulated, Imogen blinked back a few confused tears. "You don't have to . . . We can just . . . get to it." She wanted—no—*needed* this to be over before she lost her nerve. A heated curiosity had bloomed within her, and crawled over her skin. She felt like a wanton. Not like a whore, but like a lover. And she knew whatever he did to her just now was utterly dangerous.

Dangerous, because she didn't want him to stop.

He'd awakened something, some wicked need, and she

knew that feeling anything but revulsion with him would only intensify her shame later.

He blinked her into focus, scrutinizing her with his unsettlingly astute eyes for someone in his state, while his hands steadied her at her waist. "I assume you don't have many . . . customers who care to give you pleasure."

Imogen bit her kiss-abraded lip before answering carefully. "I . . . can't say that I have."

His eyes warmed, melting the copper to a smoldering liquid. He pressed his nose against hers before kissing her lightly in an affectionate gesture that nearly undid her.

"Do you want to know why I chose you tonight? Why I paid the twenty quid? I mean, other than your exotic beauty, of course?"

He was being a flirt, but Imogen still couldn't stop the pleased blush from claiming her flesh.

"Your eyes." He reached up, running a thumb beneath where thick kohl liner accentuated the shape. "While they are lovely, they are tired. Strained. You looked as though you've had a rather difficult go of things."

Imogen swept her lashes down, disturbed that she'd given away so much. She pressed her lips together against the tide of tears his kindness threatened to unleash, and swallowed them down, nearly forgetting their intimate pose for a moment.

"I've had a rather trying week," he muttered. "I'm certain you've heard about it."

She nodded, a pang of sympathy permeating her own misery.

His finger trailed down her cheek, to her jaw, and across the bare expanse of her chest, encouraging her to look up at him again now that she'd composed herself.

Lord, but she'd never accustom herself to the beauty that assaulted her each time she saw his face.

"I came here tonight hoping to drink enough to forget . . ." His own eyes became suspiciously liquid, and he took his own moment to grapple with his composure. His voice was huskier as he continued, deeper, if at all possible. "I want us *both* to enjoy this indulgence. This oblivion. I want this night to be a reprieve . . . because the dawn brings everything back, doesn't it? Duty does not allow for sorrow or weariness. I'll have to go to—" He caught himself in time, clenching his teeth against words that would escape him. "It doesn't matter where I'm going. What I'm saying is that the world will churn on, despite what we've lost. Despite what we've gained . . . what we want or—don't want, in any case."

Brimming with empathy for the naked grief in his eyes, Imogen brought her hands to his face, cupping his hard jaw. The man had lost his family, and even the coldest soldier or spy had to mourn in his own way.

"Take your pleasure, Cole," she whispered. "Don't worry about mine."

He was right about one thing, no one else ever did.

He breathed out on a shudder. "Here." Grasping her hand, he guided it down between their bodies until he wrapped her fingers around the surprisingly hot flesh of his cock. Her small hand barely fit around the velvety skin encasing the rod of steel beneath.

Her eyes widened in alarm. What did he want her to do with it?

"Now you see," he said on a breathless groan. "It's better that I make you come. That I make you ready. Even the most experienced . . . ladies have difficulty sometimes."

Imogen swallowed her apprehension and pulled her fingers from around him.

Though she appreciated that he'd done his best to avoid referring to her as a whore.

His arms snaked around her as he pulled her close. "Let me," he commanded, and stole her breath with another kiss. "Let us *share* pleasure, as though we were lovers instead of strangers."

He didn't explore or caress her body again. Merely delved into the fine nest of hair between her legs and stroked into her folds with merciless fingers. Imogen gasped and trembled, but it was he who sucked a labored breath through his clenched teeth.

His other hand held her fast, again gripping the flesh of her hip while his rough-skinned fingers turned slick as her body coated them in desire. A lightning-quick pleasure speared her as he trailed past a cluster of sensation. He didn't linger there, but slipped over and through the folds with light, playful gestures.

Her belly became tight as an aching, pulsing void of need opened up within her womb. Unbidden, her hips followed his clever fingers, seeking after that first, arousing stroke again with undulating demand. He fondled and separated her, teased and tantalized her, all the while keeping her mouth occupied with his questing tongue.

Her breath came in gasps, then pants, and then little mewls of wordless delight as he finally stroked at the right spot again, and once again, until her fingernails bit into his shoulders as an insistent, burning pleasure began to seize upon her.

"Cole?" she whimpered, clutching at him, almost afraid of whatever it was that locked every muscle from her sternum down into uncontrolled pulses.

"Yes," he growled into her mouth. "Fucking come for me. That's it."

The gathering storm broke upon her with scream-provoking intensity. Tears sprang to her eyes as she curled around him, her thighs clenching his as though she rode a powerful steed rather than wave after wave of unimaginable pleasure. Convinced there was magic in his hands, she opened her mouth to tell him so, but all that escaped her was a low cry. Or maybe nothing. She couldn't tell. Or remember. Or care.

When it became too much, too intense, she bit down on the meat right below where his neck met his shoulder and he made that sound again. That dark, savage groan that became a growl in a chest as large and cavernous as his.

But he seemed to understand, as his ministrations gentled until his fingers only whispered across that bud of sensation in a tremor-inducing caress before letting his hand fall away.

"Christ, you're exquisite," he panted, his eyes a little unfocused, his skin flushed and his body one long knot of tension. "You're ready," he gritted out. "Now."

In one graceful move he lifted her, rotated them both, and tossed her onto her back. His body was so big on top of her, pressing her legs almost uncomfortably wide. She wanted to tell him to wait, to give her a moment, but he distracted her with another deep, long kiss.

He released unintelligible words into her mouth, and Imogen knew them to be harsh and filthy. His eyes had glazed over completely now, as though his wits had deserted him, leaving her with nothing but this beast of lust and need.

He lifted himself, arched his neck, and on a smooth, brutal thrust, he was inside her, ripping through the feeble barrier of her virginity as though it didn't exist, and separating muscles unused to intrusion. The sound he made was more roar than growl, and drowned out her whimper of protestation. Tears sprang to her eyes, and she bit down on her cheek hard enough to taste blood by the time he'd ceased his endless plunge.

Because of his height she buried her face in the crook of his neck, doing her best to breathe through the pain. To hide her tears, lest she displease him.

"Jesus," he cursed. "Tight."

He slid away and pushed forward again, this time gaining more ground, a hot, searing brand against her untried flesh. She could feel her body trying to adjust, molding around him.

"Too . . . tight . . ." he panted. His movements shortened, became less graceful and more frenzied. Her sex felt like a knot of tension and fire, though something beneath the discomfort whispered at the pleasure his hands had introduced her to. She wondered, as her body began to relax, as his penetrations became shallower, if that incomparable bliss would come for her again.

If *she* would come again.

With a low moan, his body seized and he pulled out of her, still pumping his sex between their bodies before great tremors rolled over him, forcing his head back with what looked like racking, almost painful convulsions as warm, wet moisture coated her hip.

Imogen turned her head to look away, feeling like an intruder on an intimate moment, even though that moment was her own. She watched the muscles of his arm, braced beside her head, as they clenched and flexed, forcing vivid veins to the surface of his straining skin. She'd never seen something so beautifully sensual in her entire life.

As with every violent storm, the aftermath hung heavy and silent as they each willed their bodies back under their control. He held himself above her, still but for his chest heaving against hers. She thought he'd whispered something like "Never." But the word was lost to the darkness.

It was done. What was left of her innocence had been taken. No, not taken.

Bought.

Imogen decided that the sacrifice of her virginity had been ultimately worth it. A few seconds of pain in trade for an entire year of freedom. For an entire lifetime of loneliness. For the safety of her sister.

For twenty pounds sterling.

Tenderly, Trenwyth bent to kiss her, and some of her dark thoughts dissipated. There had been pleasure too. Illicit, unimaginable pleasure wrought by his brutal, gentle, masculine, skilled hands.

With a groan, he lifted himself off her and reached for a cloth hanging from the basin. It was red, like everything else in this room, and would hide the blood of her virginity. Cleaning himself without bothering to look, he handed a second one to her, respecting her privacy as she wiped the leavings of his pleasure from her hip, grateful he'd taken precautions against pregnancy.

It wouldn't do to have the first child of the Duke of Trenwyth born the bastard of a prostitute.

She expected him to leave then, to dress and abandon her to the task of pulling herself together.

Instead, he prowled, completely nude, back into the

bed. He reached for her and unhooked the stays of her corset in a few rough, jerking motions.

"What are you doing?" she demanded, swatting at him ineffectually.

"This," he said by way of patient explanation, yanking her chemise off.

"Don't . . . what . . . you . . . Oh!"

Somehow completely bare, her arms clutched over her breasts, he dragged her up to the pillows like some loutish, ham-fisted beast, and settled her on her back.

She lifted a knee and crossed it over herself in an absurd attempt at modesty.

He looked at her then, just knelt above her, all naked sinew and strength, and watched her with those hot, languorous eyes. A possessive sound of satiation rumbled from his throat. Something undeniably masculine, and at once oddly bestial, both a purr and a growl, she thought.

Ceaselessly inquisitive hands roamed her languidly, found little intimate places she'd never before paid much notice. The divots beside her knee, the quivering skin beneath her belly button, the sensitive hollows of her visible ribs. Places she'd not considered sensual before this moment.

"You should eat more," he admonished, his attractive features arranging themselves with displeasure.

Imogen gave him a tight smile and nodded her complacency, biting her lip to keep from informing him that an empty larder and three empty bellies do not a voluptuous lover make. She'd love to eat more than scraps not fit for an alley cat. But that wasn't his concern, nor was it something she wanted to consider now. Hunger didn't present a problem at the moment. In fact, a sense of supreme satisfaction lingered in every organ and limb.

Trenwyth's hand curved over the slight swell of her hip exposed by her barely modest posture. He traced a little shape found on the swell of her buttock, a mark she'd had since birth.

"Has anyone ever told you this looks precisely like our island?" he asked, bending down to press delighted lips to the mark.

"No," she admitted shyly. No one but her mother had ever seen the shape, let alone remarked upon it, but it wouldn't do to tell him that.

"I do believe I just kissed you somewhere near Cornwall." His lips moved slightly to the right and north. "And here's Edinburgh." He pressed his warm mouth to her again, eliciting delicious shivers of sensation along her skin, raising little needles of gooseflesh.

He crawled up her body, nuzzling at her nose with his before sealing his lips to hers in a rather pleasant, if casual kiss. "How very patriotic of you to carry such a representation upon your person," he teased with a breathtaking half-grin. "And on such a lovely spot. I commend you on behalf of your queen and country."

Despite herself—despite everything—shy mirth tugged Imogen's lips into an answering smile.

That is until he moved her arms from where they shielded her modesty before burrowing his rather tousled head against her breasts and settling his body around her.

Dear Lord. He meant to . . . *sleep* with her.

His great body heaved with such a sigh, she didn't ever think he'd cease exhaling until finally it ended on a sound of—dare she think?—contentment.

"Thank you." He yawned. His hand settled over her breast, and Imogen tried not to be embarrassed by the way it barely filled his palm, let alone his long fingers. Though he didn't seem to mind. In fact, his hold there had a rather possessive quality to it.

Or perhaps she only imagined it did.

"You can't know what you've done . . ." His slur became more pronounced now, as exhaustion settled over his big body. "You've turned this nightmare of a day into . . . something else."

Moved by his words, she covered his hand on her chest with her own, wondering if he could feel the heart beating right above her breast. "I know we're not speaking of it," she ventured. "But I'm very sorry for your loss, all the same."

He became dreadfully still, and her heart gave an extra thud.

"You know . . . everyone keeps *congratulating* me," he finally said as though he couldn't believe it. "I've lost . . . nearly every person who ever meant a fucking thing to me, and all anyone can talk about is my good fortune at being the youngest of three and still inheriting the ducal title and all of Trenwyth."

Imogen couldn't think of a thing to say to that, mostly because she agreed that the sentiment was deplorable.

"I *loved* my brother," he said darkly. "He and Hamish Mackenzie were—*are*—the closest people in the world to me. And my father . . . he was so dear, so upright and stalwart and strangely sentimental for a man. I'll miss him."

The hollow note creeping into his voice broke her heart. "And your mother?"

"Of course. Of course my mother. We weren't particularly close, but I loved her. And she loved me, in her own way, I suspect. Though she loved Robert the most, as I caused her no end of trouble as a boy. He was the heir, and I was the spare, as they say." The caustic sound he made tickled her bare skin. "If she'd—lived, she'd just *detest* that I'm the duke now." His laugh contained a suspicious hitch.

"I'm certain she'd be proud of you." Imogen knew nothing of the sort, but she desperately wanted to lend him some comfort.

He nuzzled in closer, and something warm melted her heart.

"I don't want to be a duke," he lamented around a yawn. "I never did."

"You're likely the first man to ever say that."

That sound again. Like a laugh, but not quite.

Imogen contemplated the loss of her own father. A kind man, when he remembered to come home. When he hadn't left them to gamble and drink away all the money. Leaving them with nothing. "Fathers." She sighed. "They don't always leave us the legacy we are prepared for, that's for certain. The best thing we can do is try to muddle through, I suppose. Try our hardest to make the best of things and not give a fig what anyone else has to say about it. You grieve as long as you like, Collin Talmage, and anyone who has a thing to say can go hang."

"You are a rare find, Ginny," he murmured, and nuzzled her breast.

"How's that?" Imogen found that she rather liked the warm weight of his body chasing the chill of the spring night.

"A genuine person in a world full of deceit."

Touched, she squeezed his hand and his fingers threaded with hers.

"Is Ginny your real name?" he queried.

"No," she confessed.

"You'll have to tell me what it is." His words were

barely intelligible now, and Imogen didn't have to wait long until a soft snore vibrated against her skin.

"It's Imogen," she whispered. A tear slid into her hair as she realized she'd shared the most physical and emotional intimacy she'd ever known with a man who didn't even know her name. They'd never even been introduced, and likely never would be. "My name is Imogen Pritchard, Your Grace. It's a pleasure to make your acquaintance."

CHAPTER THREE

London, August 1877, A Year Later

"The Duke of Trenwyth Lives!" Every one of the empire's ubiquitous newspapers from the *Times* to the *Telegraph* had some variation of the exact same front-page headline. As she scurried away from Charing Cross Station, Imogen burned to stop and devour every detail, but she was due at St. Margaret's Royal Hospital in ten minutes, and Dr. Fowler was nothing if not a stickler for punctuality.

A pinprick of light appeared upon the ever-darkening canvas of her disposition. Collin Talmage was *alive*. Imogen had followed the saga of his disappearance the prior year a little more breathlessly than the rest of the nation. She'd held the night they'd shared as a treasured secret in her memory—and in her heart—as everyone from Buckingham Palace to the military, to the Criminal Investigations Division of Scotland Yard had searched for England's favorite son.

Imogen had reluctantly left Trenwyth sleeping soundly

in room 17 of the Bare Kitten last spring, and hurried to her shift at St. Margaret's, much as she was doing now. From what the papers had gleaned over the year spent searching for him, Trenwyth had boarded a ship bound for the Indies that afternoon and had never been heard from again. Rampant speculation had spread like a pernicious disease through the local and international press. Had he been lost to some Oriental jungle and the savages living there? Killed in the skirmishes between the Ottoman Turks and the Russians? Defected to the obscene wealth of a profligate sultan? Or made his own little tribal kingdom somewhere in the wild desert, complete with a harem to do his bidding?

Eventually the crown had put a stop to the articles, though the more liberal newspapers still ran a piece now and again on the alternately scandalous and mysterious life of the vanished duke, Collin Talmage. As the third child of one of the noblest and wealthiest families in all of Britain, he'd spent his youth as a reprobate and a wastrel, squandering his allowance on expensive courtesans, parties, and the kinds of pleasures not strictly allowed by imperial law. Eventually, his desperate father had bought him a commission in the military, and this was where journalists spent most of their time and energy. Because after a short time beneath the command of Lieutenant Colonel Liam Mackenzie—the man they called the Demon Highlander—Collin Talmage's rank and regiment became increasingly opaque. Articles and editorials often remarked upon how odd it was that a peer of the realm—a man in the direct line of succession—should be sent on a military expedition, most especially so soon after the deaths of his parents and brother. Did the demise of the

Talmage family have anything to do with Collin's disappearance? Had *he* anything to do with their deaths?

The papers screamed the word his compatriots had whispered that long-ago night in the Bare Kitten.

Spy.

Imogen often searched her memory of that night, and could still recall the way he'd avoided revealing his destination, or his objective. Just as often—maybe more so—she'd prayed for his safety, for his comfort. The Duke of Trenwyth might have been any number of things in his life, but he'd been kind to her. Generous. They'd shared something in that room above the Bare Kitten, an intimacy that surpassed the physical. And while he likely never thought of it, his kindness had meant the very world to her.

By the time she mounted the back stairs of St. Margaret's, Imogen was exactly eleven minutes late according to the watch she had pinned to her bodice. She'd certainly be hearing about this. Stashing her gloves, bag, and sundries into her designated cupboard in the nurses' changing room, she seized her apron and cap and lunged for the door. Her heels made mismatched clips on the stone floor of the back hall as she tied a starched white apron over her black frock. The sole of her left shoe had come loose ages ago, and she couldn't afford a trip to the cobbler. Making a note to pilfer some paste from the storage room again, she swung to the right and hurried up the back stairs. She had her cap affixed to the crown of her head by the time she reached the second floor. She never worked the surgical theater, so she kept climbing, past the crowded patient wards on the third floor, and toward her post on the top level where the private wings were located.

St. Margaret's was a rather exclusive hospital, only

treating patients who thereby had the means to afford it, but the back stairs usually bustled with staff. Use of the grand front entry stairs was restricted to patients, family, and the occasional doctor or visiting patron who would subsidize a new wing or a particular mode of research.

So distracted by her thoughts of Trenwyth, Imogen didn't particularly notice that she'd not met another soul on the stairs until she'd already cleared two flights.

Where was everyone? Could it be that providence, for once, was on her side and she could make it all the way to her post without Head Nurse Gibby or Dr. Fowler noting her tardiness? She increased her speed, using the banister to give her extra momentum as she careened to the fourth floor. All she had to do was make it down the long hall of private rooms to the South Wing nurses' station and begin mixing the morning tinctures and medications before anyone noticed. She'd stop in to Lord Anstruther's room first. Everyone knew of their fondness for each other, and would believe that she tarried with the elderly earl before beginning her duties as was her habit.

Reaching the top of the stairs, she lunged around the corner, then clamped her hand over her mouth in order to prevent a sound of surprise from escaping. She didn't, however, stop in time to avoid a slight collision with Gwen Fitzgibbon, her counterpart in the North Wing.

Gwen, a stout, quick-witted Irish girl, instantly caught Imogen, then pushed her back against the wall with one strong arm. The instinct to resist died immediately when Imogen realized that nearly the entire staff of St. Margaret's was crowded into the hall, and thusly lined against the wall in a parody of regimental posture.

It seemed a miracle to have so many bodies in her ward making hardly a sound, or perhaps the hammer of her heart blocked any noise. She'd caught the suggestion of a voluminous black skirt and a great many black and red coats toward the end of the hall before Gwen had saved her. But Imogen couldn't make out the goings-on from this distance, and didn't dare move until her breath returned to normal.

Gwen tilted her dark head toward Imogen, eyes the color of cobalt sparkling with excitement and awe. " 'Tis Her *Royal Majesty* and Mr. Disraeli consulting with Dr. Fowler." She injected as much marvel into the breathy whisper as was possible.

"What?" Imogen gasped in a breath. The Queen of England *and* the prime minister? She let her head fall back against the wall. Of all the bloody days for her to be delayed, why *not* when Queen Victoria and Benjamin Disraeli stood in front of her station?

Bugger. Was she going to get the sack in front of the English monarch and her retinue? Was it too late to throw herself back down the stairs?

"Aye." Gwen continued, gesturing to the sovereign mostly obscured by a circle of royal yeomen, her personal bodyguards. "She's here to check in on her distant cousin, or haven't you heard?"

"Her cousin?" Imogen's heart split in two with the violence of a hatchet strike. One half relief, the other fear. All her blood seemed to be pooling in her limbs, turning them hot and numb. "You don't mean—" She couldn't bring herself to speak his name, even in a whisper, lest she prematurely conjure impending disaster.

Trenwyth was alive. *Thank God* he was alive.

And if he recognized her, he could ruin everything.

"Aye, Collin Talmage, the Duke of Trenwyth, in this very hospital," Gwen affirmed.

Imogen's hand flew to her corset where it seemed to inhibit her lungs from expanding at all.

"We're not like to be introduced, though." The girl deflated with a long, breathy sigh.

"Why not?" Imogen asked alertly.

"The duke is a right mess. I didn't catch all of what the doctor said, but I did hear that he is afflicted with typhus."

Imogen's hand moved from her lungs to her heart at the word. "No," she whispered.

Gwen nodded. "Aye. After all this time. After everything it seems they did to bring him home. They don't expect him to survive the night."

Home from where? Hazarding a break in decorum, Imogen craned her neck to glance down the long hall of the South Wing. The royal entourage painted bold, stark renderings against the hallway painted institutional white.

Queen Victoria, a stout, imposing woman bedecked in unfathomable yards of silk, stood like a black pistil within the crimson-clad petals of her vanguard. The register of her voice carried down the hall as she consulted with Dr. Fowler, but the words remained unintelligible. If the queen's commanding words didn't reach the landing of the stairs, surely Imogen's careful whispers wouldn't disturb Her Majesty.

"Did they mention where he's been all this time?" she asked Gwen, who'd returned to staring at the monarch with a mixture of awe and ambiguity. As an Irish Catholic, Gwen had likely been born with a distrust of the English crown. "What did you mean when you said 'after everything they'd done to bring him home'?"

"Don't you take the paper?" Gwen glanced back impatiently.

"I'm afraid I slept in rather late this morning." After an extra boisterous night at the Bare Kitten, she'd been dead to the world until Isobel had to wake her, likely saving her job.

"Well." Gwen adopted a conspiratorial posture. "The official story, according to the London press, is that he'd contracted typhus while exploring the jungles of India . . ." She trailed off dramatically, and Imogen wanted to shake her and every one of her blarney-speaking relatives for their bardic tendencies. Then she caught herself. Why was she being like this? Voracious, impatient, almost desperate for any information she could glean about a man she barely knew.

A duke who could ruin her. Who—some would argue—already *had*.

"You have reason not to believe the story?" Imogen prompted, fighting to keep the impatience from elevating the volume of her voice.

"Half the royal army's in the Indies, aren't they?" Gwen said pointedly. "Why, then, send the Demon Highlander after Trenwyth?"

"Who knows?" Troubled, Imogen chewed on her lip. "But if—"

"Nurse Pritchard." Dr. Fowler's voice carried down the length of the hall as he broke from the queen and searched the hall of anxious faces for her own. "Nurse Pritchard, step forward, please."

Imogen would have done so the first time he'd uttered her name, if the very marrow hadn't frozen in her bones.

Gwen, always the helpful friend, gave her an encouraging push—or rather a shove—into Dr. Fowler's path.

"Ah, Nurse Pritchard, there you are." Dr. Fowler's balding pate shone beneath the gaslights, perspiration the only sign of distress in the usually imperturbable man. As if the daunting chief physician at St. Margaret's weren't enough to incite a bout of trembling, the queen trailing in his wake threatened Imogen with a bout of the vapors.

Certain of her imminent and utter devastation, Imogen attempted a perfect curtsy, though her unsteady legs only executed an adequate one. "Your Majesty. Dr. Fowler."

"I noted in your file this morning that you claim to have previously been afflicted with typhus." Dr. Fowler looked down his beakish nose at her, his eyes flashing with unspoken warnings.

"I have, sir." She glanced down at the floor, unable to meet anyone's eyes for very long, lest they read her shameful secrets hidden there.

"Typhus tends to spread in an institution such as this, and it would not do to risk an epidemic. As you're the only staff nurse that has overcome the disease, you are now immune to it. Therefore I'm assigning you as the Duke of Trenwyth's personal nurse."

So many emotions, from gladness to panic, crowded into Imogen's throat, preventing a reply.

"She seems like a very correct and demure person, Dr. Fowler." Queen Victoria regarded Imogen from clear, round eyes, her shrewd assessment as cutting as her words were kind.

"Thank you, Your Majesty." Imogen managed not to stammer.

"It is of the utmost importance, Nurse Pritchard, that Trenwyth receive only the best of care. He is a hero of the empire, and we mandate that he survive. Are we understood?" The queen enunciated every one of her syllables with solemnity and abject clarity.

Bugger. Imogen swallowed the unladylike curse and

nodded, again robbed of her ability to speak. Little more than half of those afflicted with typhus survived the disease. Would she be blamed if Trenwyth succumbed?

"I'll do my utmost not to fail you, Your Majesty."

"One hopes that's enough," the queen clipped.

"Dr. Longhurst is in with His Grace; give them a quarter hour to finish washing and dressing him before you enter." Dr. Fowler's uncompromisingly stern voice always gave her a case of the fidgets, and Imogen clutched her skirts to avoid them now.

"Of course, sir." Should she curtsy again?

"Above all things, we must be proper," the queen agreed. "Come, Dr. Fowler, we will discuss a few details of a delicate nature in your office." By the time she'd finished talking, she was halfway to the stairs.

"Just so, Your Majesty." Casting Imogen a voluminous look, he hurried after her, barking at the staff to resume their duties.

As they dispersed, Imogen exchanged a look of sheer amazement with Gwen, deciding to use her quarter hour wisely. Hurrying three doors down from her nurse's station, she turned the latch and slipped inside, panting as though she'd sprinted a league.

"Ah, my dear Miss Pritchard!" Everyone in the world should hear their name enunciated with such warm and earnest enthusiasm, Imogen decided. It did wonders for the soul.

"Lord Anstruther." She greeted him, with mirroring pleasure as she bustled into the paradoxically opulent gloom of his private quarters. The frail, septuagenarian earl all but disappeared into the bed beneath a pile of blankets. His head and thin shoulders, swathed in a dark silk dressing gown, were scooped into a sitting position by a mountain of pillows. "How do you fare this morning?" Imogen queried with a sad smile, reminded of what a merciless brigand time was to them all. "Describe how you feel so I may record it on your chart."

"Like a steam engine has taken residence in my chest, but never you mind that." He lifted a hand to wave in front of him, and Imogen made a note of how blue the paper-thin skin of his fingers had become. "I assume you've brought me your copy of the reclining bacchante sculpture?" He made a grand show of tilting his head this way and that, as though to spy something hidden behind her.

Bugger, she'd promised that she'd sketch Jean-Louis Durand's scandalous sculpture for the earl on Saturday, when it was her habit to visit the Grand Gallery. They had it on loan for a very short time before it was returned to its French salon. A fellow artist, Anstruther had lamented to her that he was too unwell to visit the unveiling, and Imogen had said she'd do her best to immortalize it for him in all its indecent detail. Instead, she'd been forced to put in an extra shift at the Bare Kitten.

"No, my lord, and I do apologize. I was unable to find my way to the gallery." She was equally unable to stand his disappointment, so she busied herself with his assessment so she didn't have to look into his soft brown eyes. "I came to inform you that I won't be in to see you for a while, as I'm going to be nursing someone with typhus, and I dare not bring that misery to your room."

"Typhus, you say?" His brows were two silver-white bushes separated by surprise and inquiry.

Imogen leaned down to take his pulse, but covered the gesture with an air of conspiracy. "I don't know if you've heard, but His Grace, the Duke of Trenwyth, is here in this hospital."

"Trenwyth? You mean they found that scamp? Little Collin Talmage?" His thin face split into a wrinkled grin.

She tried to keep the skepticism from her features. No one with eyes in their heads could call Trenwyth *little*.

"I've been worried about the boy," the old man confessed. "Lived next to Trenwyth Hall my entire life. I knew his grandfather, by Jove, I even knew his great-grandfather. Outlived them all, and what do you think of that?" He curled his mustache between two fingers before he broke into a fit of coughs that concerned Imogen a great deal. "Typhus, you say? Aren't you putting yourself in a great deal of danger on his behalf?"

She shook her head. "I've already had it."

"Still . . . Bring me Dr. Fowler, I'll demand he find someone else."

Imogen made a gesture of helplessness, touched by his concern for her. "I'm afraid you'll have to take it up with the queen, as she only just left."

"The queen, you say? Well, doesn't that just take the bright spot out of my week?" He visibly deflated, then seemed to come to a decision. "Why don't you visit me anyway? There's no cure for old age, or for what I've contracted. What's typhus when there's *art* to be discussed?"

Imogen's heart tugged at the note of loneliness in his voice. "Dear Lord Anstruther, you know I would never put any of my patients in danger, least of all my favorite." She attempted to charm him.

He snorted. "You'll take one look at Trenwyth and change your mind about that, my dear, typhus or no. Handsome as the devil and afflicted with a similar set of morals, that's Trenwyth."

Struck by sudden curiosity, Imogen lowered herself to the edge of his bed. "You knew—*know* him well?"

"Watched the Talmage children grow, Sarah and I did." Sarah, his wife, had been gone a long fifteen years, and still the man pined for her. "She was particularly fond of Collin," he recalled. "Lad would pop over for a peppermint whenever she was in the garden and tarry round her skirts, that is, until he started chasing skirts of his own. A bit starving for female affection, if you ask me. Mother was a cold fish, God rest her soul."

Imogen smiled. "He was a good boy, then?"

"Cole? Good? Not at all! But my Sarah always did have a soft spot for us rakes and ne'er-do-wells." His eyes sparkled at her. "We never did have children, I suppose she enjoyed her time with the boy. Even wept a bit when he went into Her Majesty's Service. She was mighty proud of him."

"They say he contracted the disease in the Indies," Imogen prompted, drinking in every detail.

True to his nature, Anstruther took the bait. "My valet, Cheever, got his hands on an American paper," he bragged. "Januarius MacGahan wrote that he witnessed a man fitting Trenwyth's description fighting like the very devil during the April Uprising in Bulgaria. Claims to have seen him dragged off by the Ottomans, he did."

"But . . . the Ottomans deny that the April Uprising even happened," Imogen speculated. "Surely they would have killed Trenwyth if he was witness to it, wouldn't they?"

"Perhaps not if he's a royal." He shrugged. "Maybe they were paid his weight in gold for ransom." The excitement and the conversation had the earl dissolving into a fit of coughs. The cancer was now in his lungs and there was naught to be done but make him comfortable. Only God knew when it would take him.

Checking her watch, Imogen stood. "I'll send Gwen in with a compress and your tonic," she said, hoping her bright tone would smother the grief already welling in her chest. "I vow to bring you my rendering just as soon as . . . as I can.

"Give us a kiss then." He offered his cheek, and she complied. His skin was cool, dry, and thin beneath her lips.

"And take good care our boy Trenwyth," Anstruther admonished. "Does the realm no good to lose that entire family. They are among the few noble families that deserved that designation."

"As are you, my lord."

Imogen stood in front of the closed door to Trenwyth's room paralyzed by indecision. Dr. Longhurst's voice filtered through the wall as he labored over the duke, likely assisted by a male orderly, and Imogen thanked her stars that she had more time to stall.

She burned to see Trenwyth for herself. And she dreaded it.

A delicately pretty, fair-haired nurse bustled past her with an armful of linen that, by the smell, had more on them than merely blood. If the girl was going to the laundry, she'd be passing right by Gwen's station. Imogen struggled to remember her name, as the nurse had only recently been hired. She knew they'd been introduced, but this nurse worked on the third floor in the more crowded wards. Her name started with an *M,* didn't it? Maggie, Mary . . .

"Molly," she remembered aloud. "Your name *is* Molly, am I right?"

Startled, the girl whirled in surprise, and dropped the linens. "Look what you made me do!" Her brashness, as much as her accent, pegged her as being born no farther south than Yorkshire. She knelt to carefully gather up the linens, her face scrunched in a grimace of disgust. "If these stain the carpets, I'll be sure that you clean them, not I. Though why they put carpets in a hospital where blood is the least despicable of the substances that might stain them, I'll never guess. Some idiot toff wot thinks he knows something likely demanded it beneath his lofty feet. And don't *we* always have to cow to what *they* say?"

Imogen blinked, taken aback by the woman's vitriolic outburst.

"I—I do apologize, let me help." She started for the bundle, but was shooed away.

"Stay where you are," Molly demanded. "I'll not be getting typhus along with a reprimand should the Dragon come by."

Imogen softened a bit for the girl, who must have had a run-in with Brenda Gibby, the head nurse of the fourth floor. In truth, Imogen feared the woman dubbed "the Dragon" more than she did Ezio del Toro, and that fear was mighty.

"I haven't been in His Grace's room yet, you're not in any danger of contracting—"

"I can't lollygag about, I've work to do, *your* work now that you'll be locked up in there," Molly quipped shortly, eyeing her with wary gray mistrust as she stood with her bundle. "You weren't about to add to it, were you?"

Imogen gave her a conciliatory look. "I was going to ask if you'd send Nurse Gwen Fitzgibbon to Lord Anstruther's room on your way to the laundry. I don't know if I'll make it to the North Wing and back in time."

"Might as well," Molly said acerbically after a moment, and Imogen was almost surprised she agreed. "Those other of us always used to envy you fourth-floor girls, you know, working up here with your betters. But now that I've a taste of what it's like, I'll never complain again."

Imogen very much doubted that, as complaining seemed to be a particular talent of Molly's. Though it was nice to hear that someone appreciated the stressors that came with treating the rich and demanding, not to mention living up to the impossibly high standards of conduct expected of the fourth floor.

It was, in a word, exhausting.

As Molly departed without another acid remark, Imogen turned back to the closed door, on the other side of which was a man she'd dreamed about every night for the better part of a year.

Collin Talmage. Or, as she still referred to him in her private thoughts, *Cole*.

She raised her hand to tap softly on the door when it was wrenched open, nearly startling her to death.

"Dr. Longhurst." Imogen gasped at the young doctor, who did likewise, as though she'd surprised him in equal measure. She'd heard Dr. Fowler say that Albert Longhurst was the most brilliant medical mind of the century, and she heartily believed it. Imogen pitied him, though, as it seemed that Dr. Longhurst often lived within that brilliant mind, and rarely glanced out to detect the rest of the world. A young, enthusiastic man, he spoke in quick, clipped sentences, eschewing rhetoric in the extreme. At times, he left out entire words altogether.

"Nurse Pritchard. You shouldn't be here. It's typhus." A lock of hair the color of hot chocolate curled against his forehead and kept falling into eyes the color of oak leaves in the late summer. Imogen very much doubted that Dr. Longhurst remembered to go to the barber very often, though his disheveled appearance didn't decrease his attractiveness.

"Because I've already survived typhus, Dr. Fowler assigned me as His Grace's personal nurse."

"Oh." His eyes brightened, and he swiped at his hair as though only just noticing that he'd forgotten to groom this morning. "Very well, then. Do come in." He drew the door open wider and stepped out of her path. "You know William? He's also survived typhus, and will be helping you care for Lord Trenwyth."

"Of course, hello."

"Nurse Pritchard." William, a young, sandy-haired lad, nodded to her. "I'll step out now, but just tug on this bell-pull 'ere if you need me, and I'll be back faster than you can say 'bob's yer uncle.'"

"Thank you." Imogen barely heard a word the cockney lad said, let alone noted his departure, so intent was she on the sleeping man almost as white as the sheets tucked around his prone form.

Cole.

The spare yet expensive room disappeared as she ventured closer, afraid to blink lest the shallow rise and fall of his chest cease. "How . . . how is he?" She didn't even fight to keep the catch from her voice.

"Rather dim-witted, I'm afraid, but strong as an ox and willing to help."

It took her a moment to process that Longhurst had misunderstood her meaning. "No, not William. I mean Trenwyth."

"Ah." He trailed her to the bedside. "I'll admit the prognosis isn't good. His fever refuses to break. Tried everything." He sighed, as though Trenwyth's fever were being purposely recalcitrant and tiresome to his patience.

"Were the duke as strong as he should be, a man in his prime, I'd give him a better chance. But malnourished as he is, and with the rest of his injuries . . ." He let the sentence die, as it contained words unnecessary to utter.

Imogen stared down at Trenwyth's face as he slept in a kind of fitful, feverish torpor. Beneath thin blankets, his limbs twitched restlessly and his eyes rolled behind their lids.

She devoured the sight of him, absorbing the features she knew, and acquainting herself with the alarming changes. The grooves in his forehead and branching from his eyes had deepened more than they should in a year. His pallor accentuated the hollows beneath his strong cheekbones, turning them gaunt to the point of skeletal. But she recognized his face, his dear, familiar, *beautiful* face, and thanked God that he'd made it home.

To her.

Information processed slowly through the depths of her emotion and she latched on to the last thing Dr. Longhurst had said.

"The *rest* of his injuries?" She echoed his words in a query.

Instead of informing her of his clinical assessment, Longhurst grasped the edge of the coverlet and threw it wide, allowing her to see for herself.

"Dear. *God.*" Her voice broke on the exclamation.

"God had nothing to do with what happened to this man." Even Dr. Longhurst, a colleague she knew to be rational and sensible to the point of stoic, injected an extra note of emotion into his voice at the ghastly sight of Trenwyth's body.

"W-why?" Imogen whispered.

More bruises covered Trenwyth's long form than unmarked flesh. His hipbones jutted against the thin white linen of the undergarment draped to grant him a modicum of modesty. He was malnourished, emaciated, and had obviously been tortured. His skin, once a hue of gold to rival the sunlit barley fields in August, now reminded her of the pale wax she had to peel from the top of an unopened bottle of Ravencroft Scotch. Though his cuts and abrasions had already been stitched and wrapped, the angriest bruises suggested he'd spent a great deal of time bound by coarse rope, indenting at his neck, his ankles and wris—.

Imogen closed her eyes, assaulted by a wave of anger, compassion, and disbelief.

His left hand, it was . . . gone.

CHAPTER FOUR

"You're not going to cry, are you?" Panic edged into Dr. Longhurst's voice.

"No." Imogen sniffed, fearing that at any moment she might be proved a liar. It was all she could do to tear her horrified gaze from the rounded, bandage-wrapped wrist. "But . . . how did this happen? *Who* did this to him?"

Trenwyth shivered, though a sheen of sweat glossed his skin, and Imogen helped Dr. Longhurst to cover him as he murmured strange and nonsensical things.

"Know what I believe?" Longhurst asked in his abbreviated way, looking about them as though to assure their privacy. "The Ottoman Turks. Now help me open the windows. There's new evidence that fresh, clean air is beneficial to those with fevers this high, and all of our antipyretic efforts have been thwarted."

Dazed, Imogen trailed after Dr. Longhurst, surprised how reluctant she was to leave Trenwyth's side, even to perform this little task. "The Ottomans?" He'd been the second one only this hour to deduce that. "Did you also read the American papers?"

He gave her a queer sort of look. "No, but I've spent time among the Persians and the Turkish people, studying some of their chemical and medical advancements. While I respect and enjoyed them very much, I've also seen what they do to their enemies. Have you ever heard of Sharia law?"

"I'm afraid not."

"If a man is considered a thief, it is the practice of certain sects to relieve him of the offending hand."

"How . . . barbaric." She winced.

"About as barbaric as what we Westerners do, believe you me."

Her own hand flew to her chest. Had Trenwyth run afoul of the Ottomans? Had he, indeed, been part of the April Uprising? Had he been a prisoner all this time? An entire year . . . She couldn't bear the thought of so much suffering, only to end up like this.

"Will Dr. Fowler mind the open windows, do you think?" she queried, desperate to inject some sense of normalcy into the conversation, lest he perceive her particular distress over Trenwyth's condition. Crisp, spring air swirled in, carrying the sweet scent of puffed carameled corn and cinnamon pastries sold by street vendors. The aroma was underscored by the more pervasive, unpleasant odors of the city such as coal smoke, horses, and the preferably unidentifiable bouquet of the Thames.

"Fowler can hang if he does," Longhurst said evenly. "If the medical journals say this is best, then he should be paying them more mind than his backward traditions."

Imogen silently agreed, returning to Cole's bedside and checking his chart. He'd been given every treatment possible to combat his condition. The ice baths, tinctures, teas, and so forth had produced little to no effect. "What else needs to be done for him, Dr. Longhurst?"

To her utter surprise, the doctor rested a hand on her shoulder. "All we can do now is make him comfortable. And pray, if you do that sort of thing. Though his bandages may need changing in short order."

"I would be most anxious to assist while you—"

"I don't mean to seem . . . crude or unfeeling, Nurse Pritchard, but unlike you I've never had typhus. The less time I spend in here the better. For my patients and myself. If you could do as much on your own as necessary . . ."

Suddenly the thought of being alone with Trenwyth appealed to her very much. "Of course, Doctor. If you would, please send William up with some marrow broth, bandages, ice, and water?"

Longhurst nodded, assessing her with what she would call an earnest look before lowering his hand from her shoulder. "Do call me if—*when* his condition changes."

"Yes, sir." Imogen barely noted his leaving as the gravity of his words struck her with new trepidation. Trenwyth couldn't, indeed, remain in this limbo of fever and illness. He'd either recover eventually or . . .

No. Shoving any grief-inducing words from her mind, she bent over him, resting a hand on his forehead. Touching him seemed surreal after all this time.

He was so incredibly hot, it astonished her that his perspiration didn't instantly turn to steam.

Until she'd seen him, her greatest fear had been such a selfish one. That he would take one look at her, and remember who she was. That he would tell everyone that she'd been his prostitute, and she'd be dismissed on the spot. Now, a dread more insidious than that weaved its cold way through her as she hovered over him as though to shield him from the grim reaper.

She feared for his life most of all.

The man had been scoundrel and saint. Heathen and hero. A dangerous man and a deferential lover.

And now . . .

She brushed sweat-slicked hair away from his broad forehead, the most tender sentiment filling her chest nigh to bursting. Now he needed her again.

"You are going to live, Cole," she whispered to him. "I'll make certain of it."

Typhus, a nasty disease they had called gaol fever in the not-too-distant past, preyed upon those that lived in squalor and drank putrid water. Then, the infection spread, like it had to those in the Pritchards' close and dingy apartments so long ago when she'd battled the miserable disease.

Rarely did someone like Trenwyth contract it. Someone healthy, adult, and well fed.

How deplorable the conditions must have been in whatever hell he'd been rescued from.

William arrived with the items she'd requested, and Imogen instantly got to work. She knew the duke would find it uncomfortable, but in order to bring his temperature under control, she'd need to rub him down with the ice thoroughly and often.

"Does he need use of the necessary, Nurse Pritchard? He hasn't since he arrived."

Imogen checked, frowning. "No, I'll ring for you if he does."

Refusing William's offer of further assistance, she

waited until the door clicked closed again, and peeled the sheet back from Trenwyth's body, now damp with his sweat.

Try as she might, it was difficult not to despair as she dipped her soft cloth in the icy water and began bathing his forehead with it. He flinched at first, but then his head turned toward her touch, as though it brought him relief.

In her cherished memory, Trenwyth was such an imposing man, almost inhuman in the perfection of his physique and abilities. Often, on her days off, she'd stroll through Hyde Park, pausing to consider the statue of Achilles at the Wellington Monument, and appreciating the physical similarities between the Greek hero and her one-time lover.

Now, his flesh hung from sinew that clung more tightly to his thick bones. He was so tall, so naturally powerful, that his malnourishment was all the more horrid and conspicuous. She ran her cloth behind his neck and then to the front, tracing a poorly healed scar that reached from his clavicle to his shoulder. It hadn't been there a year ago. Nor had the strange cluster of round, puckered skin that looked like pebbles had lodged into his flesh and subsequently been dug out. What could have caused such a scar? Trenwyth would, no doubt, have many more once the gashes and cuts now marking him healed.

If they had the chance to.

His murmuring became more insistent, escaping his dry, cracked lips on tortured sighs and groans. He still wasn't coherent, and what few words she did catch disturbed and chilled her. *March. Bayonets. Dig . . .*

Babies.

Deciphering the horrors locked in his mind seemed too dreadful to contemplate. Dipping the cloth in the ice water once more, she spread it over the long range of his torso, interrupted by his many visible ribs and the uneven knots of his abdominals. He contracted, groaned, and then relaxed as the jarring cold became comfortingly cool.

"I'm sorry to cause you any distress, Cole," she whispered to him, checking beneath a bandage on his bicep and deciding that it did need changing. Peeling it off, she spread iodine over the neat stitches, and redressed it with clean bandages from her tray. "I'm doing this to keep you alive. I know you must be tired, so very tired, but can you fight a little while longer? I'll fight too. Whatever it takes."

"Ginny?"

Her name—her *Kitten* name—on his lips startled her so much that she surged to her feet and glanced around the empty room. Elation that he spoke, that he recognized her voice even after so long, was quickly followed by a grave trepidation.

He made a sound of distress, his head turning this way and that as though looking for a familiar face in a crowd. The limb from which his hand had been taken flailed out. The subsequent groan that escaped him could have almost been a whimper had it been produced by a smaller chest. It was the sound of one forsaken. Low and desperate.

It broke her heart into gossamer pieces.

"Ginny," he called, louder this time, and she could do nothing but answer him.

"I'm here, Cole," she soothed, as she sat down beside him on the bed. "I'm here. Do you remember me?" She shouldn't be touched but, bleeding heart that she was, she couldn't seem to help herself.

Leaning over him, she took an ice chip from a crystal glass, and pressed it against his lower lip, letting it melt into his mouth. Pleased that he swallowed, she lifted the cloth warmed by his torso and submerged it back into the basin.

"Ginny." His right hand burrowed into the rough folds of her uniform skirt and clung there with astonishing force for one so ill. "The world was on fire, Ginny," he moaned. "The world was on fire, and I thought I was in hell."

"I know," she whispered, again wiping his unruly hair from where it was plastered to his burning forehead. She *didn't* know—couldn't comprehend—but desperately wanted to lend him some comfort. Some understanding.

"But it was the snow. The snow . . ." He pulled at her skirts, becoming more agitated. "Hell isn't fire, Ginny. It's ice."

"Shhhhh," she soothed, swallowing the lump in her throat that threatened to restrict her breath. She couldn't think of a thing to say but, "You're safe now," which seemed like a tired and overused consolation.

And wasn't entirely true.

If he'd had a terrible experience with ice, then her ministrations must be akin to torture, but how *else* could she keep his dangerous temperature from cooking him alive?

"I'm sorry," she whispered through eyes blurred with tears as she took the frigid cloth and, this time, wrapped his feet with it, attempting to draw the heat from his head.

He hissed and repeated her name. Then his breath caught, and every one of his muscles seemed to tighten. Imogen watched helplessly as his bruised, pale body convulsed for a moment, and was glad that he was too weak to kick out at her. Thank God the typhus hadn't produced the rash that most often accompanied the fever. When she'd been afflicted, she remembered her skin feeling like little beastly ants were slowly eating her flesh away. It had been unspeakably miserable.

Trenwyth had been spared that, at least.

She crooned soft things to him as she melted another ice chip on his mouth, painting his lips with it, and allowing the water to trickle inside. This he seemed to tolerate well, and even sighed when she produced another.

"I dreamed of you," he rasped through a throat abraded by desert sand and pain. "I dreamed of blood. And you."

"I dreamed of you too," she confessed, pressing her hand to his forehead once more. She'd thought it impossible, but he felt even warmer than before.

"Bugger," she muttered, and stood.

"No." He pulled her back to the bed with surprising strength.

"Hush, Cole, hush now," she soothed, reaching down to uncurl his fingers from her skirts. It seemed that her voice lowered to a whisper every time she said his name; the intimacy of it felt wicked on her tongue. She should be calling him Your Grace, even in private, but the familiarity seemed a nominal sin considering the circumstances. "I'm going to change your bandage." She kept talking, as it seemed to appease him and calm his increasingly shallow breaths. "Then we'll see if you can keep down some bone broth and tea."

Settling herself on the other side of him, she stretched his left arm out so his wrist hung over the edge of the bed. She intended to use the flat-sided scissors to cut the bandage off, but the moment the scissors touched the edge of the bandage he groaned and flinched expansively. Had Imogen worse reflexes, he could have been cut.

She decided to unwrap it, instead, the chore taking her extra long because of his severe reaction each time she exerted even the smallest amount of pressure.

Imogen liked to think of herself as a seasoned and

stouthearted nurse by now, incapable of disgust, but she gasped when she uncovered Trenwyth's mangled wrist. The wound was not fresh, indeed, it was more healed than not. It became apparent from the haphazard stitching of the skin, and the misshapen form, that it hadn't been properly cared for at all.

Battling her temper along with a fresh wave of pity, she reached for the iodine, applying it to the wound.

She barely ducked a vicious strike as he screamed in pain. Imogen stared down at him in helpless frustration as a suspicion began to form.

Fever, pallidness, delirium, and muscle contractions . . . all symptoms of typhus. But so was a rash that covered the entire body, and there was generally a dry and hacking cough, which Trenwyth didn't have. Granted, his breathing was shallow, and his pulse weak . . . but didn't William say he hadn't released any water since he'd arrived?

Dropping the iodine, Imogen ran from the room in search of Dr. Fowler. Trenwyth didn't have typhus but something just as deadly, if not worse.

CHAPTER FIVE

"Nurse Pritchard, I shouldn't think you prone to such ridiculous bouts of female hysteria." Dr. Fowler was a rather jowly man for one so thin. The extra skin drooped from his cheeks, punctuating his supercilious frown. "The diagnosis is typhus. Every medical professional who's cared for Lord Trenwyth from India to here has agreed that this is a textbook case."

That was assuming Trenwyth actually traveled from India and not Bulgaria or Constantinople like the evidence might suggest.

"So you didn't make the initial diagnosis yourself?" Imogen pressed.

"Careful, Nurse Pritchard, you are on dangerous ground." Displeasure snapped from eyes also afflicted with loose skin.

"I wouldn't dream of meaning any disrespect, Dr. Fowler," Imogen began, "but I believe I've made a strong case for septicemia. If you'd only witnessed how His Grace reacted when I touched his wrist—"

"The poor man had his hand hacked off," Fowler interrupted impatiently. "Or sawed off, judging by the sight of it, of *course* it still causes him pain."

"Yes, but his pain seemed rather extreme and—"

"Is the site swollen, Nurse Pritchard?" He regarded her with such obvious disdain, she could have been a rodent in need of extermination.

"Not that I can tell, but it's so poorly healed that—"

"Is it visibly quite red or extraordinarily warm to the touch?"

"His entire body is quite warm to the touch." She'd not actually been hysterical when he'd accused her of it, but Imogen could now hear the desperation creeping into her voice.

"But the wound is not red, is it? There is no abscess or evident swelling."

She didn't want to cede the point, but she dare not lie. "If you'd only take a moment to come with me so that I can show you, I might be able to better express—"

"You're treating me as though I didn't examine the wound for *myself*." The director put undue emphasis on the word. "Are you insinuating that I have been somehow derelict in my assessment?"

"I would never presume, but could we not at least perform a procedure to fix the damaged wrist and create a smoother limb? Then we'd know for certain, and if I'm mistaken, then at least His Grace lives more comfortably."

"Nonsense! I cannot in good conscience submit such an ailing patient to the risks of the surgical theater," he blustered. "I'd lose all credibility, and the ability to practice medicine. No, no, dear girl. Besides, the aesthetics of what's left of Trenwyth's arm are the least of his problems. He'll likely not live long enough to notice—"

Impassioned, Imogen slapped her hands on his grand mahogany desk and splayed them open, leaning low over his seated form. "He cannot be allowed to die, Dr. Fowler. It is our duty to do *all* that we can. To explore every angle and at least consider alternate diagnoses and treatment. What if I'm right? Isn't it at least worth looking again?"

"I believe I know what is going on here," Dr. Fowler said after regarding her for an uncomfortably long time. He rose from his desk, and Imogen had to stop herself from taking a step back. She stood to face him, like David squaring off with Goliath. Only without a slingshot. Or an army. Or any real expertise.

Bugger.

"I understand our beloved Majesty tasked you with Trenwyth's survival. She is an imposing and powerful woman, but even *she* cannot control the course of disease. The duke is in God's hands now. The odds of him enduring this illness are insignificant at best." Fowler crossed his extravagant office to open the door, dismissing her entirely. "Don't take this so hard, my dear. Your concern and enthusiasm do you credit, and I promise there will be no reprisal on you should the duke expire. Your job is to keep him clean and comfortable, and to leave the diagnoses to the doctors."

Imogen didn't trust herself to move. Her entire body shook with equal measures of fear and rage. She abhorred conflict, was petrified of it. But worse than that, she despised ignorant, egotistical men who'd rather see someone die than have their opinions questioned by someone of inferior rank.

By a woman.

God's hands, indeed. Cole was in their hands, in *her* hands, and they should be doing everything they could. How did Dr. Fowler not comprehend that?

"Good day, Nurse Pritchard."

Imogen fled the room, not trusting herself to reply.

By the time she found Dr. Longhurst in the laboratory, her lungs fought for every breath impeded by her corset and a band of desperation.

"You *have* to *do* something, or he's going to die!" she demanded.

"Nurse Pritchard?" Longhurst blinked at her from behind goggles that turned his dark green eyes positively owlish with astonishment and caused his unruly chocolate curls to gather comically high on his crown. "Say what?"

"Col—His Grace, I believe his affliction is septicemia, not typhus. I think his wrist is infected and making him ill and that no one has noticed until now."

Carefully, as though handling something volatile, Longhurst set the beaker he'd been inspecting on one of the many workbenches strewn about the room. Imogen navigated them like a maze.

"I watched Dr. Fowler change the dressing, myself." His eyes moved behind the goggles as though scrutinizing the exact same thing in his memory. "No abscess. No evidence of infection or putridity. No vein discoloration. Though . . . presence of abnormal discomfort for a wound not entirely recent." His gaze snapped to her, assessing her with clinical precision. "Explain your theory."

She'd have to keep this brief to retain his attention. "As you know, I've survived typhus, I'm intimately familiar with its symptoms. There's almost always a very painful rash. It feels as though your chest is full of cotton, and you want to cough and cough, but you expel nothing. And then there's . . . digestive complaints, which are unpleasant and embarrassing, to say the least."

"You don't have to explain the disease to me, Pritchard. I've noted it enough." Impatiently, Longhurst threw the cuffs of his shirtsleeves and began to roll them to the elbow. "I have a great deal of work to do."

Terrified that she might be bashing up against the wall of another masculine ego, she hurried on. "My point is, Trenwyth has exhibited *only one* of these symptoms, and only a little. He's wheezing more than coughing. It's just not the same. If it were just the absence of the rash, or that he had the rash but not the cough, then I would assume it was just an abnormal manifestation of the disease. But the absence of both symptoms?"

He considered it a moment, nodded curtly, and removed his goggles. "So, why septicemia?"

"You, *yourself,* noted the pain in his arm. His fever is spiking ever higher, and he's having an increasingly difficult time breathing. His pulse is both quickening and weakening, almost to a flutter. William said he hasn't used the necessary once. All these symptoms point to a terrible infection."

Longhurst hurried to the door on long legs. "I'll examine Trenwyth again. If all is as you noted, we'll inform Dr. Fowler and prepare the surgical theater."

"I already told Dr. Fowler. He won't hear of it." Imogen seized his arm. "I fear, Dr. Longhurst, that if you take this to him, we'll both be reprimanded. And worse, he'll forbid us to treat the duke."

"Fowler," Longhurst spat, as though the name disgusted him. "How a man that stupid was chosen to run such a facility boggles the mind. The blowhard can raise funds, but is utter shit at practicing medicine." He flicked her a conciliatory look from behind lashes long and thick for a man. "Excuse my vulgarity."

"I agree." Imogen sighed out a breath of relief. "Will you help Trenwyth? I think you're his only hope."

"I'm more chemist than surgeon. This isn't really my purview." He glanced about the laboratory, indecision disturbing the tranquility of his features. "If I performed an unauthorized procedure, I could lose my position."

"And if you don't, a man could lose his *life*!" Imogen cried.

For the first time since she'd known him, Longhurst's eyes altered from sharp to soft as they alighted on her face. "You are right to remind me of that," he conceded. "Come, let us see to your patient."

When she was a young girl, Imogen's family had a cat named Iris, who'd given birth to a litter of kittens. One of the kittens, Icarus, had taken a particular shine to her and followed her everywhere, going so far as to join her in the bath. At night, it would curl up on her chest and Imogen would hold perfectly still, marveling at the speed of the tiny sleeping animal's breaths. Once, she'd even attempted to mimic the short motions of the creature's chest, and found it impossible to maintain.

Now, hovering over Longhurst as he examined Trenwyth, Imogen despaired to note that the duke's breath was every bit as fast and shallow as Icarus's had been long ago. This time, when Longhurst palpated the wrist, Cole's body jerked and spasmed, but only a raw sound escaped. It was as though he couldn't produce the air for a scream any longer.

Time was running out, she thought with despair.

Longhurst looked up at her, his eyes as serious as she'd ever seen them. "Prepare the anesthesia and surgical kit," he ordered hoarsely. "And hope that it is not too late."

CHAPTER SIX

Over the years, the definition of hell made many transitions in Cole's perspective. As a young man, it had been a nebulous place of dubious origin. Some underworld created by old and religious men to threaten those with rebellious spirits and inquiring minds into submission. His mother had been fond of the place as a probable destination for his eternal soul, and had taken every opportunity to inform him thus.

As a soldier, hell had become a tangible thing. The battlefield. Where weapons forged in fire ground men forged of earth into so much meat. Cut living flesh down to nothing but elements and offal that, once dried, returned to dust.

It had been impossible for Cole to imagine anything more hellish, until the smoke had cleared on April 20, 1877. The April Uprising. Hell had become an endless, punishing march to an Ottoman prison somewhere between Bulgaria and Constantinople. A year became an eternity of tedium interrupted by bouts of torture. Where Cole had learned that a youth spent in pursuit of the most exquisite pleasure could be balanced in such a short time with equally exquisite pain. That torment could be as consuming as an orgasm, the veins in his body dilating to allow the pain to flow into his every limb, to set fire to his every nerve. Suspending his muscles with the helpless, pulsating sensation until his body was no longer his own. No matter how valiantly he fought it, groans and screams spilled from him as freely as his blood.

In hell, he'd lost an intrinsic part of himself.

And then he'd lost his hand.

He'd endured, because despite whatever fresh terror the day would hold, the night would bring her . . .

Ginny.

A ridiculous name, really. Rather boozy and lowbrow, come to think of it. Didn't suit her at all. The sultry, exotic waif with a riot of shimmering ebony curls. Eyes lined with dark kohl that sparkled like tiger's eye gems from her porcelain skin. She'd been long, lean, and sinuous, but her grace and sensuality hadn't been the practiced, come-hither seductions of most of the women in her profession. She hadn't draped herself over him like a smothering blanket of perfume and sex, one hand on his cod and the other in his purse. *No*. She'd been wary and uncertain, like a baby doe he'd had to coax to eat from his . . .

Well, never mind from what.

On nights when the cold would seep deeper than his bones, into his very soul, he would remember how warm it had been inside her. How she'd clung to him, and buried her face against his neck. How she'd shuddered with release over him before he took her, those cat's-eyes wide with wonder.

When his gaolers would cut him, would ask him questions he could not answer in a tongue he did not speak, creating reasons to torture him, he would detach himself.

And find her.

He'd go to her in that room, the room the color of blood, and he'd lie in her arms. Her small limbs, as delicate and feeble as a bird's, somehow sheltering him from his pain. Her voice, a tentative whisper, would soothe him and sometimes strengthen him. He'd remember how fiercely she'd given him permission to grieve.

To feel.

Ginny. A prostitute. A creature of a cold and often brutal profession. And yet she'd shown him more genuine warmth than he'd been privy to in a lifetime. She'd been more than a whore to him that night.

She'd been a friend.

And during his year in hell, she'd become something indescribably more precious than that. Not a saint, per se, but a sanctuary. Her features—blurred by a dim lantern, makeup, and a bottle of whisky—were made even more opaque by time and tribulation. But the memory of her soft lips, her dark hair, and unparalleled touch had climbed inside of him. Had created her own place in a heart growing ever more bitter and bleak.

Ginny. He would find her, he vowed. He'd duck into the Bare Kitten out of the damp London night, and there she'd be. Her face would melt into a smile, because she knew he'd come for her. To claim her. To take her away from a life of objectification and mistreatment.

He'd only have to endure. To survive.

Today, hell was no longer a place, but a state of being. His prison no longer consisted of four walls guarded by unspeakably cruel men, and yet he remained confined.

Trapped.

He could have battled the blinding pain in his wrist. Pain had been a foe he'd vanquished well and often. He'd conquered all that threatened to destroy him. The despair of another sunrise lost to a place so foreign and cruel. The insidious fear that the world you knew had forgotten you in this place, and you no longer had a home. The horror and disbelief of looking down at a body that was once yours, and not at all recognizing it.

But the heat of fever had taken him prisoner, pulled him away from himself and thrust him into an inescapable delirium. Then, with the inevitability of mortality, the chills followed, seizing him up in such force, his bones surged and rattled. Reality became nebulous, and time a fabrication of madness, until the more he tried to cling to the memory of Ginny, *his Ginny*, the more she became a diaphanous specter.

His world had become a nothing but a gray cloud of pain. He would dream that his blood was turning black, tentacles of the putrid stuff sprouting from his apendage-less wrists and reaching up to poison his heart. Agony consumed everything, the fever burned away all hope. All thought, dreams, or memory. Until he could no longer visit his sanctuary. Until he could no longer conjure her face. He gave himself over to the mist, melded with the pain, and ceased to fight.

That's when she said his name.

She called for him through the cloying mist. Her voice followed by waves of cool pressure on his skin bringing blessed relief. She told him to fight, begged him to live, and a fire ignited inside of him again. Frantic, he reached for her. He desperately fought against a mire threatening to swallow him, immobilizing his limbs.

He tried. *God,* how he tried. How had she found him in hell? She didn't belong here, but he couldn't bring himself to let her go.

A male voice joined hers. Grating and unwelcome. Pain accompanied it and their voices became more frenetic.

Cole tried to snarl, to warn the man away from his woman, but he couldn't summon the breath. A lake of fire and brimstone drowned him before he could summon her name again, and dragged him down into darkness.

Imogen spent three days with her heart palpitating so intensely she could barely function. So very much was at stake, and the anticipation of disaster overcame everything, driving her halfway to madness.

The only reason she retained her job was because she'd been right. During the emergency procedure, Dr. Longhurst found infection not only in Trenwyth's muscle tissue, but also in his bone. He'd done what he could, but the fever still refused to subside, and the fear was that too much damage had already been done.

Trenwyth's death would not only be a tragedy that could have been prevented, but also the impetus for so much more calamity. Dr. Fowler would have an excuse to be rid of Longhurst and herself, and he made it no secret that doing so would cause him extreme pleasure.

Men like him hated nothing so much as the proof of their own folly. Even though Imogen mentioned no word to the staff about his refusal to perform the procedure, he still pierced her with his repugnant glare whenever she was unable to avoid his presence.

Her nights became a blur of chaos and catastrophe. Anxiety and exhaustion made her clumsy and forgetful.

Del Toro threatened that if she spilled something on one more patron, or broke another dish, he'd have to start *charging* her to work for him.

It seemed that the thread of balance she'd woven into her life had become as tenuous as Trenwyth's survival. Any moment now, the thread could snap. *Any moment* and the fingertips by which she clung to the edge of the abyss would lose their desperate grip, and she'd shatter at the end of an absurdly short fall.

"Any news, dear girl?" Lord Anstruther queried as he'd done every day when she'd brought him his tea and paper. "Any change?" He looked more brittle than ever before, the edge of his lips tinged in blue.

"I'm afraid not, my lord." She gave him the same answer, and they shared a moment of frustrated concern for Trenwyth. "He's breathing steadily, perhaps a bit less agitated, but he still refuses to wake."

"Well, *I* refuse to die until he wakes, and that's my last word." Anstruther lifted his arms so she could set his tray across his lap, simultaneously wagging his finger toward the ceiling.

"Have you taken to issuing edicts to God?" she teased.

"Only to Sarah." He winked at her. "I'll leave it to my dearly departed beloved to organize the afterlife for me. If the Lord is so omnipotent, he'll know ahead of time that there's no arguing with her."

Even in her distracted and fatigued state, the wicked earl was able to pull a laugh from her. "Are you certain it's a good idea to wax so blasphemous at a time like this?"

"It's the only option of vice I have left to me." His wit was interrupted by a wheezing breath. "I haven't the capability for much sin in or out of this bed these days."

Fighting a smile, she adjusted his pillows, made him

another poultice for his chest, applying it with a warm, moist wrap.

"You take such good care of me, Nurse Pritchard," he said with uncharacteristic solemnity. "I'd be more miserable under the care of anyone else. I don't suffer fools, you see, and you're not just kind, but you're sharp and not easy to astonish. A rare trait among women of my rank. You remind me of my Sarah."

This wasn't the first time she'd heard this from him, but the compliment never ceased to flatter her, as he clearly held his late wife in such lofty esteem.

"If you'll pardon my vulgarity, it occurred to me that you may not have been able to bring me the renderings you promised due to lack of . . . that is . . . insufficient funds." His eyes darted away from her, as his noble reticence to discuss money reminded her of just how distant their worlds were from each other. "I had Cheever procure several sketchbooks, canvases, and instruments by which the commission could be accomplished."

His gaze was equal parts hopeful and abashed, and Imogen couldn't remember ever finding someone quite so charming in her entire life. How could she tell him that his concern over her financial status was only half of the cause for her delay? The extra time she'd spent caring for Trenwyth already cut into her clandestine profession at the Bare Kitten. In the estimation of a highborn man, a few evenings spent at the museum once her shift at the hospital ended should be nothing at all. A pleasure rather than a chore. Had she her druthers, he'd be absolutely correct.

But her life was exceedingly more complicated than he was capable of imagining. And she barely had the time or strength anymore to lament that she wasn't the artist she'd hoped to be.

"Well, you've succeeded in astonishing me, Lord Anstruther, but surely it is not appropriate for me to accept such a gift."

"Bah." He made the same face he did when swallowing his bitter tinctures from the apothecary. "When you're my age and rank, my dear, just about any eccentricity is permitted."

That produced another laugh, though this one shaded with regret.

"I'd compensate you for your time, of course." He cleared his throat, again uncomfortable at the mention of funds.

So much gratitude for his kindness welled within her heart, her chest literally ached with it. "It's not that at all, my lord, only—"

Dr. Longhurst burst into the earl's private room without so much as a knock, startling him into a fit of coughs. "Nurse Pritchard! It's Trenwyth. He's awake." Without processing the information, Imogen went to Anstruther, but the old man waved her off.

"Go," he wheezed. "I told you . . . *He'd* listen . . . to Sarah." Again the earl pointed to the ceiling.

It was almost enough to make a believer out of her as she followed Dr. Longhurst into the hall.

The door to Trenwyth's room stood open, and light spilled from it along with a cacophony of voices. Dr. Fowler was in there, she could tell from his jowly voice as he ordered other staff around the room. William entered before her with a tray of tea and broth.

All noise was smothered by her blood pounding between her ears as Imogen's dread surged as powerfully as her euphoria. What if Trenwyth remembered her? He'd recognized her voice as Ginny's in his feverish delirium.

He'd called to her, dreamt of her, clung to her like she was his salvation, and that very admission evoked trills of foreign and ridiculous hope.

But . . . what if in consciousness, she was nothing more to him than a whore? What if he revealed her secrets to a room full of her employers? Of men. She'd lose everything.

Just as quickly as the fear presented itself, she excised it. How could she consider herself at a time like this, when a man she'd fought to save had miraculously pulled through?

Because it was not only herself she had to consider. She had her mother to support, and her sister to protect. They had no one else. They relied on her absolutely.

Dr. Fowler had sent for Trenwyth's sister, Lady Russell, but she was traveling with her husband on the Continent, and they'd not heard a word from her.

Which meant . . . Cole had no one either.

Not true, Imogen decided. He had *her,* and there was no chance she'd let him go through his dreadful recovery alone. She'd nurse him back to health. She'd be a source of strength, knowledge, and of encouragement. No part of her would be denied to him. Her assistance, her body, her hands, *her heart* if he wanted it.

Imogen knew he'd owned a part of it since that night they'd spent together. It would take little more than a kind word and that devastating smile to coax the rest of it into his strong hands.

Hand. He only had the one. She'd help him get used to that as well. She'd fetch and carry what he could not. She would—

All sentient thoughts scattered like a flock of startled birds when she rounded the frame of his door.

Had Imogen passed him on the street, she would not have recognized him. Certainly, there was the jaw she'd shaved smooth only this morning. Aristocratic angles and masculine stubbornness clenched against a sip of tea William held to lips that remained pressed together. His hair wanted a cut, though she'd washed and shaped it after a fashion. It fell across eyes that bore no resemblance to the molten fire she remembered. They were now more feral than fierce, but dull too. Dull and empty. As if everything that had once made him Collin Talmage, Duke of Trenwyth, had been taken, leaving only this coarse and rather lupine creature in his stead.

Shadows seemed to gather around him that had nothing to do with the fact that Molly drew the curtains closed against the spring afternoon.

"Your Grace," Longhurst said, leading Imogen into the room. "Might Nurse Pritchard persuade you to take your tea, or broth if you prefer?"

Unable to breathe, Imogen stared in slack-jawed stupefaction.

Trenwyth's eyes flicked over her and fixed back onto Longhurst. He'd considered her only for the time it took a grain of sand to pass through an hourglass, but it was enough to set Imogen's limbs to trembling. Not for the reasons she predicted either. Those eyes, once so full of assessing wit, predatory confidence, and not a little pain, were now only strident wells of immeasurable nothingness.

"Why would she?" His dry voice resembled a growl, but lacked an iota of inflection.

"Why, indeed?" Fowler muttered from where he stood over the duke, his arms crossed in what Imogen translated to be a rather defensive stance.

She winced, but stood her ground, unable to tear her

eyes away from the dear sight of him. Alive. Awake. His left arm, still heavily bandaged, was secured to his chest with a sling draped from his wide shoulder. He had regained some color beneath his chapped and weather-beaten skin.

He was battered, bruised, and still every bit as beautiful as she remembered.

"Nurse Pritchard is the reason you're alive," Longhurst informed him.

"Hardly!" Fowler unfolded his arms, his hands falling to clench at his sides.

"She, alone, diagnosed you," Longhurst reasoned. "We all thought you had typhus. She fought for you. For your survival. And won, obviously."

Trenwyth's head swiveled on his neck with almost unnatural slowness until he'd speared her with a glare that froze the blood in her veins. "Did she?"

It wasn't gratitude that arranged his features, but accusation.

Longhurst's regard, in contrast, glowed with uncharacteristic warmth. "She is to be commended," he murmured.

No one said a thing for an uncomfortably long time.

Conscious of her drab uniform and the severe knot of hair beneath her cap, Imogen smoothed her apron as she stepped forward, trying again to catch Trenwyth's eye. "If the tea isn't to your liking, I could bring you another—"

"I want nothing from you," Trenwyth said shortly without looking at her. "I despise tea. I'll take coffee."

Stung, Imogen stepped back. This wasn't at all what she'd expected.

"Stimulants are not recommended for recent surgery patients," Longhurst informed him. "Perhaps in time—"

"Where is my man?" Trenwyth's cold copper eyes searched the faces of all those gathered in his room. All but hers.

"Who?" Fowler asked.

"Sean O'Mara, my valet, did he return from . . . ?" For a moment the duke looked confused, then resolute as though he'd remembered something, until the shadows and spite settled back around him like a cloak. "Is he alive?" he asked tightly.

"He'll be sent for straightaway, Your Grace." Longhurst bowed to him, watching him intently. "He's now employed with Scotland Yard under Sir Carlton Morley. In the meantime, allow Nurse Pritchard to administer your opiate tincture. For the pain in your wrist."

Trenwyth's lip curled back from his teeth in a cruel sneer. "That plain-faced twit won't come near me, and neither will you, sawbones."

"Beg your pardon?" Longhurst said in a way that made it clear that pardon wasn't being begged, but demanded.

"You won't drug my wits from me, not when I've just regained them." The duke met Longhurst's challenging gaze with dark censure.

"But your arm," Imogen couldn't stop herself from protesting. "The pain will be unimaginable once the Laudanum we've already administered completely wears off. Worse than it is now. You'll want to take all precaution against it." It must be pain causing him to act like this. For he was not the Trenwyth she remembered.

His eyes were slivers of disdain when he looked at her again. "I don't have to *imagine* what it'll be like. Think you I'm afraid of pain?"

Imogen pictured the many scars and wounds that, even now, turned his entire topography into a map of torment.

Of course, after being through so much, how could he possibly remain unchanged?

"No, Your Grace, but perhaps something topical? I could—"

"You've done enough. Get out."

Longhurst took a protective step toward her, his brows drawn down with mystification. "Your Grace?"

"Everyone. *Out*." The teacup William had returned to his tray shattered on the wall above her head, showering her with lukewarm droplets. "Get me O'Mara," Trenwyth roared, upsetting his tray with one powerful swipe.

Molly shrieked and fled to the hall.

As Longhurst and William surged forward to subdue the furious duke, Fowler grabbed a speechless Imogen by her elbow and dragged her into the hall.

"Pack your things, Miss Pritchard, you no longer work for St. Margaret's Royal Hospital."

Still too stunned for words, she blinked dumbly up into the bags drooping from Fowler's bitter eyes for a moment too long. "But . . . what have I done?"

"You are being dismissed for gross insubordination." His *s*'s protracted like that of a viper as though he took reptilian pleasure in the words.

"You mean with the duke?"

"You were told to leave it alone, to leave him alone, and you deliberately went behind my back and convinced *Longhurst* to perform a procedure without my permission."

"But he survived because of that," she argued.

"Doesn't matter, what if the next patient dies because you now think that since you were right the once, you know more than the attending physicians? The London medical community is already afflicted with too many angels of death, Nurse Pritchard, we don't need one more."

He referred, of course, to the nurses who often euthanized their terminally or chronically ill patients. Some called them angels. Others called them murderers.

She was neither.

"Please, Dr. Fowler," she begged. "I've never done anything like that. This is the first and—I promise—the only time I've ever disobeyed an order. I won't do it again. I swear. Just don't let me go. I have a family to support."

"You should have thought of them before you made a fool of me." He released her roughly and she stumbled. "Molly, fetch me all the orderlies and nurses on the floor. We'll need help subduing Trenwyth, and someone will need to escort Miss Pritchard off the premises."

"Yes, Doctor." Molly cast her an unpleasant look as she scrambled to comply.

Imogen's eyes latched onto Lord Anstruther's door down the hall. "Can I at least be permitted to say goodbye to—"

"You will be permitted to do what you like, Miss Pritchard, so long as it's not on these premises." He held up his hand as she opened her mouth to plead for mercy. "Before you ask, don't even consider requesting references, as none will be forthcoming. Good day to you, Miss Pritchard." He substituted "miss" for "nurse," making it clear that it was no longer her title.

Oh God, nothing had at all gone as she'd hoped or as she'd feared. Her greatest fear should not have been that Trenwyth remembered her.

It should have been that he'd not recognize her at all.

CHAPTER SEVEN

Imogen didn't remember that she'd abandoned her things in her cupboard at the hospital until halfway through her shift at the Bare Kitten. She couldn't even recall who'd escorted her out. She'd barely felt the chill of the misting rain until she'd wandered the streets for an hour. Incredulity had given way to numbness, and then despair. She couldn't bring herself to return home. Couldn't watch her mother try to keep the house and cook the meals and do the shopping on rheumatic knees that no longer wanted to work. Couldn't watch her sister, dear, pretty Isobel, try to make herself look presentable for school and tell her that she might just have to go to the factory instead. She couldn't face her failure in their eyes. She'd saved the life of a wealthy, ungrateful duke and, in doing so, lost the only income that kept them afloat. It amazed her how short a distance it was from St. Margaret's in the West End to the Bare Kitten on St. James's Street, and yet, how they seemed to occupy separate worlds.

Her world was only this now, Imogen thought as she looked around the dingy opulence of the place she loathed. Sweeping rubbish and a broken glass from the disgusting floor, she did her very best not to resent everyone and everything. Her father, for leaving them in this diminished position. Her sister for being younger and innocent and in need of protection. Her mother for being feeble and ill and reliant upon her. Dr. Fowler for his irrational ego and damnable pride. Trenwyth for making love to her. For making her care for him. For not recognizing her.

And most of all, herself. Because, regardless of everything, this was her fault.

"While you're down there on your hands and knees, why don't you clean this with your mouth?" the drunken man who'd broken the glass suggested as he cupped himself lewdly. His companions erupted into hilarity disproportionate to the wit, as a table of drunken men was wont to do.

Imogen stood, her broom in one hand and dustpan in the other. "I'll get you a new glass," she offered dryly, trying to avoid the disgusting sight of the spittle studding his beard. She turned away, making for the rubbish bin behind the bar.

"How much for this one, del Toro?" The man slapped her behind as she passed him. "She seems obedient. I like that."

Del Toro paused from where he enjoyed his imported cigar in the corner. "She's my serving bird," he answered easily. "She's not for sale, Barton. But help yourself to any of my kittens, sir, at a discount since it's a slow night."

"Not for sale, everyone's for sale!" Barton argued. "How much, and I'll pay it?"

Del Toro's eyes flickered over her, and he sent her a

secret smile that curdled like sour milk in her stomach. "Someone once paid twenty pounds for her." He blew a perfect ring of smoke. "You can have her for that much."

"Ha! That's an entire bargeload of shit, del Toro. She in'nt worth twenty shillings, tits that small."

"My hand to God." Del Toro enjoyed his own story with a hearty laugh. "Believe me or don't."

"Who was the doffer wot paid it?" Barton challenged.

"Now, Barton, what would your wife think if I went around disclosing my clientele?" Del Toro was without scruples, certainly, but not without savvy. "A man in my business must be discreet." He gave Imogen a wink, but tossed his head toward the bar in a silent order to get back to work.

Discarding the shards of the glass into the rubbish bin, she stowed the broom and dustpan and returned to fill the odious Mr. Barton another drink.

"I'll do it, Ginny." Jeremy Carson flashed that kind, boyish smile of his and, not for the first time, Imogen noted that his cobalt eyes seemed to have witnessed ages. "I'll deal with your table if you deal with that, though I don't know that I'm doing you any favors." He pointed to a puddle of vomit left beneath a table of old and grumbling men who'd decided now was a good time to settle the bill.

Sighing, Ginny decided she'd rather clean up vomit than serve human excrement like Mr. Barton.

"It's a full moon tonight," Jeremy mused seriously. "They say it makes people do strange and terrible things. Best watch yourself, Ginny."

"Thank you, Jeremy." She mustered a grateful smile, and went in search of a pail.

She spent the night working through her predicament

in her head. Rent was due in a week, and she'd not have it. The larder was full—well—as full as it ever was, and they wouldn't starve if they were careful for at least two weeks. Maybe she could apply for another nursing position at a different hospital. She didn't have references, but if she wasn't mistaken, Dr. Longhurst held her in some respect. Perhaps she could convince him to write an unofficial letter of recommendation.

The thought cheered her slightly as she emptied the rubbish bins into the can in the side alley out back. Her arm ached from the strain as she used one to clutch her shawl over her wig to keep the curls from loosening in the rain. All she had to do was wait until Dr. Longhurst finished his shift at St. Margaret's and catch him as he left. She could even pen the letter for him and persuade him to sign it, and then she wouldn't have to rely on him to remember—

Rough hands grabbed her by the scruff of the neck and bent her farther forward, forcing her head over the foul-smelling bin.

Imogen cried out, but a big body bent over hers, clapping another hand over her mouth and forcing her to breathe in the stench of the rubbish.

"If you're not for sale, then I'll take you for free." Barton's breath smelled of cigarettes and gin, an odor foul enough to rival that of the rot beneath her. Fear, disgust, and the stench had bile crawling up the back of Imogen's throat. She swallowed it and a scream, knowing neither could escape her covered mouth.

She tried to bite him, to rear back so the bin's edge wouldn't cut into the tender flesh of her belly, but he jerked her head to the side so roughly that she feared he'd break her neck should he try it again.

"Struggle and I'll make you regret it. Scream and I'll knock you unconscious," he warned, and began to gather her skirts behind her.

If she *didn't* fight him, she'd regret it all her life.

Going limp, she once again swallowed her revulsion and reached into the bin, rummaging frantically until she found what she'd been searching for. A shard of the glass he'd broken earlier.

Palming it, she waited for him to shift in order to undo his trousers. When he did, she jerked her body around and struck at him. The glass cut her too, but she knew she'd found her mark when he grunted and released her. The makeshift weapon caught him in the ribs, beneath his arm. Painful, but not fatal.

Not deep enough.

He struck back then, his sharp fist opening a cut on her lip and collapsing her to the dirty stones of the alley. Explosions of darkness in different shades danced in her periphery, and Imogen clung to consciousness as fervently as she clung to the sharp glass in her hand.

"Even the law knows you cannot rape a whore," he slurred, bending over her, fist cocked to strike again. "When I'm through, you'll—"

She didn't allow him to finish his threat. Lunging forward, she slammed the glass into his neck, right above the clavicle. He screamed then and jerked away, leaving the thick shard of glass in her viselike grip.

Warm blood sprayed her from the wound, until he covered it with his hand, stanching the flow.

Terrified, desperate, Imogen surged past him, hoping to escape.

"Wait!" Barton grabbed for her, his meaty hand twining

in her shawl. Yanking back as hard as he could, the shawl came away in his hand.

Dropping the shard of glass, Imogen reached for the door, ready to go for help.

"You've killed me," Barton gasped, as he slumped down against the brick wall. Blood ran down his shirt, his vest. So much blood. "You've killed me, you devious cunt." His voice held no fury, only incredulity.

Imogen knew he was right. If he didn't get help in minutes, he'd bleed out there in the alleyway. But if she went for help and he didn't survive, she could hang for his death.

The alley door yanked open, and Jeremy's light eyes widened as he nearly collided with her.

"Ginny? Good God, what's happened?" His hand closed over her shoulder, his skinny arms long enough to reach the distance.

"Bitch stuck me," Barton accused weakly. "Fetch the doctor or I'm done for."

"Yes, go for help," Ginny said, though her chest was heaving as though she'd run a league. The knowledge that she was as dead as the man who'd attacked her lit a fire beneath her feet. She had to get away. She had to warn her family.

Whirling, she wrenched out of Jeremy's grasp, gathered her skirts and bolted.

"Ginny, wait!" He grabbed for her shoulder again and came away with her dark wig tangled in his fingers. Imogen only looked back once as she fled. She saw Barton, barely conscious, perched against the brick, and Jeremy, staring at the wig in his hands with horrified aversion, as though he'd pulled a limp dead animal from her head.

He looked up at her, confusion and disbelief mingling

in his young eyes, and she knew what he saw. Her hair, gold washed with strawberries, her mother would say, tumbling past her shoulders and darkening with moisture.

"Get help," she cried again, before plunging into the rain-soaked London night.

CHAPTER EIGHT

Imogen didn't stop running until her lungs threatened to burst. The streets were sparsely populated due to the time and the weather, but not deserted. Twice she had to turn down dangerous-looking alleys to avoid a foot patrolman on his beat. Luckily for her, the rain kept most people's gazes directed at the cobblestones from beneath their hats and umbrellas.

She fought for breath as she took refuge beneath a dark overhang across from the train station. Looking down, she gasped at the sight of so much blood on her hands, not all of it hers. She held them out to the rain, watched and trembled as the storm attempted to clean her open palms, turning the crimson wells into a pink watercolor. The gash in her hand was long but not deep, and had begun to throb now that her all-consuming panic had subsided to a bone-rattling anguish.

She let the wall hold her up for a moment so she could think. So she could breathe.

Imogen wanted to run home, to warn her family, but she would frighten them looking like this. Not only half-dressed, but covered in a man's blood.

A man she'd murdered.

Not only would she upset and shame them, the police would come for her as soon as they were summoned to the Bare Kitten. Del Toro wouldn't protect her, this she knew.

Should she warn them? Should she wait?

Had she killed him? The answer would mean the difference between a prison cell and a noose.

Imogen's lip smarted where he'd struck her, and it tasted of rain and copper when she tested it with her tongue. The storm had washed away the spray of Barton's blood from her bosom, but not the stains on her low-cut bodice. She had no shawl to cover herself, and the cold seeped into her bones. The rain turned her hair into heavy, limp strings, and she didn't even want to think about what her makeup must look like.

She had nowhere to run. No one to go to. There would be no getting on that train. Someone would surely stop her in this state.

Unless . . . unless she could change and clean up. She'd left her things at the hospital, hadn't she? She knew she had a clean black uniform frock in her cupboard and, while she was there, she could doctor her palm and her lip and hopefully formulate a plan. She kept a few half-pennies in her cupboard in case she needed a lunch or to make the train.

Only a handful of night nurses and one doctor on the ground floor would be in residence now. The wings were not overflowing at the moment and stingy Dr. Fowler didn't like the expense of extra night staff.

Gwen might be on shift, and Imogen was fairly certain she could trust her friend. Besides, she hadn't been able to say good-bye.

She might have to say good-bye to everyone now.

The grim reality threatened the strength of her knees, and Imogen knew that if she sank to the ground, she'd never rise again. So she summoned what remained of her fortitude, arranged the wet sheets of her hair to conceal what she could of the bloodstains, and plunged back into the storm.

Imogen infiltrated the hospital easily, knowing which doors would be unlocked or unguarded. She navigated the dark halls silent as a specter, though she left trails of rainwater in her wake. Pilfering bandages and supplies, she cleaned and bound the cut on her palm first, so as not to leave blood on anything else.

Her reflection in the mirror brought hot tears to her eyes. They scalded her numb, cold cheeks as they escaped. She hadn't cried about the man she may have killed. Nor did she weep at the pain of her wounds or the cold of the rain. Surely she'd expected tears to run at the prospect of losing her family, of losing her life, but her eyes were the only parts of her that remained suspiciously dry as she fled through the storm.

Until now.

Until she spied the pale, wan mask of skeletal terror that stared back at her from over the washbasin. The kohl with which she'd lined her eyes and darkened her lashes streaked all the way to her chin. Her upper lip was split and swollen to twice its usual size, but only on the left side. It bled no longer, which was a small mercy. Her fair hair, matted with rain, hung in limp tangles.

Blood. Blood stained the almost translucent, sky-blue

bodice of her dress. It turned the gauzy fabric into a lat-
ticework of violence.

A fugitive sob burst from her as she grabbed at a cloth
and soap and began to scrub. She shook with turbulent
emotion as she uncovered her light freckles from beneath
the powder that she'd used to turn her skin to flawless porcelain. Tears turned her muddy hazel eyes a sharper shade
she could almost call green. When she'd finished, she recognized the pale, plain woman staring back at her. Wide-
eyed and shivering. A sharp nose slashing over her mouth
pinched with pain and cold, her already full lip swollen
to an almost comical size.

A plain-faced twit. Wasn't that what Trenwyth had
called her? She wondered what he would say if he could
see her now. She *was* plain. And gaunt. Her shoulders
little more than sharp angles and her clavicles threatened
to slice through her skin.

Something twisted deep in her gut. Something so cheer-
less and desolate, she gasped. The death of her future,
perhaps. The bitterness of a trusted, happy memory turning
to ash.

Sniffing in a bracing breath, Imogen found her cupboard, reached inside, and found . . .

Nothing.

No frock, no small purse of three halfpennies. No extra
stockings, petticoats, or aprons. Someone had taken her
things, or had thrown them on the rubbish heap.

Imogen's breath left her in a bleak rasp as her last bit
of hope flickered out.

Abruptly, she knew what to do. She hated herself for it.
Even as she stood, gathered her sodden skirts, and tiptoed
toward the stairs, she actively loathed the crime she was
about to commit. But the thought of her sister starving

pushed her up the first flight, and the image of her mother breaking down at the news of her daughter's crimes propelled her up the second.

Lord Anstruther, that dear, wonderful, dying man, had been nothing but kind and generous to her.

And she was about to rob him.

In the drawer at his bedside table he kept what he called "a bag for trifles." Enough coin to tip a delivery boy, or to send with his valet to fetch or buy something.

Enough coin to keep her entire family for a month. Longer if they were even more frugal than usual. She could find her sister on her route to school and slip her the money, taking just enough to make her own escape and figure a plan from there.

It was all she could do now. Anstruther would barely notice the coins' absence, but it would buy Imogen and Isobel time to figure out their next step.

The carpets and the storm muffled the sounds of her movement as she crept down the fourth-floor hall. Rainwater still squished in her slippers, but not quite so loudly now. Imogen couldn't believe what she was about to do. That she even considered something so utterly deplorable.

And yet, here she was.

Anstruther's room was located very close to the nurses' station, which was tucked back into a room of its own, and she slowed to an incremental tiptoe as she neared. Flinching when the handle of the earl's door clicked open, she eased inside and pressed it closed with infinite care.

With the drapes drawn against the tempestuous night, the darkness was absolute. Imogen preferred it that way. She'd maneuvered these rooms in the dark for years.

Lord Anstruther's even, wheezing breaths broke her heart. She inched forward, trembling more from careful strain now than her cold, sodden garments. All the while, prayers for his peace, for his comfort, flowed through her as she used his bedpost as a guide, then slid to the nightstand.

She was better at this than expected, she thought. Made nary a sound as she eased the drawer open and reached her fingertips inside, quickly finding the silk satchel and tracing the rigid outlines of several coins. Now only to lift it without making a—

"If you're the angel of death come to take me, be quicker about it. One should think you're on a schedule." Anstruther's voice, raspy with sleep, still conveyed his everpresent good humor.

Imogen froze and squeezed her eyes shut, her heart slamming into her throat, and then diving to her stomach.

A match struck and a wick hissed as it caught. In that moment, Imogen knew it was over. All was lost. Anstruther would ring the bell for the nurse, they'd call for Scotland Yard, and men with shackles would come for her. She knew this, because while her will screamed at her to run, her legs hadn't the strength left to make it very far. She'd reached the limits of her capability.

"Nurse Pritchard? What's this? What the devil are you doing? What in God's name are you wearing?" His rapid-fire questions all pierced her as she wordlessly pulled her empty hand from the drawer and shut it with an audible click.

"I was after your coin, Lord Anstruther," she admitted in a surprisingly even voice.

"Look at me, dear girl." The earl's order was quiet, but threaded with that absolute authority that belonged to those born to dictate.

Slowly, Imogen turned to him, every muscle of her

features fighting to stay smooth through the quivering tension. She let out an uneven breath as she met his clear, kind eyes. "I'm desperate," she said tightly, hating the tear that tickled its way down her face. "I'm stupid . . . and I'm sorry."

"There's blood on your dress, if you can call *that* a dress." He slid his eyes away, obviously more scandalized at her state of dishabille than shocked at her admission. "Is it yours?"

It took her an absurd moment to consider if he inquired of her ownership of the dress or the blood, but decided to answer about the latter.

"No, my lord, the blood is not mine."

He took a long moment to observe her, eyes snagging on her matted hair, her split lip, her sodden dress and bandaged hand.

"You may call the authorities, my lord." She glanced down, unable to stand his regard. "I'll not stop you."

"Fetch that lap robe and cover yourself, Nurse Pritchard," he directed instead. "You're showing enough flesh to send my feeble heart into conniptions. I'm dying, not dead. Good Lord."

Hurrying to comply, Imogen huddled into the soft, warm lap robe and clutched it to her.

"Now," he continued. "I'll stay my hand with the authorities if you pull that chair close and tell me why you were caught with your hand in my purse, whose blood is on your bodice, who struck you, and why you're dressed like . . . well, like you'd charge a penny a dance."

Perhaps it was because in all her life, she'd been acquainted with many men who'd call themselves gentlemen, but she'd never before met a truly *gentle man*. Someone who'd have her cover up rather than reveal herself. Who'd use a euphemism before calling her a whore. Surprised and humbled, she did exactly as he'd instructed.

Her story poured from her like a final confession. She told him of her mother and sister, of their two-room flat that smelled of fish and despair. She spoke of her father's debt and her indentured servitude at the Bare Kitten. Recounting her dismissal from St. Margaret's, her attack, and the probable dead body they were likely even now taking from the alley.

Anstruther listened without interruption. Only his mustache twitched as he made little tsking sounds of distress from time to time.

Imogen didn't weep until she reached the part where she'd planned to steal from him. To take his money and meet Isobel on her way to school, slipping her the coin before she disappeared, hoping to find anonymity somewhere. Here the tears flowed freely. Tears of shame, of sorrow, and of helplessness.

He was quiet a moment after she'd finished her tale, and she couldn't bring herself to look at him. Imogen couldn't say why, exactly, but she'd left Trenwyth out of her story. She said nothing about the night with him. About the connection they'd had before he returned an ill and changed man.

She knew that if she took that regret out to examine it, she'd disgrace herself past all repair.

"What time is it?" Lord Anstruther queried softly.

Imogen blinked up, dashing at her cheeks. "My lord?"

"It's either very late or very early, which is it?" He gestured to the pocket watch on the bedside table and she handed to him.

"Very early," he muttered, and then turned to capture her gaze with his. "You listen to me, Miss Pritchard, you have a choice of two kinds."

Imogen swallowed, but remained silent.

"I will give you that bag with all the money it contains and send you on your way right now, but I warn you that you won't get very far."

The kindness of his offer both humbled and startled her. She stared at him for a moment in dumb amazement. "What—what's the second option?" She was almost afraid to ask.

His mustache lifted in a mischievous smile. "That you marry me, of course."

Chapter Nine

London, May 1879, Nearly Two Years Later

Cole wanted to take the steel-spring blade he'd attached to the inside of his prosthesis and shove it through Liam Mackenzie's brawny neck. Not because the Marquess of Ravencroft was his enemy. It was simply that every word from his former commanding officer's mouth dripped like acid into the dark, empty void where his heart had once been.

"I'm telling ye, Trenwyth, it's like she never existed." The dark Scotsman helped himself to some Scotch from his own distillery kept in a crystal decanter on the sideboard of Cole's private study. "If I didna know ye better, were ye not so relentless, I'd think her naught more than a dream. Some figment of fantasy ye'd conjured to keep yerself sane in that piece of hell."

Cole turned away and released the top few buttons of his shirt, not wanting the monstrously large marquess to see him choking on his disappointment.

Where are you, Ginny?

"She's starting to *seem* like a ghost," he confessed. "I've lived a lifetime in the three years since she and I . . ." Drifting to the study window, he pulled back the drapes and braced his right forearm against the pane, avoiding his reflection.

"It's been so long," Ravencroft murmured gruffly. "Why do ye torture yerself still by persisting in this hopeless search?"

"Perhaps I've become accustomed to torture." His eyes refused to focus on the tableau in front of him, instead gazing into the murky, blood-soaked images of the past. "That prison. That hell. She provided me a piece of heaven there. She occupied that place in my mind that they couldn't get to. That they couldn't take from me. She's there still, but even I'm beginning to fear that she was a delusion. A construct. Something . . . someone I needed at the time, but never truly existed."

Reaching for her was like trying to grasp at the sea with his bare hand.

"I've spent so long searching for her, and yet I fear that I'd pass her in the street and not recognize her."

Ginny. A beautiful, raven-haired specter. Her features blurred until he only possessed the descriptive words, but not the image. Obscured by drink, darkness, and the passing of too many days, his memory of her lived everywhere but in his eyes. He could recall how astonishingly small she'd felt beneath his hands. Little more than flesh and bone. Her skin the color of moonlight and softer than Indian cashmere. Her eyes had been huge in her thin, delicate features. Anytime he tried, Cole could conjure the kindness he'd found in their depths, the hesitant desire, the fear and the fondness. So why not their color? She'd been wearing so much makeup that night . . .

He remembered the sweet tremble of her voice, hardly above a gentle whisper, and yet threaded with conviction and compassion. How he craved that now. That quiet place inside she'd taken him. He'd never known peace like that before, and certainly not since.

A loud crash from outside stole his attention, and he looked in time to see his loathsome neighbor in her garden, screeching like a madwoman and shaking her skirts as she ducked and danced. An easel, canvas, and chair rocked from where they'd been upended in her panicked frenzy. She let out another inhuman squeal, half call for help, half war cry as she snatched a rolled-up paper of some kind and began wildly striking the air with it.

Peace, it seemed, was to be eternally denied him. Most especially with *her* living next door.

What the devil was she doing? Battling some insidious insect, no doubt, Cole surmised with a bemused grunt. He found himself rooting for the bug, so strong was his dislike of the woman.

"Well, the lass is nowhere to be found on this island, I can tell ye that." Ravencroft let out a heavy breath. "Probably not on the Continent either. We've searched Paris, Berlin, Vienna, Rome, all the places a woman of her . . . industry might seek her fortune."

"We?" Cole glanced over his shoulder, his eyebrow lifted.

The man they'd christened the Demon Highlander gave what might have been called a guilty shrug. "I have an . . . associate with more connections in that world than I. I've enlisted his aid."

"An . . . associate?" Cole echoed.

"He's someone I trust. The Earl of Northwalk."

"You mean Dorian Blackwell, the Blackheart of Ben

More?" Trenwyth corrected tightly. "And here I'd thought you smarter than to trust the most notorious criminal in the empire. Just because he's managed to snag the Townsend heiress no more makes him an earl than stepping in the mud makes me an urchin."

Case in point, Lady Anstruther out there among her tea roses, lavender, and forget-me-nots. A countess by all rights, but resembling nothing close to a lady.

"Blackwell has more noble blood than ye'd think," the Scotsman muttered.

Turning away from the stormy look on Ravencroft's hard features, Cole noted that the woman had succeeded in swatting the abhorrent swarming creature to the ground, and was now grinding it into the stone path with the heel of her boot.

His mother would have been mortified to share a property line with such a disgrace. He was merely annoyed.

"I went back to the Bare Kitten when I returned from the Americas recently," Cole continued. He'd searched for Ginny through logbooks at Ellis Island, New York, where many immigrants landed, and continued his search far into the interior. He'd searched for himself too, but came up empty-handed in both regards. "The old proprietor, Ezio del Toro, seems to have retired back to Sicily. The barkeep, a Mr. Carson, owns the place now, though how a lad that young—and apparently witless—could afford it is beyond me. He worked alongside Ginny for a few months, and barely remembers her name, let alone where she lived or who her people were."

"I'm still not convinced that del Toro bastard didna lie to us when he said he never knew her last name," Ravencroft speculated. "He was a shifty tub of lard if I ever met one. I always thought he knew more than he let on."

The laird's words reflected Cole's own suspicions. He had gone to the Bare Kitten the moment he was well enough to walk again. Del Toro had pretended not to remember Ginny at first, and then when he was caught out, confessed that he'd hired her not too long ago. He'd subsequently let her go because she'd attacked a customer. Though which customer, he couldn't recall.

Not for the first time, Cole had wished he'd killed the greasy man right then and there. It would be no less than he deserved. Usually men didn't lie to him, not when he had his good hand wrapped around their throats and the sharp metal of his hidden wrist-blade at their sacs. But back when he'd confronted the pimp and game-maker, he'd been barely released from the hospital. Weak, frail, and desperate.

What if del Toro had lied to him? What if the man had more guile than Cole had credited him with? What if . . . he'd kept Ginny for himself? Taken her to Sicily, perhaps.

The very idea made Cole's skin crawl and his stomach clench. Every lead had gone cold, and the woman he'd pined for these past three years had simply vanished into the London mists.

"Perhaps your associate, Blackwell, has contacts in Sicily, and could find del Toro for me. I think it might bare new leads, interrogating him once more."

"After this long, Trenwyth, the odds of finding her are approaching nil. Not one of the whores who worked with her stayed at the Bare Kitten. None of them remembered much about her either," Ravencroft said carefully as he drew up behind him. "Och, I'm not accustomed to speaking to the back of a man's head, Yer Grace," he chided. "Are ye admiring yer own reflection in that window, or have ye found something that's better to look at than my brutish face?"

"Neither." Trenwyth opened the drapes further to share the view. "I was simply watching my insipid neighbor make as much of a disaster of trying to paint as she does of everything else."

Ravencroft peered over his shoulder past the hedgerows that hid a stone and iron fence, on the other side of which the Countess Anstruther had wrestled her canvas and easel back into place. She currently settled herself into her uprighted chair, spreading a stained apron over her blindingly pink skirts.

The marquess gave a low whistle. "Well now, that's a bonny view ye have there."

"Her?" Cole snorted. "*Hardly.* She's nothing more than a grasping opportunist that can afford a garish wardrobe."

"She's not wearing much of that wardrobe now." Ravencroft chuckled. "Ye canna say ye hadna noticed."

"Dressed or not, she is *beneath* my notice."

Only . . . she wasn't.

He'd noticed the day he'd returned to Trenwyth Hall that if the weather was clear, Lady Anstruther habitually took advantage of the light in her garden. Almost every afternoon she'd pack her art supplies into the sunlight, eschewing the help of servants, and set up in this very spot. The canvas would face the sun to the west, and she'd sit facing the east. The room he'd picked for his study happened to give Cole a perfect view of her. How could he help but *notice* her?

He *noticed* that, if the day was warm, she'd strip off her blouse, painting only in her chemise and corset as she did now. He *noticed* that she hadn't the sense to use a lawn umbrella or parasol, so what occasional sun London enjoyed tinted her skin an unfashionable shade and darkened the freckles that marred her nose. He *noticed* that her hair was too golden to be called red, and too red to be called blond.

He even *noticed* her vivid expression of emotions that he'd never again hoped to experience as she daintily pressed her brush to the canvas with the most whimsical, almost unbridled movements. Inspiration. Nostalgia. Contentment . . .

Peace.

Lord, how it irked him. How little he regarded her, but how much he *noticed* her.

"I take it ye're not friendly neighbors?" Ravencroft surmised.

Cole made a caustic sound. "Her late husband, Lord Anstruther, was a particularly decent man. She some-*bloody*-how got her claws into him as the old man—seventy if he was a day—malingered on his deathbed. They were married only nine months before he expired, and now she is the sole proprietor of his fortune, as he had no heir, and his estate was not entailed."

"Is that right?" Ravencroft asked, conveying only mild interest. "I suppose that's an infrequent occurrence among our class."

"There's the rub. The woman *has* no class. No family, title, or money. The daughter of an impoverished merchant, she was his nurse at St. Margaret's, if you'd believe it. I've looked into her a little to see if I could wrest Anstruther's legacy from her, but the documentation is ironclad. She certainly helped him put his affairs in order before she likely helped him to the grave."

"That's a substantial accusation," Ravencroft remarked.

"More a speculation than accusation," Cole admitted.

"But I'd stake a rather mighty wager on it." From Cole's vantage, he could trace the errant breezes that riffled through the glinting fall of her unbound hair as though carefully choosing which strands to pull away from her shoulders and across her heart-shaped face. She tucked at it with a long and graceful finger, stained with blue, and she left a streak of it in her hair that she didn't seem to be aware of. "She's even presented her younger sister to society, to the queen!" he scoffed. "Pretty girl, but who would lower themselves to have her?"

Ravencroft shifted more to his right, leaning farther into the window to catch a better view. "Ye can never tell these days," he stated blithely. "The Anstruther fortune may not be as vast as our own estates, but it is significant. I imagine many impoverished noble families might come up to scratch. The world is changing. More and more land-owning peers are forced to swallow their pride in favor of a much-needed dowry. The little sister of a countess might look better to us blue bloods than shipping an heiress from America."

Though his face tightened in a grimace, Cole ceded the point. "I suppose, but . . . a *nurse*? It's just so bloody obvious. The man was still mad for his saint of a dead wife. I can only imagine that lust or lunacy could have driven Anstruther to marry again, and if that was the case, couldn't the man have found a decent-looking debutante who'd know what to do with his legacy?"

"Who would settle for decent-looking, when a man could have a ripe beauty like that making his last few months on this earth merry?" The laird chuckled. "I love my wife's mind, her wit, and her soul, but they're not what I'm appreciating when she's trouncing about with no blouse on." He gestured to the shamelessly garbed woman, who now held a paintbrush in her teeth as she used a cloth to correct some mistake on the canvas.

Cole supposed some men would find her beautiful. Indeed, they might see the way the sun had moved the shadow of an elm to dapple her bare shoulder in dancing silhouettes and appreciate the honeyed hue of her smooth flesh. Or they'd find the arch of her darker russet brow charming as it accentuated the depths of her concentration. Perhaps the bow of her full lips would be considered excruciatingly sensual to some as she nibbled on the tip of her paintbrush whilst inspecting her work.

But not him. He preferred midnight curls to straight, fair locks, and porcelain skin, not freckles and honey. Slim, shy wraiths enticed him. Not the hearty type that romped out of doors practically in the altogether.

If she was beautiful, it was like a viper was beautiful. Best to be appreciated from afar, and given a very wide berth.

"Perhaps ye shouldna be so hard on the old man's memory," Ravencroft admonished lightly. "I've noted this sort of thing too many times in my life as an officer to discount it. Nurses and soldiers, ye ken? There's something about the gentle healing touch of a pretty, kindhearted woman that a man who's been kissed by death canna seem to resist. It evokes a powerful emotion . . . obsessive even." Flicking Cole a meaningful glance, he dared, "Besides, nursing is a great deal more respectable profession than whoring, wouldna ye agree?"

Cole's returning glare was full of warning, though he had no retort when presented with his own hypocrisy.

"Doona mistake my point for censure or judgment." Ravencroft put up his hands as though to ward against attack. Even so, his features remained as good-natured as the savage-looking Scot could attain. "I've fallen prey to the curse, myself. I've married a woman who'd been in an asylum, after all. Disgraced, besmirched, and dishonored, she still makes an excellent marchioness."

"Yes, well. She'd have to possess a certifiable measure of insanity to consider marrying the Demon Highlander," Cole retorted, with no real heat in his scorn.

Trenwyth actively hated the contented warmth in Ravencroft's wry laugh. "Then I am to assume your recent marriage is a happy one?" he asked.

"Happy doesna seem an apt enough word," the marquess answered rather enigmatically. "Last year was . . . eventful. I lost a brother and gained a wife."

Cole crossed his arms, tucking his metal hand against his opposite bicep. They'd never spoken of it. Of the dreadful time that Laird Mackenzie had brought Major Hamish Mackenzie to the Home Office and thrown him upon the mercy of the crown. Hamish had been a monster by that time. A monster. A murderer.

A traitor.

To his crown and to Cole.

They'd charged him for innumerable war crimes, treason, and hanged him shortly before Christmas. Cole and Liam had been allowed to attend, even though the crown had outlawed public executions in 1866.

Ravencroft and Trenwyth had always respected each other. The lieutenant colonel, almost a decade Cole's senior, had been his commanding officer for a time, until Cole had taken a commission with the Special Operations Corps. Ravencroft earned his moniker, the Demon Highlander, on the open battlefield, where he dominated with the savage brutality of his Jacobite ancestors.

Cole never earned a moniker, for his brutal deeds rarely left witnesses.

On paper at the Home Office, his work was filed under diplomacy. In the field, it was no less than espionage, intelligence, and, in most cases, assassination.

It was the elder Mackenzie bastard, Hamish, who'd followed Cole into the Special Operations Corps. And then he'd betrayed him to the Turks in order to save his own skin.

Ravencroft hadn't known he'd been rescuing his own brother's victim when he'd been sent in to retrieve Cole from the Ottomans. The marquess had accompanied the American consul, the British ambassador, and the Irish-American reporter Januarius MacGahan to Bulgaria under the guise of intelligence gathering, as the Ottomans denied the Bulgarian uprising ever occurred. They'd scoured towns of once seven thousand souls with only two of their thousand left remaining. They'd searched heaps of bodies rotting in the streets with no one left to clear them. Rummaged through the decaying skulls of maidens and the babies skewered by bayonets. Fifty-eight massacred villages. Five desecrated monasteries. Thirty thousand corpses were combed through while the dogs feasted.

The aftermath of the horrors Cole had witnessed. Had battled against. And somehow survived.

Then they'd heard that more than a few important prisoners had been marched east toward Constantinople, and it had still taken several months for Ravencroft to find him. Their relationship had been forged anew when he'd dragged a beaten and emaciated Duke of Trenwyth back home.

The American journalist wrote an exposé on it, and the English press and the people began to call for answers. Oscar Wilde, Charles Darwin, Victor Hugo, they used their influence to force an investigation, for Britain, or rather, the whole of Europe to take action.

Ravencroft and Trenwyth had joined the ranks, hoping that Britain would do more than sanction the Ottomans for their villainy. As time passed, it seemed, their cause was lost in the cogs of capitalist bureaucracy.

Regardless, they'd forged a deeper acquaintance during that tumultuous time. But it wasn't until the day they both watched the man they'd once called brother kicking at the end of a rope that their bond had been solidified. Cole confided in the Scottish laird like no other. Though Ravencroft resided mostly in his Highland castle with his two children and relatively new bride, he'd still been instrumental in Cole's tireless search for Ginny.

"Are you in London for the duration?" he queried flippantly, hoping to change the course of his dark thoughts.

"Aye, my daughter Rhianna is presented to the queen and having her season. My life is naught but bloody ball gowns, ceremonies, waltzes, tedium, and yer terrible English food. I've considered impaling a few of my daughter's favorite young lads on my dirk, just to enliven the evenings if nothing else."

"Sounds bloody awful."

"'Tis." Ravencroft scratched at his ebony hair, which he kept past shoulder length. Cole surmised that it was to hide the few locks of silver that shone at the temples. "I'll be a pauper and a murderer before the season is out, mark ye me."

They both knew this to be a lie. At least the part about

becoming a pauper. Ravencroft was responsible for more deaths than almost anyone in the history of the empire, surely, but he owned some of the best land in all the Highlands. His estates and distillery were more than profitable, they were enviable.

"Havena even had a proper honeymoon," the burly Scot groused.

"A pity," Cole replied, distracted for a moment as Lady Anstruther lifted her long hair and coiled it into some sort of knot on top of her head, stabbing it through with an extra paintbrush. Lord, had her neck always been that elegant? "It's not as though you need to get an heir on her or anything," he muttered, shifting a little to relieve an uncomfortable tightness in his trousers.

"If ye'd met my wife, ye'd understand my need to drag her away from all distraction and keep her naked for days in some warm, exotic place. But I canna do that until my stubborn daughter has bewitched and broken every limp-wristed, useless aristocrat in this godforsaken city."

"Another ball tonight, I take it?" Cole smirked, grateful he'd escaped the peculiar responsibilities of fatherhood.

"Actually, she's chaperoned tonight by my late wife's mother, her grandmother." The marquess didn't exactly sound relieved, more resigned. "Lady Ravencroft has enticed me to attend a benefit this evening. A new charity project she's rather passionate about."

"By enticed, you mean coerced."

Ravencroft made a noncommittal sound. "I doona mind so much, it's a good cause and I hear the food will be grand. So, there's that."

Grunting in response, Cole glared down at Lady

Anstruther, reminded of another reason to dislike her. "Let's hope your wife has the sense to keep the charity down in the slums where it belongs."

"I doona grasp yer meaning." Ravencroft's voice slowed and lowered, as though he wondered whether or not to be offended on his lady-wife's behalf.

"Don't get your kilt in a bunch, I mean nothing against your beloved marchioness." Cole gestured once again out the window where the candid countess was pressing a damp cloth to cool her neck and shoulders, dipping it below her bodice. Beads of moisture glittered on her skin, as though someone had sprinkled her with stardust. Cole suddenly forgot what he'd been about to say as he traced their eventual paths over the expanse of her chest and into her décolletage.

Abruptly seized with a great thirst, he reached for his own snifter of Scotch and tossed it back in one great, scorching gulp.

"Then to whom were ye referring?" Ravencroft pressed.

"*That* woman," he spat. "If you'd believe, she has opened her mansion here in Belgravia to a handful of harlots, unfortunates, and unwed mothers."

"The conniving bitch!" Ravencroft gasped, his mocking sarcasm as thick as his burly chest.

Cole sent him a droll look. "She's trying to convert one of London's finest and most magnificent homes into a haven for pickpockets and dock whores. Everyone in the borough is in a foaming frenzy over it. They barely tolerate that actress Millie LeCour living on the other side of her because they're terrified of her husband, who I understand is another connection of your curious new associate of Blackheart fame."

"Christ, Yer high-and-mighty Grace, were ye always such a snob?" The laird nudged him with his elbow.

"Probably."

"Perhaps ye should check next door amongst the so-called handful of harlots for yer long-lost Ginny."

He already had.

"Ginny was no common prostitute. She was . . . different."

"How so?"

Cole poured himself another drink rather than answer, which opened him up for more of the laird's irritatingly astute observations.

"Could it be that the only difference yer Ginny possesses from the other . . . ladies of the evening is nothing more than that she means something to ye?"

Cole took a sip, glaring down at the Anstruther garden, desperately trying not to remember what del Toro had revealed to him that night.

The bastard had sold him her virginity.

And he'd been too drunk to notice.

Cole had been her first lover, and it tormented him to consider how many men might have had her since. That they might have used her roughly. That the kindness, the *innocence,* she'd shared with him could have been extinguished in the time they'd been apart.

Because he'd not been there.

"Look, see there?" He pointed with his prosthetic hand, unwilling to put down his glass. "That buxom wench she's embracing." Ravencroft moved in closer, peering down to observe the outrage to which he was referring. Lady Anstruther stood grasping the hands of a voluptuous woman with a stunning wealth of auburn hair. "The countess is barely dressed and receiving guests in her garden. And that other woman, she's obviously a wanton."

"Aye, that she is."

Something in Ravencroft's tone prompted Cole to glance up at the man. "You say that like you know her."

"I do. That buxom, wanton wench would be my wife, Mena Mackenzie, the Marchioness of Ravencroft."

CHAPTER TEN

If ever Imogen hated herself for being easily coerced, it was tonight. Why, oh why, had she ever allowed Millie LeCour to talk her into hostessing this event? At first, Imogen had been terrified that no one would bother to attend; now she fretted about having enough room to accommodate them all. Especially for dinner.

Upon Mena Mackenzie, Lady Ravencroft's, advice, she'd invited an excess of guests in hopes that a mere percentage of them would attend. It seemed that her initial guest list was enough to entice half the London *ton* to accept. Not only did the Demon Highlander's marchioness sponsor the event, but the powerful and controversial Earl and Countess Northwalk advertised their attendance, as did Millicent LeCour, her neighbor to the west, who happened to be the empire's most beloved celebrity.

Imogen knew she should be thrilled, not terrified.

So why couldn't she seem to shake a portent of impending doom? What if tonight turned out to be an unmitigated disaster? Wasn't the chance of catastrophe and ruination a great deal of the reason everyone was here, to gawk at the interloper, the counterfeit countess who'd snagged an earl?

Imogen's hands fidgeted in their gloves, and she wondered if they were damp enough for her guests to feel the moisture through the fabric. Antithetically, her mouth was as dry as the Sahara. Her smile had begun to shake at the corners and, not for the first time, she wondered how much longer she'd have to stand at her grand entrance and greet people who neither liked nor accepted her as one of their own.

It hadn't bothered her until now. Imogen had thought, once she'd married the Earl of Anstruther, her days of scraping and bowing to the rich and titled were over. Her plan had been to lock herself and her family inside this lovely mansion with her canvases and paints and leave the rest of the world to itself.

Apparently, she was a glutton for punishment, and found that she wasn't suited to a life of idle leisure. Without a cause, without some kind of purpose, she just couldn't seem to thrive.

Who'd have guessed?

But, had she known this evening would be the result of all her preliminary work, she might have seriously reconsidered her processes. So many people. Their bejeweled and adorned bodies winked beneath the lights, a firmament of gems. Imogen wondered if there were truly as many stars in the heavens as diamonds in London.

"Relax, darling." Millie LeCour slid her crimson-gloved arm through Imogen's and tucked her into her side. For such a diminutive woman, the ebony-haired seductress was a considerable force. Her charisma arrived three entire paces before she did, and any room that contained her seemed a hundred times more colorful. "The scent of fear is like an aphrodisiac to these people."

"Not just *these* people." The actress's inconceivably large husband was her constant shadow. Imogen blinked up at Christopher Argent, wondering just what he meant as he scanned the ballroom with the air of a predator selecting which morsel to cull from the herd. Was he insinuating that he also enjoyed the scent of fear? That couldn't be right, and yet . . .

Imogen had been acquainted with them less than a year, but she'd observed that in their marriage, Christopher Argent was the sturdy ship upon which they sailed the stormy oceans of life, but Millie was unquestionably the rudder. The auburn-haired Viking seemed content to follow his lovely wife's chaotic navigations, and their devotion to each other was as inspiring as it was envy-inducing. He seemed affable enough, his expressions only ranging from mild disinterest to faint amusement. But the enigmatic Mr. Argent often did and said things that sent a little thrill of fear sliding across the nape of Imogen's neck. She didn't know the man well, but she had the distinct notion that he was more lethal than a viper.

Ignoring her husband, Millie swept her free arm to encompass the entirety of the Anstruther mansion's grand ballroom. "I insist that you enjoy yourself, darling, the night is already a rollicking success."

"The night's barely begun," Imogen murmured, imaging the scenarios of any number of disasters.

"Precisely, the evening is full of opportunity and possibility. Come morning, all of London will be talking of nothing but your incomparable affair."

Impulsively, Imogen hugged Millie, kissing her soundly on the cheek. "You and your friends have been so kind to me, I could never repay you."

Millie's brilliant smile drew the stares of so many. "I'm lucky to have such women in my life, and am happy to share them with you, most especially in support of such a worthy cause."

Smoothing her white glove down the front of her intricate apricot dress for perhaps the millionth time, Imogen scanned the ballroom, ticking off her particular accomplishments to soothe her nerves.

With the Marchioness of Ravencroft's expert guidance, she'd draped the white marble hall in heaps of gold to match the embellishments on the Grecian columns. Billowing drapes caught the night air from windows left open to allow the late spring breezes to cool the room. Strings of lights, valances, candles, cast an ethereal glow over the crowd, accentuated by charming paper lanterns she'd had one of her boarders purchase from the Asian markets. Guests seemed to appreciate the flattering golden light, and some had already begun to turn about the floor as the orchestra cued their selections of music including Camille Saint-Saëns, Antonín Dvořák, Pyotr Ilich Tchaikovsky, and some Gilbert and Sullivan to appease the nationalists.

Speaking of the marchioness, Mena Mackenzie's statuesque figure glided toward them, draped in bronze silk that set her hair ablaze. To Imogen, she conjured Botticelli's *Birth of Venus*. Not only in her build and beauty, but in the dualism of the rather sensual divinity and kind benevolence that shone from her aspect.

Ascending the stairs to the entry landing, she held out her hands to Imogen, and greeted her with a kiss on both cheeks. "Everything is just lovely, dear," she encouraged. "And look at what a marvelous time they're all having."

Imogen had to admit, it did seem that everything was going well thus far.

"I'm intimately acquainted with that look," Mena confided. "You're certain something is about to go wrong."

Imogen frowned, pained that she was so transparent.

"I was a viscountess before I was a marchioness, and I've hosted more of these events than you can imagine. Let me assure you, your fears are not baseless. In fact, you can't completely relax until you've put out a fire, whether literal or figurative. But with our help, you'll avoid, or at least be able to conceal, any mishap or emergency before it's noticed."

"I'm praying that the mishap this afternoon counts." Imogen wryly referred to when Clara Boyle, a former fishwife who'd recently joined her employ, had shown the marchioness into the garden instead of having her wait in the parlor, without so much as an announcement. Imogen had been painting in little but her chemise and skirts, her hair twisted above her neck and her face ruddy from the heat.

Mena, of course, had been gracious and sweet, laughing off Imogen's mortification while mentioning that she lived in the Highlands where men worked the fields clad in only their kilts, boots, and the low Scottish sky.

The lapse in etiquette worried her, though, as she'd planned on making a particular point this evening. That, given the proper training, education, and opportunity, even someone from the lowliest circumstances, like a prostitute or a petty thief, could live productive, lucrative existences in society.

They only needed a chance.

"Has anyone seen my wayward husband?" Mena queried.

"I'm certain he's not arrived yet." Imogen glanced toward the door, where Mena watched expectantly. She was certain Laird Ravencroft wasn't in attendance, because the Scotsman surpassed even Christopher Argent in size, and therefore was impossible to overlook.

"It's not like him to be tardy," Mena worried. "He said he was visiting a friend here in Belgravia this afternoon, maybe you know him, the Duke of—"

"Lady Anstruther."

Imogen turned to face Cheever, whom she'd promoted to butler upon her husband's death. He hovered in a way that was both absolutely appropriate, and completely unsettling. Something had happened, she could tell by how he clasped his hands behind him.

"What is it, Cheever?" She was proud of how she kept her voice even, though her breathing had increased dramatically.

"Pardon the interruption, but there's some urgent news from Croyden, madam. Might I consult with you in the blue parlor? Should only take a moment."

Imogen felt the blood rush from her extremities, and she released her hold on Millie so she wouldn't give in to the impulse to collapse against her. "Of—of course, Cheever." Excusing herself from her guests, she made her way across the ballroom on legs as substantial as glass.

Croyden. This was bigger than a mishap. This could very well be the epic disaster she'd been fearing. *Croyden* was the code word Edward and Cheever used when discussing the Bare Kitten.

Imogen found Jeremy Carson in the blue parlor helping himself to some Turkish delight she kept in a crystal dish. He stood when she entered, and self-consciously swiped a dusting of confectioner's sugar from his trousers.

"Ginny—I mean—*Lady* Anstruther." He gave a rather exaggerated bow and tried to hide the rest of the confection in his cheek.

"Jeremy, what a pleasant surprise," Imogen lied. It wasn't that she harbored any bad feelings for the boy, quite the contrary; it was only that any news from the Bare Kitten promised to be dreadful.

Imogen was somewhat of an expert in handling dreadful news, but . . . just not tonight.

"I hope everything is well with you," she prodded gently, keeping her voice deceptively mild.

His cheek pouched over the candy somewhat ruined his crooked smile, but it was endearing all the same. "Sorry to inconvenience your ladyship, I didn't know you were having a toff to-do tonight. It's just that, there's something I think you should know."

Bracing herself, Imogen reached for the high back of the chair, gripping it until her entire hand went white. "Go on," she encouraged.

"That lofty duke, the one what lost his hand, he came round asking after you again yesterday." Jeremy took advantage of her astonishment to finish chewing his Turkish delight, and she watched the obtrusion of his Adam's apple dip as he swallowed the entire thing.

"After me?" she finally gasped.

"Well, after Ginny, but yeah." Jeremy removed his cap and held it in both hands, worrying at the rim. His hair, the color and consistency of oat straw, stuck out in wild tufts, though he'd obviously tried to tame it with pomade. "But I says to him, I says, 'Oi, I don't care what kind of title you throw around, I ain't telling you a thing.'"

"You said that to him?"

"Well, not in those precise words." He threw her a sheepish grin, revealing one gold tooth that was somehow utterly charming beneath his freckles. "But I told him that I didn't remember nothing, I hadn't seen you round, and it didn't matter how many times he came asking, my memory's not like to improve with time."

"Bless you, Jeremy." Imogen stepped around the chair and sank into it, letting the fine velvet envelop her in comfort and warmth.

"Ain't nothing, Your Ladyship." Jeremy gave her an endearing wink before placing his hat back on his head. "Though what that old cripple wants with you is a bleeding mystery, if you'll pardon my saying so."

"You don't have to call me Your Ladyship," Imogen reminded gently. "You were a friend before . . ." It wasn't that she didn't want to answer Jeremy's not-so-subtle question, it was only that she didn't want to ponder the reasons why Trenwyth would be looking for Ginny after all these years.

"I haven't heard a word from Devina, Heather, or any of the others," he said encouragingly. "They shouldn't be a danger to you." The women that had worked the Bare Kitten with her had been offered an entire year's salary to relocate, no questions asked, and they'd all taken it gladly.

"There's only . . . Barton," Jeremy reminded her soberly. "And no one's seen him since that night. No one, that is, but Flora."

Imogen had never forgiven herself for what became of Flora Latimer.

Apparently the night Imogen fought off Barton, Jeremy had chased after her until he'd lost her in the mist some blocks away from St. James's Street. Upon his return, he'd found Mr. Barton had vanished. In Imogen's frenzy, it seemed that she'd not injured him as gravely as she'd initially thought. Poor Flora Latimer, the sweet blond harlot, had had her throat slit in the cursed alley. She'd been discovered bound, sodomized, and facedown in a pool of her own blood.

Imogen wished she'd have killed Barton after all, and then he'd not have taken his rage at her out on poor Flora. He'd disappeared, of course, but he was always there, a pinprick of worry in the canvas of Imogen's new life, threatening to reappear at any moment from the shadows to ruin the entire tableau.

"Your Ladyship?"

Imogen blinked at him, startled for a moment that he still sat watching her with a particular alertness. "I'm sorry, Jeremy, what were you saying?"

"I know it's not my business, and if you don't mind my asking, but why is it you're so afraid of this Trenwyth? Is he threatening you? Is there something I can do? Because you say the word and we'll—"

"*No,*" she answered more quickly than she'd meant to. "No. It's simply that when I married the earl and became a countess, it became imperative that I leave that part of my life in the past." She tried to keep her answer as diplomatic as possible, so as not to offend him.

"I can understand that, my lady. You know what *they* say, these toffs are more hypocritical and pitiless than a whorehouse full of vicars on a Saturday night."

"Just so." Imogen laughed, in spite of herself. She'd never heard anyone say such a thing, and she hadn't any idea who these *they* were that Jeremy always quoted. But she often found herself in agreement with them.

"But not you, though." His soft brown eyes reminded her of some guileless woodland creature, and for a moment, her heart melted and everything ceased to be so perilous.

"You're utterly kind to say so, Jeremy." She stood and went to him, planting a chaste kiss on his cheek that left a fierce blush in its wake. "Through everything, you've been such a true friend."

"And always will be, Ginny." He forgot himself, seeming unable to peel his gaze from the floor.

"Call me Imogen," she offered. "It's my real name."

He looked at her as though she'd handed him a costly gift, and he had nothing to give her in return.

Embarrassed and flattered by his youthful veneration, she turned away and put some appropriate space between them. "Is there aught else I can do for you? Things at the establishment are going well?" She didn't want to offend him by offering him money, but wanted to give him the opportunity to ask should he be in need.

He seemed to want to say something, to linger, but then changed his mind. "Naw, I've interrupted a right proper to-do, din'nt I? I should let you get back to your guests."

"Well . . ." She was terrible at this part. Never knowing just what to say, how to leave things with an old acquaintance she never chanced to meet anymore. "You can't know how much I appreciate your coming here. I'm going to have Cheever give you a box of the Turkish delight to take with you. Please do call again."

"Maybe will do." He flashed her that gold-flecked smile, and sauntered toward the door. "Maybe will do."

It seemed as though the moment he left the room, the din of her guests filled the space he'd emptied. She needed to return to them.

She needed to think.

About Cole.

She'd not seen much of him since she'd left St. Margaret's, though Jeremy had alerted her that he'd come by the Bare Kitten looking for her before he'd left for America.

Now he had returned. And still hadn't forgotten her. She didn't know whether to be terrified or pleased.

In her secret self, she could admit to a bit of both.

The kindest reason for him to come looking would be that he remembered their time together with fondness. Perhaps he wanted to again pay to share her bed. Even offer to make her his mistress. Imogen had to admit that, had her circumstances remained what they were, she would have seriously considered such an offer. She'd enjoyed his illicit attentions, and even the parts that caused her pain were still worth the stability and opportunity such a position would have afforded her.

But she didn't need to reflect on options like that now. Edward had generously taken care of all such concerns, not only bribing del Toro with a small fortune, and buying the establishment for Jeremy, but going so far as to set up a six-month investment stipend for the boy. *Man,* Imogen firmly reminded herself. Baby-faced as he was, Jeremy had to be at least twenty-and-one now, only a handful of years younger than herself.

Which brought her to the most terrifying reason the Duke of Trenwyth might be looking for her . . .

What if he suspected who she really was and, instead of wanting her as his mistress, he planned to reveal her scandalous and dangerous past to those who would revel in her downfall?

Perhaps a year ago, that wouldn't have mattered, but now . . . now that she'd begun to build something, to champion a cause, it was more and more imperative that her past remain where it was.

Hidden.

The last time she'd seen Trenwyth had been at Edward's funeral in Belgravia Chapel. She'd been both heartsick and relieved as his last weeks had been miserable, and it hurt her unspeakably to watch him suffer.

Cole had glared at her the entire time. Pale and wan from his own recovery, he'd regarded her with such contempt that it had filled her with angst. At the funeral, she'd been frightened of his recognition, remaining swathed in black and heavily veiled. Lord Anstruther's peers, his military subordinates, and his friends offered her little in the way of comfort, and he'd been no different. The rebuffs had been expected, but she hadn't thought they would sting as much as they had.

Most especially his.

Though, she supposed, it was better that she avoid him. Should he truly recognize her, the life she'd built for her mother and sister would be in peril.

Now that he'd returned from his travels, she'd need to take care.

Her appearance was most certainly altered from what it had been. Her hair, of course, was a different length and color than he'd remember, but beyond even that, she'd been well cared for since her wedding. Instead of her bones protruding through her thin, dull flesh, she'd become pink-cheeked and—admittedly—well fed. The women in her family were not intrinsically delicate, but the Pritchard women had become so for lack of sustenance. Indeed, Imogen had grown hips and breasts at twenty-and-four. Her hair became glossy, and her gaunt gray eyes now sparkled over features turned golden and freckled with too much time spent in the garden. She'd even dare to call her hazel eyes green now, if the light permitted.

In fact, she doubted very much that should Ezio del Toro, himself, cross her path he'd recognize her.

Even so . . . she'd be wise to give her neighbor a wide berth, she decided as she adjusted her gloves and swept into the hall. Collin Talmage was a dangerous man. Being a prisoner of war had altered him. Not just physically, but in ways she couldn't even begin to conceive of. Perhaps in every possible way.

The thought of his loneliness caused her a pang of guilt and sorrow. Curiosity as to his motives for seeking Ginny out after all this time itched at her.

And yet, it was imperative that she keep her distance to avoid the dangerous duke at all costs, she reproached her soft and traitorous heart. Affixing a smile to her lips, she attempted to glide into the ballroom as she'd seen Millie and Mena do, their grace and confidence flowing from them in tangible waves. Though her desperate circumstances had changed, she still had Isobel to consider. Who, even now, attended Lady Caroline Witherspoon's debutante ball in hopes of meeting a husband.

In the gathering crowd, Imogen found a familiar face. "Dr. Longhurst," she exclaimed "I'm beyond pleased that you accepted my invitation!"

He made an awkward gesture, narrowly avoiding an upset of his drink as he turned to her. Though his features lit with similar pleasure, which warmed and diverted her. "Nurse—I mean, Lady Anstruther. I almost didn't attend. I'm appalling at these kinds of events. Never much of a dancer." He pulled at his collar, which was slightly askew. "Can't ignore a good cause. Or . . . the chance to see you again."

Imogen linked her arm with his and gestured to the room at large. "To see you here has made my entire evening."

He flushed a bit, and took a bracing drink. "You're being kind," he muttered uncomfortably.

"How are things at the hospital?" she queried, realizing his discomfort with familiarity.

"Same old." He slid her a speaking glance.

"Dr. Fowler?" she guessed.

"He's retiring at the end of the year, or so the rumor goes."

They shared palpable pleasure in this gossip. "That's the best news I've heard in ages."

Longhurst agreed with a grim nod. "Had I not taken an oath to do no harm, I'd be sorely tempted in his case."

"And no one at all could fault you. In fact they'd applaud you."

He sobered further as he looked down at where her arm casually linked with his. "You look . . . well," he murmured. "Better. Healthier."

"I am. On both accounts." Imogen didn't tell him that she'd been asked to serve on St. Margaret's charity committee, which was to say she'd been asked to become a sponsor of the hospital. She decided in that moment to use whatever clout her money provided her to help further Dr. Longhurst's research and career. "Did you hear that Gwen works with me now, to further my charity work?"

"A great loss to St. Margaret's," he said. "Both of you. You'd think I'd be used to your absence. Almost two years, now, since we worked together. But . . . I still find myself searching for you to assist me. You were the best nurse we ever had."

"Now it is you who are being kind," she countered warmly.

"No." He finally met her eyes, and Imogen was surprised at the admiration she read there. "No, I am not."

Suddenly flustered, she put her hand over her heart. "I trust everyone else is well?" she said a little too brightly. "William, Mrs. Gibby, Molly?"

"Haven't you heard? Molly died. Rather suddenly, or so I'm told."

Struck dumb, Imogen could only blink at him. She'd only met the nurse the once, and their interaction hadn't been pleasant, but the news still came as a shock, especially when given with such nonchalance. "Oh dear Lord. Do you know what happened?"

He shrugged. "I wasn't there. But by all accounts the circumstances were gruesome."

"Lady Anstruther!" Mena hurried to her from the far entry where she'd stood with a cluster of curiously tall, overly well hewn men. "Over here, dear, there's someone very important I'd like for you to meet."

She looked up to Dr. Longhurst, and read something strange in his demeanor. Something more than disappointment. "I—"

"Oh look," he muttered. "There's Gwen. I'll go inflict myself upon her."

"But—" It didn't seem they had finished their conversation. She felt strange about leaving things between them like this, even though nothing of consequence had been said.

Something, in fact, had been left *unsaid*.

"It was lovely to see you," he hurried, extracting himself from her grasp. "I hope to do so again. More often."

And then he retreated, and Mena Mackenzie took her arm and directed her to their cluster of acquaintances. "Lady Anstruther, you remember my husband, Laird

Liam Mackenzie, the Marquess Ravencroft." The woman said his name with such pride, such obvious affection, that Imogen couldn't help but beam at the brutish-looking Highlander.

"Welcome, Lord—er—Laird Ravencroft. Your wife is truly extraordinary."

"Aye, that she is," he agreed as he pressed her hand carefully and released it. "I hope you'll forgive my tardiness, Lady Anstruther, and again my breach of manners, but I've invited a guest tonight, only because I reckoned an extra pocketbook wouldna be dismissed from your gathering."

"You reckoned correctly." She hurried to put him at ease with a warm smile. Certainly she was overcrowded, what was one more at this juncture? The more money they raised, the better, and chances were she'd already sent whoever it was an invitation. "Any guest of the Mackenzies is *most* welcome."

"You are generous, my lady." He turned to gesture to a tall gentleman, whose broad back seemed to test the limits of his tailor's capabilities. The footman had yet to relieve him of his hat, so his coloring remained indistinguishable from where he conversed with Argent in the entry. "Lady Anstruther, allow me to introduce His Grace, Collin Talmage, Duke of Trenwyth."

Imogen fought the urge to steady herself as the entire mansion tilted. For a horrible and absurd moment, she wondered if a house could tip over on its side, even with so many weighing it down. It took every fiber of will she could possibly summon not to reach out for something to steady herself with. Instead, she fisted her hands into her skirts and summoned her shaking smile.

It died when he turned at the sound of his name.

Apparently, in the time since he'd returned, he'd not only recovered from his illness and injury, he'd . . . transformed. This was not the broken, fever-ravaged duke she'd seen last. Nor was he the grieving, amiable soldier she'd met at the Bare Kitten.

The man who stood before her was someone entirely new. Someone she'd be frightened to find herself alone with. In only three years, he'd aged maybe a decade, but not in the way her late husband had aged. He'd . . . grown somehow, in size and strength. The long elegance of the man she'd shared a bed with had been built upon with undeniable sinew and muscle. He wasn't as brutish as Argent, or as brawny as Ravencroft, but to pack such muscle on a man so unfathomably tall would go against the rules of both God and nature.

As he towered above them both.

His features had weathered, darkened, and Imogen became certain that his beauty had acquired that savage cast in the untamed Americas.

"*Lady* Anstruther." His voice put undue emphasis on the word, as though he thought it a personal joke.

Lord, whatever could that mean? What did he know?

"Your Grace," she breathed, and shamed herself by clearing the fear from her throat with a very unladylike sound. "Welcome, Your Grace," she attempted once more, this time with greater success, offering a trembling hand to him.

Prowling closer, he reached for her outstretched fingers.

The hard press of metal against her glove startled her, but she covered her astonishment by gripping the steel to maintain stability until he pressed her knuckles to his lips.

Those lips. Every single part of her remembered those lips. No more than a hard slash across harder features. No longer lifted with masculine confidence, but twisted with cynical arrogance. The change mystified and bemused her, and when he brushed that mouth over her knuckles, a shiver full of unidentified fears and pleasures overtook every bone she possessed. He'd taken her hand with his prosthetic one to purposely unsettle her, of this she was certain.

He watched her with those eyes, those molten copper eyes, tracking her every movement like a scientist would a specimen beneath his microscope.

In that moment, Imogen knew. She was the creature this beast, this wolf, had chosen to cull from the glittering herd. From behind the elegant veneer of the illustrious duke, cousin to the queen, herself, peered the eyes of a predator. Calculating. Hungry.

Lethal.

A footman appeared, quickly whisking away his hat and coat, and then Cheever melted from the limbo where well-trained, innocuous servants resided in complete invisibility.

"Worry not, my lady, the dining arrangements are being reestablished."

"Arrangements?" she echoed, before an emergent horror washed over her in prickles of heat. Of course, as a duke, Trenwyth was the highest-ranking peer in attendance. He'd expect the place of honor at the evening meal.

At the side of the hostess.

CHAPTER ELEVEN

It felt like a sacrilege to be blessed with such decadent food, and unable to manage a single bite. Imogen had never been a persnickety diner, but the thought of swallowing something, even the soup, past the lump of unease lodged in her throat seemed too monumental a task.

Despite her awkwardness, conversation over the main course flowed with gaiety and ease, much to the credit of her illustrious and intriguing guests. From her place at the head of the main banquet table, she could easily follow the conversation of those closest to her while blithely ignoring Trenwyth, who towered to her right.

Custom dictated that he escort her into dinner, which he had. She'd taken his left side, and slid her hand over his offered arm with a sense of both nostalgia and trepidation. These arms had held her once, held her like she was a precious thing. How surreal that she should be touching him now. How strange that he didn't remember. That she couldn't articulate, even to herself, the sense of possession mingled with unfamiliarity that had swept over her with confounding potency. He'd been strong when she'd known him, but not this strong. He'd been stolid, but not this morose. He'd been extraordinarily handsome, but not this . . . she struggled to find the word. Fierce? Rugged? Primitive?

She remembered comparing him to a wolf, sleek and lupine, a pure and potent predator. Now, the comparison still applied, but there was something even more primordial in the way he moved, less domesticated somehow. As though he might rip his suit to shreds at any moment and devour her.

Shutting her eyes against the admittedly sensual thrill that struck her at the thought, she reminded herself to breathe deeply and do her best to navigate the evening with grace and patience.

It would all be over soon.

Straps of some kind made curious grooves beneath his suit coat, and she wondered why he'd bind something so high when it was only his hand missing. Had more of the limb been removed? Imogen hadn't realized she fingered the bindings with idle curiosity until she chanced a peek at him from beneath her lashes.

He'd been watching her fingers from the corner of his eye, that hard mouth drawn into a pained sort of frown.

Sufficiently mortified, Imogen wished that had been the worst faux pas she'd made in regard to the duke.

She'd previously instructed the kitchen staff to prepare his meal in bite-sized portions making certain he could consume whatever course they served him with one hand. Unfortunately, this resulted in him being served an already—and quite artfully, in her opinion—arranged plate while others served themselves according to custom. Instead of looking pleased at her thoughtfulness, he glared at her, making no compunctions about the fact that she'd gravely insulted and perhaps humiliated him.

Imogen had tried to avoid interaction with him all through dinner, careful not to advertise to her other guests that she did so. So many questions, fears, sensations, and scenarios coursed through her until she felt as though she might succumb to the utter torment of it. She focused on breathing, and did her best to follow the conversation.

On Trenwyth's right, she'd placed Edith Houghton, the Viscountess Broadmore, a pretty young widow who attended as her first event out of mourning. Imogen would hate if the woman guessed that she'd been placed there as the only other unaccompanied guest at the table to even out the conversation, but the coquettish woman seemed delighted to have Trenwyth as a dinner companion.

Imogen pretended it didn't irk her to watch the viscountess simper and giggle as she twirled a golden ringlet around her still-gloved finger. Who wore gloves to the dinner table anyway? The woman probably had warts, she thought unkindly.

Dorian Blackwell, whom she'd seated on the other side of the Viscountess Broadmore, also wore his gloves while he dined, so perhaps it wasn't the breach in etiquette she'd previously thought. She was hardly an expert, essentially an outsider among this particular class.

On her left, Lord Ravencroft and his wife sat abreast of Christopher and Millie, and—so surrounded—Imogen allowed those who were already acquainted with the duke to entertain him.

Though Dorian Blackwell was the Earl of Northwalk, she noted that his closest associates still referred to him as merely "Blackwell." Clad though he was in impeccable dinner attire, and possessed of a rather charming wit,

Imogen still couldn't help but sense that she'd invited the devil, himself, to dine at her table each time she chanced a glance in his direction. It wasn't merely his size, the black-as-pitch hair, the eye patch, or the rather cruel cast of his handsome features. It was the vicious gleam in his good eye that belied his amiable manners. Or perhaps the way he assessed every person in his vicinity as one would an acquisition rather than a human being. It was terrifying enough, being introduced to the so-called Blackheart of Ben More, but having him silently catalogue her with that frighteningly intelligent, calculating eye was an experience she'd rather not often repeat.

If Blackwell was the devil, his wife, Farah, was his counterweight in every respect. A small, delicate, angelic beauty with silver-blond hair, kind gray eyes, and a gentle but inordinately capable demeanor.

"What do you make of this modern-day pirate currently terrorizing the Mediterranean, Trenwyth?" Blackwell queried in his dark voice. "This man who calls himself the Rook?"

The duke considered the question for a moment too long, his jaw flexing in the most distracting way over a perfectly formed bite of seared duck breast with figged port demi-glace.

"He's rumored to be a savage, villainous slave trader." Lady Broadmore reached her long neck over her dinner plate as she said this, as though taking them into her confidence. "I've heard he's British, and only steals cargo from North Africa and the Continent, so why should we worry about him at all, so long as he stays clear of the Channel and the English fleet?"

What an insipid thing to say, Imogen thought, trying

to remember why she'd invited the inane woman in the first place.

"He originated in the South China Seas where it is known he conducted a great deal of violence against English vessels," Dorian answered dryly, making it clear that he shared Imogen's plummeting opinion of the woman. "He marauded the Bay of Bengal for a time, then the Arabian Sea. I say the fact that he's moved as close as the Mediterranean is cause for great concern, indeed."

"Besides, not only British ships feed our empire's economy, and not only British lives are of consequence." Imogen couldn't stop herself from censuring the vapid viscountess in her own subtle way.

Blackwell turned his head to regard her with that unsettling astuteness, before nodding his approval. "Well said, Lady Anstruther."

Unused to compliments of any kind, especially for her opinion, Imogen barely stopped herself from pressing a hand to her cheek to feel the blush she was certain stained it.

"I think his story is far too apocryphal." Trenwyth finally answered the original question, after wiping his mouth with a linen. "The high seas aren't what they were a century ago, ruled by pirates like the Barbarossa brothers, Sir Francis Drake, and Blackbeard. The East India Company has been completely dissolved—you were involved some years ago, Ravencroft, if I'm not mistaken?"

The Scotsman shrugged a giant shoulder, though his dark eyes twinkled. "I canna confirm nor deny."

"Shipping is mostly steam powered now," Trenwyth continued. "And cargo very heavily guarded. The probability is that this Rook, or whatever he calls himself, paddles around on a clipper and takes easy foreign prey, and then spreads his own legend with embellishments as thick as Devonshire cream."

Farah Blackwell set her knife down, aiming a disarming smile at Trenwyth. "I don't know, Your Grace, I haven't seen any evidence that steam-powered ships have done to piracy what steam engines did to highwaymen. Essentially, render them obsolete."

"I thought you were fond of highwaymen." Blackwell frowned down at his wife.

"Only one in particular," she replied, running a finger along his arm.

If a man could have purred like a cat, the Blackheart of Ben More certainly would have in that moment.

Imogen felt something inside her go soft at the sight of them. To be surrounded by such love, such devotion, it was enough to make one hope . . .

Edith put a hand to her breasts, which were threatening to escape her bright pink gown. "But, the papers say that he cuts the . . . the *scalps* off his enemies and hangs them from his flagpole, just like those savages in America."

"You should *always* believe what you read in the paper," Argent said in his unique, toneless way that made one wonder if he was being supportive or derisive.

Though the sarcasm was evident in this case.

Millie smothered a smile and said, "Illusory or not, it's imperative someone find out who this Rook character is, and what he wants."

"Why would it matter what he wants?" Mena queried, dabbing at a bit of sauce that had dripped on her diamond bracelet. "The crown is not in the habit of rewarding criminals and fiends, or giving in to their demands."

"Is that so?" Blackwell lifted a cheeky brow and everyone laughed as though enjoying a shared secret.

"Well, I think Millie raises an excellent question," Farah replied. "In my experience, in law enforcement and otherwise, the key to catching a criminal, or to reforming one, is to first identify his motivation. Once that is ascertained, then you have the key to his every move."

Blackwell scowled without umbrage, before returning to Trenwyth. "I asked you, specifically, because I know you're still very active with the Home Office, and I was curious as to their take on the Rook situation."

All turned to look at the duke, who seemed to choose his words very carefully, plucking them from the darkness where state secrets were well kept, and leaving what shadows needed to remain. "As far as the Home Office is concerned, there isn't a situation as of yet . . . Though what worries them the most is the utter lack of available intelligence on the man. He's British, or claims to be, but no one knows who he is or where he came from. He literally has no name. No past that we can find. It's like he just . . . appeared from the sea one day."

"Like Aphrodite," Imogen mused.

Trenwyth's gaze snapped to hers, and he studied her long enough to incite little shivers of heat down her spine.

"Aphrodite?" Edith laughed, loudly enough to draw censuring glances from the other guests. "What utter nonsense, Lady Anstruther. We're discussing a pirate, not a goddess."

"If I'm not mistaken, Aphrodite was said to have been created of sea foam and magic," Imogen countered. "That was the parallel I was making."

"You mean you actually paid attention to your Greek

tutor?" Edith rolled her eyes heavenward and took another bite. "Tell me we're not inflicted with another bluestocking."

"Not exactly." She'd never had the opportunity to study Greek or any other language. She'd had no governess, and only a rather rudimentary education before attending nursing school. But she'd chanced to see the painting of Venus by Henri Pierre Picou at a gallery, and had been so moved, she'd simply had to devour everything she could about the Roman goddess of love and, of course, her Grecian counterpart, Aphrodite. Though she'd let the haughty viscountess think what she liked.

Imogen tried some of the main course as the conversation proceeded around her. She was able to wash it down with a bit of wine and let out a sigh of relief as some of the strain began to unstitch from her muscles.

How grand and extraordinary these people were. She appreciated their acumen and intelligence, but also their progressive principles. Not only did the men converse with conviction and compassion, but they also listened *with interest* when their wives spoke. They respected their views and opinions, and discussed them with as much candor as they would any man's.

It was all rather unsettling, while at the same time very inspiring.

They not only approved of her cause, they championed it. In fact, the Blackwells and the Mackenzies had already begun to draft documents for Parliament regarding hospital and prison reform. Two years prior, Dorian Blackwell had been instrumental in the Prison Act of 1877, which centralized the prison systems and brought awareness to some of the inhumane acts and egregious conditions, including those of younger offenders and children born into incarceration.

When Imogen had approached them, with Millie's help, they'd not only been receptive to her ideas, they'd been delighted. To speak of available medical care and facilities for the poor didn't at all worry her. It wasn't a subject most were unsympathetic to. But when she'd spoken of shelters for desperate women and children, for those who'd been mistreated by their spouses, or those who'd been coerced into prostitution, the response had been unexpected and overwhelming. Even the stoic and unaffected Mr. Argent had been what some might call enthusiastic . . . if they knew him well enough to tell the difference.

Her first step was to convert her home to the Lady Sarah Millburn Women's Refuge, in homage to her late husband's first wife. Once she'd established that, her next step would be to acquire property in all the boroughs of London, from Westminster to Whitechappel, and open similar facilities, staffed with medical professionals to care for the ill and ill-treated, bodyguards to protect the property from pimps and dangerous husbands, and then educators who could help the women find work or means to support themselves. Months ago, it had seemed impossible, and now, because of the success of this night, and the promise of many nights like it, the goal seemed not only possible, but attainable.

As the dessert course arrived, treacle tarts and coffee, Imogen seized upon the moment to address all those present. Standing, she tapped her silver spoon against her crystal goblet and summoned the address she'd spent an entire week memorizing.

"While you're all here, I wanted to take this opportunity to express my gratitude for your support and sustenance of this foundation. We are a blessed few, and we have a divine opportunity to care for those less fortunate. Thank you all and please enjoy the rest of your evening."

The enthusiastic applause both startled and thrilled her, and Imogen glowed when she took her seat. She suddenly found that she couldn't *wait* to tally the donations and get to work.

"A divine opportunity?" Edith wrinkled her nose and rolled her eyes. "Isn't that a diplomatic way of saying that it is our heavenly mandated duty to give to the poor?"

Offering the woman a brittle smile, Imogen refused to be cowed by her ignorance. "Isn't it, though? Be you Anglican, Catholic, Hebrew, or any number of religions, caring for the poor seems to be a rather universal edict."

"Some of us are rather more used to giving edicts than obeying them." Trenwyth followed his caustic remark with a sip of his coffee.

"Not all of us were born a duke," she gently reminded him.

"I certainly wasn't," he volleyed back.

"Perhaps not," Ravencroft said evenly. "But ye are one now, and ye have to admit to a certain amount of privilege that accompanies our nobility, whether we are the firstborn or not."

Trenwyth shook his head. "Yes, but with that privilege also comes a great amount of responsibility. Do we not care for our tenants and subordinates by providing employment? They work lands that we own and maintain at great cost. Generally the relationship is mutually beneficial, and the financial accountability always falls to us. Do we not care for the empire's economy by purchasing wares and sundries, by sponsoring various hopeless causes?"

"Hopeless causes?" Imogen echoed.

Ignoring her, he continued. "Wasn't it Machiavelli that

stated there had to be those who must need to work to make a living or society would collapse? If we privileged few supported the less fortunate instead of allowing them to work, who is served by that?"

"I'm in complete agreement with you, Your Grace," Lady Edith stated smugly. "If the upper classes didn't demand and pay for luxury, then how would the merchant classes live? And if they didn't make a living, how would they employ anyone? We provide the entire empire an extraordinary service."

Argent's cold, blue eyes narrowed. "By all means, let them eat cake."

"We're hardly discussing economics." Blackwell interjected, his gloved hands gripping his utensils just a little too tightly. "There are those, even in this room, who were born with less than nothing and still had our dignity, *our humanity* taken from us. Perhaps if someone felt it their responsibility to help, we wouldn't have struggled thusly."

Trenwyth gestured to Blackwell "But you make my point entirely, you and Argent are self-made men. There are those who would say that you've done rather well, despite your circumstances, and without charity."

Blackwell and Argent shared a look. "No one should have had to do what we did to get where we are."

Trenwyth made a derisive noise. "We've *all* done things we shouldn't have had to do. Some of us in our *own* interest." He gave Blackwell and Argent a pointed look. "And others in the interest of the empire. In the service of every British soul." He gestured to Ravencroft, punctuating his argument with his prosthetic.

It struck Imogen at that moment, how much Blackwell and Ravencroft resembled each other. Each with glittering, marble-black eyes and ebony hair. Same stubborn jaw and patrician nose. A similar cruelty of expression and sardonic brow.

The Scottish laird glanced between Trenwyth and Blackwell as though torn. Imogen knew that, like Trenwyth, he was both a peer by birth and a soldier by trade. But a tender sort of guilt touched his gaze when it alighted upon Blackwell, stirring a particular suspicion within her. Could his noble blood tie him not only to the crown, but another royal line? That of the reigning king of the London underworld?

Ravencroft, the unquestionable elder of the congregation, held his chin as he considered the growing rift at the table. A line, it seemed, was being drawn between those with inherited titles, and those without. "I see the wisdom in both of yer perspectives. Aid and service can be given in many forms. Not only by charity, but also with protection and leadership and justice. There are those of us who are expected to lead, to govern, is that not its own service?"

"Absolutely." Mena put her hand on her husband's arm, ever the peacemaker. "Also those who toil to heal and care and, of course, research ways to better our health and comfort. We can't forget those who enforce the law and even those who clean our homes and dispose of our rubbish. There are innumerable ways to contribute, and it seems to me that Lady Anstruther is only providing one more way to serve and save others for those of us who are inclined to give of their bounty."

Trenwyth set his prosthetic on the table with a heavy sound. "Some give life and limb, is that not enough?"

"Of course it is," Imogen agreed with a sense of growing panic. She hoped to God none of the other attendees were privy to the growing tension in their conversation.

Hoping to temper the glow of fury building in his eyes, she summoned her most charming smile, and was encouraged when his eyes snagged on her lips. "Of course it is, Your Grace, and such a sacrifice is only to be met with utmost gratitude. I do not disagree with you on any particular point, but in my experience there are those who work themselves into exhaustion and are still unable to better their circumstances. Most especially women. At times, they become so desperate, for one reason or another, that they cannot see a way to climb out of the hole they find themselves mired in. Often, they are oppressed by the upper classes, shunned by society, and utterly hopeless. Those are the souls I'm trying to lift from the mire. If they can only be shown a different way, a better way, perhaps they would no longer need charity."

"Your idealism is commendable." His condescension grated on her, but she didn't dare let her smile falter as, she noted, their conversation had drawn quite a bit of interest. "But whatever you're trying to achieve here, it won't work, I tell you. You simply can't take a rat off the street and expect it to behave like a well-bred hound."

Her smile suffered an instantaneous inversion. "People are hardly animals."

He snorted. "They're hardly better than."

"I beg your pardon!" she gasped.

"People must be what they *are,* what they were born to be," he said from between clenched teeth. "I've seen firsthand what happens when a bastard aspires to be a marquess." He cast a pointed glare at Ravencroft before turning back to rake her with a dark look. "Or when a commoner attempts to be a countess."

Stunned at his cruelty, the entire dining hall echoed

with expectant silence. Unable to look at Trenwyth, Imogen glanced over to Lady Broadmore, whose face shone with a smug and vicious enjoyment.

Driven past caution, Imogen allowed a victorious smile to crawl across her features, turning her smile chilly rather than warm as she decided now was the perfect time for a declaration of her own.

"If I were you, Your Grace, I'd take great care before consuming another bite, as your entire meal was prepared by rats."

A small din of confounded whispers surged through the hall as everyone surveyed their plates with uncertainty.

"That's right," Imogen continued, a surge of indignation carrying her voice to everyone. "Every single soul of my staff for this evening, from the servers, to the footmen, cooks, entertainers, decorators, builders, drivers, and valets, indeed all—save the musicians—have once upon a time, to put it indelicately, worked on the streets in one illegal capacity or another. No one would have guessed had I not revealed it to you."

Her point made, Imogen enjoyed the astonished conversation as it swelled around her. "Now that you know, Your Grace, perhaps you'd want to skip cigars and port . . . just in case you are correct and one of these so-called rats tries to poison you."

For an infinitesimal moment, violence shimmered in the air. Imogen couldn't exactly tell where it originated from, the duke, Blackwell, Argent, Ravencroft, or the few footmen who hovered nearby, many of whom had been former guests of Newgate.

An austere sort of rigidity sharpened the angles of Trenwyth's features as he leaned toward her, speaking in carefully enunciated syllables. "If there is one thing that

I've learned in my years of service to the crown, it is that people can, indeed, be trained for short bouts of time. Like rats. You can reward and punish them. You can even dress them up in finery or uniforms, until they are molded into a semblance of what you wish them to be. And the illusion might even convince those who are unaware. But believe you me, when the bullets begin to fly, when the blood flows and the explosions detonate, the rats scurry, only emerging again to pick over the rotting flesh of the brave and noble once the battle has ended. That is a constant. *That* is something you can rely on."

"But this is about life, not war," Imogen murmured, hoping to calm him.

"It speaks to your banality and ignorance that you think there is a distinction." Tossing down his napkin, Trenwyth stood and jammed a finger toward the footmen. "Sooner or later, they will bite the hand that feeds them. Better yours than mine." That said, he turned on his heel, and quit the room.

CHAPTER TWELVE

The crimson pall over Cole's vision distorted the familiar warm halls of the Anstruther mansion into something ghastly and grotesque. His every breath died in his chest, and he gulped at the tepid, indoor air, never seeming to find enough. Despite a thin bloom of sweat that burned like acid over his entire body, he shivered as though he stumbled naked through the streets of London on a winter's evening.

Out. He needed to get out. The lush halls had begun to bend and the ceiling lowered until he fought the urge to drop and crawl, lest it crush him.

A breeze cooled the beads of sweat on the back of his neck, and he whirled to face an open door, gauzy curtains fluttering over it like erstwhile ghosts. Lurching for escape, he plunged into the night and gasped in the unmistakable fragrance of lavender, evening primrose, and night-blooming jasmine. For a moment he stood on unsteady legs, panting and disoriented, eyes darting about the garden as a myriad of colors blended together in a bewildering kaleidoscope.

There. A long bench stretched into the shadows against the house, lending a view of the blossom-choked path. The limestone pathway led to a Tuscan fountain with a tiny fat satyr balancing on one cloven hoof, blowing a horn from which a steady stream of water spouted.

Cole tucked himself into those shadows, appreciating the stability of the bench beneath him, and the cool night air that soothed his raw skin.

He should leave. Should bloody well go home and exhaust himself with training, or running, or a woman. Maybe two. Until his heart stopped threatening to pound its way right out of its cage and onto the floor. Every vein was full of fire, or maybe ice. He could never tell anymore. One thing he knew for certain, he needed to survive the next several minutes before trusting himself to go anywhere.

Reaching a shaking hand into his jacket, he pulled out his pipe and tobacco, the stuff cut with a small amount of Asian ganja, which seemed to very much calm his nerves when they were in this state. His prosthesis itched and stung, the sweat beneath it causing the straps to chafe.

He needed rid of it.

"Christ," he muttered, setting the pipe down to unlatch the attachment. As unsteady as he was, the chore at which he was generally so dexterous seemed an impossible feat. Uttering a slew of curses, he bit down on the already prepared pipe and found his matches. Smoke first. Steady on. Once he stopped shaking, he'd regain his dexterity.

Striking a match on the stone, he watched the flame

flicker and dance in his trembling hand until he managed to light the pipe and draw in the first welcome breath.

Cole didn't know how long he sat there. Long enough for dinner to end, he was certain. The night enveloped him in a shroud of sweet-smelling darkness and coveted silence. Every now and again, strains from the chamber orchestra would filter to him, but blessedly the noises of revelry did not. He'd had enough of people. Enough of everything.

Ivy clung to a familiar wrought-iron fence with a stone foundation. This was not part of the manse's regular gardens in which he'd taken refuge. This was the east garden. Small, private, and walled off from the rest of the house, the east wall abutting his own estate.

Her garden.

The infuriating Lady Anstruther.

He'd thought her only a devious social climber, but it was much, much worse than that. She was, in fact, an idealist. A crusader. One of the consecrated few who'd pulled themselves out of the middle classes and wanted to reach into the gutter and pull everyone else up as well.

Curse her bleeding heart.

She couldn't possibly be so blind, could she? How was it feasible to not realize the risk she was taking, letting criminals and whores into her home? How could she maintain such a misguided faith in humanity? She must have never known cruelty. Or betrayal. She must be a stranger to brutality; the only violence inflicted upon her the errant stick of a hairpin by her lady's maid.

It occurred to him that she didn't know better. That she'd not seen the horror that was the primal man. The beast that lived inside, the rot beneath the blood and offal and clay.

He knew. Oh, he knew. He'd seen men rip each other apart for an extra piece of moldy bread. He'd watched the strong prey on the weak in the most sinful of ways. Once man was stripped of all society, civility, and dignity, even the most noble of them became animals. Savages. Beasts.

Monsters.

He knew because he'd been one of them.

Layer by layer, lash by painful lash, he'd been carved away from himself, from his humanity, until nothing but that primitive savage remained. Once he'd been rescued, the struggle to regain his sense of civility became his only imperative. When nightmares played on the backs of his eyelids every time he closed them. When he had episodes like this one, where his body betrayed his dignity, and the beast threatened to overtake the man, demanding he execute or escape. When paranoia stalked his every interaction, and suspicion became his only companion, he grasped onto the one principle he knew to be true.

Every man was an animal.

The only thing that separated them from the beasts was regulation, convention, and order. England was the grandest empire in the world because of the strident social expectations that harnessed the savage creature. That cultivated intellect and logic and tradition, eschewing the base and the prosaic.

This was necessary for the survival of mankind. Of this he was certain.

He'd experienced the alternative, had lost a part of himself to it, a part of his body, a part of his soul. It haunted his every moment, no matter how hard he tried to keep the creature at bay.

Some lived their lives closer to the beast than others, and it was better that they remain where they belonged.

Where they could prey upon each other. Breeding and cannibalizing until one of their betters came along and established dominance, order, and thereby distracted the monster. Or at least redirected it.

He wished he could make the misguided Lady Anstruther see this. That he could make them all realize. That they could know what he knew without experiencing it firsthand, as it were.

Some of them might understand. He knew Ravencroft was well acquainted with the ferocity of war. He'd been called the Demon Highlander because he'd been known to unleash his beast upon the battlefield. He'd become an unholy thing. But he was not a demon, that's what they didn't comprehend.

He was only a man.

And man was evil enough. He didn't need the help of the devil.

Case in point, these fits of wrath and unreasonable terror that made Cole want to do unspeakable things. These moments when what he feared the very most was himself. These days he felt nothing but spite and irritation. The slightest noise would set his nerves to singing, and incite his urge to strike. It was a daily battle not to act on every impulse. Not to eat, drink, or smoke too much, to fight or fuck too often.

He was barely keeping himself together. He couldn't remember the last time he'd felt peace or pity.

No, that wasn't true. He *could* remember. It had been precisely three years ago.

With Ginny.

He knew that was why he pursued her so ardently. Why, despite his convictions, he made himself a hypocrite only for her sake. Because as bitter and cynical as he became, she remained his only hope for exception. She'd been a true diamond in the rough, as they say.

An innocent whore.

What was she now? *Where* had she gone? He almost feared finding her sometimes, of giving her a chance to prove him right about the whole world. To dash what little hope he possessed. What if he found her, and she betrayed or abandoned him?

Like everyone else had.

Before he'd met her, he hadn't known he could be broken in so many ways. Now, after all he'd survived, he was pretty certain a woman he'd only known one night could finish him.

For good.

The clip of soft, light footsteps alerted him to the hurried approach of a woman before she burst into the garden much as he had. Only she took the time to turn and latch the doors softly behind her.

She passed the wall by where he sat, and hastily navigated the path to the fountain. Her dress, the exact bewildering color of the sunset, brushed at a multitude of flowers, snagging on some of them, but she didn't seem to care.

Lady Anstruther didn't stop until she'd reached the water, plunging her hands beneath the satyr's cold stream and splashing her face with it. Then she pressed damp fingers to her flushed neck. Her breath was elevated, her manner agitated as she paced the wide stone base of the fountain, visibly attempting to compose herself.

She fidgeted while she walked, her hands smoothing the intricate coils of her hair, pressing against where her corset bound her lungs, then lifting to her forehead. She tilted her face to the sky and sought the moon. Once she found it, she stilled and breathed easier, as though the soft light it bathed her in had conveyed some mystical secret.

For a moment, it was as though the moonlight had become sunlight. Her hair shone more brilliantly than it ought. A large flower ornament glittering with center gems winked from the coiffure as though held there by magic and a prayer. In the ballroom he'd thought her gown too garish, a silly ocherous flower among precious jewel tones.

But here in the garden she belonged. She . . . bloomed.

Cole hadn't realized that his mouth had dropped open until his pipe clattered to the stones, spilling ashes and cinders at his feet.

She started at the sound, turning to peer into the darkness. "W-who's there?" she asked in a tremulous whisper. "Jeremy, is that you?"

Something vicious twisted inside him. *Jeremy?* Why did that name sound familiar? Who was he to the sainted Lady Anstruther? A lover, perhaps? It surprised him how little he liked that possible development.

Instead of answering, he bent to retrieve his pipe, stamping out the smoldering coal beneath his boot heel.

And instead of fleeing, like many a frightened damsel would, she ventured closer to him, her voluminous skirts swishing softly against the stones and overgrown plants.

"Oh," she said finally when she'd drawn close enough. "It's you."

Cole could decipher little to no affect in her tone, so he remained silent, finding that his heart answered each step she took with alarming acceleration. Damn her, he'd barely calmed the excitable organ down. Though, apparently, it wasn't the only organ that seemed to react to her nearness. Adjusting his position to alleviate a disturbing tightness in his trousers, he slid deeper into the darkness toward the far side of the bench.

The daft woman mistook it as an invitation to sit next to him.

"Worry not, I didn't plan to linger." He lifted his pipe. "This seemed like the place to seek refuge from the insufferable crowd and indulge in a smoke before taking my leave."

"It seems we had similar instincts, Your Grace." She glanced around, and Cole wondered if she used the colorful flora as an excuse not to look at him. "I'm exceedingly fond of this garden. It makes an excellent refuge."

He chose not to reveal that he knew just exactly how often she made use of this sanctuary. That he could spy upon her from his study window and he'd seen more of her than she'd ever intended.

"Though I confess, I didn't expect to find you here." She seemed nervous. In the moonlight, he could make out the intensity with which she clasped her hands together in her lap.

"Obviously." He should have been chagrined to be discovered lingering on her property. "Expecting someone else, were we?" He set his pipe next to him to itch at the straps of his prosthetic. "Some clandestine rendezvous? Tell me, as a merry widow, do your tastes lean toward the gallant lord, or do you keep to the groundskeeper for a more familiar territory?"

"The groundskeeper? Hercules?" She let out a faintly amused sound, leaving the merry-widow comment alone. "Not likely, he's a rather hairy Greek man who's sixty if he's a day."

"He's younger than your first husband," he challenged. He expected her to slap him, or at least demand an apology for his ghastly behavior. But to his utter astonishment, she tossed her head and laughed, the sound full of moonlight and merriment.

"Touché," she acquiesced, a light glinting in her eyes like she'd absorbed some of the shine from the stars. "Not only does my groundskeeper speak very little English, but the dear man eats nothing but garlic. Also, I'm quite certain he bathes in olive oil, which I'll admit does stir my appetite upon a warm day when he is particularly fragrant, but only for Mediterranean fare. Nothing else, I assure you."

Struck dumb, Cole could only stare at her with agitated bemusement. Why the devil was she being so civil? He'd been a rote bastard to her, shamed and insulted her in front of her guests. And here she was dallying with him in her garden managing to be entertaining.

Christ preserve him, it was both unsettling and alluring. Too intriguing. And bloody hell, were these straps on his prosthetic made of glass shards and wool? He couldn't take his eyes off her brilliant smile as he grappled at it with his one good hand. He wanted to be rid of not only the offending object, but his clothing had begun to likewise chafe. He wished to cast it all off, and hers as well, to be clad in nothing but the night air and moonlight.

"Your Grace." She regarded him with the most absorbed expression, part assessment, and part concern. As though she truly saw him. As though she *knew* him. "Is there anything amiss? Are you . . . all right?"

The breathy quality to her unceasingly feminine voice scratched at a door in his mind that remained stubbornly closed. He'd come across a few of those doors since returning from Constantinople, and knew it best that they remained locked. Most especially when he was like this. Raw, agitated . . .

Aroused.

He held up the base of his prosthetic, strategically placing it between them as a reminder of his damage. "It's this fucking prosthesis. I've outgrown it somehow. The damned buckles are impossible and I can't get them adjusted for another week. One of the bloody straps is stuck."

She didn't so much as twitch at his profanity, startling him again by reaching for him. "Allow me to try," she offered.

He pulled it behind him, belatedly realizing the movement made him appear childish. "Don't bother," he clipped. "It's not for a lady to—"

"You've made it abundantly clear how certain you are that I am not a lady," she wryly reminded him. "Perhaps you could make allowances. I was a nurse, after all."

It was unlike Cole to be self-conscious, and yet he couldn't comprehend why the thought of her gazing upon his mangled arm incited a new bout of hesitance. "Handling an amputated limb is entirely different than fluffing the pillows of the elderly." He tossed her a severe look, warning her away.

She returned it with that steady, mysterious gaze of hers. "I know. I dealt with you and your limb from the moment you entered St. Margaret's. You threw a teacup at me."

Heat suffused his face. "That was you?"

"You don't recognize me?"

He could summon a vague recollection of a frail, freckled woman in a black uniform, but that was all. "I was just coming out of a delirious fever and opiates," he pointed out. "I barely recognized myself." He still couldn't claim to, he thought bitterly.

"Nevertheless, I was the one who discovered the infection in your limb, I was there for the surgery, and I saw to your recovery. Aside from Dr. Longhurst, I'm the person most familiar with your case, so give it over."

Cole's brows drew down at the brusque hint of authority in her voice as she opened her palm and gestured for him to comply. He wasn't used to following orders, but had somehow placed his smarting forearm in her grasp before his pride decided against it.

Then the enormity of her words slammed into him with all the force of a frigate at full speed. She'd been the nurse who'd correctly diagnosed him with septicemia rather than typhus. It was because of her that he'd survived.

He *owed* this woman his life.

Did that mean anything to him? Did it to her? She certainly hadn't mentioned it before now. Not that he'd given her the chance to. Not that he'd been particularly grateful. She'd given him his life back. This lonely existence full of waking nightmares and rage. That was why he'd thrown the teacup, because before he'd regained consciousness, Ginny had been holding him, soothing him.

When he woke, there had been only pain.

Without any decorum, Lady Anstruther rested his arm in her lap and slowly, gently pushed his suit coat and shirtsleeve up to the elbow.

Until this moment, he'd allowed no one but Dr. Longhurst and the prosthetic engineer anywhere near his arm. He'd thought such an intimacy impossible with someone he rather liked, let alone someone he—he . . . Somehow, he couldn't seem to identify a word that would properly express his ever more opaque feelings for the indomitable woman. He owed that bit of witlessness partly to the proximity of his arm to her thighs. His wrist rested on the crest of her leg, the outline tantalizing through her petticoats and skirts. His prosthesis, however, dipped into the delightful crevice between. Yet *another* reason to lament the loss of his hand, he realized. Had he fingers that worked, that still registered sensation, they'd perhaps be close enough to feel the intimate heat between her thighs.

However, had he fingers, he'd likely not get them half so close as they were.

Cole didn't care to see the expression on her face, so he watched the veins in his own arm struggle to pulse blood past the tightly strapped prosthesis. His jaw clenched so forcefully, it ached.

The moment was surreal enough to be a dream. The woman he'd deemed his nemesis ran slim, elegant fingers across the fine hairs of his tense forearm, learning the mechanisms of the prosthetic structure. He felt the ripples of that brush of flesh blossom over the entirety of his being.

"How ingenious," she marveled to herself, as though he weren't even present. "These straps are interwoven to incorporate a harness." Deftly, she undid the buckle he'd struggled with, drawing a frown from him.

"I'm aware of that," he said dryly. "I designed the piece, myself."

"Did you?" she mused. "Well, that's impressive. Why the harnesses?"

"I had it fashioned in New York by an engineer," he explained. "I'd been invited on a spelunking expedition to South America, and needed a way to secure the hook I planned to use should I require it to support my weight. The harness is buckled here, and then is secured around my torso and opposite shoulder."

"How marvelous." She peered at his chest, as though trying to see through his clothing to the topography beneath. Was it only clinical curiosity knitting her brow? "And then I assume you have different attachments you fasten to the metal base here?" She gestured to the currently empty, flat steel apparatus at the end of his wrist and the dip into which his several attachments threaded securely.

"Don't touch that," he ordered as she flirted with the release lever of his hidden blade. "Lest it stab you."

"How clever," she remarked, but left it alone.

His head buzzed and his mouth felt as dry as grit. Certainly an effect of his smoking, and not at all the intoxicating scent of the woman who'd somehow slid closer to him. Christ, did she always smell like this? Like lavender and lilacs? Probably not. They were in a garden after all; the fragrance of night-blooming buds shamelessly baring themselves to the moon like beckoning wantons was enough to smother a fellow. And yet he couldn't deny the pleasantness of it. The . . . peaceful quality of it all.

"I was glad to hear that you became quite the adventurer after your recovery," she said conversationally, returning to work on the buckle of the second strap. "I read about your hunting grizzly bear in the American West, and climbing the Tetons. Then you navigated the Amazon, didn't you? Working with that cartographer, what was his name? Morton . . . Morgan something? Is that where you went spelunking, in South America?"

"Callum Monahan," he recalled. "A fearless man." He regarded her intently. "Have you been following my travels, Lady Anstruther?" He'd almost forgotten that she was about to uncover his stump, focused only on the fact that his arm crept ever higher on her thigh.

She glanced up sharply. "Not at all, though my husband

did. Dear Edward thought so very highly of you, and he had me read the articles of your many exploits. He said you were a particular favorite of his late wife."

"Lady Sarah Millburn," he said fondly. "I fell in love with her when I was but seven years old. No offense to your husband, but I used to wish a rather tragic and early end for him as a boy of ten or so, fantasizing that his wife would seek solace in my open and ready arms. She was the only female of warm disposition I'd met until . . ." He stopped himself, not wanting nostalgia to heat the current moment. To make more of it than it was.

Not wanting to think of Ginny just now.

Odd, that. Odder still that he revealed so much. She was neither confidant nor confessor. She was the real Lady Anstruther's inadequate shadow. A grasping pretender. A usurper. He had to remember that.

She had to be his enemy, lest he start desiring her to be something else.

Desiring . . . her.

"Sarah. Now *she* was the epitome of a lady." He quite literally looked down his nose as he said this.

"As opposed to me, you mean?" She arched a brow up at him, but it accompanied a dry smirk.

"Take it how you like, but try not to be too offended. I am a man of diverse faults and deficient merits. A right proper ass, really, and most of the people I ever held in high esteem are either dead or . . . missing. Conversely, Lord and Lady Anstruther were kind people. I ardently regret their passing."

Her gaze was soft the next time she looked up at him, and a pleased little smile toyed at the corner of her lips. He had the oddest notion that she resembled a woman who'd found something she thought lost to her.

"I miss Edward every day." Her confession stunned him, and for a moment, he almost believed her. With a delicate sound of victory, she freed the buckle and was able to pull the prosthesis away. While she set it aside, Cole covered the abrupt end to his forearm with his shirt, the empty cuff a stark reminder of what wasn't there. He couldn't, however, hide his utterly relieved sigh.

If she noticed, she didn't convey it. "He seemed to recover a little toward the end." She went on as he rubbed at the tender places made raw by the tight straps. "He would sit here in the garden with me and watch me paint when he was up to it. And once I was able to take him to the museum in his wheelchair and show him some sculptures he was so keen to see . . . It was the loveliest day I can remember."

His gut twisted again with that odd and discomfiting sensation. Cole slammed a door on it, summoning all the cool disdain he possibly could. There was simply no possible way he was jealous of a dead man. The ache he felt had to be something else. His face contorted into a grimace of distaste. "You're not asking me to believe that you . . . *loved* the old codger, are you?"

"And why not?" she asked hotly. "Of course I loved him. Not as a proper wife to her husband, granted, but like . . . like a dear friend. Perhaps a daughter to her father."

"That's disgusting."

"Don't you dare," she admonished him, the almost imperceptible register of her words lending them a great deal of gravitas. "Don't you *dare* contaminate the companionship my husband and I had, or turn it into anything perverse. It was innocent."

"Innocent?" Cole echoed. "Are you saying the marriage was never . . . consummated?"

"I don't see what business that is of yours." Though her voice conveyed indignation, her eyes darted away.

He had her. Perhaps if he frightened her enough, she would cease her dreadful schemes. "You are aware that if you're a virgin, your marriage could very well be annulled."

Her eyes widened. "Certainly not posthumously."

Sensing her fear, he struck. "I might look into it. I wield a great deal of influence, or hadn't you noticed?"

"Why—why would you do such a thing?" she whispered, as though he'd wounded her.

"Because it'd be what you deserve. Shame on you, beguiling a decent old man on his deathbed, turning his ancestral home into little better than a brothel, and not even a useful one at that."

Her features hardened, lips drawing into a tight line. "It should be beneath you to bully me thus." She stood, obliging him to do the same. "I'll have you know that I'm *not* a virgin, so you'll not be able to carry through with your threats."

Not a virgin? Some foreign, dark emotion drew the corners of his lips down. "Why does that not surprise me?"

The look she gave him brimmed with an irony he didn't comprehend, but now he was too irritated to consider it. She made a caustic, brittle sound, wrapping her arms around herself as she did so, hunching against the evening breeze as though the world had become too cold.

"I'm not going to let you stop me, you know," she said archly. "This charity is my purpose, my passion. I may not be able to save every unfortunate, but it won't stop me from doing what I can."

She had spirit, he'd give her that. But perhaps if logic and adversity wouldn't dissuade her, dread might.

Cole stepped toward her, using his height to crowd her, forcing her to take a step back toward the doors. "You are such a little thing in a big, cruel world," he murmured menacingly. "How will you manage all this, alone and defenseless?"

She took another step backward as he stalked her, but thrust her chin to a haughty angle. "I'll manage quite well," she said tartly. "We all have our impediments, don't we?" Her eyes flicked to his empty cuff, and Cole felt the beast stir within him.

It wanted at her with a violence he'd never before felt.

His hand found its way to her throat. Her startled gasp both shamed and inflamed him. It was the only way he could make her see, the only possible way for him to force her to comprehend the mortal danger she was putting herself in.

"I will spoil you at every turn," he snarled.

"I would expect no less from you." By now, she had to tilt her head back rather far to look up at him, pressing the column of her throat against his hand.

"It would take nothing to destroy you." He tightened his fingers ever so slightly, and the telltale jump of her pulse belied her unwavering audacity.

"Better men than you have tried," she remonstrated, her eyes blazing green with a maelstrom of her own primitive emotions. "Yet here I stand."

"You are a fool if you think any of those people in there are going to help you save every gutter whore from here to the East End once they realize you're planning on bringing them *here*."

She gave him a level look. "You surprise me, Your

Grace, I rather expected you to have higher opinions of whores, as you are reported to spend an inordinate amount of time in their company."

He leered at her. "I appreciate whores very much and like them to be what they are instead of striving for a title."

Her eyes narrowed to glittering slits of wrath. "You should hear what they have to say about titled men. Apparently blue blood has a difficult time finding its way to the correct appendage. And even if it does, the experience rarely lasts long enough to be worth the trouble."

She gasped a bit when her back found the panes of the door, but to her credit, her eyes never ceased burning up into his.

"The whores I've known have never left my company unsatisfied," he purred, his finger drifting south, to curve over the delectable flesh at her nape, the sharp arrow of her clavicle, pointing down. Down toward the breasts now surging toward him with each troubled breath.

"How wonderful for you." She mocked an impressed expression, but not before something else flickered over her features. Fear. Sadness. And something else . . . something that disappeared as quickly as it had materialized. "I suppose they're paid not to complain. And I happen to know the ones who feign pleasure are better compensated."

He made a droll sound. "I rather think I'm not too dense to decipher real pleasure from false."

She lifted a lovely bare shoulder and rolled her eyes heavenward. "Every man assumes thusly."

How was it that such a lovely, soft woman had such a sharp tongue? It was like being bitten by a butterfly. Most women would have been shocked into catatonia by this conversation, or at the very least reduced to tears. His hand was around her neck, for the love of Christ . . . or it had been. Now it was decidedly not. It had drifted and explored . . . which should have distressed *her* more than it did him.

But the countess Anstruther met his dark look with a mulish one of her own. God, it had been a long time since he'd felt so frustrated, so infuriated.

It was . . . rather glorious.

The scant air between them shifted, becoming heavy with promise, insinuation, and more than a little danger. "How is it, Lady Anstruther, that you know so much of my intimate exploits? Interested?" He punctuated the word *intimate* by leaning forward and catching his weight on his elbow, hovering above her. A moth's wing wouldn't have survived between them.

"It's only the worst-kept secret in the realm." She rolled her eyes again, but her voice was certainly breathier than before, contradicting her pretense of remaining unaffected. "Everyone knows who you are and the manner in which you conduct yourself. The prodigal duke. The tragic hero. Gossip columns report what kind of powder you prefer to clean your teeth with, let alone the more salacious aspects of your life. Everyone knows how you've taken your second chance and done your best to ruin it in the most reckless, ridiculous ways possible. It's an insult to those of us who toiled so hard to save you."

"They bloody well know nothing," he growled. "And I credit you with even less intellect than I first did if you believe what you read in the papers."

"If not for a reporter, you'd never have been rescued," she argued.

"I'm certain you're feeling that your life would be a

great deal easier had I not been found." He meant to push away from her, to stalk out of her home and her life, but something about her expression froze him in place. Between the blood-soaked battlefields and messy assassinations, the numerous hospitals and even the Turkish prison, he couldn't remember ever seeing such a deeply, truly wounded expression.

"You can't even hope to *imagine* how I feel about it." Her faint words carried a thread of steel, and so much pain he could no longer stand to look her in the eye.

Glancing down, his gaze snagged on her now-exposed throat as it struggled to swallow some incomprehensibly powerful emotion. Such a graceful neck. Soft and lovely with fragile, thin skin. The most delicate place. Well . . . among them. There were others.

Like the insides of her wrists. Or her thighs.

Her lips. Lips that might welcome him, that might part for him if he took them.

His head dipped low, his body curled around her. So small. So slight. And yet so warm.

Her tremulous breath brushed at his face, her features frozen. Paralyzed. Though her small, pink tongue slipped over her lower lip, leaving a delicious gleam of moisture there.

Fuck, suddenly he wanted to—

Surging up to her toes, she slammed her lips against his with such force their teeth almost clattered together.

Cole couldn't have been more shocked if she'd taken a knife and stabbed him in the heart. Either way, that traitorous heart ceased beating. She not only stole his wits, she took his breath for good measure.

This was no searching, probing kiss from an aroused

woman seeking stimulation or validation of his feelings. No exploration of sensual attraction nor the expression of tender affection. This was something hard. Something angry and wild. The explosive moment held them suspended in time, the frustrated heat of it searing its way from his lips to his cock. With this kiss, she seized control of the moment. Exerting her wishes upon him. She demonstrated to him with a definitive, unmitigated action that she was a creature in command of her own will.

He'd been so wrong about her. At first he'd thought her devious and scheming. Then perhaps sweet and simple, unaware and out of her depth.

But no.

This was no bright-eyed do-gooder latched to his mouth with all the craven audacity she could muster. She was a woman of desire, of spirit and determination. She was like a wild American mustang yet to be broken to a master's hand.

Sweet Christ, did he ever want to ride her until they were both slick with sweat and pleasure. Until she was slack-limbed and docile.

The moment he decided to deepen the kiss, she ended it.

A new pallor flushed her skin as she held a hand to her lips. He realized with a hot stab in the pit of his stomach that she was as shocked as he by the electric current of arousal between them.

She recovered astonishingly well, her multicolored eyes glittering with triumph as they narrowed at him. "Don't get any mistaken ideas of my intentions, *Your Grace*," she said. "I merely wanted to see if your taste was as bitter as your conversation." She gathered her skirts and made to push past him, her voice hitched with telltale breathlessness. "Now if you'll excuse me, I—"

"Shut up," Cole commanded, as he crowded her back against the door and captured her mouth again.

He wasn't finished with her.

Cole made his kiss everything hers hadn't been. Wet, probing, and utterly wicked. Though he had to brace himself against the door so his weakened knees wouldn't have to support them both, he summoned all the skill and expertise she'd accused him of having and wielded it against her lips.

He licked at the seam of her mouth, more of a warning than an inquiry, before he claimed it with his tongue. In truth, he half expected her to bite him.

But she didn't.

The moment a dark groan manifested in his throat, she came alive in his arms, clinging to his shoulders for stability. As he drank deeply from the well of shocking pleasure in her kiss, he found with sinister delight that her tongue tangled with his instead of retreating. Her mouth was hot and her lips so infinitely soft, he almost couldn't believe they were real.

A part of him realized he'd conjured a firestorm in that moment. That everything that had been shattered and cold within him melted in an instant inferno, becoming liquid and incomprehensively hot. Ready to be molded into a weapon. Made to thrust. To penetrate.

And here was an opponent worth the battle.

With a ragged sound, she broke the kiss, ripping her mouth from his and surging to the side, out of his grasp. With clumsy, shaking hands she wiped at her mouth as though to erase any trace of him.

She stared at him in open accusation, her features twisted with dire anguish. "*Why* did you come here to-night?" she demanded with a half-sob. Her eyes, though suspiciously bright, remained empty of tears and full of antipathy. "Do you enjoy tormenting me so, that you would dedicate an entire evening to my humiliation?"

Cole pushed away from the door, turning from her and taking the time it took retrieving his prosthetic from the bench to collect himself. Why *had* he come? Why was he acting like this? Why, when his mind recoiled from her, did his flesh seem to crave her? It was as though his body betrayed him in her presence. He'd never had such a strong physical reaction to a woman he hardly knew. At least not since . . .

"Ravencroft wanted me to attend, and since I owe the man my life, I find it hard to deny him anything." He answered her question with as much nonchalance as he could muster.

"Need I remind you that I *also* saved your life," she railed. "And yet you have no compunctions about degrading me and threatening to take everything I have."

Was that how she regarded his kiss? As a degradation?

"What have I done to you?" she cried. "Why must you be so beastly?"

We must be what we are, he thought. *Beasts.*

"I don't like what you are doing here." He turned on her, summoning his reserves of malice to coat the nerves that had become raw and exposed by their interaction. "I don't like the noise of your renovations. I don't want to live next door to whores, vagrants, and pickpockets. I don't want to deal with the risks their associations bring into this neighborhood. I want *peace*, woman. Why can't you understand that?"

"Is your peace and quiet worth a beaten woman's life? Or a frightened child's safety?" she asked, once again impassioned.

"Whatever it's worth, I've paid twice the price. I've *earned* it." He brandished his prosthetic at her. "You want to save all the whores in London, fine, just do it elsewhere."

"These women, they're not *just whores,* not merely a collection of orifices for your amusement. Some of them are mothers. Or daughters turned out by the very family who was supposed to protect them. They're human *beings.*"

"You don't think I know that?" he bit out.

"Do you? If you truly believed in their worth as women, you'd treat them with compassion instead of contempt. With affection rather than acrimony."

"You know some big words for such a small woman."

"And you have a small mind for such a big man," she volleyed back, raking him with a disgusted glare. "I can't believe I ever—" She pressed her lips closed, her little fists balled with fury.

"You ever . . . what?" he finally asked when the silence stretched longer than he was willing to bear.

"Nothing," she breathed, turning against the door to open it. "If you'll excuse me, I need to return to my guests."

Like hell would she escape him with this left unfinished. "You can't believe you ever what? Kissed me? Saved my life?" he demanded, seizing her arm.

She looked at his hand with sufficient contempt. "I can't believe I ever welcomed you into my home. In the future I'll make certain the door is barred to you."

He released her immediately. "No great loss."

"To either of us," she agreed, and escaped into the house.

It took Cole a full minute to find his breath again, and another to gather the strength in his legs. He shook with so many fragmented emotions he couldn't even begin to identify them.

Imogen Millburn, Lady Anstruther, was more dangerous than he could have ever imagined. For she brought out something in him he'd promised he'd left in that prison cell along with his hand.

That wild, primitive beast. A starving, wolfish creature who wanted to do nothing more than stalk and prowl. To leap and snare. To feast and fuck.

This beast was no duke. He was no man raised with genteel civility, with a care for the expense of things or the consequence of his actions. This beast was no longer dormant within him, but prowling beneath the surface of his skin, wanting to mark his territory.

And he'd found a delectable morsel just now, one he was in danger of acquiring a taste for.

CHAPTER THIRTEEN

It wasn't a long walk from Mayfair to Belgravia, but Chief Inspector Carlton Morley went on horseback, his haste due to the brutal murder at the Anstruther manse. The fact that the Anstruther residence abutted the Grecian-style monolithic dwelling that belonged to Britain's former most prolific assassin, Christopher Argent, didn't at all set his mind at ease.

Just because Argent worked for Scotland Yard now didn't mean the man had stopped killing.

Spilling blood became a delicious addiction if one wasn't careful, Morley reflected.

He should know.

Argent clattered up to the Anstruther gate behind him on his own bay steed. The strident assassin-turned-lawman having fetched him at dawn, a mere hour after Morley had collapsed into bed.

He would like to have claimed that something common like a woman or a troubling case had kept him up into the wee hours of the morning. But he couldn't. It had, in fact, been the spilling of blood. His new and dangerous addiction. These nocturnal goings-on would put him in an early grave, of that he was certain.

But there was no help for it now. No stopping him.

"You look like the devil used you for his mistress last night." Argent slid off his bay and tossed the reins to the same footman Morley had. "Have you taken to some new and dangerous vice?"

The observant assassin's insight was his greatest asset in the investigative field, but Morley cursed it this morning. "If I believed in the devil, I'd think you his bastard, Argent," Morley quipped.

"A better sire then some I've known," the former assassin replied gravely.

On this they agreed.

"I wouldn't have stirred you had I not known you'd want to see this." Argent pulled out a notebook, a standard practice for all investigators. Unless a man could organize his thoughts and recall them as perfectly as Dorian Blackwell, he needed to write them down. "It isn't every day a countess is found raped and strangled to death in a Belgravia terrace garden."

"Lady Broadmore was a *viscountess,* Argent," Morley corrected, nodding to the constable who held open the gate. "Lady Anstruther is a countess."

Argent shrugged, scratching at the russet shadow-beard stubbling his hard jaw with a heavy hand. "Never was very good at telling the difference," he said casually. "Never much cared to learn."

"You'll need to learn the law and structures if you want to thrive in this society, Inspector," Morley assessed.

"Scotland Yard isn't the underworld. Everything must be aboveboard." Even as he said this, Morley called himself nine kinds of liar. As an inspector, his words represented an absolute truth. As for his nighttime employment . . . such was not the case. Though, he had to admit, an intimate acquaintance with strictures and laws did help one to break them.

Argent slid him an even look. "Survival is a talent of mine, Morley, or have you forgotten?"

Morley hadn't forgotten that once, a long time past, Argent had stabbed him and saved his life all in the course of one night. "All I remember is that it is better that we are allies than enemies."

"Better for whom?" Argent didn't smile exactly, but his cold blue eyes danced with amusement.

"For the both of us, I imagine."

"Do you know what I think, Morley?" The assassin turned to him at the base of the entry stairs.

"No one can quite tell what you think, Argent. Inscrutability is one of your few merits."

Argent ignored his attempt at levity. "I think you allow people to underestimate you, in fact, I think you encourage it."

Suddenly uncomfortable, Morley turned toward the steps. "We haven't time to dally, not when there's been a murder."

"Dead bodies keep." Argent gripped his shoulder, squeezing the muscle found there. "You tailor your jackets to hide the strength in your shoulders. It is the source of much speculation between Blackwell and me, why a powerful man would conceal his power rather than wield it."

Morley shrugged the big hand off, pulling an air of nonchalance around him like a cloak. "I wield as much influence as I desire," he hedged. "Besides, elegance is the male fashion, is it not?"

Argent was not amused. "You soften your vowels like a born gentleman, but walk with the light-footed swagger of a thief from the East End. You've been a soldier, a killer, the best marksman in the Royal Highland Watch, or so they say. You were no one until the queen knighted you for your bravery, *Sir* Carlton Morley. Your past is as clear as steam in a pall of coal smoke."

"What are you getting at, Argent?" All levity fled the interaction.

"It's less about what I'm getting at, and more about what you're up to . . ." Argent lifted a skeptical brow. "You're a walking corpse these days. A man who eats little and sleeps even less. The others are starting to think you're a man possessed, but I've seen that look before. You are a man *obsessed*. The question is, with what?"

Morley decided to tell the truth. "I'm a man obsessed with justice, Argent."

"There are many forms of justice."

Returning the hard stare with one of his own, Morley stepped closer. "So there is."

"Does your justice have anything to do with the exonerated criminals disappearing with alarming frequency—"

"Leave. It. *Alone*." Morley enunciated every syllable in a whisper threaded with steel.

Those eerie arctic eyes narrowed, and the two men stood toe-to-toe, nose to nose, each muscle bunched with tension, blood feeding the essence of violence into each breath.

Most men hadn't a prayer against Christopher Argent,

but the assassin had one thing right . . . Morley was a man used to being underestimated.

And often used that to his advantage.

What Argent didn't know could hurt him very badly, indeed.

Eventually, Argent stepped aside, his mild look returning as he swept his hand toward the grand entry. "To the task at hand."

Morley inspected the exterior of the Anstruther manse, willing the fire in his blood to die. The house was an elegant, eighteen-room dark stone structure that drew the eye away from the uniform white grand houses dominating the aristocratic neighborhood of Belgravia. At this early hour, the lords and ladies of the *ton* hadn't yet stirred from their overstuffed beds, many of them having whiled away the night at some useless revelry or other. Most of them would have tucked in at the same early hour he did, but the idle rich needn't wake until noon.

They placed the safety of their borough in his hands, and that was a responsibility that never slept.

And neither did he.

"Tell me what you know," he ordered as they mounted the front steps.

"Lady Anstruther hosted a charity event last night which, as her next-door neighbor, I attended. The guest list had more lords and ladies than *Burke's Peerage*. The deceased *vis*countess was seated near the head of our table between the Duke of Trenwyth and Dorian Blackwell. If you ask me, she was a tittering, ill-tempered quim."

"I'll thank you to bite your vulgar tongue when we're in the presence of the countess," Morley admonished.

"You're welcome to bite my vulgar ass, and I'll say what I like," Argent volleyed back tonelessly. "Besides,

Lady Anstruther is friends with my wife, and acquainted with my vulgar tongue."

It was Morley's turn to lift a brow.

"Not in *that* way." Argent scowled, returning to consult his notes. "The body was found by Lady Anstruther's younger sister, a Miss Isobel Pritchard, as she came home from some husband-hunting ball right before dawn."

Pritchard . . . Why did that name tug at his memory?

They found Imogen Millburn, Countess Anstruther, and Isobel clinging to each other for support in a parlor the color of spring mint leaves and marigolds.

They stood when the butler, a rather rotund man named Cheever, announced him.

Identical pairs of round hazel eyes stared over at him. From what Morley surmised, the sisters resembled each other in everything but affect. Though both were fair-haired and delicately structured, the elder sister, Lady Anstruther, looked at him with the weary gaze of a woman who had seen much. Including, if he was not mistaken, death.

How unexpected.

Young Isobel held a handkerchief to her pale cheeks, catching the tears streaming from eyes rimmed red with woe.

"Chief Inspector." Still clad in a voluminous lavender night robe decorated with violet flowers, Lady Anstruther stepped toward him with her hand outstretched. A remarkably casual gesture for a countess. "Thank you for coming."

"My lady." Morley bent over her hand, noting that the other was still a captive of Isobel's desperate grasp. "I'm very sorry for this distressing situation. Who would you prefer to show me the body?"

"I'll show you to the garden," the countess answered steadily. "It's just through here."

"Imogen, no!" Isobel protested, tugging on her sister's hand. "You shouldn't have to look again, it's too, too horrible."

Lady Anstruther only kissed her sister's cheek, distracting her while she pried the girl's white-fingered grasp from her hand. "Isobel, darling, it would be polite to offer Chief Inspector Morley and Mr. Argent a cup of tea, would it not?" she asked gently.

"Tea?" The pale girl, who looked no older than seventeen, blinked as though she'd never heard the word before.

"I like mine brewed strong as Turkish coffee," Argent said softly.

Unsurprisingly, her ploy worked, and the young woman seemed to return from whatever stupor fear and fatality had created. "We—we have coffee, if you prefer it to tea, Mr. Argent." Her own smile was shy and watery as she smoothed the skirts of her rumpled peach ball gown that confirmed that she hadn't been to bed yet.

"That would be grand."

Lady Anstruther took immediate advantage of her sister's distraction. "This way, Chief Inspector."

He followed her out of the parlor and down a hall choked with art and antiques toward two French doors that presumably led to the terrace garden. A pair of constables in their blue uniforms stood vigil at the doors. Their eyes upon Lady Anstruther in her nightclothes, as modest as they were, still glittered with both intrigue and hunger.

It hadn't escaped Morley's notice that she was, indeed, an uncommonly lovely woman. Her hair a stunning gold, shaded with tones of red. Her eyes a gentle confusion of greens, golds, and darker hues. Her robe outlined a slight body with delicate curves.

His notice of her beauty was more a detection of it, than anything. He looked at her not like a man would a woman, but like an inspector would a suspect. Or a witness.

Nothing more.

This confirmed a dilemma he'd been contemplating for quite some time. Something was wrong with him. Something grave and serious.

But he hadn't time to brood about it now.

"How long have you been acquainted with Lady Broadmore, the victim?" he queried, staring down the constables until they noticed, panicked, and found something on their boots worth very close inspection.

"I only became acquainted with her for the first time last night," Lady Anstruther replied. "I realized immediately that further acquaintance would be undesired by either of us."

"That's a brave confession to make about the woman who was murdered in your garden."

"I am not her murderer. What have I to fear?"

"She was found on your property. There are accounts of you quarreling with this woman. Lady Anstruther, as of right now you are first on our list of suspects."

"While we didn't quarrel, exactly, we certainly didn't agree on anything." Lady Anstruther picked her way carefully through a short path choked with wildflowers and swept to the side, soberly gesturing down at the deceased.

Something Morley thought long-dead flared inside of him. A memory, one he held locked in the dark vault where his heart had once been, transposed itself onto the murdered viscountess.

A golden-haired beauty prone in peaceful repose. Indeed, one could believe her sleeping, were it not for the unnatural stillness of her breast. For the blue tingeing her lips and the gray painting her skin the color of the slate sky.

Death used a rather obvious palette.

In his memory, the girl's body was tainted with sludge and silt from the river Thames, discarded beneath a bridge in Southwark rather than swathed in sunlight next to a playful fountain. A coarse frock had barely covered the evidence of her brutal death instead of a ball gown of magenta silk.

But the woman on the shore of the Thames had bruises on her thighs . . . and blood.

Caroline. His beloved sister. His twin.

She'd also been strangled to death and discarded like so much rubbish.

A familiar white rage drowned out everything but the evidence. Tattered undergarments, shredded to ribbons, floated limply in the Anstruther fountain. The countess's skirts were twisted above her knees, though her silk stockings and slippers remained intact.

All evidence pointed to rape . . . but he'd require the body examined before he could be certain. Once his suspicion was confirmed, he could mobilize.

He'd conduct his inquest, find the culprit, and make certain justice was meted out.

Justice. It wasn't a new obsession. Only an intensifying one.

A gentle voice permeated the roaring in his ears. "Chief Inspector? Sir?" The past melted from his vision, and the concerned features of Lady Anstruther replaced them.

"Are you all right? You've gone rather pale." She placed a hand on his sleeve, observing him with steady, watchful eyes.

Needing an anchor for his fervent thoughts, he reached into his coat pocket, and smoothed his thumb across the perforations of the sealed letter he found there. Perhaps he'd consult with Dr. Francis Aubrey-Dencourt. The man was not only a medical genius, but specialized in forensic medicine. Their professional correspondence had become ambiguously personal of late. Dare he say, more than just friendly? And while he didn't care to examine the sense of indulgence he felt over the good doctor's letters, he didn't feel that asking for a favor would be out of the question.

"Pardon me," he said shortly, searching for a brief explanation. "I hurried here without breakfasting first."

"Of course." She released his arm, patting his sleeve. "Allow me to call for Cheever, and he'll have Cook send up extra breakfast."

"No need." Narrowing his eyes, he stayed the woman by grasping her arm.

She stilled like a rabbit caught in a snare, and Morley deduced that she was no stranger to violence. "I must say, I find your composure remarkable, Lady Anstruther. Does the fact that a woman was found murdered and sexually assaulted in your garden not at all disturb you?"

At this, Lady Anstruther winced and wrapped her arms around her middle in an oddly childlike gesture. "Chief Inspector Morley, I assure you I'm not only disturbed by this, I'm horrified and revolted. But, I confess that this isn't the most upsetting thing to have happened in the course of my life. And, as I'm sure you'll find out upon further investigation, before my fortuitous marriage to the earl, I was employed as a nurse at St. Margaret's Royal Hospital. So, you see, this is also not my first experience with death, even one so gruesome as this."

Morley searched her eyes and found only sincerity and regret. Either the woman was in earnest, or she was a better actress than Argent's wife, Millie LeCour.

He noted the capable delicacy of her hands, and silently compared it to the wide span and thickness of the finger marks marring the vicountess's neck. Whether Lady Anstruther was involved or not, she certainly hadn't assaulted and strangled the victim.

"I need to establish just when this occurred," he stated. "Do you recall the last time you saw Lady Broadmore?"

"It would have been at dinner," she recalled, wrinkling a troubled forehead. "So, perhaps half past nine o'clock. Since we didn't get along, I assumed she'd left early."

"You assumed? You did not see her leave?"

Her eyes shifted away from his. "I—I'd had a trying evening, you see, so I came here, to the garden to compose myself."

"And how long did you tarry in the garden?"

"Not long, maybe a quarter hour or less, but I didn't see the viscountess after that." She slid a glance to the body and closed her eyes briefly. "The ball ended around half past two, and I went straight to bed. I believe this happened sometime between then and when Isobel and my mother returned home at five. Isobel gave Mother a sleeping powder, and came down here for some tea and to take in the air. That's when she found . . . when we sent for Mr. Argent."

Morley nodded, making a notation of the times in his notepad. "So to your knowledge, you were the absolute last person alone in the garden before your sister arrived home early this morning to find Lady Broadmore like this?" he clarified.

A heavy, protracted silence caused him to look up and find that all the color had drained from the countess's face.

"Lady Anstruther," he pressed. "This is very important. Who was the last person you identified in the garden?"

Lifting her chin over a difficult swallow, she looked to the stately pale mansion towering over her garden wall. "Collin Talmage," she answered in a quivering voice. "The Duke of Trenwyth."

It took a herculean amount of will on Cole's part not to swipe the entire mess of intelligence paperwork into the fireplace and tell the Home Office to go hang themselves. Even one-handed, he was still more capable than half the agents in the field, and he'd been relegated to little better than a fucking secretary.

A secretary with a lofty title and a great deal of power and influence, but even so.

He was not cut out for shuffling papers and making weighty assessments. He'd been born a man of action, more comfortable with decisions made in the moment and acted upon decisively.

Besides, he couldn't focus on something so pedestrian as paperwork. Not with a cockstand that seemed to appear every other minute. Incidentally, the precise rate that the memory of last night's encounter with Lady Anstruther forced its way into his mind

Perhaps now was a good time to call upon Argent and schedule a sparring session. Restless aggression simmered beneath his skin, and his neighbor was the only man who didn't take his rank or deformity into account. To the cold, logical bastard, Trenwyth's impediment was all the more reason to train. To become stronger. Faster.

Harder.

On this, they both agreed.

In a world that preyed upon the weak, one must turn his encumbrance into power, or be consumed by it.

Consummation. Now there was a concept upon which he'd rather not dwell. Though, he had been. For three years past he'd been obsessed by the memory of a very specific consummation.

Except for last night. A new and unsettling beauty had diverted his thoughts, abducted his dreams. For so long he'd been the devotee of nostalgia. But now a lovely, outspoken idealist had absconded with his closely guarded reminiscence and replaced it with new and distressing interactions upon which to reflect.

Lady Anstruther. *Imogen.*

Cole took many liberties with her in his thoughts, the very least of which was her name.

Why was it that he couldn't seem to conjure Ginny's face, no matter how hard he attempted it? But the intrepid countess's features inserted themselves into every moment since they'd parted, waking or otherwise.

He knew the answer, of course. Not only because she'd kissed him, but because *she'd* seen *him*. There in her garden, she'd used the moonlight to illuminate him, and she'd asked him if he was all right. Not like most posed the question, as though they'd queried a thousand people a thousand times. But as though she wanted the answer. Like it meant something to her.

Like he'd meant something to her.

And he'd wanted to tell her, hadn't he? That he, in fact, resembled nothing close to all right. That he seethed one moment, and was completely numb the next. He wanted to confess that he hated the entire world. That he hated himself, most of all. That he remembered how to *survive*, but not at all how to *live*.

He'd wanted to give voice to his greatest fear, that he'd be this . . . this shadow of a man until he finally decided to end his own life. Because there were no fresh wonders left. Nothing to conquer. Nothing worth protecting. Nothing to fight for.

Nothing to live for.

That the night would only ever be too dark and full of remembered suffering. That the day would only ever be too bright and too loud. That all his moments would bleed into the next and time would steal his memories, just like it did that of Ginny's face. And he'd forever yearn for what he'd never again attain. Because not only was he not worthy. He was not capable.

He'd wanted to say all of that. To confess his weaknesses to her. Because weakness didn't seem to be something that concerned Lady Anstruther in the least. While she wasn't as delicate as some, she was a small woman. He'd felt her fragility beneath his hand, her susceptibility to be easily broken. It had stirred in him something he'd thought lost to the world. Some strange and disquieting instinct he was loath to name. Something possessive. Protective.

In a base world where people were easy to read and even easier to predict, a woman like her was a rare find, indeed. She was truly an enigma. Someone who, after amassing a fortune, seemed intent upon giving it away and asking others to do the same.

But for what purpose? There was no such thing as an altruist, everyone knew that. So why couldn't he figure her out? She was as rare and puzzling as the mighty Grecian Sphinx.

He'd told her all the reasons he didn't want her to procede with this charitable scheme of hers.

All but one.

That being the risk to her own safety.

Because while he had no love for the woman, he was starting to think he had less contempt for her than he initially determined. She'd been kind. Until he'd pushed her past the level of her own tolerance. Which, if he was honest, had always been a particular talent of his.

Then she'd been shockingly impetuous. Incredibly carnal.

Cole didn't think himself capable of shock anymore. He'd been a rake in his younger days, and even worse since his tragedies.

He'd sought to drown his emptiness in pleasure, and found that the more he tried to fill it, the more fathomless the void became.

Propelled by a sense of shame, Cole stalked to the sideboard and reached for the Scotch, something he'd been doing with alarming frequency these days.

Argent's familiar voice reached him through the open window.

Her window. The portal to the Anstruther garden.

What the devil? Seized by curiosity, he looked down to see not only Argent's wide back standing by the satyr fountain, but facing him, a man he also recognized on sight. Sir Carlton Morley, a knight and a marksman he'd briefly known maybe a decade ago. If memory served, he was now the chief inspector at Scotland Yard. Was he a supporter of Lady Anstruther's schemes?

That didn't seem likely; from what he remembered, the

man was a stern and stoic traditionalist. A gentleman of militaristic focus and priestlike self-control who could shoot the eye of a needle at fifty paces. He always wondered why Morley should become a lawman, seeing as they didn't carry firearms.

Morley moved to the side, inspecting the fountain. In doing so, he uncovered a sight that sent Cole's heart slamming against its cage.

Morning light glinted off pale hair. A prone woman in a bright dress askew among the wildflowers. Her skirt bunched to her knees.

Cole had seen enough of death to recognize it. Without thinking, he bolted, reaching the door before his tumbler of Scotch spilled to the carpet.

CHAPTER FOURTEEN

Imogen had suppressed her tears for so long, her throat ached and her head throbbed. Her home, her sanctuary, and the refuge she had been trying so long to build for others had been infiltrated, *desecrated* by death and brutality.

Perched on the shaded bench she'd shared with Trenwyth the prior evening, she watched as Inspectors Argent and Morley conducted their investigation.

Imogen refused to look in the fountain, where the evidence of sexual brutality floated on the surface, stitched with sullied white lilies.

Poor Lady Broadmore. How terrified she must have been. Did she try to call for help? Had her ordeal been quick or drawn out? Had she been violated before her death? Or after? Imogen put her head in her hands. She'd slept through someone's assault and *murder*. How would she ever forgive herself? She'd been so angry. So heated and then humiliated by Cole that she'd spent the rest of the night attempting to salvage the evening, and had barely given the absent Lady Broadmore another thought.

She'd gone up to bed after everyone had left and all donations had been tallied with a sense of smug satisfaction. Despite Trenwyth's dire fit of public temper and Lady Broadmore's ignorant comments, she'd done better than she'd ever predicted. A small, spiteful part of her had wanted to make sure they knew of her success. To prove that she would neither be intimidated nor dissuaded. That she'd moved others to action and charity despite their best efforts to sabotage her.

She should have looked for her missing guest. She might have noticed, then, that Lady Broadmore's cape and pelisse were still in the cloakroom, but the woman was nowhere to be found. The villain had been *in her home* as she'd gone to sleep, blissfully unaware of the ghastly crime being committed on her own property.

Imogen blinked up, unable to believe her eyes for a moment as Trenwyth materialized across her garden. Where *he* came from, she could only guess. She was sitting by the garden door and surely would have seen him arrive from the house.

Hair and eyes blazing like burnished ore, he surged against Argent's and Morley's restraining holds until his wide, restless gaze latched upon her, and the flame flickered out upon an expression she'd almost identify as relief.

Dear God, what was he telling them? Why did the way he was looking at her now make her want to clutch her robe closed to the throat? She felt so exposed to him, even in her modest nightgown and wrapper. It was easy to fear that the force of his masculinity gave him some sort of inhuman capability. She absurdly worried that he could see through not just her clothing, but also the secrets that shrouded her very existence. She'd been naked in front of him once before.

But never truly exposed.

Though, she'd been unutterably stupid last night, kissing him like she had. It had been a dangerous move. One born of impulse and anger. And it could have cost her everything.

What if he'd remembered her from her kiss? He and Ginny had never kissed like that. But that had been before. Before he'd been captured. Before she almost killed a man.

Before a woman was murdered in her garden.

Imogen stood on quivering legs and made her way toward them. Why should he look so wild and concerned when he'd made his feelings about her irrevocably clear? Where had he come from?

Strange and precarious suspicion lanced her as she sidled around the horrific scene. Had their interaction pushed him past the edge of sanity? Could *he* have been the one to—

Trenwyth's head snapped up at something the chief inspector said, his temper sparking from his eyes as though Morley's last words had been a blacksmith's hammer, and he the tempered steel on an anvil.

With a burst of strength and speed, he shoved past the two men and stalked to her, the inspectors quick on his heels.

"You think *I* did this?" he thundered at her.

"I never said that." Imogen put an ineffectual hand up, as though to ward off an attack. To her utter surprise, it worked. He stopped a few paces from her, his hand curled tightly at his side, and his prosthetic gleaming like pewter in the morning sunlight. "I only told the inspectors the truth. That you were the last person I was aware of in this garden, and that you threatened to make certain my venture failed."

"This is certainly one way to see to that," Morley remarked, his alert blue gaze making studious calculations of Trenwyth's every move and expression.

"Yes, but not *my* way," the duke managed from between clenched teeth. "I would never—how could you even think—" He blinked, his hard mouth pressing into a hyphen.

He was remembering what he'd done to her in the garden, Imogen was certain. His hand at her throat. His body against hers. The menace he'd used to attempt to frighten her away from her current path. The way he'd dominated her with his kiss.

His gaze flickered over to the fountain, but not before she noted a lick of regret behind the temper. Perhaps even shame.

Good. He should be ashamed of his behavior.

"No one is accusing you of rape and murder, Trenwyth." Argent's dry inflection broke the tension of the moment.

"Not as of yet," Morley amended, earning him a sharp look from both men.

"We're establishing a timeline," Argent continued. "Could you tell us how long you tarried in the garden after Lady Anstruther left you alone?"

They didn't remark on the scandal that would be caused by the very fact they'd been in the garden alone together, and for that, Imogen was unfailingly grateful.

"I left immediately," he clipped, lifting a brow at her. "As it was made abundantly clear I was no longer welcome on the premises."

"A definitive that remains unchanged," Imogen stated, folding her arms over her breasts as something made them tighten painfully. A chill in the morning air, not the one in his glare, surely.

"Lady Anstruther, can you think of anyone who has recently expressed displeasure with you?" Morley asked.

"With me?" Imogen blinked, unsure of his meaning.

"Any enemies or antagonists you're aware of?" he prodded gently.

"You mean aside from the one standing right next to you?" She gestured to the duke with her chin, unwilling to uncross her arms. Not only was she shielding herself, but she felt as though her own grip might be the only thing keeping her together.

Thunder rolled in the distance, as though Trenwyth had conjured it by the storm building in his countenance. The sound matched the violence in his posture. "I can prove I didn't kill Lady Broadmore." His glare reminded her of the glint of light on a lethal blade.

"By all means," Argent invited.

Trenwyth stalked to the body and bent one long knee. "Look at the finger marks here." Without hesitation, he laid his fingers over the bruises on Lady Broadmore's neck. Not only did it demonstrate that his hand was much too large to match the perpetrator's, but . . . "Whoever strangled this woman used *both* hands."

Nearly blown over by a tempest of relief, Imogen stared down at his skeletal silver left hand, not because of the anomaly, but because it illustrated the changes in the man standing in her garden. Once, that hand had been upon her. Warm and gentle. Then hot and demanding. Now it was gone, replaced by a cold and unyielding object, shaped by fire and force and unimaginable things. Who knew what it was capable of? Because, it seemed, it had about as much warmth and feeling as the man who wielded it.

At least he was no murderer. Well . . . not last night, at least.

"Lady Anstruther." Morley interrupted her troubling thoughts. "Was there anyone else in attendance at your charity ball last night who you think could have been capable of something like this?"

Oh dear Lord, it was the question she'd been dreading. "Well . . . um. What do you mean exactly by '*capable*'?" she hedged.

The sound Trenwyth made could have turned the Thames into a desert wasteland. "Correct me if I'm wrong, Argent, but last night was a veritable Who's Who of London's vicious and bloodthirsty."

Imogen huffed. "I wouldn't go so far as to say—"

"Take your pick, Sir Morley," he interrupted. "The Blackheart of Ben More. The Demon Highlander. Along with various and sundry of their contacts and associates." He directed a look full of unsavory meaning at Argent. "Also, according to the countess here, the entire household staff consisted of cutthroats and criminals."

Morley's fair brows climbed his forehead. "Is this true?"

"*Former* criminals," Imogen remonstrated. "They are reformed, sir. And I'm mostly certain there isn't a cutthroat among them."

"Mostly?"

"Well, one can't ever be confident of the true nature of a man, can one?" She cast a withering look of her own at the duke. If there weren't so many witnesses, *she* might just be capable of murder at the moment.

"It is not my experience, Lady Anstruther, that criminals are in the habit of reformation." Morley said gently.

Argent made an ironic noise, which he resolutely ignored.

"But I—"

"I trust you have a list of these employees?" Morley pressed.

"Of course." Deflated, Imogen couldn't bring herself to look over at Trenwyth. "I'll have Cheever procure it for you." The words tasted of bitter defeat.

"Might I inquire as to what exactly *you* are doing at the scene of a brutal crime?" Morley turned on Trenwyth. "Were you somehow otherwise connected with Lady Broadmore?"

Imogen wished she wasn't as interested in the answer as the inspectors seemed to be, though she didn't at all want to investigate her motivation for being so.

"I never met her before last night," he claimed, shifting uncomfortably.

"How did you get into my garden?" Imogen couldn't stop herself from demanding. "The gate is secured with a chain and the only other way is from inside the house."

The cad had the grace to achieve a sheepish expression, and bugger if it wasn't appealing. "Twenty-five years ago our elm succeeded in rupturing the fence." He gestured to a giant tree that spanned the stone base of the fence. "There is a section crumbled away large enough for a man to fit through at the base. I've been using it to visit Lord and Lady Anstruther since I was a boy as neither they nor my parents seemed inclined to mend the rift. It's a tight fit now, but I managed from my own garden."

"But . . . why?" Imogen breathed.

Trenwyth cast the poor victim a troubled look before pointing up to his adjacent home. "My study window overlooks the Anstruther garden. When I chanced to glimpse over, I noted the body and thought—"

Imogen's breath caught in time to the death of his sentence.

"You thought it might have been Lady Anstruther," Argent finished.

Trenwyth said nothing.

Morley moved to stand next to Lady Broadmore and lifted his face to the window Trenwyth had indicated. "From this trajectory and distance, your conclusion is not remarkable. In fact, the resemblance between the deceased and Lady Anstruther is noteworthy in a case such as this."

"It . . . it is?" Appalled, Imogen had to force herself to look down at the slumberous expression forever frozen upon the poor woman's features. "How so?"

"You are both fair-haired and slight of build," Argent assessed. "You wore dresses of comparable color."

"Not so." She grasped for something, for anything to crush this ridiculous train of speculation. "If you remember, my gown was apricot, and hers is most decidedly coral."

She met a collection of blank stares and profusely cursed the entire male sex. Mostly because they'd only just established their own point. The masculine palette, famously simpler than that of the feminine, would certainly have a difficult time deciphering the difference between the colors unless one was an artist. These men were used to the assessment of only one primary color.

Bloodred.

Additionally, the moonlight had been the only illumination in the garden last night, as she'd left the gas lamps unlit to dissuade anyone from venturing into her sanctuary. Which left Imogen with no choice but to concede that Lady Broadmore's fate may have, in fact, been meant for *her*.

"Oh my God." Imogen turned away from them, and only managed to stagger a handful of steps before fainting into a carpet of unsuspecting poppies.

CHAPTER FIFTEEN

To Cole, carrying Lady Anstruther was like hauling a bolt of silk, limp and unwieldy, but not without its tactile pleasures.

The forensic doctor arrived just as she fell, and Cole barely even remembered offering to carry her inside until she was somehow gathered like a sleeping child in his arms. He swept her into the solarium and carefully lowered her onto a chaise. Supporting her back with his right hand, he made to slide the other from beneath her, when an unwelcome tug stopped him. Upon closer inspection, it became apparent that some of the joints and bolts of his metal hand had become entangled in her hair.

Lucifer's bollocks. Cole gritted his teeth against a frustrated sound as he realized he'd have to slide his arm farther beneath her to disentangle himself.

His heart still hadn't normalized from the bolt of terror he'd sustained when he'd seen Lady Broadmore. He'd truly thought . . . well, it didn't bear consideration now.

Now that he knew Lady Anstruther was alive, he needed to escape her. For both of their sakes.

He arranged a pillow underneath her head and lowered to his knees, allowing the chaise to support all her weight as he burrowed his arm under her shoulder until the offending hand was accessible. Leaning over her, he gingerly worked on freeing the errant strands without breaking or ripping them on his prosthetic.

Though her hair was thick and lush, it felt as fine as goose down. This would have aided his efforts if the press of her against him didn't somehow affect his dexterity.

He checked their surroundings surreptitiously, acknowledging the scandalous intimacy of their postures. Though only their torsos were touching, it would look to anyone who should chance upon them as if he might have her locked in an impassioned embrace.

And who could blame him, he thought as he gazed down at her.

At her proximity, his flesh had become suffused with a heat that traveled all the way to his cock, filling it with warm need. The memory of last night was too fresh, the taste of her had yet to fade. The primal hunger still growled within him. His heartbeat toppled over itself as his gaze locked onto her pale, perfect lips.

They'd been a lush pink before she'd fainted.

Christ preserve him, he was a rank pervert for lusting after an unconscious woman covered in soil and crushed poppies. And when a dead woman lay on the other side of that wall.

He attacked the tangles caught in his joints with renewed vigor, taking the utmost care to be gentle in his haste.

Her scent invaded his lungs. Lavender and lilacs. Bitter and sweet. The combination intoxicated him as it mingled with the particular scent of her flesh. Warmer than a flower, muskier than the earth.

Her shallow yet even breaths feathered over his cheek in damp little puffs, and Cole battled a slew of disquieting and humiliating urges. Ones that somehow reached beyond the primitive.

As a virile man, he should want nothing *more* than to ravish her. To hone in on the press of her soft breasts to his chest and to fantasize about all the indignities a mouth so lush could perform upon his person.

And he did. Sweet Christ, he *did*.

But he also was strangely aware that if he turned his neck just so, his rough cheek would press against her astoundingly smooth one. Her neck, just below him, was the perfect size and placement to rest his weary chin. Her hair was a sheet of smooth silk the color of the sunlight behind the pall of coal smoke on a still London day. Though caught in the cogs of his metal prosthetic, it sifted through his fingers as fluid as water.

Her color returned in slow increments, roses dusting her prominent cheekbones.

Lord but she was lovely. He'd never truly stopped to study her before, especially not up so close. Never had he seen such flawless skin. Not even upon the pallid women who'd rather die than allow a glimmer of sunlight to pierce their parasols.

She was covered in the sun, burnished that unfashionable shade of honey, and dusted with a sparse array of freckles. Why was porcelain skin so admired, anyway? Who had gazed upon a sun-kissed beauty with such vivacious hues and wished her to be one of the colorless waifs so ubiquitous in England?

An imbecile, he decided.

You did, his inner voice reminded him.

Ginny had been white as the driven snow, and it had suited her. He'd pined for her pale delicacy and the contrast of her dark, unruly locks.

But the woman beneath him was a different shade. Her shape, her scent, even her manner was quite singular, and the sun worshipped her for it.

How queer that he should like to do the same. That he should want to peel the garments from her if only to ascertain just how much of her was burnished dusky and how much remained pale.

He thought about kissing all the places the sun had touched.

And then the places left untouched.

She did not remain placid in his arms for long. Her lids twitched and trembled, her fingers curled against his vest a heart-stopping moment before her multifaceted irises were uncovered, and she regarded him with an unfocused gaze.

Cole froze like a thief caught in torchlight.

Then she whispered the absolute last thing he expected.

"Hello."

"You fainted," he blurted rather witlessly, then cringed.

"Don't be silly," she gently admonished with a tongue that sounded heavy. "I don't faint."

"You did today," he gently explained. "Now be still, my prosthetic is tangled in your hair. I'm almost free."

"You're tangled in my . . ." A wrinkle appeared between her brows and she was silent for a protracted moment.

"I carried you here when you fainted," he repeated.

She put a hand to her forehead. "I fainted?"

"That's what I said." Had she sustained a head wound?

"I fainted . . . because . . . someone wants to hurt me," she whispered. "Maybe even . . . murder me."

"That isn't going to happen." The words left him with more vehemence than even he realized he felt. But as she blinked up at him in uncertain assessment, he realized he was in earnest. This woman was not the Machiavellian opportunist he'd initially judged her to be. And even if she were, no one deserved what had befallen Lady Broadmore.

She winced as he accidentally tugged at a lock of her hair in his struggles.

"Forgive me," he muttered, feeling both awkward and churlish.

"Of course I forgive you," she replied, and he had the absurd notion she meant she'd forgiven him for more than just the damage he'd inflicted to her scalp just now.

Turning to look, she reached up and covered his fingers with hers. "Let me," she gently admonished, and proceeded to untangle her own hair in three deft movements.

To his astonishment, she sat up when he did, following his movements, keeping them close. Somehow, she retained a hold on his prosthetic, and her gentle grasp held him more captive than any chain or manacle ever had.

Silently she plucked at a few solitary strands of her hair that had broken off and remained entwined in the intricate metalwork, and allowed them to drift to the carpet beneath them.

Cole remained motionless as his senses abruptly sharpened, his body tensed as everything became louder, clearer, as though he'd awoken from some bewildering dream, or surfaced from beneath the water. The tick of the ornate clock on the mantel raced his pounding heart.

The soft butter and sage hues of the solarium somehow became more vivid. The sunlight shafting in through the open windows broke upon her with a brilliance he'd never before seen.

And when she spoke, her voice was like a melancholy concerto, filtering through him as only music was capable. The vibrations plucking at his very soul.

"It pains me that we humans can be so terribly *inhumane* to one another." Her fingers wandered from his cold, metallic hand to the round fitting. Sliding beneath his cuffs, they didn't stop until she met his flesh. "What horrors we can wreak on someone who is more or less exactly like ourselves. The lies we conjure to justify the infliction of such deeds." Her damp eyes met his, swimming with a potent emotion that made him catch his breath over an answering burn in his own throat. "It hurts my heart," she whispered, and blinked out a tear that swiftly fell from her chin.

Gentle thunder growled in the distance, warning that their sunshine was not to last.

Cole's heart reverberated in time to the gathering storm. Were her tears for Lady Broadmore? Or for the mangled wrist she held in her hand. "Are you not afraid of me?" Cole breathed. "Of this?" He glanced down to where she touched him, the sensation more intimate than if she'd reached into his trousers.

She shook her head, her fingers threading through the fine hairs on his arm, drifting upward. "There was a time that I was afraid of the whole world," she said. "But not you."

"Maybe you should be," he warned. If she knew what he was thinking right now. If she realized how close he was to ripping her night robe off her . . . Despite the mess in the backyard, or the open doors, or the inherent wrongness of it all.

He wanted his mouth on hers again. He wanted her beneath him, just as she'd been, her sweet breath on his damp flesh as he took her.

How the devil did this fucking happen?

"All right," she relented. "Perhaps I fear you a *little*." Her lashes shielded her expressive eyes from him. "Most especially after last night. But I also . . ." She didn't seem to be capable of finishing her sentence as she stared at the metal hand in her lap.

"Do *not* pity me." A cold warning crept into his voice.

"You're in no danger of that," she said flippantly. "I know how strong and capable you are. Since your . . . ordeal, you've climbed mountains and forged through oceans. You're more formidable and fearsome than you've ever been." She made an amused sound. "I don't pity you, Your Grace, only the people who have to spend a great deal of time in your churlish company."

He deserved that. Cole frowned until he noted the glimmer of mischief in her eye and the slight quirk of her lip. She was teasing him.

"I'm glad you can smile today," he said, and meant it.

Instantly, her smile died as she glanced at the window, reminded of the horror being investigated in her own garden. "I just can't understand how a man can be so cruel to a woman, how he can take something more helpless than he and destroy her with such violence."

"That is because you do not understand what it is to be a man."

"Apparently," she said bitterly. "I mean, yes, we women are generally smaller and softer than you, but why does that make us less than human in your eyes? Or less capable?"

"It doesn't." Did she mean, him, personally? Or all of mankind? Cole wasn't certain he was ready to defend those of his sex to her.

"But it *does*," she insisted. "If I were a man, would you so strongly object to my charitable undertakings?"

"Yes, I would. But we've already established that I am an unmitigated bastard. That has nothing to do with your sex," he reasoned.

She balled her hand into a little fist, her expression turning fierce. "You haven't any idea the strength it takes to be a woman. In my experience, it is *men* who are the weaker sex. Either too undisciplined to control their baser, primal instincts or, conversely, they are too fragile to endure the discomfort of honesty or integrity. Yet women endure and survive by whatever means we are able. And still we are either property or playthings. We have as much use in the eyes of the law as a cow or a fertile plot of land. It is not wrong to mistreat us. To objectify us. To shame and demand things of us and bend us to your will. That is your right as a man and our duty as a woman. Is it any wonder the world is in chaos?" A verdant fire snapped in her eyes, and Cole recognized a great deal of fear behind the anger. He pondered a moment, his entire being focused on the warmth of her hand as she clutched at him, seemingly unaware that she did so. What a little activist she was. So fierce.

"You know what I think?" he finally said. "Men are terrified that were they to hand over power to women, they'd be humiliated at what a better job you'd do of everything. If you look at it, some of the most peaceful, prosperous times in our empire's history have been when a great woman occupied the throne. Elizabeth, for example, and our own Victoria, of course. Not many men have ruled so wisely."

The reluctant smile she gave him melted some of the ice bricked in his chest. "You continually surprise me, Your Grace."

"I propose that, under the circumstances, we can dispense with all that," he murmured. "In private you can call me Collin if you wish."

"Collin?" She wrinkled her nose. "Is that what your friends call you?"

"It isn't, actually."

She made an expectant gesture, as though she'd already known. But how could she have done?

"Cole," he blurted. "My friends call me Cole."

"Cole." Her eyes crinkled at the sides, signifying that he'd pleased her. "We're not exactly friends, are we?"

That brought a wry smile to his face. "I'd rather we no longer be enemies."

"I'd like that as well," she replied, her face shining with genuine satisfaction. "And you may call me Imogen."

He wanted to say her name. Wanted to test the intimacy on his tongue, so lush and lovely was the word. But the way she looked at him now, the light in her hazel eyes masking something dark and haunted opened a tender ache in his chest he'd not known since . . .

"You are so dreadfully kind," he accused. "So good. Do you never hold a grudge? Do you not hate anyone?"

"I don't know if I'm capable of hatred." She glanced outside, as though testing her theory. "I firmly believe that hatred is a disease. And one does not cure a disease by propagating it, does one? I believe, I *know*, that kindness can be infectious too. And that is something worth diffusion. That is why I am attempting this undertaking. To show kindness to those who don't know the meaning of the word."

"Even now?" he marveled. "After what happened last night?"

"Especially after what happened last night," she said gravely. "Though I do believe I'll need to hire more protection . . . perhaps Mr. Argent is aware of someone."

"I don't know if you're intrepidly courageous or just fantastically daft."

"Let's agree on the former, because then we can remain civil." A hard glint of warning underscored the levity in her voice. "For a moment there, I thought you had remembered how."

"Remembered?" he scoffed. "It is a vast assumption on your part that I've ever demonstrated civility in the first place."

"No it isn't," she argued, solemnity replacing all humor. "I know that you're capable of kindness."

Cole didn't have time to puzzle over the volumes of meaning in her regard.

"How fares your wrist?" She deftly changed the subject, turning his arm until it faced upward and inspecting the straps much like she'd done in the garden. "Does it still trouble you as it did last night?"

"It'll keep." It did bother him still, but not so much as the tender concern knitting her brow, or the probing gentleness of her touch.

Amusement dimpled her cheek, which he was glad to notice regained more color by the second. "Such a masculine response," she murmured demurely. To illustrate her teasing, no doubt. "I believe I can procure a salve of comfrey, lavender, and a fractionated oil that will soothe

the irritation. I'll send my maid, Lillian, to deliver it when I'm able." She glanced uncertainly out the window, then visibly set her chin and met his gaze with the steady capability and authority of a Major General, or a long-time nurse. "You should apply it at least twice daily, and most liberally at night. It would be best if you avoid wearing your ill-fitting prosthesis unless absolutely necessary until it can be adjusted to avoid exacerbation."

Something pleasant glided through him. Something other than awareness, frustration, or even desire.

He dare not call it admiration. He dare not call it that . . .

"You must have been an extraordinary nurse," he blurted. "I can see why Anstruther didn't want to relinquish your care of him."

His compliment seemed to startle her just as intensely as it did himself. Her eyes, turned an intriguing shade of sage by the room's décor, became positively owlish and unblinking.

It was Cole who ultimately looked away, searching for safer ground. "I'll admit to having had very few women in my society with any amount of employment experience," he said conversationally. "What was it like, being a nurse?"

Imogen withdrew her hand from inside his cuff, as if barely realizing the improper amount of time she'd spent with her hand against his skin. After a thoughtful silence, she answered softly, "Messy. Difficult. Sad . . . Infuriating and utterly fulfilling."

"Do you miss it?" he asked, before he could think of a reason not to.

"Sometimes. Though I think I am more suited to what I am doing now," she said carefully. "I believe I was always meant to help those in need. I want to do everything in my power to alleviate pain."

He nodded as he silently watched her deft, elegant fingers secure his cufflink. He had to admit that, despite his protestations, there was nobility in her cause. Her intentions were ceaselessly honorable, he knew that now. Finished with his cufflink, she laid her hand over the one with which Cole braced himself on the cushion beside her knee.

"What was it like being a sp—a soldier?" she corrected herself before calling him a spy.

He searched her gaze, waiting for the familiar savage, chaotic emotions to well within him when he thought of his military career these days.

They didn't. In fact, a strange sort of half-smile tugged at his lips. "Messy. Difficult. Sad . . . Infuriating and utterly fulfilling."

She smiled without parting her lips, an expression as sad as it was genuine. "It seems that we've both waged our share of battles. Mine against time and disease, and yours against the enemies of the empire."

"It's a wonder either of us have any fight left," he agreed.

"I only seem to in your presence." She made a gesture of exasperated amusement. "I'm glad we've called a sort of ceasefire for the moment."

"I imagine we've both seen enough blood to last a lifetime," Cole murmured. He'd not meant for his statement to bring them back to the grim happenings in her garden, but it did. They both glanced toward the window, and a bleak vulnerability seized Imogen's features with such sorrow, Cole fought the sudden and disquieting urge to pull her close.

"Your Grace." Morley beckoned from the door. "A moment."

"Excuse me." It disturbed Cole, how little he wanted to leave the room. How strange and solitary he felt at the prospect of losing Imogen's proximity.

"I'll go check on Isobel." Lady Anstruther stood and reatreated, and Cole watched her go, grappling with stunning regret.

Resolutely, he followed the chief inspector back into the garden.

Morley glanced back toward the window of the solarium. "She doesn't seem to like you, overmuch."

Cole made a wry sound. "The feeling is mutual. Or, it was. We seem to have . . . reconciled our differences for the moment."

"I'm glad to hear it." Morley nodded. "You see, I know that you were in Her Majesty's Special Operations Corps. I understand that surveillance and . . . assassination were your particular specialties."

Even from across the path, Argent's head perked at the word *assassination*. They'd known this was something they'd had in common ages ago; it was why they now sparred together. It was difficult in a world like theirs to find a man with a similar competency for killing.

"The worst kept secret in all of London, apparently," Cole lamented. "I'm the spy everyone recognizes."

"In this case, that might be a boon." Morley studied him in that quiet way he had, the one that made a man feel more like a target than a companion.

"Tell me you're joking."

"It's possible that Lady Anstruther has a dangerous enemy. One that might be dissuaded if it were known she were under your protection." The volumes of expectation in Morley's words were unmistakable.

Cole grimaced as he considered it. Half the London elite had witnessed her embarrassment at his treatment of her the night before. No one would believe her to be defended by him.

"What did you do or say that made her comfortable enough to all but accuse you of this?" Morley motioned to the strangled woman.

Trenwyth remembered the delicate feel of Imogen's throat beneath his hand the night before. The captured thrum of her pulse, the soft press of her sinuous body. The incomparable taste of her.

She must have been terrified.

He watched silently as Lady Broadmore was covered and moved to a stretcher, suddenly weak with gladness that it wasn't Imogen or her sister. "I've been an ass," he admitted to both Morley and himself. Looking up into the unsettling, perceptive eyes of the chief inspector, he asked, "Do you have any clear idea of who could have done this? Any suspects of initial interest?"

Morley sighed and lifted a paper in his hand. "This list certainly helps, but no. I'll have to look deeper into Lady Broadmore's personal life, but I believe that this is connected to Lady Anstruther. Though—" He broke off, his gaze becoming remote.

"Yes?" Cole demanded sharply.

"There are some very strange similarities to another unsolved murder case that's nearly two years old. A prostitute was found strangled, which, unfortunately, is an omnipresent crime in this city. But the parallels to Lady Broadmore's case are salient. The fact that her eyes were closed is unique, though not unprecedented, as though the killer wanted to pretend she was sleeping rather than dead."

Argent lifted a dubious russet brow. "That isn't much to go on."

"That and her . . . undergarments are completely ripped away," Morley continued with an uncomfortable gesture. "As I'm certain you're aware, lady's underthings are sewn with an opening between the legs. Rather makes the entire—er—area accessible, doesn't it? So why strip only that article away, and not the rest of her garments?"

With a perplexed frown, he stepped to the stretcher and lifted the white sheet. "Also, the utter lack of previous or subsequent violence is worth noting. She hasn't a bruise anywhere on her body but her neck. Rape is generally a violent affair, more violent than sexual if you ask me. But in this case, and the one I referenced, dominance doesn't seem to be the motivation. It's almost as though the perpetrator would be a lover." Covering Lady Broadmore's visage, he stood and faced them. "Though . . . what a murder of a viscountess in Belgravia and that of a kitten of St. James's Street have to do with each other is rather baffling."

Something inside Cole snapped, and he stalked to Morley, seizing his arm. "Kitten? Two years ago? Who was the victim?"

Morley tensed; the muscle bunching beneath his hand was thicker than Cole had expected. He stared at Cole as though he'd sprouted horns, but he answered the question after a moment of frank consideration. "Can't say I remember the name just now. Florence or Fiona or something . . . though that was her given name on her birth record. These prostitutes are generally in the habit of ascribing themselves, and each other, clever pseudonyms and the like."

"Ginny?" Cole pressed desperately. "Could her name have been Ginny?"

Morley's eyes sharpened, and Cole wondered if his entire world might be sliced to shreds by the man's next words. "That name does sound familiar. In fact, I believe it was brought up that evening. I'll have to consult the case file and it's in a different borough, over at the records office at number Four Whitehall Place, Scotland Yard."

"I want that file," Cole growled.

Morley attempted to shrug him off, but Cole's grip was ironclad.

Argent moved behind Morley, his shoulders bunched in readiness. "Careful, Trenwyth," he warned.

"I *will* see it," Cole gritted through his teeth. "Try to keep it from me."

"Why would you want to?" Argent queried, studying him as he would a newly discovered species of man, with interest and a bit of hesitation.

Realizing he was getting nowhere, Cole released the chief inspector and turned toward the fountain, glad to see its gruesome contents had been removed. "I visited the Bare Kitten before . . ." He held up his left arm. "There was a . . . woman, Ginny, with whom I spent the night. I . . . took something of hers all that time ago, and I wanted to . . ." Christ, this was difficult.

"What did you take?" Morley queried.

Her virtue. It wasn't like he could return it to her, but he could somehow make amends. He might even do what he could to make an honest woman out of her. A prostitute duchess, wouldn't that beat all?

"That is *my* business. But if she's . . . dead I . . ." *God.*

Had he been searching for her ghost all this time? Had his tragedy become hers, as well? The very thought slammed into him with the weight of a blacksmith hammer, threatening to break him at the core. His knees weakened as grief and fear washed over his skin and filled his mouth with the taste of bitter gall.

"Tell you what, Trenwyth. I'll request the file from wherever it's been archived, and when it's in my hands I'll invite you down to my office to peruse its contents."

Cole forced himself to turn back to the man and speak to him, even though all he wanted to do was break something. "I'd very much appreciate it."

"You are owed, for your sacrifice in the field, if nothing else." Morley's gaze flicked to his hand.

"How long do you think it'll take?" Cole pressed.

"I'll contact you the day after next."

"Until then." He nodded to both men before making his way back toward the tree. He knew he should take his leave of Lady Anstruther, but it somehow seemed wrong to do so, because of his body's rather aggressive reaction to her nearness.

He'd never promised any kind of fidelity to Ginny, that he knew. But if he had, whatever happened to him in the presence of Imogen would have been nothing short of a sin.

Please, God, he prayed for the first time since his faith had bled out of him in a pit of hell in Constantinople. *Don't let her be dead. Not like this.* If Ginny had been the victim of a crime similar to the one he'd witnessed today, Cole knew it would be the end of him.

For his last vestige of hope would die just as violently. And there would truly be nothing left.

CHAPTER SIXTEEN

To Imogen, sleep was as elusive as the stars behind storm clouds these days. She knew it was there, where it had always been, but her exhausted mind remained restless and churning. A factory of predictions and anxieties.

Once upon a time, she would have wandered her garden in search of peace, refuge, and a bit of bracing fresh air. Now it had become something else. The stage of a murder. A murder that was perhaps meant for her.

She'd think it imprudent to be wandering through the garden now were two policemen not stationed at her home, one within and one patrolling the grounds outside. Chief Inspector Morley promised her the best Scotland Yard had to offer, leaving her with a blithe and burly Irishman named Sean O'Mara, and also a rather dashing North African gentleman, Roman Rathbone, whose marble-dark eyes gleamed in a way that suggested he'd spent more of his years misbehaving than enforcing the law. Imogen had warily sensed a spark of significant attraction from both men in regard to Isobel.

She'd have to watch for that, as her sister was obviously too young and tender for either of their attentions.

The full summer moon hung low and heavy in the clear night sky, and Imogen pulled her wrapper close against a moist chill that chased away the heat of the day. On nights such as this, torches and lanterns were not needed, as the moon provided enough illumination once the eyes adjusted to the silver-white gleam.

Though Lady Broadmore's body had been taken to the morgue, and no blood was spilled, the base of the satyr fountain still seemed tainted. Stained by something more gory than blood, more sinister than even death.

Imogen skirted the fountain altogether, padding down a path that wound through wildflowers as she measured the many possible sources of threats to her life and family.

Not Trenwyth, she thought with relief. He'd become many unfamiliar and dangerous things in their time apart, but not a rapist. Not a murderer of the innocent and helpless.

"So who, then?" she asked the moon in a soft whisper. And *why*? Supposing Lady Broadmore's death truly had anything to do with her, the question became all about motivation, didn't it? Had the murder been meant to protect her? Or in some sort of morbid effigy of her?

Imogen thought of her beloved childhood cat, Icarus. He'd adored her, and to demonstrate that high regard, he'd often leave the corpses of little birds or mice at the foot of her bed. He'd sit next to them, amber eyes gleaming with pride and satisfaction, awaiting her prompt and expected adulation.

Was this the message the killer had intended? Lady

Broadmore had seemed bent on making an enemy of Imogen. Had one of the men in her employ or—dare she think it?—a guest left her a gruesome gift in the form of her adversary's corpse?

The other more frightening possibility was that the killer had, indeed, mistaken Lady Broadmore for Imogen in the dark. Once he'd gotten his hands on her and discovered his mistake, he had still carried out his dastardly crime upon the wrong woman.

This seemed most likely the case. Imogen chewed on her lip as she contemplated the next question very carefully.

Who wanted her dead?

Barton was always a possibility. Though she'd been certain at the time that she'd stabbed him in the artery, perhaps she'd been mistaken. He'd never been found. What if he'd been stalking the shadows all this time, waiting to finish what he'd started in that terrifying alley behind the Bare Kitten? If he'd let his anger fester nearly two years to an obsessive point, it made perfect sense that he should return for her with the intention of carrying out his rape and mortal revenge.

She really should have notified the inspectors of him. They had the list of former criminals in their possession, and the chance remained that it could be one of them. However, she'd unfairly left out a significant piece of the puzzle.

Because Trenwyth had been there. Because she still wasn't certain that she was safe from a charge of murder.

And because if she made it known, even to the police, that she'd once been a Kitten of St. James's Street, everything she had worked for would be ruined. Her charity disgraced. Poor Isobel would be a pariah. She might lose the patronage and friendship of Millie, Farah, and Mena.

Indeed, though she'd made a brittle truce with Cole this very afternoon, he still might carry through with his threat to bring into question the validity of her marriage to Lord Anstruther.

He'd be so angry with her for lying to him. She was certain of that now.

Lord, what a mess she seemed to make of everything. She'd been a fool to think that she could run from her troubles. That money and a title would erase the misdeeds of her past.

That she wouldn't make new and grave mistakes.

Who else had had access to her garden that night? Only all of London, she thought woefully. Even a few characters from her past. Jeremy Carson, the sweet barkeep who misquoted just about everyone. Dr. Longhurst, a dark horse afflicted with brilliance. A brilliance accompanied by a certain amount of awkwardness in society. A touch of cold indifference, as when he'd informed her of poor Molly's death.

Was it possible he . . .

The unmistakable sound of flesh connecting with flesh in aggression broke her reverie, and she abruptly realized she'd drifted close to the stone and iron fence that separated her garden from that of Trenwyth Hall.

Her breath accelerated in time with her heart as she drifted close enough to rest her hand upon the ivy crawling the iron trellis, and impeding her view. Grunts and growls provided a lethal melody to the percussion of violent strikes that she felt down to her very bones.

What was going on? Had Inspector O'Mara chased an assailant onto the grounds of Trenwyth Hall? Had the duke, himself, found someone in his own garden?

Imogen attempted to part the thick ivy, but was

thwarted by her lack of strength. Then she remembered what Cole had said when he'd appeared in the garden that morning. The ancient tree, not twelve paces away, hid a passage between their properties.

She didn't know what time it was; late enough that dew had begun to collect on the moss beneath her feet as she hurried to duck beneath the ponderous branches of the Wych elm. Reaching the trunk, she instantly noted the part where the stone and mortar had crumbled away; leaving enough space for someone to shimmy through. Though how a man of Trenwyth's size managed remained a mystery to the laws of man and nature.

She could feel the striations of the tree bark snag at her shawl as she shimmied through the fissure and held close to the stone wall. Crouching down, she peered from beneath the low-hanging branches and caught her breath as her mind struggled to process the magnitude of what she saw. The sheer masculine brutality of it.

Cole brawled, but not with a murderer.

Or perhaps she was wrong about that. In fact, she became certain she was, because two men who moved and struck like this were physically made for little else but systematic execution.

The moonlight reflected off the golden warmth of his naked torso, and burnished his bronze hair in a shroud of silver beams. He seemed to shimmer like a mirage, the illusion made more severe by the incomprehensible speed with which he moved against his opponent.

Christopher Argent, of all people.

The grounds of Trenwyth Hall were decidedly more grass than garden, and the two men fought each other clad in naught but loose trousers. Like Imogen, even their feet were bare.

Ducking a brutal blow, Cole tucked his lithe body and rolled out of Argent's reach, unfolding to stand a great distance off. They circled each other like predators fighting over territory, eyes gleaming and feral, teeth bared, and muscles knotted. Each looking for a weakness in the other to exploit and finding none.

Judging by the sweat slicking their hair at the temples and creating a rather intriguing sheen on their scandalously bared flesh, they'd been at this play for quite some time. Each held what looked like blunted metal knives in their right hands.

A thin line of blood dripped from Trenwyth's eyebrow, following the line of his temple, but he hardly seemed to note its existence.

Imogen knew she should not be watching this, but she couldn't help but play the dishonorable voyeur to such an emollient moment. Violence was about to explode between them, and a shameful, primitive part of her wanted to watch the detonation.

For the artistic value, if nothing else.

These men, locked in a timeless engagement, were not built for this era of elegance and refinement. They were creatures of combat and carnage, their muscles crafted in layered ropes and swells advertising a strength born of hardship and labor.

And both men had scars. Such awful scars that Imogen had to clear a sheen of sorrow from her eyes with a few rapid blinks.

Argent's back was to her, but the pale giant's topography was a map of torture. A web of once-burned skin covered one entire shoulder like a plate of gruesome armor. A myriad of puckered wounds suggested several battles with a knife. And maybe a bullet or two.

Millie LeCour's stoic husband was certainly more than he seemed.

Imogen couldn't help but catalogue the differences between the two men. Argent's decidedly wider shoulders buttressed a bulk not often seen on this island. Surely he came from Viking stock, his skin pink with exertion and lightly freckled. His hair darker than copper but lighter than wine. He moved with an ease not often seen on men of his size. As though the elements made room for his passage and prepared for the brutal force he brought with him.

Trenwyth, on the other hand, stood taller than any man had a right to be. His sinew was forced to stretch over thick bones and layered with veins. His abdomen seemed to have one more flexed ripple than his opponent's, and Imogen's gaze hungrily followed the line between them until it ran into a waistband.

He stalked and circled on bent knees, the predatory savagery on his face contradicted by a calculating gleam in his lupine eyes. Here was the wolf she recognized from that long-ago day in the Bare Kitten. Generally so stoic and self-contained, so certain of his uncontested reign.

And yet. He had to perfect his skill, didn't he? To remain at the head, a leader and noble, he must keep his mind and body honed to a dagger's point.

Watching them was a lot like Imogen would imagine watching a wolf fighting with a bear. Each of them crafted for killing, but in entirely different fashions.

As they circled, the moonlight illuminated different parts of Cole's body. A shallow slash on his neck. A perfect round bullet wound in his shoulder. A labyrinth of raised and welted scars scattered in violent chaos across his entire trunk, both front and back.

She remembered some of his scars from before his

incarceration, the visual narrative of a soldier's life. But most of them, indeed, the most horrific, had been inflicted whilst he suffered in a foreign prison, subject to the basest cruelties imaginable.

Cole's left arm corded, the metallic hand glinting in the moonlight as he lifted it, the buckles strapped tightly to his thick forearm.

How extraordinary, Imogen thought. That he should use his prosthesis as a weapon. That he should turn his hindrance into strength. She remembered the coiled blade hidden at the wrist, and wondered if he'd ever chanced to use it. She remained crouched beneath the ancient tree on unsteady legs. It was like watching a dance, the steps brutish and heavy, but requiring just as much mastery of motion. In this waltz, one misstep had eternal consequences.

Without any sound or warning, Argent lunged forward, aiming low with his knife in an attack so quick and deadly, Imogen was left wondering if he couldn't shove the blunted weapon right through a man's heart by way of brute force.

She needn't have worried, Cole waited until the last possible moment before parrying, using Argent's bulk against him and sidestepping the attack. Argent seemed to anticipate the move, and performed some sleight of hand, the knife appearing in his left and jabbing once again at Trenwyth, even though he was slightly off balance.

This forced the duke to throw his body back, his left arm crossing his chest to bat away the trajectory of the knife aimed at his throat. He performed a simultaneous attack as he blocked, but the thrust went wild, missing its mark.

"You're distracted," Argent accused.

"Am I?" Trenwyth baited.

This exchange gave Argent the time he needed to regain his balance, and he took no occasion to savor it, but struck like a coiled viper, the weapon aimed directly beneath Trenwyth's sternum.

Now squared to his opponent, Cole caught Argent's outstretched arm by crossing both of his in front of his body. He maneuvered the weapon out and away from danger, and turned against the extended arm to plant an elbow in Argent's jaw with a gasp-inducing crack.

Imogen's hands flew to her mouth, barely containing her cry of astonishment.

Argent caught the knife-wielding hand that closely followed, and spat blood on the grass. The men strained and grappled for an instant, their movements concealed by the substantial shadows they both created with their magnificent bodies.

After a heart-pounding struggle, they both froze, locked in some painful-looking impasse.

"You're distracted, and you're dead," Argent said victoriously, a bit more breathlessly than before.

"Am I?" Trenwyth repeated.

The blunted blade glinted against his neck as Argent made a slashing motion.

"So I am," the duke relented, and then made a gesture that directed attention to where he held his own blade.

Scandalously high against Argent's inner thigh where the femoral artery would spill all his blood in less than two minutes.

"So are you." It might have been the first time Imogen had ever heard a smile in Cole's voice. At least, the first time in almost three years.

Their sparring ended with a draw, and the men separated with a handshake, then each used the back of their

hands to wipe blood from their faces in an eerily synchro-
nized manner.

"Care to divulge what's troubling you?" Argent
prompted mildly.

"What makes you think I'm troubled?" Trenwyth
bent to gather other discarded sparring implements such
as canes of bamboo, fencing swords, and their knives.
He returned them to a sturdy trunk at the foot of the
garden stairs.

Imogen knew she should go, but had to remind herself
to even so much as blink. His sleek, powerful beauty mesmerized her into stillness, hypnotized, nay, seduced by
the potency of his masculinity.

Argent assisted, though he paused to study Trenwyth
whilst he was unaware. "If I've learned anything in my
life, Your Grace, it's this: if you watch people long enough,
they reveal themselves to you."

"Your Grace. What a ridiculous moniker," Cole murmured bitterly. "You and I have known very little grace
in life, Argent. And we possess even less. I wonder if such
a thing exists."

"It does," Argent affirmed in his toneless way. "I've
found it with my wife. My mother had it. Most women are
built with an extra element of grace. It is because of men
like us that they need it, I think." He elbowed Trenwyth
in the ribs, as though to mark the rare occasion upon
which he employed humor.

Ridding himself of his burden of weapons, Cole looked
down at his hands. One streaked with his blood, the other
with the metallic reflection of the cold moon. "Blood
and steel. These are the only elements I recognize anymore. I only find grace in a single memory. A memory of
a woman who gave it to me once. In that, I fear, is my

tragedy. I wonder if reminiscence has smothered my sense of reality."

Argent contemplated that for a moment. "It is only human to prize most what we have lost."

"I *know* that." Cole made an impatient gesture, directed more at himself than his companion. "It's a tactic I've used against others countless times. And so . . . I should be above that base impulse, should I not?"

Argent shrugged. "Even remarkable people are subject to human banality."

"I seem to be imprisoned by it," Cole said bitterly.

The big, stoic man brought his hand to his auburn hair, looking about as though seeking permission from the darkness to say what he did next. "More than most, I understand that a prison can keep you long after you're released. That a man, locked away, becomes an animal. And that animal walks with you into freedom, until freedom becomes confining. It is . . . not an easy thing."

When Cole glanced over at Argent, the careful expression on his face caused an ache to well in Imogen's chest so painful that she clutched at it.

"It is exactly as you say. My mind has become a sort of prison. The walls are bricks mortared with remembered screams. The bars lock me in with remembered torments. My body squirms to be rid of it all. Of me. Of the past. And the disgust I feel drenches me until a vague sort of numbness takes over . . . and erases me altogether. I want to tear myself apart. Or others. Or the entire world. I feel at once violent and apathetic and—" He broke off, his hand curling into a fist.

"And you are looking for the one person you think can hold you together," Argent finished for him.

"Yes."

That one broken word shattered any semblance of Imogen's composure. Tears made tracks of fire down her cheeks, and her heart thundered so loudly it was a miracle that both superlative men couldn't hear it.

Imogen ducked further into the shield of the tree as Argent turned to look past her house toward his own, hunkered on the other side. Millie was, no doubt, slumbering within, awaiting her husband's return.

"Don't stop until you find her," Argent said with more ferocity than she'd ever credited him for.

"What if she's nowhere to be found?"

"I would burn this empire to the ground if Millie were taken from me. I would scour the world until fate swallowed me whole and hell tried to claim me, as it surely will."

"I feel as you do. But I only knew her for the space of a night . . . It seems ludicrous, doesn't it? I should have my head examined."

"Sometimes it only takes one night to fill a chamber you thought empty." Argent thumped Cole on the chest, above his heart.

The duke nodded, turning so Imogen could no longer see his face. "I was going to ask Dorian Blackwell for his aid, but I think I made an enemy of him."

Argent made a sardonic sound. "Dorian never forgets a thing, but his own bit of grace has taught him to forgive. I'll talk to him on your behalf."

Feeling as though she'd stolen enough luck to remain concealed, Imogen sneaked back into her garden on trembling legs, holding in sobs that threatened to reveal her. She didn't know what terrified her more. That Cole would find her and reveal the clandestine life she'd been forced to live . . .

Or how very much a part of her yearned to be found.

But it was impossible now, wasn't it? He'd never forgive her secrets, or worse, wouldn't believe her. She had details of their night together locked into her memory, of course. She could prove that she'd been Ginny.

Oh God, was she even considering this lunacy? Was the risk worth the recompense?

Her heart bled for Cole, for all the suffering he'd endured these past years. But every encounter they'd ever had as duke and countess had been fraught with antagonism. He disliked almost everything about her.

Once, long ago, they'd been no more than a soldier going off to war and the woman he'd paid for comfort. If he transposed her with his memory of Ginny, which emotion would win his heart? Would his nostalgia be strong enough to smother his fury? His distaste for what she'd become?

And if it did, what would he expect of her once he knew? Sex? Love? Marriage? She wasn't Ginny anymore. Her love could not be bought for twenty pounds.

Neither was she the desperate Imogen Pritchard. She hadn't been for a long time. She was capable of showing him plenty of grace, of forgiveness and kindness and . . . maybe love. But what could he provide her other than the title of duchess? Which, if she was honest, meant absolutely nothing to her.

Assuming he even offered for her. That he didn't destroy her in a fit of wrath.

He'd certainly made it clear that he couldn't accept what she'd chosen to do with her life, and she wasn't willing to let her purpose go. Not even for him.

So what was her next move? She could pray that Dorian Blackwell wasn't as crafty and well connected as they seemed to think. But something told her it was only a matter of time. Once upon a time she would have fled England, and a selfish part of her wished that she could. But she couldn't abandon the ladies and children already in her care and employ.

She needed to stay and fight. Fight for their safety and survival.

And, above all, fight that aching part of herself that yearned for him to come and claim her.

CHAPTER SEVENTEEN

Your Grace,

After careful inspection of the case file we discussed, I've come to the conclusion that the murder of a one Flora Latimer and that of Lady Broadmore have enough similarities to give the connection further consideration. I have decided to cast the net of investigation wider, and sent requests to the Scotland Yard branches of other boroughs for information on any such similar atrocities. According to a witness, the attacker was likely a man named Mr. Barton who has subsequently disappeared. As to your association with this "Ginny," I have yet been unable to confirm her existence, let alone her connection to the victim, but I can tell you that it is notated that Flora Latimer used some sort of chemical dye to make her hair gold. However, the file clearly states she had naturally dark hair and green eyes.

I have found, however, that a Devina Rosa worked at the Bare Kitten at the time, and is now one of the infamous courtesans they call the horse-breakers of Hyde Park. Perhaps she remembers your Ginny. I hope this information helps you, though I fear it can confirm neither your fears nor your wishes.

My sincerest regrets,
Sir Carlton Morley

With a vicious curse, Cole had crumpled the letter in his hand and tossed it into the fire. He'd learned in his days in prison that hope could be wielded as a cruelty. Never had that been truer than this moment. He didn't know whether to rejoice or grieve and that, in itself, was a certain kind of hell. Stalking to his study window, he'd whipped aside the drapes and glanced down to find a particular garden empty of a particular countess. The sun was high and warm today, the air still and tepid. Why the devil wasn't she painting?

A frown weighed down his features as he rang for his jacket and hat and ordered his horse, cantering to Hyde Park to seek out this Devina creature, and the answers she might provide him.

Answers, it seemed, were to be as elusive as anything else he sought. Contentment, tranquility . . .

Sleep.

He dare not even reach for happiness.

After considerable time, charm, and expense, he gleaned that Devina had moved on, finding a rich protector whose name no one knew, and was installed comfortably somewhere out of his reach. Upon learning this, Cole had turned his horse's head toward Rotten Row, the long raceway at the east of Hyde Park, and galloped until they were both panting, hot, and exhausted. Still, it didn't quell the burn of helpless fury whipping through his chest as uncontrollably as a wildfire.

He'd find this Devina, if he had to tear London apart stone by ancient stone.

The rare sunlight did little to help his dark mood, though the exertion did quiet the violent urges. Somewhat.

Ignoring the hails of sycophantic lesser nobles, the calls of desperate mothers with eligible daughters, and others of the *ton* who crowded into Hyde Park during the season for no other reason than to see and be seen, Cole trotted toward the Mayfair park entrance. Perhaps he'd go into the Home Office and find out what he could about Devina. She was a Spanish migrant, this he knew, and there would have to be some record of her—

A rather violent shade of purple skirt fluttered in his periphery, interrupting his thoughts and turning his head. Only one woman he knew wore such unapologetically vibrant colors. And there sat the countess Anstruther in profile, perched forward on a long stone bench. Though, rather than applying the paintbrush in her hand to the canvas in front of her, she stared at some mysterious point in the distance.

Violet satin ribbons fluttered from her hat in the same errant breeze that caught red-gold tendrils escaping her intricate coiffure. The rest of her remained as still as the statue of Achilles she regarded with more morose perturbation than artistic appreciation.

Cole deliberated for a moment before deciding he should definitely leave.

He slid from the saddle, planting his boots in the soft grass.

He should avoid Countess Anstruther and her compelling presence, he admonished himself while simultaneously tossing his reins to an awaiting stable hand, along with a few coins.

As his long stride brought him nearer to her, he noticed a pinch between her brows and new shadows beneath her eyes that hadn't previously been there. It wouldn't be prudent to interrupt her, especially in such a public venue. Cheever, the old goat, lounged behind her in a lawn chair with a paper, so it wasn't as though she was left unattended.

She appeared tired, Cole noted. Tired and a little gloomy. Well, *he* certainly wasn't a harbinger of cheer, and shouldn't even consider getting any closer . . .

She glanced up at him the moment his shadow crossed her canvas. Her eyes crinkled in that way that made him sure she was pleased, though he couldn't imagine why she would be.

"Cole."

His heart tripped at the sound of his name on her lips, and he managed a curt nod.

"What an agreeable surprise." Scooping extra skirts beneath her, she made space for him on the bench.

"Is it?" It discomfited him just how much he wanted the radiance in her eyes to be genuine. Because when she looked at him, the shadows he'd just noted were replaced by a warm light. He found it extraordinary. Confounding, but extraordinary nonetheless.

"How striking you look," she remarked, and didn't give him a moment to process the abrupt spurt of pleasure at the words before she turned to Cheever. "Would you very much mind procuring the three of us some lemonade from the stand at the entry? His Grace seems uncomfortably hot."

Cheever folded the paper just so, setting it on his seat

before bowing to them both. "Of course, my lady. Your Grace." His stride was that of a much younger man as he left them.

"Do sit," she invited. "The shade here is excellent."

"I really should be going," he excused, and then somehow they were nearly at eye level as the sun-warmed stone of the bench caught him when he sat. What was it about her that drew him like this? It was as though he was a ship tossed about in a storm, and she a siren luring him to his fate. In her presence, his body was consistently at odds with his mind, and refused to obey him in any regard.

"Though we are little better than strangers, you always seem to treat me as though you know me," he remarked.

"And yet it seems I know nothing about you," she challenged.

It could have been the dappled sunlight, the distraction she provided from his consistent disappointment, the mysterious glint in her eye, or some odd combination of all of these variables that summoned a rakish mischief within him he'd thought forever lost.

"I am an open book," he declared with false solemnity.

"You are *anything* but that," she laughed.

He made a sound of mock outrage. "Ask me any question you please, and suffer the consequences of my absolute candor."

She pretended to give it some thought. "Speaking of books, then. Who is your most beloved author?"

"Shakespeare, obviously."

She cast him a dubious look. "Which play?"

It was his turn to give it some thought and answered with a defiant smirk, "The one wherein the parent dies and someone goes mad."

"That's nearly all of them." Her eyes danced with

mirth. "So much for candor. I'm beginning to doubt you know Shakespeare at all."

Cole plucked from his memory one of the numerous sonnets he'd devoured as a child.

" 'Love is not love which alters when it alteration finds, Or bends with the remover to remove, O no! it is an ever-fixed mark that looks on tempests and is never shaken . . .' " He let the words trail away as their significance pierced him with solemnity.

" 'Love alters not with his brief hours and weeks,' " she finished breathlessly, the paintbrush trembling in her hand. " 'But bears it out even to the edge of doom.' "

Their eyes locked and held as Cole's mind churned with the same frenzy his stallion's hooves had only minutes prior. Was that what he was doing? Bearing out his obsessive need for Ginny, even to the edge of his own doom? What would the bard have to say about his behavior? he wondered. Would he have censured Cole for pining after Ginny all this time? Or for forgetting to do so when thusly engaged with the Lady Anstruther?

"I stand both corrected and astonished," she admitted, seemingly impervious to his thoughts. "I, too, love Shakespeare. Though I enjoy his words more when performed than the reading of them. To be honest, Isobel is the great reader in our family, as I tend to appreciate more visual modalities." She gestured to her painting.

"I can't find fault in that," he murmured, unable to tear his eyes from the vision she made. A violet blooming in the shade of their tree. "There is much to appreciate."

A pretty pink blush stained her high cheekbones, and she lowered bashful lashes. "You've been riding today." She swept some horsehair from his jacket, and Cole could almost hear the scandalized gasps of the noble matrons passing in their expensive carriages. He loved that she seemed to care even less than he did. "It is my most fervent regret that I never had the chance to learn the equestrian arts."

His first instinct was to offer to teach her, and then he realized what the sight of her on horseback would do to him. She was a lithe woman, and proximity to her rolling hips and her bottom bouncing in a saddle might just be the death of him.

Shifting away from her, he gestured to the nude Achilles statue, the hero's only adornment, other than a sword and shield, an intimately placed fig leaf. "You abandoned your garden today in search of more . . . stimulating inspiration for your art?"

An impish dimple appeared in her cheek. "I've always been fond of this statue," she admitted. "On a day like this, I like the play of the sunlight on the darker bronze of his musculature."

Cole swallowed around a dry tongue as he watched her gaze trace the exposed lines of Achilles' form with naked admiration.

"More of your passion for Greek mythology?"

She shook her head, surprising him yet again with her audacity, even as her lashes swept down. "No, actually, he . . . reminds me of someone."

"The Duke of Wellington, I presume? The thing was cast in his honor though, obviously, not in his image."

"No." She glanced back up at the imposing statue, and Cole had the absurd notion that she was studiously avoiding his gaze. "Someone else."

Cole glared at the statue with a renewed distaste for it. It reminded her of someone . . . Someone she'd apparently experienced in flagrante delicto.

Were he a lesser man he'd be jealous.

But he wasn't.

Not in the least.

Though he had to admit it a balm to his ego that his physique could rival that of Achilles, at least, this particular rendering of him. The one she so admired. He couldn't help but wonder what her aesthetic eye would capture if she were to gaze upon him so revealed. Would she see his strength and sinew, or only his impediment?

"I like his stance most of all," she said, studying it as though she'd done so a thousand times before. "It's as though the sculptor captured the heartbeat before a great triumph. His shield is brandished in a way that leaves no question that he deflected the blow of his enemy. His sword is readying for a maneuver that he's mastered. One can almost complete the moment in one's mind in all its fierce victory, even though other variables are missing." She finally turned to him, eyes shining with the fanatical enjoyment he'd often envied in the intellectual set.

"It's the mark of a great artist, don't you think? To still convey what is *not* captured on the canvas, or . . . in the clay or stone, as the case may be. It's a talent to which I aspire."

For a moment, Cole forgot where they were or what they were talking about. All he could do was gape at her, as though seeing her for the first time. He could stare into her eyes all day and never catalogue all the hues. The ring at the center of her irises was decidedly brown, and then bled with color to the verdant edge. From a distance, the sunlight turned them green, the moonlight burnished them a silvery-gray, and her tears made them murky as the Thames in a storm.

By what magic, he had no idea, but Lord, did he enjoy the spectacle.

Grace, he realized, was something this woman had in spades.

"And here I thought you merely painted the landscape of your garden," he murmured, discomfited that his voice seemed to have lowered a few unnecessary octaves.

Her brow puckered again, as it seemed to do when she was distressed. "If I'm honest, I've been unable to enjoy my garden since . . ."

"Lady Broadmore?" he guessed.

She nodded, again avoiding his gaze. "And also, I confess I've had the distinct feeling that I'm being spied upon when I'm out there."

A guilty flush stole from beneath his collar. He'd spent more time than usual at the window with the intent of watching her, but for no other reason than Morley had asked him to, of course.

"Though, I suppose, venturing from the safety and anonymity of my gardens probably does me some good. I not only challenge myself artistically this way, but I endeavor into the unknown potential of the day." She summoned a sunny smile for him, and again his heart sputtered. "For example, I might chance to meet a newly mended acquaintance, or notice an art gallery I hadn't previously visited."

Or happen to be an easy target for an enterprising murderous rapist.

Cole scowled, then opened his mouth to admonish her for her carelessness, but somehow he couldn't bring himself to cause the death of one more of her winsome smiles.

Instead he said, "As a soldier I had little need or care for the arts. I'm curious, if I were to happen upon a gallery, which paintings are the ones most worth my time and admiration?"

She gave her answer less consideration than he expected. "The paintings with the dustiest frames."

"Pardon?"

Her smile disappeared regardless of his efforts, and Cole immediately missed it. "Often, when a gallery has a showing, there are those paintings that are advertised by some great master, the ones that draw the largest crowds. Then, the walls are frequently scattered with others of lesser acknowledgment." She plucked at a loose thread in the violet lace overskirt, her gaze ever more distant. "Patrons often walk past those other paintings with a single-minded idea that the only worthy piece of art is the one coveted by others. But those paintings, the ones with the dusty frames . . . someone must appreciate them, mustn't they? Someone should give a thought for them, for the visionary who created them. Else they are returned to the shadows. To a basement somewhere. Locked away. Quite forgotten." The whites of her eyes turned pink as the lids washed with tears. "Sometimes I can't bear the thought of it."

She sniffed, removing her gloves to catch the tears with her fingers before they fell. "Forgive me, Your Grace, I must still be overwrought. Surely you didn't come here to watch me weep like a silly schoolgirl. Somehow, I can't seem to help myself. It's not at all like me. I've never—"

Before he realized what he was doing, Cole caught her bare hand in his, and brought it to his lips. His eyes didn't stray from her face as he kissed the moisture from her fingers, tasting the salt of her sorrow.

Her breath quickened behind her stays, and her gaze darted about the crowded park as though only just realizing what an exhibition they made. "Please don't be kind to me," she begged in a husky whisper. "I'll fall apart in front of everyone. I'll humiliate us both."

Reluctantly, he released her hand, wishing more than anything that they were alone, that he could pull her against him. That he could shield her tender feelings from all danger with his body, and hold her wounded heart encased in the empty cage of his own chest.

Holy fucking Christ. This was dire. He needed to depart, but how could he leave her like this? He had stridden into her day, wishing to share in her sunshine, and somehow managed to rain all over it.

God, he was a loathsome brute.

He tried to think of something, anything, to bring her smile back. And realized that not only did he not know much about her, he knew precious little about women in general. Usually, he had to do little more than look at a woman and cock his head to bring her hither. And then she was all titters, flirts, and occasionally more. Imogen was a different sort of lady, to be sure, but a woman all the same. So . . . a compliment, perhaps, would do the trick. "Your dress is . . . it's very bright."

She looked down at it with a rueful twist to her full lips.

"I meant, in an appealing fashion," he rushed. "It was how I recognized you in the crowd. Why is it that you always wear so much color, even during the afternoon, when every other lady is swathed in white or pastels?"

She spread her silk skirts and fondled a layer of lace as she glanced out at the coiffed and coddled women twirling their parasols and pretending not to watch them with raptorlike interest.

"It's not that I don't like pastels," she mused, then paused and squinted as though looking for guidance from far away. "I think that people like you and I have a . . . unique understanding of just how dreary and sometimes . . . ghastly the world can be, do you agree?"

He dipped his chin, feeling that he'd far missed his mark where cheering her was concerned.

"After Edward died and I was in mourning, I went through a period of time where I looked at everything through a pall of gray. I trusted no one. I resented everyone. I was listless and irritable and expected the worst of any situation. It was a rather dreadful few months."

"I didn't realize his loss was that much of a tragedy to you," Cole admitted, remembering how cold he'd been to her at the funeral and castigating himself for it.

"It wasn't *only* that," she confessed. "Before I married him, I lived a life full of such . . . well, of difficulty and disappointment. I hadn't been privy to much in the way of kindness or beauty or . . ." She paused to give him a searching look. "Or pleasure."

Even the word on her lips sent a thrill of lust through him. Would that he could show her pleasure. That he could give it. Take it. God, what he could do to her. If only—

If only his heart didn't belong to another.

"Anyway, the moment I came out of mourning for Edward, I burned all my black dresses, and ordered a new trousseau in all the brightest colors of the spectrum imaginable. I wear them at my leisure, to remind myself that for all the gray in the London sky, there's always color to be found. A smile to give. A kindness to share. A sunny day to look forward to. Or at the very least . . . a bright dress to wear. You see, Cole, if I cannot find that color, if there is no bright spot, then I must become one."

"And so you have," he murmured, distressed by the tenderness welling inside of him. "Like an oil painting in a gallery of watercolors."

"Exactly that." A delighted smile spread slowly over

her face, chasing away the sadness, eliciting something so achingly sweet within him, he had to turn away.

"It's not just the dresses, you know," she continued earnestly. "It's sort of an entire way of life I've found. The charity. My family. And art, of course. It all grants me something like happiness, I think."

He envied her in that moment, that she could create something so elusive. Something he'd convinced himself he couldn't have unless he found what had vanished.

Or whom.

Suddenly he realized how foolish it was to pin one's hopes for redemption on a memory. But . . . if he didn't have that, have Ginny, then what was he left with? A great empty house and an emptier life.

"I wonder what advice you would give to someone mired in that gray place. What if they've lost the ability to feel anything but enmity? To expect nothing but betrayal? To see nothing but shadows and darkness?" Even as he said this, he knew it to be an admission he'd given to no one else. Why should he confide in her like this? Why should he lay his troubled thoughts at her feet for her to tread upon when they were little better than strangers. Barely more civil than enemies. A few nights ago he'd been vowing her demise. Now he was seeking her advice?

Perhaps he *should* have his head examined.

"I believe you find your way out of the mire with small but consistent victories," she mused, giving him a sad smile. "But you must look for the light, as it will not always find you. You must stop to marvel at commonplace miracles. You must find wonder in the mundane. To me it's like weeding through a cacophony to find a melody, and then learning to hum along."

A brittle and bedeviled emotion coursed through him,

and he had to gather his composure in order to meet her gentle gaze. She couldn't possibly know, could she? The maelstrom of angst and rage he grappled with just to pry himself out of his restless bed. The despair that seemed heavier than any load that had previously tested the strength of his shoulders. The alarming and imaginary pain in his missing hand. The endless stretch of lonely days. He was a man who had everything. Money, power, influence, charm, and almost unparalleled physical prowess, despite his injury.

And still he was filled with emptiness. Alone in a crowded room. A soldier without a war. A spy without a mark.

Except here. Now. On this bench with this woman. The beast within him was still and perhaps for the first time since he'd returned from Constantinople he was . . . himself.

Finally, he felt the sunlight break through the gray.

Her searching look became a speaking one as her gaze seemed to delve into his, reaching through his opaque memories and smothered pain, into the depths of his very soul. She wove a spell that had him leaning toward her like a serpent mesmerized by an exotic charmer.

"Happiness, it's a foreign tune to me now," he admitted. "A melody I no longer remember how to play."

"If you look for vagaries, enemies, and misery wherever you are, you're certain to find them, aren't you?" she murmured. "But what if you looked closer? Deeper? Might you not find something new?" Her lashes dipped and lifted to unfurl an ardent sentiment that bemused and entranced him. It was something like expectation, and something like anxiety.

"Or . . ." Her voice wavered hesitantly. "Perhaps recognize something you'd considered lost?"

He stared at her for a breathless moment, something stirring inside of his confounded memory. Something sweet and also crimson.

"Your lemonade, my lady, Your Grace." The moment was broken, the door of his memory slammed with a sense of abrupt permanence as Cheever handed him the cold beverage. "I was even able to find a vendor with a block of ice. I hope you don't mind that I took the liberty of the indulgence."

"Not at all, Cheever." Imogen couldn't have sounded more delighted as she took the glass, already glimmering with droplets of moisture, and held it aloft for a toast. "To small victories and brighter days."

Amused, Cole touched the rim of his glass to hers. "To reclaiming what we've lost."

Was he mistaken, or had she paled significantly at his words? He studied her over the rim of his glass as the sweet and tart refreshment mingled on his tongue. What did she know of loss? he wondered. It haunted his every step. He'd lost everyone he'd ever called family. He'd lost parts of himself he'd never again regain. Not only his hand, but his heart. Indeed, parts of his immortal soul. Chipped away by the things he'd done in the name of his queen and country, by the tortures inflicted by cruel enemies, and by the betrayal of those he trusted the most.

Perhaps it was why he could admit to himself that he wanted her. That he admired her and, God forgive him, was even beginning to *like* her.

But no matter how much goodness she demonstrated, he couldn't bring himself to trust her. Though her smile was open, her eyes held a mystery. A secret to rival that of the Mona Lisa, he suspected.

Would that he knew what it was. Did it have something to do with Achilles? he wondered, turning to glare at the statue with renewed distaste. Not the myth, but the man who drew her to paint his effigy?

The one who tormented her memory.

Had he betrayed her? Or had she lost him in some other way? To death, to another, to whatever cruel vagary of fate sentiment had inflicted upon her.

Was he the reason she was no longer a virgin?

Sunlight fragmented as the glass in Imogen's hand shattered, dousing her and him in glacial, sticky liquid a mere moment before a weight landed against his chest with a resounding thud.

Cole caught it before it could fall to his lap, and held up a rock about half the size of his palm. Someone had thrown it, but at which one of them?

"Sweet Christ," he cursed. "Are you all right?"

She sat blinking at the jagged remnants of her beverage in her hand for a few stunned moments, then looked down at her soiled gown, now glittering with shards of glass. "I—I think so."

Cheever, who'd leaped out of his chair, pointed down the footpath that led toward the west gate. "Look there," he cried. "The blackguard is getting away!"

A fleeing man in a drab felt derby hat and beige plaid jacket weaved through an array of carriages and astonished onlookers.

Cole was on his feet, wishing they could surge as fast as his rage. "Get her home safe," he commanded Cheever over his shoulder, already in pursuit. He'd not met many men with legs as long as his, and they ate up significant ground as he pounded after the assailant. He shoved aside useless gawkers, cursing them for doing nothing to help. What was wrong with the upper classes, not one of them lifting a finger to help protect one of their own?

He leaped over a row of hedges, and even jumped into the door of an open landau carriage that idled in his way, hurtling to the other side.

Cole knew he'd need his horse if he ever had a chance of catching the bastard, but it didn't stop him from giving chase. Devil take the man, he'd have to have quite the arm to have thrown a stone from such a great distance. He disappeared into the crowds of Oxford Street before Cole could close the gap, escaping into the press of humanity.

Cole stood at the gate, searching this way and that, but Oxford Street and the Mayfair Borough were simply crafted to confound and enrage a pursuer with any number of alleys, side streets, hackneys, and buildings in which to disappear.

The foul words that escaped him sent a few women into a fit of vapors. He ignored the clamor of the aftermath. Jogging against a slew of people anxious to leave the park after such a happening, he returned to the bench to find it empty. Even the art supplies had been swept away, and Cole applauded Cheever for taking his orders and clearing his mistress from the open.

Imogen would be safe for the moment, with her carriage driver, a footman, and the butler all on alert.

A wisp of violet caught his eye, and Cole stooped to retrieve a delicate silk glove from beneath the bench. Tucking it in his left breast pocket, he hurried to retrieve his horse from where it was being cooled down on Rotten Row. That accomplished, he mounted and trotted for the opposite gate of the mass exodus.

This confirmed it. Someone was after Imogen. But who? And why? Unfortunately, a woman with a cause like hers could amass any number of enemies, from violent husbands, to even more unscrupulous street criminals; both denied the women to whom she offered refuge.

Perhaps this was what he'd warned her about, the vile and base violence of her charges bleeding into the playgrounds of the upper classes. Turning in his saddle, he cast one last look at Achilles, the bronzed and naked hero seeming to mock him. To shield her secrets.

Perhaps . . . Cole wondered. Perhaps Lady Anstruther had other enemies. Ones that followed her from a life of lower-class drudgery into the peerage. It struck him, then how very little he or anyone else seemed to know about her.

Pulling his horse to a stop, he reached into his pocket and extracted her glove from where it rested against his heart. He marveled at the size of it, only fitting the width of four fingers where her wrist would go. Giving in to a rash and impulsive urge, he brought the glove to his nose, letting the silk brush against his lips. He hunted for her scent, lilacs and lavender, and filled his chest when he found it.

Imogen. She held him quite transfixed. Be she a sphinx, a siren, or a snake charmer, he decided it was time he found out more about his bewitching neighbor.

For her own good, if nothing else.

CHAPTER EIGHTEEN

"I really think he's going to kill me this time." Heather's frantic wail barely registered against the vicious clamor at the door to the Anstruther mansion. "I couldn't stay with him. I couldn't do the things he wanted me to, not anymore."

Imogen held the buxom woman against her shoulder, wondering if it was the blood from the prostitute's nose or the woman's tears that soaked her bodice. It had only been a day since the incident at Hyde Park, and her nerves didn't seem sufficiently fortified for another dangerous crisis.

"How many men are out there?" Cheever demanded, holding himself against the door.

"I don't know!" Heather sobbed. "I counted maybe three or four when I was running, but O'Toole called for more of his men to join the chase. And it was getting dark."

Imogen held her former adversary from the Bare Kitten

closer, marveling at the strange and frightening turns life sometimes made.

"I know I was ghastly to ye, Ginny, and I don't deserve yer protection, but *please* help me. I had nowhere else to turn." The desperate woman clung to her, and Imogen forgave her immediately.

"You will address the countess as my lady when in this household, madam," Cheever admonished with a sniff.

"I'm sorry, my lady." Heather nodded, sufficiently chastised, and the fact that the old Celtic fire that used to blaze from her eyes had been extinguished caused Imogen no small amount of concern.

"There's no need for that, Cheever, I'm sure—"

Another pounding knock was followed by a door-rattling crash, as though someone had hurled themselves against it.

"And I'm sorry I brought this to yer doorstep." Heather sniffed, only just seeming to notice the blood running from her swelling nose down her mouth and chin. She swiped at it with a soiled-gloved hand, but only managed to smear it. "But when I heard ye was taking in whores like me, I thought ye might forgive what's past between us."

Another rattle shook the rafters of the giant sturdy house. "Return what's mine!" screamed a harsh Irish voice from the other side. "That crafty trollop needs to face the consequences due a thieving whore!"

"Begone, sir!" Imogen called back. "Or I'll be forced to send for the police."

A bark of cruel male laughter from several men met her threat. "You'll have to go through us to get to them, darlin'. And I don't see that ending well for you."

"Not a copper for miles," another scoffed.

Imogen cringed as they called her bluff. Of all the days

for something like this to happen. A riot of dockworkers had erupted in Southwark and threatened to spill over the bridge into Westminster. Morley and Argent had called Rathbone and O'Mara away. Violent deaths had already been reported, fires started, and all of Scotland Yard rushed to contain the chaos before the pavement of industry ran red with the blood of hundreds.

They had left not only Imogen unprotected, but also the rest of the city. If ever there was an opportune moment to commit a crime, it was today.

"His name's Johnny O'Toole," Heather said. "He's been terrorizing Piccadilly, beating us girls when we don't give him what he thinks he's due. Bringing us rough men and taking the extra he charges for the deviant things they do to us. The bastard calls it protection." She spat. "He found out that I put his new girl, Tess, on a train back to Brighton. She was *twelve*. She didn't want this life. Not after what he did to her."

"Is that why he broke your nose?" Imogen asked.

"Aye. And he meant to do worse had I not walloped him one with my shoe and fled." She lifted her skirts to show Imogen a grimy foot with ripped stockings, and Cheever couldn't contain his gasp of distress at the improper sight of her ankle.

Imogen handed Heather off to Gwen, who'd recently joined her in her charitable ventures, as she'd tired of working for the odious Dr. Fowler at St. Margaret's. This hadn't been the first time Imogen's work had called for the care of a nurse, and with two more buildings already purchased, she'd begun to hire more staff.

"Take her upstairs to one of the back washrooms," she said gently, then turned back to the door, summoning all the resolve and courage she possibly could.

"Don't go out there!" Heather surged forward, flattening herself against the seam of the two solid grand doors.

"Open up, or we'll break it down!" The warning burst against the entry right before another heavy blow tested the strength of the frame.

"I'm getting the hunting rifle," Cheever threatened

"You think we don't have a gun?" O'Toole volleyed back. "You'd better be a good shot, old man."

"They have more weapons than just that. Knives, clubs, knuckles. Don't ye have footmen?" Heather cast her gaze around for someone else. "Someone who can help?"

Imogen puffed out her cheeks on a beleaguered breath. "Usually . . . yes. But it's Sunday. Most the staff has today as a half-day and, since it was quiet, I let them have it all off." That had been before O'Mara and Rathbone had been called away. She dearly regretted the decision now. "The majority went to church with my mother and sister, I think, this afternoon. And then off to call on friends and family."

Impeccable timing, she reprimanded herself, as per usual.

Bugger. What am I to do now? How could she keep everyone safe?

She peeled Heather from the door just as a shot rang out, then another, splintering through the wood and miraculously missing them.

"Everyone, upstairs," she ordered over the screams, once again shoving Heather toward Gwen. "Now."

The window next to the entry broke, glass erupting like sparks in the light of the gas lamps. Imogen screamed and covered her hair as some of the shards rained down on her.

As the women retreated up the grand staircase, Imogen fled to the left, toward the solarium and the doors to the back garden. She might not be able to run for the police, but she now knew that she happened to have one of the empire's most dangerous men as a neighbor. She realized this would greatly help his case against her, but she saw no choice but to seek his protection.

"Cheever, go with them!" she cried as the old man puffed along next to her, his fine shoes sliding on the marble floors.

"If you think I'm leaving you to these brigands, my lady, you're mad."

There wasn't a word in the world to describe her relief.

Until she heard the screams.

A second volley of gunshots had Imogen pressing herself against the hallway wall for whatever cover it could provide. She listened in frozen terror to wet and concussive sounds echoing from beyond the broken window.

No one breached it to invade her home, as was surely their purpose in breaking it.

She crept closer, glass crunching beneath her boots.

A masculine scream, cut abruptly short, preceded the shocking appearance of a body flying past the window next to the entry. Imogen could have been mistaken, but it appeared that his neck hung completely limp from his shoulders. As though his spine no longer held it aloft.

Another gunshot caused her to duck and instinctively cover her head. Then came the unmistakable sound of a weapon penetrating flesh. Again and again.

Someone *else* was out there.

Imogen knew who it was even before he bellowed her name and broke the door open in two powerful kicks.

Cole stilled when his feral eyes found her, roaming every inch as though searching for a wound. The doorway framed him like a portal to purgatory, and he stood like an avenging archangel come to wreak a wrath no less than biblical.

The swells of his powerful chest heaved against the white of his shirtsleeves now blotched and stained with blood. The blade on his prosthesis was extended past the motionless metal fingers, and blood dripped from it into a thick crimson puddle on the marble floor.

The pistol he gripped in his right hand did a sweep of the entry. "Did any of them get in?" He snarled the question, as he strode past her, checking every shadow, searching every nook. "Did they touch you? Are you hurt?"

"No," Imogen breathed as she made her way to the door on wooden legs. Her wide stone porch had become like a battlefield, the blood of four corpses mingling in a syrupy fall down her steps. Two of them had their throats slit. Another bled from too many stab wounds to count. A neat round hole penetrated the forehead of a man perched like a scarecrow across the banister.

She didn't even bring herself to look at the dead body in her hedges.

Arms weak with tremors in the aftermath of such an incident, she managed to slowly push both doors closed on the gruesome scene, and gathered her fortitude to face the lethal man behind her.

Their eyes locked, his blazing with an amber fire, hers, no doubt, gathering a defiant storm. She knew what he was thinking, and she hadn't a single defense against it. His jaw clenched and released and his lips thinned, edged with white.

All Imogen could do as they squared off with each other like duelists was wish he didn't look so blasted magnificent. Framed by the gentle opulence of her home, his aristocratic features sharpened into something savage. Something not altogether human.

He was stained with the blood of her enemies. He'd just *killed* to protect her. Five men.

This changed . . . everything.

She didn't know what to do. Who to send for. It was all so utterly appalling.

A soft, rhythmic tap was a metronome in the charged silence, and Imogen looked down to see yet another puddle of blood pooling beneath him on the floor, this one from below a growing red stain high on the sleeve of his good arm.

"You're hurt," she accused, going to him. This she could help with. This she could fix. She might not know what to do with the dead, but she could heal a wound.

"Cheever, I have to get him to the washroom."

Cheever nodded, a great deal paler than usual. He seemed to summon extra reserves of determination right in front of her eyes, and tugged at the front of his vest as though deciding something. "I'll see to the . . . disorder out front, my lady, whilst you see to the duke."

"Thank you, Cheever." She sighed. "I can't thank you enough."

He managed a curt nod. "I'll call over to Welton, Mr. Argent's butler. I have it on good authority that he's no stranger to this sort of . . . particular mess." With a rather bewildered air, he clipped away toward the west entry, avoiding the front door.

Imogen hurried past the duke without acknowledging him; half afraid he'd seize her and do her some mischief now that he'd saved her. She'd made it halfway down the hall toward the back stairs before realizing he hadn't so much as twitched a muscle.

"Follow me," she prompted.

For a minute, it didn't seem like he would. Then the metallic sound of the pistol returning to dormancy preceded the heavy falls of his boots coming closer.

She turned away, willing her frantic heart to slow as she led him past the blue parlor where she'd met Jeremy, past the study, the library, and—

Hurrying to a door left ajar, she seized the latch, pulled it closed, and hastily locked it. She, alone, had the key to this room, and had somehow left it ajar in her absent-minded fog this morning.

Guiltily, she glanced back at Cole, who seemed more occupied with trying not to drip blood on her rugs than noticing her movements. "This way." She gestured down the staircase. "Gwen is nursing a wounded woman in the upstairs washroom. I have some extra medical supplies in a room off the kitchens."

Better that he not see Heather, lest he recognize her from the Bare Kitten.

His silence was heavy as he followed her down, and her awareness of him prickled along the nape of her neck and all the way down her spine. They passed the kitchens, the butler's pantry, the housekeeper's office, the laundry, and the larder to a small room with a pair of large sinks. The room was dim and boasted only one grimy window above the basins, so Imogen lit the wick of a lamp and turned it high.

Cole stood in the doorway as she bustled about. It felt as though he consumed all the air, all the space, until none was left for her.

She gathered tincture of benzoin, a stitching needle and thread, bandages, and water, painfully aware of her unusually clumsy manner and trembling limbs. Forcing herself to take deep breaths, she willed her hands to cease their tremors. It wouldn't do to stitch a wound with unsteady fingers.

She pulled a rough bench in front of her, and gestured to it. "Do you need help removing your shirt?" she asked brusquely.

He shook his head, reaching up to deftly undo his buttons with one hand.

Imogen had to turn away as he exposed the heavy muscles of his chest, and made herself busy with preparations. He was so strong, built by brutal ancestors, a childhood and youth free of hunger, and the training to become a soldier and spy.

It was hard to look at him now, hard to see the rendering of so much masculine beauty made more so by the predatory grace he wielded to terrifying perfection.

He'd killed for her.

Why did that make her breasts tight and heavy? Why did a thrill of unnerving heat bloom beneath the dread and repulsion?

She felt rather than heard him approach, and tensed until the creak of the bench alerted her that he'd settled his considerable frame upon it.

Night fell entirely as she turned to him. Wind buffeted the city, causing the bones of the stately mansion to creak and groan. A clock chimed in the distance, marking the long moments she stood with her hands hovering above his flesh, suddenly unsure of what to do.

It wasn't that she'd forgotten that that broad, strong back looked like burnished bronze in the dim lantern light. It was only that she'd underestimated the effect the sight of it would have on her. The masculine terrain bunched and flexed as he settled, his back ramrod straight awaiting her ministrations.

This wasn't a man who gave his back to many; the show of trust actually humbled her enough to break her apprehensive fascination.

The gash was higher up on his shoulder than she'd realized, and deep, as well.

"I have to clean it," she warned, readying the cloth to press against the flayed skin. "It might hurt a little."

"It always does," he rumbled shortly.

Right. He had evidence of more stitched and healed wounds than an entire battalion of adventurous children.

He didn't so much as flinch as she pressed the cloth against the open cut. Though when she lightly gripped his shoulder with her other hand to stabilize it, the muscle beneath her finger twitched and tensed.

In the disturbingly quiet room, their elevated breaths made a strange symphony. Fury radiated from him in palpable waves, and Imogen knew she was the cause of it.

"I know what just happened vindicates what you've been warning me against all along," she relented. "But don't say it," she pleaded. "Please, not yet."

He said nothing, remaining unnaturally still as she gently and efficiently worked to stop the bleeding so she could stitch him closed. The duke would get his wish, she thought with a defeated sigh. She'd need to empty her house of its desperate occupants. It was no longer safe for those who sought refuge here. With all haste, she'd move them to one of the other residences she'd acquired, even though they might be overrun. Gwen and Heather, a bevy of maids, and a few mothers seeking refuge with their children in the East Wing would have to be relocated. It would create instability, but something had to be done until blood ceased staining her doorstep.

The silence stretched until she felt her nerves would break. She handed him a dry cloth with which to clean the blood from his blade.

Finally, he asked, "Are you not . . . horrified at what I've done?"

She should be. She knew that. But . . .

"Those men were evil. They thought nothing of prostituting children and beating a woman half to death. They deserved what you did to them, and worse."

His shoulder jerked as a sharp exhalation of amusement left him. "And here I thought you nothing but a bleeding heart with a sharp tongue. I didn't realize how fierce you were, my lady."

"There is much you do not know about me," she challenged gently. "Even the moon has an entire side we never chance to see."

"The dark side." His words were quiet and smooth as velvet.

"Indeed."

"I didn't think you acquainted with darkness." Though she couldn't see him, she heard the humorless smile in his voice. "I'm beginning to find that I was wrong."

"I know the darkness all too well," she admitted as she blotted at the blood that was beginning to slow. "I know there's a place, a solitary place deep within. One where you, alone, can go and carry those thoughts, fears, and memories you can share with no one. Even you rarely visit, because it is a place from which it is difficult to return . . ."

He shifted on the bench, his hand curling into a fist. Less, she realized, from the pain in his shoulder and more from the impact of her words. "I lived in that place while they . . ." He broke off and the tendons in his jaw flexed. "Sometimes I fear I never escaped it. That this reality is a construct and I'll wake to find myself back in prison."

Swallowing a lump in her throat, she checked to find that the bleeding had been sufficiently controlled for her to stitch. Turning away from him, she silently threaded the needle and then returned to apply it. He sat motionless as she pierced his flesh and pulled the thread through, bringing the edges of the wound back together. He'd need at least seven stitches, maybe more. While she worked, Imogen glanced often at his profile. Jaw tight, veins twitching at his temples. The hair at his nape was damp, though whether from a recent bath, exertion, or pain, she couldn't tell.

"What happened to you in Constantinople?" She whispered the question that had haunted her for nearly three years. The moment she blurted it, she wanted to take it back. She was already causing him physical pain. Must she pick at his mental wounds as well?

Something told her she had to know. That he needed to share. That whatever torment had turned her gentle lover into this hard, compassionless man was worth unburdening.

His voice was deceptively light as he answered. "If I told you, you'd never sleep quietly again."

"I don't sleep quietly now," she confessed.

Air compressed out of him in a scoff. Though whether amused or bitter, she couldn't tell without seeing his features.

"You are nocturnal, then?"

"I suppose you could say that." Imogen hesitated, and then decided that perhaps a revelation about herself would help him along. "The sun goes down and my mind seems to come to life. Sometimes for the better when I'm filled with artistic inspiration and can paint until dawn. And other times, I'll construct scenarios and anxieties that are pure foolishness. I've taken up brooding of late, usually whilst raiding the kitchens or the liquor cabinet. The Brontes would be very proud." She paused. "About the brooding and the drinking, not the snacking."

"What does a woman like you brood about, I wonder?" he asked, with no little interest.

"Oh, lots of things. My mother's health, my sister's future, and the women I'm trying to protect. The recent murder in my garden . . ." *The secrets I'm keeping,* she thought to herself.

"Not the past, then?" he stated tonelessly. "Not a man?"

Only you, she wanted to say.

"Sometimes, I see light burning at Trenwyth at all hours," she hedged, not wanting to discuss the past, lest she confess something she was not ready to reveal. "And I know that we are awake together, and I'll sip my gin and wonder if you are drinking, as well."

"Gin?" This was the first word he'd said with inflection, and it was that of distaste. "You can afford the best sherry, port, wine, and brandy money can buy and you sip *gin*?" He turned his head to spear her with a dubious look.

She shrugged, careful not to tug unduly at the stitching in her hand. "I know it's not considered in good taste for our class, but I'm a little fond of it, all told."

"Can't imagine why," he muttered, facing forward again.

"This is going to sound silly, but it's the juniper, I think. You know that delicious smell of a freshly cut Christmas tree? Juniper reminds me of that, a little, and so gin makes me feel like I'm tasting Christmas."

He let out a grunt, though she again had a hard time telling if it was born of amusement, derision, or pain as she pulled yet another stitch through his arm.

"I drink Scotch, mostly," he said after a time. "Raven-croft's is a particular favorite, though I had a valet who turned me on to fine Irish whiskey, as well."

"O'Mara?"

"Yes."

"He's a cheeky sort."

"You have no idea," he commiserated. "Keep him away from your maids."

"I have my hands full keeping him away from my sister."

"God help you." The irony in his voice was laced with a thread of humor, and Imogen's heart lifted a little.

"Well," she ventured, now that some of the tension had dispelled. "Now that we've established we're both nocturnal creatures, if you ever need a conspirator with which to brood or to drink, I'll offer my excellent company in both regards. If I'm not mistaken, you can see my kitchen light from your study."

The suggested impropriety of her rash invitation worried her almost as much as the danger of his increased proximity posed to her secrets.

"You would not welcome my company when I am in such a state." The shadows had reclaimed him, and Imogen mourned.

"Do you revisit that place in your nightmares?" she queried, feeling both concerned and bold. "Is that why you do not sleep?"

"Yes," he said darkly.

"You can tell me, Cole," she whispered, fearing that, even as she said the words, he'd deny her.

"There are no words to convey my time in that place," he said after a contemplative moment. "It made Newgate seem like a palace. Filth is too clean a word. Despair is too happy a word. Cruelty is too kind a word. Perhaps if you imagine endless days in a room hot as a furnace, bearing witness to things so unimaginably horrific that you close your eyes hoping to escape *into* a nightmare . . . that might begin to convey my time there."

Imogen couldn't think of a thing to say, couldn't trust her voice past the tight emotions crowding her throat, so she remained quiet and moved on to another stitch. Her silence seemed to encourage him, and he continued in a flat, toneless voice, as though he addressed someone far away, or dictated a letter.

"I thought I knew grief before then. I thought I knew pain. I was a soldier and a spy, after all. I'd lost my entire family. But I came to understand that before that year, I never knew a man could be broken in so many ways. My captors, they wanted me to beg for the barest scraps of dignity, but I refused and so I was denied even those scraps."

Why? she wondered, and didn't realize she'd breathed the word out loud until he answered her in a hard, mordant tone.

"I am the Duke of Trenwyth. I beg for *nothing*. I bend my knee to no one but the queen."

"You told them this?" she marveled.

"Of course I did."

"And they didn't kill you?"

He lifted his shoulders in a devil-may-care motion, which reminded him of what she was doing to his shoulder, and he stilled. "I'm convinced it is my rank that kept me alive. They were trying to coerce Her Majesty and

Prime Minister Disraeli into a secret treaty, and I think they succeeded."

Imogen had never paid much mind to politics until her acquaintance and subsequent marriage to Lord Anstruther. His fondness for her reading the paper to him not only amused her, but kept her informed as well. Britain had not been a great friend to the Ottomans, though they had been allies against the Russians in the Crimean War. However, that bond was beginning to fray, and both empires had broken faith. The April Uprising had been the proverbial nail in the coffin, forcing the crown and Parliament to withdraw all military and financial support from the Ottomans. The British Navy had sat idly by as the Russians exacted costly revenge on the Ottoman Empire. It seemed that the Duke of Trenwyth had been just the leverage the Ottomans had needed to force Disraeli's hand. That and the island of Cyprus, granted to England by the Cyprus Convention in secret in 1878.

"It must have made you very angry," she supposed aloud.

He made another sound devoid of any mirth. "You can't *imagine* the rage." His fist tightened, sending a resounding ripple up the muscles in his arm and bunching the shoulder upon which she worked. "It is my only companion these days."

She tied off the knot she was working on, and began the final stitch. "Is that why you so value your silence and solitude?" she ventured. "Because you share it with your rage?"

His chin dipped, though she couldn't say it was a definitive nod in the affirmative. "Men like me spend our time containing within ourselves the worst of man and nature. All the lusts, the avarice, the fury and the pain; if

I revealed them, if I indulged them, I would be weak. I would become the animal they tried to make of me. After dedicating my day to such a struggle, there isn't much left of me for anything else."

Heart aching, Imogen fought the urge to lean in to him, to console him with a press of her forehead against his. Instead she worked on keeping her hand steady as she finished stitching him and reached into the basin of warm water for a cloth to clean the blood from his arm and back.

"Perhaps you might consider that your pain isn't weakness," she posited. Covered by the cloth, her fingers traced the swell of his bicep, the curious indents created by so many muscles working in tandem. "In your particular struggle lies a very unique form of strength." She dipped the cloth back into the water, which came away pink as she wrung it out. "Sometimes, the widest shoulders carry the heaviest burdens," she murmured, trailing the cloth along the nape of his neck. His great body shuddered in response, and a different tension seemed to bunch the muscles there. "You're not an animal, Cole, you're a hero."

His back expanded as he filled his lungs with what seemed to be a painful breath. "You. Don't. Know. You can't imagine."

"I *don't* know," she agreed. "I do not profess to comprehend your suffering. I simply cannot." She cast about for an idea and caught one immediately. "Maybe there are those who can. Other wounded soldiers like you. Men who feel broken, who had pieces of their minds and bodies taken from them by their enemies."

"They didn't take my hand."

"What?" She couldn't have heard him right. Perhaps the blood heating her ears prevented her from understanding him correctly.

"They didn't take my hand," he repeated between his teeth.

Stunned, her cloth stilled upon his back. "Then . . . who . . . ?"

"I did."

Imogen couldn't remember another moment in her entire life she'd been more absolutely stupefied.

"That . . . you . . . why?" She wished she could see his face, that she could read his expression, but her body refused to obey any of her commands.

"At night they'd chain us to the wall so they didn't have to post guards. These cuffs were no hinged iron, but some Asian steelwork that, to me, seemed like magic at the time. When Ravencroft broke into the prison to extract me, we both worked on unhinging it, but someone saw us and raised the alarm." He lifted his left arm, holding the cold steel in front of his face as though inspecting a memory. "It was our only chance. Escape or both die in that prison . . . or worse. We winched my arm, I took the Scotsman's dirk, and he helped me saw through my wrist."

"Oh dear God," she gasped.

His head snapped to the side. "I told you not to pity me," he snarled over his shoulder.

Imogen snatched her hand from his shoulder, quick as one would from a growling hound. "You can't command things like that," she reproached in a quavering voice. "How can I help but feel sympathy for someone who's undergone such suffering?" She bent to pick up the white cloth, forever stained with his blood, and shook it at him like a scolding nanny. "Pity is not disgrace, it is *compassion*. And compassion is something that *everyone* deserves."

He stood then, rising to his intimidating height, and took a step toward the door without so much as a by-your-leave. "Not one such as I."

"*Especially* you," she insisted.

He whirled on her then, a wolf of wrath and rage. An animal too fierce to be caged. Lord, how did men erect walls thick enough to contain such a man?

They hadn't.

He'd escaped them.

"Do you know how many people I've murdered?" he spat. "How many have suffered because of me?"

Imogen shook her head, placing her hand to contain a fugitive heart. He thrust his mismatched hands toward her. "When your hands are stained with enough blood, it becomes a part of you. Past your own veins and meat. Past your bones and marrow. It doesn't stop until it stains your soul."

"I don't believe that," Imogen said stubbornly. "Not of you!"

"What do you know about it? Have you ever killed a man?"

She hesitated. Unable to conjure an honest answer. Because in truth, she didn't know. She may have. She still might be called to account for it.

"That's what I thought." Eyes narrowed and lips pulled into a cruel sneer, he made a derisive gesture at her. "Don't turn your compassion to me, woman. I'm beyond your grace, I think."

He turned to leave.

"*No.*" Something in her voice froze him mid-step. Maybe it was the defiance. Maybe it was the deference. She'd never know, and it really didn't matter. Squaring her shoulders and lifting her chin, she took a step toward him.

"Those men you killed on my porch were beyond grace. But *not* you."

A gilded fire turned his eyes an unnatural shade. "How dare you presume to—"

"I can presume to do or say what I wish. This is my home and that is my thread in your arm, so you will listen." Her logic wasn't sound, but effective, she thought, as his teeth snapped shut with an audible clack. His nostrils continued to flare in warning as he crossed two long, impressive arms over an equally imposing chest.

Imogen had to admit that his stature and stance stole a little of her bluster, but . . . as they said, *in for a penny* . . .

She cleared fear out of her throat and pressed on. "You can't presume to know the fate of your soul. That isn't for you to decide. All I know is that the blackest of hearts can find grace. You can't have fought with such ferocity, you can't have—done what you did to survive if you didn't believe that somewhere in your heart." Emboldened by his silence, she took a step toward him, gentling her voice a little. "Life, with all its perils and torments, still belongs to the living. We have a responsibility to *live* it. You should not waste it by giving over to bleak despair."

"Nor should you risk it by being reckless and getting in over your head," he snapped, staring down his haughty nose at her.

Imogen flinched. She didn't want to be cowed or submissive, but the events of the day had her so rattled, she only managed to hold her proud shoulder aloft. "No matter what you do or say, I *cannot* turn away those who need my help. It is simply not in my nature. Call me a fool if you wish, but I am what I am. And it's not that I am incapable of change, but unwilling. I know there is more suffering than I could ever contain, but my life's purpose is to save who I can."

He stared out at her from eyes ablaze for one moment to many before saying, "So long as you don't try to save me."

She crossed her own arms over her chest. "You are neither above nor below my consideration. I'll do as I like," she challenged.

The air between them thickened and shifted until it sang with violence and expectation. His broad silhouette blocked the only escape, and it occurred to Imogen that she might have spoken too rashly, the moment before he began to stalk closer, closing the distance between them.

"You should tell me to leave," he growled from low in his chest. "Order me out, woman. I am not a good man. And I'm tempted to prove it to you by doing a dire thing."

She'd like to say that she stood her ground, but suddenly she found herself against the sink, without a memory of retreating the few steps backward. "Being a good man doesn't mean doing the right thing all the time." Her voice had taken on a breathy quality she didn't at all recognize. "There are two halves to our natures, are there not? Light and dark, good and evil, the angel and devil."

He kicked the bench aside and prowled closer, pure, wicked intent etched into features made savage by lamplight and lust. "Which one are you?"

"I am no angel, Cole, of that you can be certain."

"Then it seems we are both damned." In one graceful surge of movement, he was upon her, his lips landing against hers before his powerful body followed suit.

He crowded and overwhelmed her, taking every inch of space and filling it with himself. His chest crushed against her breasts, his knee forced its way between her thighs. A thick rod quickened where he pressed his hips against her.

Kissing Cole was like kissing the night. His potent darkness consumed everything as his lips consumed her. His tongue made a conquest of her mouth, tangling with hers in wet, long strokes.

But his hand . . . his hand was infinitely more gentle as it cupped the back of her head, still leaving no doubt that she was his prisoner. His fingers laced in her hair, more beseeching and urgent than punishing.

Scalding heat poured like molten ore from his mouth into her. It spread in a flush over her skin, and traveled through her blood with significant haste and languid desire at the same time, pooling between her legs in a release of warmth.

Imogen clung to him as he, quite literally, kissed the wits right out of her.

His every muscle was drawn drum-tight as he rhythmically surged against her in harmony to the plunge and retraction of his tongue. He made a sound so foreign to her; Imogen could only identify it as a violent sort of appreciation.

Her throat produced a husky answer that seemed to both thrill and comfort him.

Abruptly, his behavior shifted from wrath to worship. The hand at the back of her head began to tremble as it smoothed over her hair. His tongue retracted as he dragged his mouth across hers in sweet, drugging pulls. Every breath they shared was a benediction, and he whispered something she didn't quite catch against her.

His kisses held an element they hadn't in that room at the Bare Kitten all those years ago. Something dangerous. Something more possessive and uninhibited.

He was no longer merely smooth muscle and lithe grace. He was teeth and bristle and unfathomable need. He nibbled at her lower lip with a sharpness that sent a shock of sensation straight to her sex.

She was drowning in him, or maybe immolating, she couldn't rightly be sure. Waves of hot desire broke upon her. His. Hers. She didn't seem to be able to differentiate.

His hand charted the curve of her back, her waist, and was frustrated by the bustle beneath her skirts which he gripped as though to tear the entire garment asunder.

Imogen had decided she'd let him when a scream pierced the close, humid air they'd created in the tucked-away room.

They both froze, their lips tearing from each other's, tensing like foxes whose burrow had been found by the hounds.

Dear God. Someone had returned home before Welton and poor Cheever had managed to clear the carnage.

The shrill scream sounded again, very close. So close, that there was no chance it came from upstairs at the front of the house. Cole surged for the door, ordering her to stay where she was.

Ignoring him, Imogen scrambled at his heels on knees weakened by desire and then fortified by adrenaline.

She'd been right, she realized. The scream hadn't come from the front of the house, but the servants' entrance down the same hall. There, in front of the door, Cook, two footmen, and a chambermaid were huddled around something they'd found at the entry.

"What's happened?" Trenwyth demanded.

The congregation gaped at him in slack-jawed silence for a full minute. The only sound that of the maid's quiet sobs. Whether it was shock at whatever had caused the scream, or that of finding a half-naked duke in the servants' hall, it was anyone's guess.

"Dammit, someone speak up," he ordered, sweeping closer.

Cook, a thin woman, despite the elegant richness of her fare, noticed Imogen and put up a hand. "No, my lady, don't come any closer!" she warned. "You'll not want to see this."

Trenwyth shouldered past them, paying no heed to his wound. Imogen skirted him, noting the way his lips thinned and skin tightened.

"What?" she queried anxiously. "What is it?"

"Imogen, don't—" he began, throwing an arm out to catch her.

But he was too late. She glimpsed what was perhaps the most gruesome thing she'd seen that day.

There, on the stoop, neck wrapped with the ghastly familiar neckerchief—the one she'd stained with blood when she'd stabbed Mr. Barton—was the body of a tiny, strangled kitten.

CHAPTER NINETEEN

Sir Carlton Morley stood at the head of neat rows of dead bodies in the morgue like the professor of a particularly macabre classroom. Hands clasped just a little too tightly behind him. Eyes narrowed in deep, almost painful consideration.

Today, London was a city of tears.

Twenty people had been killed in the iron strikes, one of his own constables among them. Dozens of injured overwhelmed area doctors and hospitals. And then . . . there was the inevitable chaos that accompanied a city-wide incident of this magnitude. Looters and thieves took advantage of an absent police force in other parts of the city. Women had been assaulted. Offices and shops overrun.

Five of these bodies—some laid out on discarded wood pallets as they'd run out of tables—were victims of the Duke of Trenwyth's considerable wrath.

And who could blame him?

Lady Anstruther's property had been invaded, and Trenwyth had seen fit to take justice into his own hands. There'd been no one else. It was time to face the facts; Scotland Yard was miserably inundated and underfunded.

Something more had to be done. Something drastic and effective. Perhaps it was time to stop trusting in the infinitely slow-turning cogs of the justice system.

His nose twitched at the mingling odors of astringent, preservatives, gas lamps, and so much death. Above this room, the clamor of loved ones waiting to identify their dead, of constables and coppers doing their best to keep the peace, and sundry other souls in need of justice awaited his appearance.

It wasn't that he hid down here, in this concrete purgatory where the dead only spent a short time, he'd merely come here to think. He'd come here to plan. Often, the departed made better company than the living. They were certainly quieter.

Morley checked his watch, and surveyed the dead with a demeanor anyone would have identified as dispassionate.

Little did they know.

As a soldier, he had created a comparable number of corpses with his own rifle. Each felled with a vital shot. The lungs, the brain, or the heart were all organs of affect that, once pierced, became utterly useless. Both literally and figuratively.

His heart had been broken too many times to count, and there were times he feared it ceased to beat. But his lungs and body were strong. His mind sharp. And those could be used in tandem to make a most effective weapon. A weapon that could be wielded in times like this, against men who incited violence. Against those who oppressed the people. And anyone who would prey upon the innocent.

Something had to be done . . .

What he needed was a strategy. What he *needed* was an army.

Morley didn't have to look back as the men he'd been expecting filtered through the door one by one. He identified them each by their stride, by their particular scents, and by the indefinable energy he'd trained himself to recognize. As a child, he'd learned to read people, to see things that no one else saw, to observe a shift in nature, expression, or intent. As a man, he'd used that skill to be aware of those in his immediate vicinity, as he observed the rest of the world at a distance over the barrel of a long-range rifle.

Trenwyth entered first, as he was used to doing so by nature of his rank. His long stride remained unmatched by any man Morley had yet to meet, though he prowled with the light step of a spy. The duke was a particularly lethal combination of paradoxes. Patient and volatile. Principled and vicious. A nobleman, but by no means a gentleman.

To Morley, he was a wolf. The feral ancestor of man's closest companion. A creature that often seemed most approachable, trustworthy even, but who would think nothing of ripping your throat out for the sheer pleasure of it.

As evidenced by the corpses they'd retrieved from the Anstruther mansion.

Dorian Blackwell followed Trenwyth, his expensive shoes producing an arrogant staccato on the spare floor. He was a man who hid from no one. His power evident. His name legendary. He could meld with the shadows, when necessary, but his style had always been rather elaborate. He was a man who understood both the physical and psychological benefits of warfare and terror, and had used them to his distinct advantage his entire life.

To Morley, he was a panther. Ebony-haired and black-eyed, ruling from his lofty perch, from which he only descended when the prey was ripe enough to strike his fancy.

Christopher Argent made no noise as he followed his former employer into the domain of his current one. Like Trenwyth, he stepped with the economy of movement needed to avoid detection, though Morley always noted his presence as a rather sinister black void. To have his back turned to Argent felt a little like he imagined it would when death came to call. The kiss of a chill vibrating the hair on his body to attention the moment before the scythe fell.

To Morley, Argent was a viper. The red of his hair a warning that one strike would mean death. The cold, reptilian gaze, the deceptively relaxed coil of his muscle, and the shocking speed of his exotic combat training marked him a most efficient killer.

Liam Mackenzie, the last of their clandestine gathering, shut the door behind him, his heavy steps muffled by boots made of the softest stag hide. Warriors like him just didn't exist in this age of elegance and industry. He possessed little to none of the shadowy grace and superlative wit of his companions. He spoke his mind, revealed his emotions, and ate the heart of any that dared oppose him, after he ripped it from their chests with his freakishly large bare hands. He was the descendant of the fierce Picts who became rebel Jacobites, his blood fortified with that of long-ago Viking invaders.

To Morley he was a bear of a man, the kind hunted to extinction on this island ages ago. A gentle beast to his family, but a ferocious, unstoppable alpha predator with a vengeful streak as long as Hadrian's Wall.

These men were all brutally efficient predators. Most of them nocturnal in nature. And recently he'd joined their ranks. Or, rather, he was about to ask them to join his.

Morley wondered where he fit in this pantheon of predators. A bird of prey, perhaps. An eagle-eyed raptor who kept watch on his city from the rooftops, and used his unnaturally honed senses to swoop upon his prey with brisk efficiency. He was neither as large as Ravencroft, as skilled as Argent, as feared and connected as Blackwell, nor did he wield as much physical and social power as Trenwyth.

However, he had a little of all of these traits. And he possessed something he was convinced many of these men did not.

A conscience. Or, more aptly, a purpose. He'd once been one of the nameless, innumerable criminal siphons on the city, and now he'd been dubbed her protector.

Her guardian.

And he feared the job was too large for one man . . . as evidenced by the room packed to the rafters with the dead.

Dorian Blackwell spoke first, his cultured accent learned rather than bred, and suffused with sardonic darkness. "Let me be the first to say, Morley, that I vow none of this blood was spilled by me. I spent the day at Covent Garden with my wife and children, and can produce many witnesses."

A pang pierced Morley at the mention of Farah Blackwell. The kind, lovely, capable woman who'd once worked as a clerk at Scotland Yard. In her quiet, gentle way, she'd stolen Morley's heart five years prior.

And just as amiably, she'd broken it.

The years dulled the pain of her loss, but never quite

erased it. Every time he saw his former nemesis with the fair-haired beauty on his arm, the wound opened anew. Their day at Covent Garden could have been his. Those children, his children, their little heads crowned with fair locks rather than dark ones.

Trenwyth stepped forward, pulling back one of the sheets providing the corpses what dignity they could. "I can't say the same," he said dryly. "I can claim a handful of these and each one deserved what they got and more."

"You don't have to fear any legal repercussions, Trenwyth, that's not why I called you here."

To his surprise, Trenwyth made a dry sound of mirth. "I am once removed from a royal duke, Chief Inspector, I could slaughter anyone I pleased in the middle of Westminster and leave their corpses in the street without fear of legal reprisal."

Morley thought he heard someone mutter, "Lucky bastard," but couldn't identify whom. Probably Argent.

"Isna that precisely what ye did this evening?" Ravencroft helpfully pointed out.

Trenwyth sent the Highlander a dark smirk, rife with self-satisfaction. "So it is."

Blackwell turned to Morley, assessing him with the eye not covered by a patch. "Not that it isn't always a right pleasure to see you, Chief Inspector, but might I ask why you've convened this conclave of degenerates?"

"And in a morgue, no less," Trenwyth added. "I assume you're trying to make some kind of point?"

"What I'm trying to do is avoid public speculation," Morley said dryly.

"Then you shouldn't have assembled us all in one place," Blackwell scoffed. "We are each of us identifiable. Either famous or infamous."

"Quite," Morley clipped, unimpressed. "It is not because of your notoriety that I gathered you. Each of you has a very specialized skill set. That, and a compelling reason to use them on behalf of someone who may be in need."

"Speak plainly, Captain," the Scottish laird ordered, using his former military rank rather than his current title. "I doona ken what yer getting at."

"The lady Anstruther is in apparent danger." Morley didn't miss how Trenwyth's glare turned from a cool copper to a blaze of hellfire at his words. "Because each of you shares with Lady Anstruther your more intimate connections—"

"Ye mean our women," Ravencroft clarified. "Our wives."

"Precisely," Morley continued. "I'm requesting your assistance in apprehending the threat against her."

"I'm in," Argent said immediately, his cold blue eyes glinting arctic. "I don't like the violence today at the house next to mine. Lady Anstruther is a favorite of my wife's, and she's been kind to my stepson. He paints with her sometimes in her garden. It would distress them both if harm were to come to her."

Blackwell looked bored, as though he'd already figured out the future direction of the entire conversation. "I'm certain you're aware that on Thursday next, Lady Anstruther is helping Farah to host another one of her charity balls, this one in support of their communal project, a home for wayward boys in Lambeth."

Morley nodded. He *was* aware. "Indeed, it is that exact event where I hope to catch this reprobate in the act. To draw him out. With the four of you there and on alert, there is a much better chance of—"

Trenwyth stepped forward, his eyes glinting as dangerously as a blade. "I'll be damned before you use Lady Anstruther as bait for a violent sadist."

"She's in danger from this threat no matter where she is." Morley reasoned. "As evidenced by the morbid 'gift' he left on her property, the bastard is demonstrating that even her *home* isn't completely safe. A structure that large is impossible to fortify without a small battalion, and we simply don't have the resources."

A storm gathered on Trenwyth's features. "If she needs someone to protect her home, I've more than established that I'm capable—"

"She's specifically requested that it *not* be you," Morley cut in.

The duke perceptively flinched, though Morley ascertained that a shadow of guilt and comprehension crossed Trenwyth's demeanor before he summoned an opaque façade.

"I have O'Mara in the home, whom I know both you and I trust with our lives. Rathbone patrols the grounds, and nothing gets past his notice."

"Even still," Trenwyth bit out. "I'm to be her escort to the ball."

Morley realized that the duke's feelings for the woman had progressed beyond mere neighborly concern for a kindhearted widow. He was acting like Morley would expect any of the other present men would in regard to their ladies.

Interesting, that.

"Have you discussed this arrangement with Lady Anstruther?" Morley asked hesitantly.

"There's nothing to discuss," Trenwyth stated. "If she's

to attend, I'm taking her, or she can bloody well stay locked in the house."

Knowing looks slid between the men behind Trenwyth's back, accompanied by the smirks of those who'd been in just his position. Felt the same frustrated possession, and lost the battle to it.

Was it possible that Trenwyth was in love with Lady Anstruther? He'd been there earlier that night, had discovered the strangled kitten alongside her and her staff. The bodies of five men paid tribute to the ardency of his protective instincts toward her.

What if Trenwyth knew that she was becoming an invaluable piece to a puzzle involving a serial murderer? Would he still feel the same about her?

Morley debated long and hard whether to include the present company in his theory. Over the past three years, slim, fair-haired women in their twenties had been strangled and molested in an eerily similar fashion and in alarming numbers. The problem was, until Trenwyth had requested that Morley look into the disappearance of his lady friend, Ginny, no one had connected the murders. They occurred in very separate parts of the city and to women who had no prior connection to each other.

The latest victim, Lady Broadmore, for example, wouldn't be caught dead in the company of Flora Latimer, the first victim, the prostitute found strangled at the Bare Kitten. Then there'd been Rose Tarlly, a charwoman who'd lived off Old Fenchurch Street. Ann Keaton, a nanny who worked in a more genteel neighborhood two blocks down from the capital building. And finally, Molly Crane, a nurse at St. Margaret's Royal Hospital.

Morley had been at a loss to figure just how the killer

selected these women other than their strikingly similar appearances. Until a few hours ago, when he remembered that Lady Anstruther had introduced her sister as Miss Isobel Pritchard.

The name had struck a hollow chord in his memory he'd not placed until going over the case files. Lord Edward Millburn, Earl Anstruther, had incited quite a scandal some two years ago when he married a Miss Imogen Pritchard, his nurse at St. Margaret's Royal Hospital.

And so the first connection was made. Imogen, Lady Anstruther, had worked with one victim at the hospital, and another was found in her own garden.

Could be a coincidence, Morley had reasoned. Not a likely one, but a possibility. That was, until just a few hours ago, when a kitten had been left in gruesome effigy.

A kitten . . . found strangled *behind* her home. And one of the famous kittens of St. James's Street found strangled in the alley *behind* the Bare Kitten.

He'd be a fool to ignore that as coincidence. He was many things, but a fool was not one of them.

All he had to do was figure out how the countess Anstruther, or the nurse Pritchard, was linked to one or all of the other victims . . . His only option was to dangle her in the open like a morsel ripe for the picking, and wait for the fiend to strike. In the meantime, he'd do his best to connect the dots.

Start at the beginning, he thought. It was time to pay another visit to the Bare Kitten.

CHAPTER TWENTY

Imogen had fully expected the daggers aimed at her from Trenwyth's glare as they trundled over the cobblestone streets of Westminster in the duke's fine carriage. In the days after their encounter with O'Toole—and then each other belowstairs—Cole had done his utmost to maneuver some time alone with her.

Thus far, she'd deftly been able to avoid him. Then, for a few days, he'd been conspicuously absent. Silent. Though every time she looked to the east, there he was. A specter in a window, his gaze burning down at her.

Chief Inspector Morley had called two days ago to inform her that Trenwyth had accepted the assignment to escort her to the charity ball.

It wasn't her lack of desire to be alone with Cole that inspired the rude and desperate actions she'd taken. It was the presence of desire, that traitorous, pervasive, and primitive emotion, that had prompted her to invite Lord and Lady Ravencroft to accompany them the short distance from her home to that of Farah and Dorian Blackwell's residence.

She'd sensed Cole's displeasure immediately when she'd descended the stairs arm in arm with Mena. She'd sensed his *desire* as well. Lady Ravencroft's shimmering blue gown set off the brilliance of Imogen's crimson silks. Never in her life had Imogen felt more beautiful.

When he lifted his chin to watch her, his ever-tense jaw had slackened and his wolfish gaze roamed her body, leaving no place untouched. Imogen could feel herself turning as red as the Anstruther rubies dripping over her clavicles, and resting in a tear-drop point between her breasts. His gaze lingered there, his lips pressing together as though to stem the rush of involuntary hunger.

She'd not seen that look on his face in three long years. The heavy-lidded veneration of a lover. The abject, unabashed appreciation of a man who'd tested a sip of honeyed wine, and was ready to devour every last drop.

To slow the gallop of her runaway heart, Imogen tried to transpose the bare-chested barbarian in her basement onto the suave and haughty duke that stood before her, resplendent in white-tie finery.

When that was a miserable failure, she'd informed him that she'd invited his acquaintances, Lord and Lady Ravencroft, to accompany them as she was certain his ducal carriage could accommodate them all.

He'd not been fast enough to hide his scowl from her before he'd informed the Mackenzie laird and his wife that he was, of course, delighted. Judging by the uncomfortable tension in the carriage, he was about as delighted to see them as a vampire was to see the sunrise.

He'd planned on being alone with her.

She planned to never again allow that, as each time they spent alone together seemed to result in a kiss.

And those kisses were becoming more and more dangerous.

Imogen managed to avoid his dark regard, doing her best to keep up a stilted conversation with Mena regarding marriage prospects for the season for Isobel and Mena's stepdaughter, Rhianna.

Ravencroft and Trenwyth sat uncomfortably close, the combined width of their shoulders forced to touch, even though pressing against the walls of the spacious coach. Though Imogen avoided looking directly at the duke, she sometimes caught the marquess Ravencroft sliding curious and amused glances at Trenwyth from beneath heavy ebony brows. He wasn't a man given to much mirth, Imogen gathered, but the ghost of a smirk quirked the corner of his full lips. As though he'd guessed the entire situation.

When the coach arrived at the Northwalk mansion in Mayfair, Ravencroft leaped out and brushed the footman aside, offering his own wife assistance from the carriage.

This obliged Trenwyth to do the same. In a lithe movement, he ducked from the coach and turned, offering her both of his hands for support.

Imogen stared at them. Since he wore pristine white gloves, it was nearly impossible to tell the difference, but for the unnatural stillness of his left. Or perhaps it only seemed thus as his right fingers twitched with impatience.

Reaching for him, Imogen found herself seized and abruptly swept to the ground, her waist supported by one strong, warm hand, and a cold steel one. Just as swiftly as she'd been pulled into his arms, she was released, before anyone really had a chance to notice the breach of conduct.

Feeling dazed and a little breathless, Imogen blinked up at Trenwyth, who gestured down the grand path to the entry in an "after you" motion. She made a sour face at him and said nothing as she made her way on unsteady legs toward the mansion. This was how it would be between them, she lamented. Their every interaction fraught with intensity and underscored with unfulfilled need.

Imogen envied him. It was unfair that he remembered so little of what transpired between them on the night he'd paid her for pleasure, and had given it in return.

She remembered everything, and sometimes that memory tormented her to the brink of a sweet and aching madness. He'd awakened within her a fiendish, feverish sort of need that night, which she'd done her best to ignore ever since. Never to indulge. Nor to reminisce.

But every time he touched her, carried her, confounded and kissed her, the fever had been rekindled in ever-increasing increments. Sometimes, when she was alone at night, she'd toss and writhe in heated agony, kicking off her damp covers in a fit of frustration. Yearning for another, warmer, more substantial weight upon her. Remembering how their sweat had mingled and their muscles strained. Wondering if making love to Cole now would resemble anything like what it had been so long ago.

Wondering if she wanted it to.

They'd arrived at the Backwell manse a bit early, as Imogen had requested, so that she and Farah Blackwell could consult upon last-minute preparations for the event. Usually, the men left them alone to do so, but as Mena, Farah, Millie, and Imogen wandered the house, inspecting the preparations and so on, they noted a very badly concealed entourage.

"I do believe our procession has acquired a vanguard," Mena remarked from behind her glass of champagne, her green eyes dancing with merriment.

Using a poorly ruffled valance as an excuse to glance over at their hovering husbands, Farah giggled as she picked and fluffed at the bit of cloth. "I do believe you're right, dear. You don't think they actually imagine they're being subtle, do you?"

As the men noted they were being observed, they suddenly became absorbed in an expensive John Constable painting to which Dorian directed their respective attentions.

"Your husband certainly has excellent taste in art," Imogen ventured, placing her empty champagne flute on a servant's tray and happily accepting another.

"My husband wouldn't know Renaissance from Rococo," Farah scoffed.

"Nor mine," Millie blithely agreed, her midnight eyes narrowing.

"*I* acquired that painting and he's never before noticed it." Farah narrowed her eyes. "Now I know they're up to something. The question is, what?"

"I fear their odd behavior is my fault." Imogen sighed miserably.

"Oh?" Millie arched a quizzical brow as she sipped her champagne. Diamonds winked from rings she'd slid over the lavender gloves perfectly complementing her paisley purple gown. "Do tell. I love a bit of intrigue."

Imogen took a few bracing swallows of her own champagne before explaining in a halting voice, "Chief Inspector Morley thinks that there is perhaps a serial murderer after me."

"Is that so?" Farah exclaimed. "Is that why he actually accepted one of my social invitations for once? Well, that explains everything, doesn't it?"

Imogen gaped at the countess, trying to process her calm reaction to the news.

"It's a good calculation on Sir Morley's part that, due to what happened to poor Lady Broadmore, the killer might be inclined to strike again at a similar event," Mena postulated reasonably.

"Yes," Millie agreed with an enthusiastic nod. "And of course he'd have notified Christopher and present male company for . . . obvious reasons."

"I feel like a half-wit," Imogen admitted. "But the reasons aren't so obvious to me."

The women shared a look. Farah nodded with a gentle smile, and they each surrounded Imogen in a sort of conspiratory huddle as they pretended to resume their inspection.

Farah slipped an arm through Imogen's, the silver of the countess's glove complementing the ruby silk of her own. "Surely you've heard that my Dorian is . . . somewhat notorious."

"The Blackheart of Ben More, you mean?" Imogen blurted, and then decided that two glasses of champagne should be enough so early in the evening.

"Indeed," Farah said with a wry smile. "Millie, Mena, and I share a distinct and singular friendship as the men we love are brothers, either by blood bond or bloodshed."

"Blood bond, in my case," Mena supplied.

"And bloodshed, in mine," Millie finished, with a proud and rather fierce glance of adoration in the direction of the auburn-haired Viking.

Imogen had yet to recover her wits, but she realized

that her suspicions regarding the familial resemblance between the laird of the Mackenzie clan and Dorian Blackwell were confirmed.

"Each of our husbands, in their own way, have their
demons," Farah continued solemnly.

"Those demons have sometimes spurred our men to
do . . . questionable things in the past," Mena confessed.
"But those skills they have acquired along the way are
most . . . effective when wielded in protection of those
they love."

Imogen thought that Mena's use of the word *questionable* had to be the understatement of the century. She remembered the lethal skill and power Argent had wielded
against Trenwyth as they sparred. She'd read about the
Demon Highlander in the papers to dear Edward, and remembered that the man had infiltrated an Ottoman prison
on his own. Also, she was quite certain Dorian Blackwell hadn't acquired his moniker, his influence, his fortune, and sinister eye patch in his wife's lovely parlor.

Millie put her hand on Imogen's other arm. "Each of
us has our own story of peril and danger," she confided
with twinkling eyes. "Either from, because of, or in spite
of our men, but they've always protected us. And Morley
knows Trenwyth will protect you, too."

"Trenwyth is fast becoming a part of their blood broth-
erhood," Farah observed. "Which, of course, means you're
one of us."

"A sister in all but name," Mena agreed.

"You're not like the other missish, useless noblewomen
the *ton* spits out every season," Millie said heartily. "You
help us achieve the good we want to. You have a quick
mind, a tough hide, and a kind heart. All of which are
needed if you are to take on men like them."

Imogen had to clear the gratitude out of her throat before she could speak. "You are so very kind," she said. "But neither Trenwyth nor I are interested in 'taking on' one another. He is only here as my escort because Morley recruited him."

Millie let out an undignified snort. "I'd wager my entire fortune that is not at all the reason Trenwyth accompanied you tonight."

"Pardon my saying so." Mena smiled gently. "But it is very clear that Trenwyth would take you on whatever surface you'd permit him to."

"Mena!" Farah laughed. "The uncouth Highlands are certainly rubbing off on you."

The marchioness's secret, self-satisfied smile had to be the loveliest thing Imogen had seen in some time.

"There is too much that stands in the way of a relationship between Trenwyth and me," Imogen breathed as she glanced over at the man who stood taller than his companions, the lamplight gilding his neat hair a familiar shade. Tinting her memory in sadness and longing. "There are too many shadows in the past, too much pain, and too many secrets."

"Be careful of secrets," Mena warned. "They can ruin everything."

Imogen nodded, and found herself with another glass of champagne in her hand as the women decided to turn their attentions to the arriving guests. She was well aware that secrets could ruin everything between her and Cole.

They already had.

The color of Imogen's gown forced Cole to admit that crimson would always remind him of fucking. It also occurred to him that for a man doing his best to avoid said activity, her choice of dresses was a damned irritant. She looked like a sin wrapped in confectionary paper. The entire torturous night, a verse from the Bible, of all things, repeated in his head, leaving trails of madness.

Watch and pray that you may not enter into temptation. The spirit, indeed, is willing . . .

"But the flesh is weak," he concluded, his eyes glued to the graceful lordling twirling Imogen about the dance floor in a perfect waltz.

"What was that, Your Grace?" Colonel Percival Rollins, Lord Winderton, tugged at the corner of a mustache curled in such a way that the jowly man seemed to be perpetually smiling.

"Nothing," Cole replied. "Please continue."

"I was saying the the Rook took a horsewhip to a Prussian lord not a week ago," the man blustered. "If he has no respect for nobility then, mark me, the British aristocracy is next, by Jove."

Cole made a noncommittal sound of dismay as he allowed the old man's dialogue to fade into his periphery. He had chosen this spot by the fireplace as a perfect vantage because he could survey the entire ballroom, each point of entry, and glance into the gaming room. The drawback was having to mingle with the circle of men gossiping like a gaggle of matrons about the latest antics of the Rook.

That, and watching Imogen work through her full dance card on legs made increasingly unsteady by the bottomless glass of champagne that seemed threaded to her fingers. Cole wasn't the only one to notice. The men who held her in their arms for the waltz took liberties with her that no one would dare with a countess in control of her wits. Their bodies pressed too close, their hands slid too low on her waist, shaping the delicate swell of her hip. They charmed and cajoled her, praised and appreciated her, and she seemed to treat each one with more interest than the last. She clung to them, using them to hold her aloft as she spun and danced and laughed.

All the while avoiding *him* like he had some form of leprosy.

It was enough to make his hand twitch with provocation. It hadn't been so long since he'd broken bones with nothing but his brute strength. How he *longed* to do it now. Here. Every finger that trailed along her waist, every arm that pulled her in close. It would be but nothing to snap them, a few deft movements, really. Practiced and relished. The sounds wet and sharp.

Oh yes, this was a pleasant fantasy. A violent one, granted. But it filled him with an odd sort of delight.

Two more dances. Two dances and she'd be his. Even though he was her escort, custom dictated that he dance with her but once. Only courting couples waltzed twice at the same social gathering, and a third turn about the floor was tantamount to declaring marital intentions.

And how could he possibly have any intentions toward her, when he'd spent the previous week searching for another woman?

He'd found that Devina had been taken by her lover to Paris. He'd dispatched someone after her, but a reply could take weeks. Blackwell had reported that Ezio del Toro had died of natural causes a few months prior, and further investigation had revealed no one of Ginny's age or description in residence at his villa, or in his employ. In fact, his mistress had been a robust Russian woman who'd robbed him blind by the end.

He'd like to say that it was his conversation with Argent that had spurred another manic sweep of the isles and beyond for Ginny, only to be frustrated at every turn.

However, if he was honest . . . he had to admit that it had been the kiss he'd shared with Lady Anstruther in that tiny dark room belowstairs.

There had been power in that kiss. Something that had alternately awakened his beast, and soothed it. To Cole, it had felt as though they'd somehow transposed parts of themselves to the other through the searing contact of their lips. She'd reacted to his passion with a fire he'd not anticipated, with a wildness he'd not known she'd possessed. For his part, his animal desperation had been tempered by a curious tenderness. A sense of warmth and familiarity he'd not thought to find. He lusted after Lady Anstruther from the first moment he'd seen her, he could admit that now. However, the description of his regard for her had suddenly become quite obscure. It went beyond the physical now, past the temporal. He . . . respected her. Enjoyed her, even when they were in disagreement.

Which was most of the time.

She stimulated him, body and mind. When she didn't provoke him utterly, she comforted him. His arrogance and bitter guile was met with patience and also strength, if not sympathy.

Imogen spent as much time standing up to him as she did encouraging him. Surely that was . . . admirable.

Admiration. There was an applicable word. There was so much to admire about her. Indeed, some of the things he'd initially found infuriating now seemed to stoke his approbation. Her courage and pluck. Her ceaseless optimism. Her apparent disregard for policy and convention. All traits the Talmage family would have scorned and scoffed at had they still abided with him in Trenwyth Hall.

His father would have pitied her for her ignorant idealism and low birth. His mother would have accused her of smiling too openly and speaking her mind too often. His sister would disparage her flagrant style and her nerve to marry above her station.

And he'd done all of those things, hadn't he? Every one. Because he'd been raised to believe thusly, and because he'd needed reasons not to like her.

But Robert . . . dear Robert. His elder brother, his most ardent enthusiast and faithful friend. The true and deserving heir to the Trenwyth title . . .

He would have *loved* her.

Introverted and circumspect, Robert had been drawn to all things bold and beautiful. He'd had the heart of an artist. Abstract and soft. The soul of a philosopher. Fair and contemplative.

Lord, they'd have been perfect for each other.

A curious ache gathered in Cole's throat as he followed the vibrant crimson blot Imogen had become through a suspicious film that obscured his vision. Had life not taken Robert from him, had grief not driven him into Ginny's arms, had Cole not been broken in a foreign prison . . . would he and his brother have competed for the lovely widow Anstruther's attentions? Possibly.

Probably.

Who would have won?

"I say, Trenwyth, you look a little peaked." The colonel interrupted his reverie. "Are you quite all right?"

"Just fine, Colonel," he muttered as something in his mind clicked soundly into place. "Excuse me." He stepped around the man, intent on only one thing.

He'd investigated Lady Anstruther, as well, in these days they'd spent apart. She'd been born Imogen Pritchard to a comfortable childhood in a firmly middle-class building off Sloane Street in the city. Then her father, overloaded with debts, had moved his family to Wapping, where their circumstances had continued to decline. He hadn't been able to figure how she made her way through nursing college, but she'd worked for St. Margaret's for only a handful of years before meeting Lord Anstruther. By all accounts, until becoming a countess, her life hadn't been that extraordinary.

She'd spoken of darkness, though. Of tragedy and disappointment. Not like someone who'd lost a little money, but someone who'd had a great deal else taken from her.

But what? And by whom?

A mystery, she was. A mystery wrapped in crimson silks. One he intended to uncover.

Until now, Imogen had been little more to him than an alluring nuisance. A needling temptation. An unwanted distraction.

But circumstances weren't improving in that regard. Indeed, the prior night he'd dreamed they were in that crimson room, back there in the Bare Kitten. And instead of a pale, waifish, raven-haired Ginny, shyly blossoming to his touch, there had been Imogen. A golden-red lioness. A strong, lithe, and wild thing. A huntress in her own right, sun-kissed freckles and wanton lips.

In his dream, she'd claimed him. Scorched him with her kisses. Scared him with her touch. When he'd awakened, his seed ready to burst from him, it had taken barely a brush of his hand to find a sharp and aching release.

It had felt like betrayal at the time. Perhaps because of the startling inevitability the dream had validated. He desperately searched for Ginny one more time.

One *last* time.

Perhaps Ginny *had* been the Kitten name of poor Flora Latimer. Perhaps she'd died violently and he'd not been there to save her. His soul shriveled and bled at the thought. There was the chance that she'd moved on, somehow. That she'd created a new identity and a new life for herself. And if that was the case, it meant she didn't want him to find her.

God knew, he'd searched everywhere. The Americas, the Continent, here in London.

Whatever had become of her, he hadn't been able to be of assistance. But here was a woman in danger, a woman in need. One who set him ablaze. At times with fury, and other times warmth.

But always with desire.

Convention be damned, this next dance belonged to him no matter what it said on her card, and he intended to claim it. Because if he had to watch one more perfumed whelp put his soft hands on her, he'd open throats right in the middle of the Northwalk ballroom.

He didn't wait for the dance to end, nor did he excuse himself before cutting in. It was merely that a dark-haired fop was twirling her to Chopin one moment, and in two or three deft movements, Cole had taken his place, leaving the other man stumbling toward the fireplace.

He did it without even spilling her champagne, he noted smugly as he led her in an effortless waltz. She didn't flinch as her fingers gripped his alloy ones. She was warm silk against him, and her body fit into his arms with a magical sort of ease.

Like she belonged there.

Cole swallowed heavily and pulled her closer than any man had dared that night.

Her eyes were two wide hazel orbs, the chandeliers gleaming off a gaze made cloudy by inebriation. *"Your Grace,"* she admonished with an oddly endearing slur. "I *hardly* think that was called for. Lord West . . . Westcher . . . Westireton . . ." Her brow furrowed.

"Westershireton," he supplied helpfully.

"Well, in any case, he isn't trying to murder me, he's just *shy*." Her voice carried to the couple to their right who peered at them as though not quite believing what they'd heard.

Trenwyth covered her gaffe with a forced laugh.

"Lord, but you're handsome when you smile," she breathed. Then hiccupped.

"How many glasses of champagne have you had?" he asked from between his teeth.

She looked up as though the memory floated somewhere above her head, which caused her to misstep. He easily caught her and covered the move.

"Only one," she slurred guiltily.

"One?"

"Only this one." Her pouty lips drew down until she resembled a child expecting a severe reprimand. "Though I've lost count of how many times they've refilled it. Please don't lecture me— What are you doing?"

He gripped her in a way that made it impossible for her not to follow him as he led them into the crowd at a deceptively leisurely pace. "I'm taking you elsewhere before everyone realizes how drunk you are, and the night is ruined."

"Am I drunk?" she queried.

"Undoubtedly."

"I've never been drunk before," she said, casting a

wistful gaze into her glass. "Champagne hardly tastes as strong as gin. Though I probably should have stopped when I started feeling the bubbles all the way to my toes."

"Do try not to speak nonsense until I get you out of here," he muttered, fighting a wry sort of amusement as he wrested the glass from her hand and set it on the tray of a passing servant.

Though the ballroom was overcrowded and the rest of the company increasingly inebriated, Cole knew they were already a bit of a spectacle and in danger of becoming a full-on exhibition. His searching gaze found Blackwell by the pillar at the entry, enjoying a cross breeze and a glass of something expensive. The canny bastard understood the question in Cole's eyes immediately, glancing down at the countess nearly teetering on her feet. Dorian made a gesture with his dark head toward a door on the south wall, and stepped forward to call the attention of the gathering for yet another toast to his dear wife.

The congregation thus distracted, Cole half led, half dragged Imogen through the appropriate door and down a dark and eerily empty hall. Securing her to him with his left arm, he tried to ignore the breasts crushed against his side, or the way her head lolled rather sweetly onto his shoulder.

"*We're* not spinning anymore," she informed him with a sigh. "But everything else still is."

He tried a few doors and found them locked, until one gave way beneath his grip. Dragging her inside with him, he shut the door and threw the skeleton-key lock, shrouding them in sudden darkness.

"Oh no." The shadows seemed to draw her from her stupor as she squirmed clumsily in his arms.

"Hold still," he commanded gently.

"No," she gasped, twisting in his grasp like he'd seen many recalcitrant children do in the arms of a firm nanny. "No, this is wrong. I *can't* be alone with you. I simply can't."

"Why not? You know I won't hurt you."

"You don't understand." Her fervor increased, her arms flailing out. "It is not I who is in danger. But *you*. We can't be here, not alone."

A spear of trepidation pierced him at her words, and he subdued her easily, shackling her arms to her sides. "Why, dammit?" he demanded. "What are you afraid of, woman, *tell me*. Did you see someone? Were you threatened?" She had nothing to fear. No one else would touch her tonight. On that they could both rely.

"I'm afraid . . . I'm afraid I'll kiss you again," she lamented. "I seem to keep doing that when we're alone in the dark. And then you'll get angry. You'll say or do something improper. Or something bad will happen right after."

Cole felt every muscle in his abdomen curl against her as he bit out a harsh, unfamiliar, repetitive sound.

"Oh, *please* don't laugh," she begged. "It feels too . . . delicious. I can barely resist you when you're an ill-tempered brute, how do I have any chance if you're laughing?"

He hadn't recognized laughter. It had been too long since he'd experienced it.

Delicious. She certainly had the right of it. Everything about this moment suddenly took on a rather epicurean atmosphere. The close room warm with the heady breath of a summer's night. The creamy delight of her bare arms beneath his hand. The scent of her blooming around him, warm and floral. Suddenly he was Adam in the Garden of Eden, confronted with temptation, with a fruit too ripe and enticing to be denied. He shouldn't taste her. Not like this, when her wits belonged to champagne, and her body belonged to him.

As his eyes adjusted to the darkness, he found that they were in a study of some kind, the furniture hulking and sturdy and decidedly masculine. The drapes had been left drawn open, the clear night casting the dark blue of the room in a silvery moonstone finish.

"I won't get angry," he soothed, allowing his grip to become more cradling then commanding. "And I won't let anything bad happen."

She froze in his arms. "What about the kissing?" she asked dubiously.

Concealing his smile in the darkness, Cole let his head drop to settle beside hers, nuzzling into her hair, reveling in the scent of it, in the softness of the skin beneath.

"I can't make any promises about the kissing."

CHAPTER TWENTY-ONE

The night had been an enemy to Cole until this moment. A time and place where shadows loomed and remembered terror lurked. He couldn't rightly tell which was worse. The nightmares he had when asleep . . .

Or awake.

In the past, he hated how darkness seemed to sharpen his every instinct, to heighten his other senses, intensifying sound, underscoring scents, and increasing the sensitivity of his skin.

But now . . . when the noise was the sweet hitch of Imogen's desperate inhalations as she turned into him. When the fragrance was champagne and berries on the hot breath that feathered against his neck and jaw. When the sensation was her silk-clad hand twining into the short locks at his nape, raising the hairs everywhere else on his body into vibrating awareness . . . well, he couldn't say he minded the darkness so very much.

Only that he wished to see her face. To read the desire in her eyes.

He settled both his hands at her waist, noticing the slight clicks and creaks the hinges of his prosthesis made with the movement.

"You didn't promise not to say or do something improper," she prompted.

"I think we both know I'm about to do something very improper, indeed."

Aroused, inflamed, Cole pulled her in closer, fitting her to him. Her body melded into his, the soft shape that of an hourglass. He lowered his lips to play across her bare shoulder and hunt for the downy skin of her neck.

He knew once his lips found hers, all semblance of honor and control would vanish like the stars behind low London clouds. He wanted to prolong this moment, with her pliant and willing in his arms. An almost innocent honesty bloomed between them. Yes, he wanted to keep this moment forever, to roll it up and wrap it in ribbons made of moonbeams and store it in that place they'd spoken of before. That secret place deep within, the one only he could visit.

Except, now he thought he might keep her there, too.

An errant sound escaped her as he found the sensitive hollow of her throat. Her fingers kneaded at his scalp and she tipped more heavily against him. "I—I've changed my mind," she informed him unsteadily. "You may kiss me now."

Her lips found his temple, clumsily questing lower for his mouth, which he denied her.

"How fickle you are, Lady Anstruther," he teased low and soft against her ear.

"I assure you, I am not," she promised. "It's only that, if my lips aren't occupied, I might say something I shouldn't."

Dear God, did he want to occupy her lips. In ways that would shock her. In ways that might upset and alarm her. Oh Christ, if only . . .

Clamping down on the salacious beast that threatened the tenderness of the moment, he, instead, focused on the satin glove warmed by her palm, currently shaping his jaw with a soft caress.

"You can tell me anything," he said gruffly, turning his head to nuzzle into her palm like a wolf demanding affection. Using his teeth, he captured the tiny seam at the tip of her longest finger and pulled it loose. He did this to four fingers before the glove slid free of her hand.

Cole tucked it in his pocket, thinking that he was beginning to start quite a collection of her gloves. "Do you know what I like about you?" he queried, charting the indent of her waist as his hand made its way up her spine. He thrilled to the little tremors of muscle he detected beneath his hand. "Your inability to hide what you feel. Your emotions radiate from you, even in the dark. They're quite contagious, you know." He caught a soft lobe between his lips and nudged with his teeth.

Her gasp melted into a moan. "You don't know what I hide," she panted. "You can never know."

"Why?" He licked at the hollow behind her ear that tasted of salt and softness.

"Because," she breathed almost imperceptibly. Then her hands lifted to his chest, pushing at him until she bent back in his arms like a bloody contortionist.

Her voice became stronger, the desperation rising above

the husky desire. "*Because*, sometimes, when one keeps so many secrets for so long, one becomes reliant on them. One's life could unravel in the wake of revelation."

"Tell me," he cajoled, tightening his hold on her. "Tell me what you fear. Tell me your secrets and I'll hold everything together."

"Must I?" she asked plaintively, melting back against him, her lips brushing along the place where his jaw met his neck. "Must the past matter so much now that you are back and I am who I am instead of who I was?"

She was making no sense, but it didn't matter. Her mouth left a moist trail down his jawline and was charting a dangerous course across his cheek toward his lips. Cole had the distinct feeling that she used the tantalizing slide of her mouth as a distraction.

Damn her lovely hide if it wasn't working.

His beast both purred and growled simultaneously as he turned his head and claimed her questing mouth. Their tongues slid against each other's in a dance of wet silk and raw, uncomplicated desire.

She could keep her fucking secrets, Cole decided, so long as she stayed like this, soft and eager against him, overwhelming his honed senses until the entire world vanished but for the two of them. The room faded and even the moon seemed to dull against the flare of desire sparking through him with all the hot, white fire of a lightning bolt. The cosmos tilted, contracted, and expanded again, leaving them suspended in an eternal firmament, lit only by tiny explosions of unfamiliar stars.

She placed her hands on either side of his jaw, one palm bare and warm, the other still gloved. Cole tasted her, devoured her, and yet her gentle grip held him utterly captive. Her hands slid down his neck, raising gooseflesh everywhere before they smoothed the swells of his chest, and tucked the lapels of his suit coat.

A quiet curse escaped him as his lungs labored beneath her palms. Shivers of lust and fire ran up and down his spine, shooting thrills and shocks to the tips of his fingers and scorching along nerve endings until he felt as though an inferno might erupt if he wasn't soon rid of his clothes.

She pulled back, and he almost didn't let her. Pressing her cheek to his, he felt a tiny hint of moisture slide between their flesh, a tear smudged by their proximity. "I would fall in love with you if you'd let me."

Her agonized whisper shook the foundations of the ground beneath his feet. They were no longer suspended in a fantastical midnight sky, but crashed back to the hard and unflinching earth, spinning and spinning in an endless orbit toward eventual oblivion.

She was here, in his arms. Not locked in a memory he couldn't fully recall, or stashed on a pedestal constructed of the past. *Here.* Offering him her gentle, honest heart.

Cole's mouth dropped open, a reply posed on the boundary of his lips like a diver at the edge of a cliff.

But as her hand stole lower, testing the turgid shape of his cock against the front of his trousers, it became apparent neither of them would ever know what he'd been about to say.

With that one caress, she'd dismantled the last of his self-control and left his humanity in the fragmented shards of moonlight on the lush carpets beneath them. His beast roared to the surface, a low sound escaping his chest before he kissed her roughly, and reached down to lift her against him.

Cole walked them both backward until something sturdy stole her weight from him. A desk. Excellent. He crowded her onto it, his tongue splaying against the heated silk inside her mouth, until her legs split to make room for his progress against her.

She clung to him as though she might still fall, her skirts bunching as she gripped him with surprisingly strong thighs, enveloping him with both her arms and legs.

Suddenly it wasn't enough. He needed flesh against his flesh. Warm skin and wet desire. He needed rhythmic movement and to watch the arching strain of her lithe muscles as she came apart for him.

He somehow rid himself of his own gloves before seizing great handfuls of her skirts, hauling them above her knees. He used his left arm to anchor her against him, and to hold her steady in the wake of what he was about to do. His right hand dragged up her thigh until he encountered the satiny skin above the ribbons of her silk stocking.

She gasped and writhed, kneading at the bunched muscles of his back as he caressed the infinitely smooth skin inside her thighs. Skin that became warmer the higher he climbed, until he reached the slit of her drawers behind which heat pulsed a wanton invitation to him.

Feeling both wicked and welcome, Cole slipped his fingers past the open seams and found the soft bit of fluff protecting her intimate heat. Both provoked and humbled, he cupped the damp mound.

Her breath left her lungs in a great whoosh, flooding his senses with champagne and sex as she rolled her hips forward, arching that lovely back just as he'd wished her to.

He murmured urgent things against her mouth, low, animal praise that was admittedly harsh and vulgar against the softness of her lips.

But his hand. His hand remained gentle as he spread

the plump petals concealing her sex and saturated his finger in the desire he found there.

Their combined exhale was a desperate, throaty invocation. Cole bent farther over her, hungrily latching to the throat she exposed as her head rolled back on her shoulders when his fingers slipped and stroked around the soft folds of her core. He relished the delicate skin. Splayed and played with her, until her hips began to roll against his teasing movements in an untried but unmistakable demand, following the deft movements of his finger with pleading little gasps.

Nuzzling a smile against her delicate throat, he grazed the tiny, throbbing pearl of her sex with a moistened fingertip. Once. Twice. Luxuriating in her shuddering response. In the way her little fists knotted in his clothes, tugging as though to rend them from his body.

She gasped his name, squirming to get closer to him. Begging him with her body to release her from her torment. Relenting, he split the delicate seam with his longest finger, finding the soft, tight place her body wept for him while simultaneously resting his thumb against the throbbing nub of sensation and need.

A low sob escaped her as he sank inside to the knuckle, her body pulling him in with tight little quivers. It amazed him that a place so small, so tight, could stretch to contain the length and girth of man.

He moved his finger inside her, testing the singular silk found only within a woman's core. He curled a knuckle ever so slightly while simultaneously smoothing at her throbbing clitoris with the pad of his thumb. She jerked and twitched as he found a soft, slow rhythm, her breathing coming in hard little pants punctuated by shaking sighs. Her body clamped around him, closing on him with sweet, velvet spasms that intensified in time to her sounds of delight.

"Cole?" she whimpered, as her hips bucked over the desk, suddenly straining against him, almost riding his hand in soft, rocking motions.

"I'm here," he soothed, dragging his mouth back to hers. "I'm here, my sweet."

"Don't. Let. Me. Go," she begged in time to the movements of his hand.

"Never," he vowed as she clawed and pulled at him, her intimate flesh clamping around him in beautiful, strong pulses.

He swallowed her ecstatic sounds with his mouth as she drenched his fingers with shudders of wet release. The feel of her pleasure both inflamed and awed him. It built and built until he wondered if it would ever end. Until he was certain he never wanted it to. This woman, this magnificent treasure . . . he wanted to give her hours of pleasure for every moment of pain she'd ever endured.

That might take a lifetime, he realized.

Was he really considering offering that lifetime to her?

When her frenzy passed, she turned her lips away from his, regaining her breath in moist little puffs while showering his face with grateful kisses, soft as a butterfly's.

Cole pulled his hand from her, clenching his eyes shut as her lips grazed his lids as well as everything else. Every muscle in his body pulled tight against the others until he feared something might snap. He needed her. He needed to be *inside* her. He knew that soft, tight channel of hers was wet enough to welcome him. That he could slip into her offered warmth and she'd pull him close to her body.

But he didn't move. Didn't dare.

She was drunk . . . and he was a fucking gentleman.
God be damned.

Cole crushed his mouth into the hair beside her ear, willing his arousal to die. Willing his beast to recede. Reminding himself that to take her now would be wrong. Would be . . .

"I missed you," her sweet voice confessed against his temple. "I missed you so awfully. I didn't feel that I had the right to, but I did. I thought of you all the time. I . . . worried for you."

In that moment, his heart melted into a tender puddle. It had only been days since they'd seen each other.

And he'd missed her too.

Unable to summon the words, he gathered her against him in a warm bundle of silk and sex and just held her close. Her heart against his, beating in tandem. They rocked a little, she with languid affection, and he with mounting, rhythmic need.

Her legs hitched higher against him, her hips pressing closer. "Cole," she whispered. "I want you to—"

A sharp knock at the door drove them apart enough for Cole to toss her skirts back over her legs.

"Come in," she said breathlessly, as though repeating an automated response she didn't really mean.

Cole fought the urge to clamp his hand over her mouth as someone tested the door latch.

"Lady Anstruther?" a feminine voice called. "Imogen, are you in there? Are you all right?"

"Oh, it's Millie." Sliding off the desk onto unsteady legs, Imogen gave a drunken lurch toward the door. "Coming!" she sang.

Cole caught her around the waist. "You absolutely *cannot*

go out there like this," he gritted against her ear. "Your hair and clothes are a mess, and your reputation will be ruined. Get rid of them."

She sagged against him a little before calling. "He says to get rid of you or I'll be ruined!"

"That's not what I—"

The rattling of the door became more urgent. "Who said that?" a separate feminine voice demanded. Cole thought he recognized the voice as Lady Northwalk's. "Imogen, who's in there with you? Are you hurt?"

"I can barely feel a thing," Imogen answered as though the information astonished none more than herself. "It didn't even hurt when he bit me."

"Bloody Christ." Cole growled the blasphemy as he really did clamp his hand over her mouth this time. "Not to worry, Lady Northwalk, she's just had a bit too much—"

"Bit you! Who bit you? Is that Trenwyth in there?" The lock was sorely tested now as the two ladies frantically grappled with it. "Open the door this very instant!"

"Just . . . give us a bloody moment," Cole growled. He needed to collect his thoughts, and to will his aching erection to subside. The squirming minx in his arms wasn't doing the least bit to help. "Hold still, damn you," he ordered against her ear.

A masculine warning sounded a breath before the door burst open beneath the weight of an auburn-haired giant.

Cole debated for a split second whether it would cause more damage to keep his hand over Imogen's mouth, or remove it. Ultimately, he decided on the latter, though he didn't relinquish his hold on her waist.

"Mr. Argent," Imogen greeted brightly, as though admitting a welcome guest into her parlor. "Whatever are you doing here?"

Argent's little ebony-haired wife rushed in behind him, glaring daggers the color of volcanic glass, followed by a concerned Lady Northwalk.

"Apparently, we're protecting your virtue," the actress snapped.

"My virtue is beyond your protection," Imogen said with a wistful sigh. "He has it already."

Argent turned on him, his arctic eyes flashing with lethal wrath.

"We didn't get that far." Trenwyth held his hand up, though guilty heat crept from beneath his high collar. "We only . . . kissed." It sounded like a lie, even to him.

"We've certainly done *much* more than that upon an evening," Imogen confessed with a rueful giggle.

He should have kept his hand on her mouth, he thought with no little regret.

"Shame on you, Your Grace." Lady Northwalk circumvented the two fuming Argents and approached. "You're supposed to be protecting her."

"I was," Cole tightened his grip on Imogen as the angelic Farah reached for her. "I *am*. Look at her; she's in no condition to be out—"

Argent stepped closer. "She's in no condition to be debauched by a mercenary, self-indulgent fuck wit. Now hand her over, and prepare to take the beating you deserve."

"Don't bother. I'm in fine condition for debauchery," Imogen protested with an increasing slur. "In fact, I feel rather sprightly."

An absurd bubble of laughter broke from Cole's throat, which he instantly regretted. Damned if she wasn't as adorable as she was irresistible.

"Give the champagne a few hours," Millie warned with

a knowing sympathy furrowing her brow. "You'll feel just the opposite."

Cole had to admit, he did deserve a beating. Not that he'd allow Argent to provide him with one. The hypocritical bastard was one to talk about the line between protection and coercion. He'd told Cole about how he'd nigh on kidnapped the woman who would become his wife.

"Chief Inspector, when did you show up?" Imogen bent toward the fair-haired man framed by the splintered doorway, wearing bemused suspicion as well as he did his evening suit.

"Just in the nick of time, I think," he said with his usual brand of measured control. "What's going on here?"

"Not to worry, no one has died," Imogen informed him earnestly.

"Yet," Argent supplemented, jabbing his finger toward Trenwyth to wordlessly warn him that they'd be returning to this point in the discussion for-fucking-certain.

Cole met his glare with a challenging one of his own, the fire in his blood shifting from arousal to aggression. "I'm taking Lady Anstruther home," he informed them.

"So you can finish what you started?" Millie spat. "Not bloody likely."

"So I can put her to bed," he explained through teeth that wouldn't unclench, and then amended upon seeing Farah Blackwell's expression of alarm. *"Alone."*

Morley stepped forward, very careful to avoid any contact with Farah, even the brush of her skirts. "Actually, Your Grace, I would speak with you."

"Can't it wait?" Cole did little to keep the impatience from his voice.

"It's about . . ." The chief inspector cast a surreptitious glance to the woman in his arms. "It's regarding the matter we discussed previously, the one on St. James's Street."

Imogen lurched forward a little when Cole's arms almost went slack as he searched the shrewd inspector's carefully closed features.

Had Morley found Ginny?

Cole fought a thousand emotions surging and ebbing like the sea in a tempest. Did he dare to hope? Did he even want to know? Should he cling to a woman—a memory— as tightly as he did to the lady in his arms? One whom he'd developed equally strong feelings for. One whom he desired with identical fervor.

Both of whom he barely knew anything about.

Reluctantly, Cole released Imogen into Farah Blackwell's waiting arms as Millie rushed forward to steady her other side.

"I'll come to check on you in the morning," he murmured into her hair as he kissed her forehead. They had much to discuss.

He had something to offer her, no matter what Morley revealed.

By now her eyes blinked with the languid sluggishness of the inebriated, though a dreamy smile touched her kiss-swollen lips. "G'night, Your Grace," she murmured, her languorous tongue making his title sound more like *Your Grashe*.

With one last warning glance over his shoulder, Argent followed the women into the hall like a hulking sentinel. Cole knew she'd be safe in their company, and yet he wasn't ready to let her out of his sight.

Glancing at Morley, he noted that the chief inspector's sharp blue eyes softened as they followed Imogen's meandering progress from the library, touched with a gentle emotion that had Cole bristling with possessive indignation.

"Is it true what they were accusing you of, Trenwyth?" The inspector dragged his eyes away from Imogen to stab Cole with a stare as obtrusive as a pushpin through a dead moth. "Did you take advantage of her?"

"No," Cole denied for what seemed like the thousandth time. "We kissed and—carried on a little, but we've done that several times sober, truth be told, not that it's any of your fucking concern." Cole ran an unsteady hand through his hair, beginning to feel like the cad they accused him of being. "Why are you so bloody protective of her, anyway?" he asked skeptically. "What is she to you?"

Something in Morley's expression flickered slightly, arresting Cole's attention. "She reminds me of someone . . . someone I once loved very much. Someone who was ill-used by men like you."

"What do you mean, men like me?"

"Noblemen. Soldiers. Predators. Anyone who could prey upon a pretty, innocent woman in desperate circumstances."

"I'm not a predator, Morley." Cole's voice became lethally soft.

"Yes you are."

"Not *that* kind. Not when it comes to her."

Morley's eyes narrowed, examining him like the same pin-wielding lepidopterist would the specimen beneath his glass.

"Lady Anstruther is precisely who I came here to discuss."

Cole blinked, wishing he had a drink in his hand. "I thought you said you were here to discuss the Kittens of St. James's Street."

Using the light spilling in from the hall, Morley opened a desk drawer, then another, until he found matches with which to light a gas lamp. That accomplished, he leaned on the desk and folded his arms in a posture of relaxed readiness. "It took me some time to ascertain the link between the murders you and I previously discussed, but I'm relatively certain I've found it . . . or rather, that I've found *her*."

Cole affected a similar posture, his brow furrowing with bemused aggravation. "You're saying these murders are linked to Lady Anstruther?"

"I'm afraid so." Morley nodded.

Cole's heart, already accelerated with arousal and anger, now kicked against his chest with the strength of a mule at this new bit of information. "How is that possible?"

"Once I realized that two of the victims had been acquainted with her, the other associations were easy to track down. Lady Broadmore, of course, was found in her garden, as you're aware. And then there was Molly Crane, the nurse who was employed at St. Margaret's with her before she became the countess. Following that thread, I investigated into Lady Anstruther's past as Imogen Pritchard."

Morley paused, glancing over at Cole as though to ascertain whether he really wanted to receive the information he was about to impart.

"And?" Cole pressed impatiently.

"I've uncovered several more victims who fit the profile. Which is to say, they are comparable to Lady Anstruther in looks, age, weight, and coloring. Working chronologically backward, I found a Miss Jane Raleigh, a spinster who lived a block over from both you and the Anstruthers some six months past. Her parents thought she'd run away with a lover, but it is my impression that she's been killed. She left with no money, none of her belongings, and I found evidence of a struggle in her garden.

"Around the time you were recovering from your ordeal in the hospital, Miss Pritchard and her family were housed for a month in downtown London near the courthouse while the Earl of Anstruther obtained a marriage license. During that month, a young and fair nanny by the name of Ann Keaton was found strangled and assaulted a mere three doors down from their apartments. Prior to that, Imogen Pritchard had worked to keep her family in rather dismal rooms near Wapping High Street. A charwoman in her building, Rose Tarlly, suffered the selfsame fate as Lady Broadmore, Miss Crane, Miss Keaton, and Miss Raleigh. Surely you see the pattern."

"I do." Cole nodded, releasing a troubled breath. "What I don't see, is a connection to the Bare Kitten, or to Ginny."

"I was getting to that," Morley muttered, shifting uncomfortably. "I can't say that the connection is strong, but I've already told you of the earliest victim, a Miss Flora Latimer, who was murdered exactly like the others."

"Yes, you mentioned that in your note."

"From what I could glean from former neighbors of the Pritchards', Mr. Pritchard, the pater of the household, was a consistent patron of the Bare Kitten. In fact, he'd run up a significant debt to the former proprietor, Ezio del Toro."

At this, Cole pushed himself away from the desk, letting his arms fall to his sides. "Did this Pritchard, Lady Anstruther's father, did he have anything to do with Ginny? Where is he now?"

"Also dead," Morley stated. "And this is where the connection becomes rather opaque. Pritchard died long before Miss Latimer or the others and, as far as I can tell, the rest of the family had no further dealings with the Bare Kitten."

"Where did you get this information?"

"The current owner of said establishment, a Mr. Jeremy Carson. He revealed the timeline to me, and it all checks out. Lady Anstruther's father died even before this Ginny began her employment there. So, like I said, the connection seems to be indistinct, if there even is one."

Agitated, Cole paced the room, something scratching at that place inside him, at the locked door in his head. A memory. A link. Something big. Something recent . . .

"Wait." He froze mid-step and whirled to face Morley. "What did you say was the name of the owner of the Bare Kitten?"

"Mr. Carson," Morley answered.

"No." Cole made a wild gesture, advancing on the inspector. "No, no, no," he said in rapid percussion, in time to the frantic pounding in his chest. "His first name, you said it was Jeremy?"

"Yes," Morley answered slowly, regarding him with some hesitation. "But you said, yourself, that you've spoken to the man."

"So I have," Cole confirmed. "But he never gave me his first name."

"I'm afraid I don't follow." Morley tugged at his white tie and high collar. "What significance does the man's first name have to do with the case?"

"It has everything to do with it." Cole could no longer stand still, no longer could he be in this house, this room. He needed to act. He needed to follow this mystery through to its end, and he had a good idea where that would be. "When I was in Lady Anstruther's garden earlier the

same night that Lady Broadmore was killed, she mistook
me for someone else in the darkness. She called me by
his name, his *first* name."

"Oh?" Morley's light brows crawled up his forehead.
"And that name was . . ."

Cole had a distinct notion that the clever detective already knew, but he wanted verbal confirmation, and so he
gave it to him with all the gravity of the giant stone of
dread sinking into his gut.

"She called me *Jeremy.*"

CHAPTER TWENTY-TWO

If Cole had learned anything from his time as a spy, it was this: A secret *always* wanted to be discovered.

He didn't know how long he stood in Imogen's garden lifting his face to the sky. Long enough for Argent and Millie to help her into bed and stand vigil for a while. He listened to them consult with O'Mara and Rathbone before returning to their own home.

He evaded their patrol, waiting for his thoughts to coalesce into some semblance of a plan, and then scatter to the cosmos, as random as the placement of the stars.

As he let a chilly summer breeze tousle his hair, he took deep, centering breaths and thought about how odd he found it that people had always attempted to find meaning in the night sky. To connect the position of the celestial bodies and turn them into what they wanted—what they *needed* to find when they looked to the stars. A fallen hero. A delineative creature. In many cases, a god or goddess.

Cole knew the constellations. He could name and identify many of them from several parts of the world. But, in truth, he'd never found what the astronomers and philosophers had. Could never truly identify the huntsman Orion, in his handful of anemic stars, nor did he see Castor or Pollux in the twin belts of Gemini. They'd been men, legends at best. Perhaps only myths created by ancient bards. Not lines drawn by primeval theologians, immortalized in the eternal beyond. If those mythical men ever lived, then they'd surely died, and they'd gone the way of all creatures.

From the time he was young, Cole realized he'd not possessed the capacity for romantic fancy. He could not draw the lines he needed to find the miraculous divine in the everyday. He understood truths that many rejected. That perspective most often designated righteousness. That most of the constructs of society were imaginary, invisible, especially to those in Orion's position. Past the sky, above the moon. If the hunter was real, were he immortalized there in the night sky as his mythology dictated, he could look down and see nothing of what men fought and killed each other over.

For country borders were merely lines on a map, not on the earth. And currency was little more than an agreed-upon idea, a value assigned to pretty minerals. An economy represented an intricate web of interests, of production and consumption, and seemed to always be destined to eventually collapse.

Because every society, every civilization, seemed to want to reject one simple and evident truth. That man for all his forward progression was still, in his being, no better than a beast. Driven by primal instincts and powerful universal hungers. Try as he might to blame his primitive carnality on various and sundry underworld demons throughout the ages, Cole believed that a man's wicked will was solely his own.

However, as he'd nursed his rather nihilistic view, buttressing it with dark life experiences, he'd begun to realize he'd overlooked one very important thing in his estimation of mankind . . .

Women.

A creature of a different sort, one fabricated from innumerable paradoxes. Both potent and persecuted. Made of equal parts fear and fairness. Wit and wisdom.

Of strength and secrets.

Certainly they had instincts and deviances of their own, but they existed generally above the cruel and bestial egocentricity of their sexual counterparts. They were constructed of kindness, of altruism, of ethics and understandings not normally possessed by men. Especially men like himself.

Imogen, he predicted, had more secrets than most. Secrets meant to be discovered, ones that would have meaning for them both.

Cole took one last look around the garden, a place he now thought of as synonymous with Imogen. The place from which she'd first captured his attention, then his lips, and eventually, his heart.

It had taken a long time for him to learn to climb after his injury, but his spelunking expedition to the Americas had been invaluable. Discarding his jacket to the bench they'd shared only days ago, he gripped the trellis with his good hand, and began to ascend.

The hook on the palm of his prosthesis attached to the harness around his torso did little better than anchor him in place as he made upward progress with his three other limbs. But he managed with almost his previous stealth. Once the second-floor balcony was in reach, he leaped over, catching the entirety of his weight with one hand. He gritted his teeth as the stitches in his shoulder strained and threatened to rip. With a foul curse and a surge of strength, he maneuvered his hook to sink into the wood railing once he steadied himself. Finding purchase with his feet, he vaulted the railing and landed in a soft crouch in the shadows of the balcony.

The first-floor locks were many and secure. The second-story doors and windows, however, were often protected with nothing better than a hook-latch.

Depressing the lever inside his prosthesis, Cole thrilled to the metallic slide of the thin blade. Carefully, he fitted it in between the balcony doors, and lifted until it released the latch with a satisfying click.

That accomplished, he retracted the blade and opened the door, entering her house as a shadow might, without notice.

He'd done this before, an infinite number of times, but never with his pulse thundering. Never with his mind so occupied.

Or his heart so vested.

How could Ginny and Imogen be connected by one young, inexperienced game-maker? Certainly, there was more than one Jeremy in the world, but the coincidence was simply too strong to ignore. A prostitute and a woman who dedicated her life to saving them . . . it wasn't much of a leap to assume that they might have known each other.

Or shared acquaintances at the very least.

If Imogen's father had been a longtime client of the Bare Kitten, if he'd owed the establishment a great deal of money, it followed that the remaining family might have some dealings with the former   or current—proprietor, and that she would be ashamed to admit said dealings to society.

Especially to an admittedly antagonistic duke.

If it was found out that the countess Anstruther was associated with a Piccadilly pimp, it would be more than a scandal. It would be her undoing.

The balcony door opened to the master suite, a room he'd expected to be hers. But as Cole crept across the plush carpets to the bedside, he was astonished to find a plump, gray-haired woman prone in slack-jawed slumber.

Her mother, he realized, as an ache bloomed in his chest. Imogen had relinquished the largest and most comfortable rooms to the woman, most likely taking residence in the countess's suites, as she would have when Earl Anstruther was still alive.

It seemed like something she would do, he thought with a reluctant half-smile, sacrifice luxury for those she loved.

Making his way into the hall, he hesitated, glancing toward what he knew to be the countess's suites merely steps away.

He would find Imogen there; her sleep aided by many glasses of champagne. Soft, pliant, and warm. Lord, how his fingers itched to open the door to her room and let the darkness decide what happened next.

But what he wouldn't find in her bed was her secrets.

They resided in a different room, of that he was certain.

The day he'd fought the gangsters on her porch, she'd led him down a long hall toward the back stairs. Upon finding a door slightly ajar, she'd quickly pulled it shut, casting him a guilty look.

He'd known in that moment that the room contained

something she hadn't wanted him to see. At the time, he'd politely pretended not to notice.

At the time, he'd not known her past was so connected to his own.

He turned to the stairs, making his way from the second floor to the ground level. Then on flat, noiseless feet he crossed the grand entry and hall to the familiar door. It didn't surprise him when he found it locked, and he effortlessly picked it, easing the door open on quiet, well-oiled hinges.

Being in the middle of the house, the room boasted no windows, and the hall outside was lit by little more than moonbeams and the wan glow of a lamp left burning for those who would make a nocturnal meander to the kitchens.

Cole got an impression of strange, mismatched angles inside the room, much like the skyline of a city from above. He fetched the lantern from the end of the hall and returned, holding the light aloft.

Paintings?

He drifted into the large, dark-paneled room, drawn forward by equal parts awe and apprehension. Here was her sanctum, the place where she kept the renderings of her mind and memory.

Her easel and tools were supported by the far wall with a chaotic sort of organization. The sketch of Achilles was propped next to them, beginning to take real form with the application of a few rough coats of heavy color.

Dusty coverlets adorned a few of the taller canvases, though just as many were left exposed. Various landscapes transported him to the countryside, and then to a back street of the East End. Others were obvious renderings of places she'd only ever seen in other paintings. Morocco or Marrakesh, the Indies, and, if he wasn't mistaken, the Alps. All painted with a wistful, yearning hand. It was as though she accepted her ignorance, and created with her brushes her own idea of a destination. Each of those landscapes had a sense of incompletion, of expectancy, as if they waited for her to travel there, to fill in the reality over the fantastical so they could be considered finished.

She was more talented than he'd realized, Cole thought. What if he took her to these places? Destinations he'd likely already traversed, but instead of his aim being entrapment and espionage, it would be nothing more than enjoyment.

Perhaps, while he watched her transpose what beauty her gentle eyes found, he'd locate that thing for which he'd been eternally searching.

Peace. Purpose. Meaning.

Love?

Though he knew that no one resided on this floor, Cole moved with the utmost care, with the sense he was on hallowed ground. An expectant stillness permeated the room, a sacred silence that both beckoned and repelled him.

Setting the lantern down on one of the many trunks scattered about the room, Cole reached for one of the covered canvases with an unsteady hand.

Secrets were always covered up and, once revealed, could never again find the darkness.

He hesitated, his fingers tuned to the coarse ridges of oil paint beneath the thin cotton.

Tell me what you fear. Tell me your secrets and I'll hold everything together. He'd promised her that a mere few hours ago.

Must I? she'd replied. *Must the past matter so much now that you are back and I am who I am instead of who I was?*

Who had she been? he wondered as his fist tightened on the cover, bunching it into his grip as he ripped it away.

He didn't stumble backward, because a man with his reflexes wasn't prone to such an enervation. Though he did have to admit that being confronted with his own brutal visage found him several paces behind where he'd revealed it.

Crimson. It once again overtook his entire field of vision, painting everything the color of blood. *No,* that wasn't it. Not everything. The color was contained within the canvas before him. Bold. Impenitent.

Unmistakable.

A tremor of potent emotion coiled around his bones, the serpentine darkness contracting until he swore the tension of his fist closing and his shoulders bunching created a tight, unnerving sound.

A crimson room. A single lamp. A naked man.

Him.

Not as he was now. Not as large, as scarred, as old, or as broken. But as he was then. *There.* At *that* moment he'd stood in *that* red room years ago both whole and heartbroken. And hungry. Starving for the affection and gentle grace granted in the last place he'd expected to find it.

Only one woman had seen him as he was depicted in that damnable painting. Eyelids half-closed with inebriated arousal. Features taut with poorly concealed grief. Long muscles tensed with barely controlled lust.

Ginny.

Gin-ny. He carefully enunciated the name in his mind as he strained to grasp a drunken image out of a past buried beneath so much brutality and blood. *Ginny . . . Imogen . . .*

He'd thought it a boozy moniker. Something to do with the back-alley gin peddled by such contemptuous swindlers as Ezio del Toro.

The memory he'd lost slammed back into him with bone-shattering speed. It climbed into his psyche. It created him, destroyed him, and then built something new from the broken pieces as he stared at the rendering of the past.

Ginny. *His* Ginny . . . had been none other than *Imogen Pritchard.*

CHAPTER TWENTY-THREE

As it turned out, Imogen reacted to excess amounts of alcohol much like her father did. That is to say, rather quickly. She'd also inherited his enviable immunity to the miserable aftereffects so many were struck with after an evening of overindulgence. A blessing, that. And possibly a curse, she supposed. Without the ghastly consequences, inebriation seemed less dangerous, and thereby had the opportunity to become more frequent. Drinking had ultimately been her father's undoing. She'd have to be mindful of that.

It was the roar of an empty stomach that drove her out of bed before the sun touched the horizon. She decided to nurse her hunger—and a lingering sense of chagrin—in the kitchen over some scraps of cold chicken, apple slices, and warm, frothy milk.

She eschewed her wrapper as the summer's night was nigh to balmy and the white nightgown Millie had selected for her was layered with lace, cotton, and silk. She was plenty warm, almost too warm, as she padded on bare feet over the luxuriously carpeted halls of the Anstruther manse. Perhaps the champagne had a little something to do with that as well.

She'd have to apologize to Christopher and Millie, she thought with a wince. They'd been so lovely. So circumspect and gentle as they'd taken her home, and Argent had given them privacy as Millie had helped her undress and tucked her in. What dear friends they were.

She'd have to make certain that Argent didn't nurse his anger toward Cole. He hadn't taken advantage of her, though he had seduced her. Just like he'd seduced her three long years ago and her traitorous body had desired the pleasure his clever fingers had produced ever since.

An insistent yawn interrupted her progress down the grand stairs, and she made up for lost time by hurrying the rest of the way on her toes. Driven by a remembrance of some fudge she'd procured in the not-too-distant past, Imogen rushed across the foyer and through the great room lit only by a few skylights.

Golden lamplight beckoned her down the long hall toward the back stairs, and she followed it past the study, the library, and—

Oh bugger.

The lamp usually left burning dimly in the hall no longer maintained its perch. The glow she'd followed came from *inside the room.*

Her room. The dark, windowless place she'd used as storage for her paintings.

Fear licked at her spine with a sharp, dreadful tongue. A stranger was inside her house. Someone who'd picked the lock to that singular room, to which she possessed the only key. Not even the housekeeper could get in there to dust, as Cheever had disapprovingly mentioned too many times.

So who? Mr. O'Mara? Or the dusky, dangerous-looking Rathbone? Didn't seem likely.

The murderer, perhaps? Barton? A stealthy criminal who'd left so many bodies, so many women, strangled in his villainous wake?

What would he want with her paintings?

Now was not the time to find out. Spinning on her bare heel, she lifted the hem of her pale nightgown and made to run away on silent toes. She'd go to the guardians Morley had appointed for her. They'd know what to do. Then she'd check on Isobel, just to make certain her sister was all right.

Three steps. She made it three measly steps before a large, frightening shadow blocked the glow of the lantern and cast the hall into darkness.

"It will do you no good to run."

The dispassionate words froze Imogen to the marble floor. She didn't have to turn around. She knew his face already. Had memorized every inch of him like a beloved poem. The meter counted by the figures used to measure his impossible height. The prose selected from the lyrical beauty of arrogant angles and brutal lines. The structure as sound as the thick bones and sinew that crafted him into something more epic than even Dante could devise.

Imogen used immeasurable, incremental movements to face him. Thinking absurdly that Dante had used the very words in his *Inferno* to describe the duke in the doorway.

Savage, rough, and stern. The wrath emanating from him did, indeed, make her veins and pulses tremble.

He knew. He'd found the painting.

"Cole, I—"

He moved like a shadow, taking her in his clutches before she could pluck a thought from the miasma of panic and arrange it into a semblance of diction. His grip was punishing as he dragged her into the room and shoved her in front of the canvas.

"What the bloody hell is this?" He gestured wildly toward his own likeness. "Tell me who you are!"

With a numb sort of detachment, Imogen studied her own painting and thought about who she *wasn't*. She'd never been a poet, for example. But she'd tried to convey in her rendering the emotion he'd elicited in her. The elegiac effect of his disappearance. The euphoria she'd experienced upon his return. The eager longing that overtook her body whenever she gave in to nostalgia. The multitude of perils the exposure of this very evidence posed to her entire existence.

His prosthetic harness pinched at her shoulder as he stood behind her, pressing his chest to her back, holding her almost aloft before a canvas nearly as tall as herself. She barely felt it. Instead her body attuned to the man. To the conflagration of his rage that served only to melt the icy daggers of his pain.

He shook her, not unlike a mechanical toy that refused to work. "Explain yourself."

"I don't think that's necessary, is it?" she replied to the painting in front of her. The Cole who looked at her like he had done in the past, with sensual invitation and gentle acceptance. Not the man of volatile fury he'd become.

He knew who she'd been. Who she was *no longer*.

"Say. The. Name. Say it!"

Imogen came to understand that the lower his voice became, the more dangerous he was. And still she refused. "You won't find her here, Cole. Only me."

He was not merely a man who held her locked in his clutches, but something almost thus. Something both human and inhuman. Much like the Minotaur, a creature with the body of a man, but whose head was ruled by a beast. A dangerous one at that.

With frantic, jerking movements, he yanked up the skirts of her nightgown, and Imogen let him. She knew what he'd find. Why he became so utterly still. There, on her buttocks, was the birthmark. The one he'd kissed and teased her about over three long years ago.

"Ginny." Though a whisper, the word was neither invocation nor benediction. But a lament. A dirge.

"I'm not her," Imogen said with strength she'd not realized she possessed. "Not anymore." Ginny had been a victim. A young and vulnerable ingénue. Untried, ignorant, and ruled by the machinations of selfish and negligent men.

She was that woman no longer.

Imogen stared up at the painting she'd finished in the first few months after she'd been married. When she'd known the broken Duke of Trenwyth was recovering in the hospital. When she had to remember all of the many reasons she couldn't go to him. Her sister, her dying husband, his faulty memory, her charity and reputation. The fact that she'd truly been nothing more to him than a whore he'd fancied one desperate, grief-stricken night.

That all seemed meaningless now.

His breathing roughened behind her, and the small hook of his prosthetic dug into the flesh of her left hip. It reminded her that they'd *both* become different people since that night she'd depicted in the crimson room.

She heard a rip. And felt the evening air kiss the small of her back as her nightgown became a casualty of his mounting rage. The atmosphere shifted, the whip of his fury lashing at her with velvet edges. She'd lied to him. For her crimes, a punishment was forthcoming, of that she could be certain.

Imogen knew that O'Mara and Rathbone still patrolled the premises in shifts. She opened her mouth to scream, but only a sob escaped. She squirmed in his unyielding grasp, and wondered why he did nothing but stand there. Holding her hostage.

The fingers of his right hand shook a little, his grip gentling from punishing to merely bruising.

Lord, he was so strong it sent little chills of fear stabbing at her, followed by thrills of heat. The muscles of his chest swelled against her back, and the buckles of a harness bit into her skin, so close were they pressed together. The sinew of his thighs beneath the soft linen of his trousers bunched against her exposed bottom. Nothing met the softness of her curves but an unending length of hard, angry male.

Lifting her arm in a panicked movement, she meant to strike at him, to poke or scratch at his eyes. Anything that would free her from his silent, terrifying grip. To attack someone behind her, she found, was nigh to impossible.

She encountered the lush hair behind his ear, threaded her fingers through it, and gave a desperate tug.

He snarled.

Then they were falling, but she didn't let him go. Neither did he relinquish his hold on her. In fact, she realized, he controlled their movement to the ground.

The carpet abraded her knees, though the descent had been slow enough not to cause her pain upon impact.

He hit his knees behind her, his left arm stealing around her middle to pull her in, bringing her bare bottom to fit neatly against the front of him. A hot, hard length pressed against the cleft of her ass, impeded only by the thin cloth of his trousers. His grip was iron against her middle; his breath volcanic against the back of her neck.

Then he bit her.

Imogen opened her mouth to cry out, but he'd already begun to lick and lave at the shoulder he'd marked, and her sound of pain escaped as a husky sigh of submission.

It was all he needed to hear.

With another rip, her soft nightgown disappeared. She turned her head to protest, but before any words escaped, he stole her breath by crushing his lips to hers.

Her fingers instantly tightened in his hair, but this time not to pull him away. But closer.

The kiss turned instantly volatile. His tongue seared its way into her mouth. It astonished Imogen that a kiss could convey so much. Unrequited need and a lifetime of desolation. His cultured manners and noble upbringing had done nothing to smother the raw, primal sin that was the soul of this man. He didn't taste her, he consumed her. Devoured her. Until Imogen wondered if she'd also forget who she'd been to him. Or who she'd become.

Too soon, he broke the kiss and bent her over the trunk, using his superior weight to keep her hostage. His hand stole between them, and after a few jerking movements, his fingers gripped her hips once again.

The heat radiating from his arousal warned her a mere breath before the blunt head of his cock kissed the folds guarding her sex. Desire flushed from her in a wet release, and she whimpered as her intimate muscles swelled in sweet anticipation. Her body was ready to accept his dominance, even though *she* might not be.

"Wait—" Her voice sounded too thin. Too low. Too husky to be her own.

"Don't stop me," he commanded, though a ribbon of desperation threaded through the order.

So she didn't.

And he didn't.

He drove inside her with rough power and searing heat. It was like he penetrated her with lightning, striking at her with his hips and injecting an indefinable current that locked every muscle into futile spasms of blistering pleasure.

She threw her head back, a sob or a scream bubbling in her throat, but his hand clamped over her mouth as his cock parted her. Filled her.

He didn't stop until he was seated deep. Deeper than he'd been before. Through a miracle of discipline and will, he held himself perfectly immobile, the bones of his hips digging into the soft flesh of her ass.

"I somehow forgot what you looked like," he finally panted against her ear, the moist heat of his breath eliciting little tremors deep within her. Tremors she knew he could feel, because his great muscles shuddered in kind. "But I never forgot how tight you were," he said from between clenched teeth. "I *never* forgot how it felt to be inside you."

Fat tears squeezed from the corners of her eyes, and found a path where his hand sealed over her mouth.

She did not cry because he hurt her. Not because he took her like this. Like an animal. Like a common whore.

But because he'd remembered. Because she'd been empty every night of her life but one, and now he filled her once more. Perhaps she'd have time to be sorry for that later. Perhaps she'd find her pride, or her purpose, and recall all the reasons this was wrong.

But for now, all she could feel was the thrum of his heartbeat through the hot, turgid flesh inside of her. All she could think was that she wanted him to *move*.

She wriggled her body against his. Pushed and strained against him. Felt the muscles of her sex grip and goad him as she begged him for pleasure with everything but her mouth.

The sound he made was victorious, and a little bit cruel.

But he did as she bade.

He pulled away. Nearly withdrew. Then slammed forward. Again. And again.

Her body opened for him each time he thrust inside, and clenched with lugubrious pulls each time he withdrew.

Imogen looked up as her body was rhythmically, *mercilessly* ground against the leather of the trunk. The man in the painting watched her with lascivious copper eyes like a deviant voyeur. He was the only lover she'd ever known, and she dimly compared him to the one fucking her now.

How different they were. The Cole she'd painted had been confident and deferential, a bit inebriated, but selfless in his giving of pleasure.

The man behind her—the man inside of her—was a singular creature. A primal beast. One driven only by primary instinct and emotion. Lust. Hurt. Need. Rage.

But besides a name, a title, and a body, both men shared one other common trait. A desire for her submission. An inexplicable need to be inside of her, for which they had each gone to rather desperate lengths.

One had paid a small fortune. The other had broken into her home.

Truth be told, she'd wanted to make love to them both. To the haughty duke and the hungry wolf.

Past the painting, beyond the glow of the lantern, and even above the darkness, she could hear hoarse, high noises of encouragement. Of joy. And was astounded when she recognized those noises as her own.

A further jolt of surprise took her as he slipped a finger inside of her mouth, then another. Her eyes widened as he used his prosthetic to press against her ass, to spread her for him, to angle deeper. The chill of the metal against her soft, warm flesh caused her to clench her muscles, and she thrilled to the harsh sound he made. Almost a bark, if a man could produce such a thing.

A rogue wave of fire and force tore through her with such frightening speed, she feared she might faint. The ferocity of it so potent, her womb contracted with it. Spasm chased spasm in relentless pulses of bliss, uncoiling with such astounding force she distantly wondered if this was what dying felt like.

She bit down on the fingers in her mouth, not breaking the skin, and the noise he made was the most inhuman sound of pleasure she'd ever heard in her life. The sound mounted to a groan, then a growl, as his cock swelled impossibly larger inside of her before it erupted, bathing her womb in a quicksilver rush of release.

She realized dimly through her own pleasure that he wasn't, in fact, growling in time to the tremors of his climax, but he was saying her name.

Her name. Not Ginny's.

Imogen.

Her liquid shivers of gratification faded before his did, and she wilted against the trunk with muscles made of melted wax. She was slick with sweat and . . . other things. Warm, languid, and thoroughly pleasured.

They were quiet for a long moment after. Their breaths diminishing in perfect synchronization. She could feel the tension leaching from her muscles and his, and she relaxed into the scandalous intimacy of the moment.

Which was why she couldn't believe he remained inside of her as he bent forward and said in the darkest voice she'd ever heard, "You lied to me."

CHAPTER TWENTY-FOUR

It was one thing to be naked and another thing entirely to be exposed. Uncovered. Laid bare.

When Cole pulled away from her—out of her—leaving his accusation stinging in her ear, Imogen thought that perhaps no one had felt as utterly naked as she did in this moment. Her secret had not only been revealed, but literally uncovered in a cloud of dust and discovery.

Rising to her knees, she glanced back in time to see him turn from her and close his trousers. Imogen didn't at all relish the thought of being on her knees as he stood over her, a tower of wrath and indictment.

So they were going to do this now, she lamented with a weighty sigh, trying to pull her thoughts back from where passion and pleasure had scattered them like shadows before the dawn. Her pristine white nightgown was a cloud of tatters, but she snatched it from the floor with limbs as heavy as the silence between them.

Gaining her feet, she faced him. Lord, but she was

tired now, and suspected that she was still perhaps a little inebriated, though whether on champagne or passion, she couldn't tell.

"I imagine you have a bevy of excuses prepared." He crossed his arms over his broad chest much like a mother would await an explanation from her unruly child.

Imogen clutched her nightgown to her breasts, letting the lace fall to her knees from the voluminous skirts. She noted the way his eyes flicked copper fire over her bare shoulders, her tousled hair, and what parts of her were left uncovered before he fixed them on some point behind her.

How could one person be both so beautiful and so bitter? It was as though he'd been kissed by some ancient god, blessed with uncommon strength and magnificence, and then cursed with loss and guile.

"Have you nothing to say for yourself?" he demanded. "You must have known I'd eventually find out."

"In truth, I hoped you wouldn't." She knew before she noted the twitch of his jaw it had been the wrong thing to say. "What I mean is, I *wanted* to tell you but there was never—"

"You had two *years.*" He stabbed the appropriate fingers into the air, effectively displaying the number while simultaneously making a foul gesture. He probably meant both. "Two *fucking*—" The fingers curled back into a fist, and Cole's head swiveled on a neck thick with straining veins, as though the need to destroy something overcame the ability to finish his sentence and he searched the room for a victim.

She took refuge behind the trunk, which only reached her thighs, so she held up a placating hand. "I know you're angry."

"You know *nothing* of what I feel."

Imogen hesitated, remembering she'd said something very like that to him once. "You don't understand what happened while you were—"

"I was scouring the fucking globe for you and you were next-bloody-door the entire *fucking* time!" With a strong sweep of his hand, the trunk that separated them went flying into the wall.

"Don't, you'll wake the house," she begged.

"We can't have that, can we?" He sneered, his handsome features arranging into a mask of ugly rage. "Can't have poor Cheever finding out his precious countess was once a two-bit whore."

All Imogen's sorrow and guilt evaporated in the heat of her indignation. "Cheever already knows," she revealed, though she had to quell a flinch as more of the color drained from his face, the lines around his hard mouth positively white. "He knows that I was bought once. One night. That you turned a virgin into a prostitute. That you paid twenty pounds. I may have sold myself to you, Your Grace, but I was *never* cheap."

"You cost me more than you know," he snarled.

"Likewise!"

His one blink too many was the only indication he gave that she'd stunned him. What she didn't know, was if the word or the vehemence with which she said it was the reason he faltered. Either way, she wasn't finished.

"You searched for Ginny, you pined for her, because she made you feel something that you'd been missing. Because she fulfilled your needs and became someone you desired. Because maybe for a moment, she made you happy. But did you ever once stop to consider *her* happiness? Her needs? *Her* desires?"

"Stop talking about her like she's dead," he growled. "You are one and the same."

"That's just it, Cole, we're nothing alike, she and I." Imogen stepped closer to the lamplight, convincing herself it was not a retreat, but an illumination. She let the lamp spin her hair into gold and shimmer across shoulders and curves so different from what they'd once been. "You remember a starving woman in a black wig with a painted face and a false name. She was pliant and afraid. Helpless and desperate. Don't you see, Cole, *I* am not *she*." Taking a trembling step forward, Imogen raised her fingers to shape over his rough, clenched jaw, hoping that her touch would soften the hard truths she spoke. "You can't know how sorry I am that you suffered on my account. But just because you bought Ginny for one night, doesn't mean that you own me. Doesn't mean that I owe you anything, least of all an explanation."

His jaw turned to iron beneath her grip the moment before he seized her wrist and ripped it away from his skin as though it had burned him. "Like hell you didn't. You owed me the *truth*, you cruel, selfish—"

"And what would have happened had I come to you? Would you have made me your mistress? Your official whore?" She wrenched her wrist away from his grasp, and to his credit, he allowed it. "You, a high-and-mighty duke, would deign to lower yourself to elevate a common prostitute? Stash her in some frilly rooms to consort with at your leisure until you tired of her, and she'd be cast off as your shameful leavings? Who would *dare* deny—"

"I would have made you my wife!" The admission seemed to startle even himself.

"Don't be ridiculous." A harsh laugh burst from her.

His expression landed somewhere between confounded and murderous.

"Consider how you've behaved toward me since you've known me as the countess Anstruther." This time it was she who advanced upon him, and though he nearly doubled her in size, she felt a stab of victory permeate her ire when he took a step back. "Tell me, exactly, when I should have revealed my tender secret to you? When you hurled your teacup at me? Or perhaps when you publicly humiliated me in front of my investors? Or threatened to ruin me in the garden, vowing to thwart my life's work at every turn. You of all people know what kind of weapon our night together could be in the hands of my enemies. You're the Duke of *bloody* Trenwyth," she cursed. "You've treated me as if I were beneath you since the day you woke after I saved. Your. *Life*. What could *possibly* make you think I'd give you the fodder to ruin mine as you'd so ardently promised to do?"

He opened his mouth, then closed it, then opened it again, his expression losing some of its heat.

"Furthermore, I'm insulted by the arrogant assumption that I'd even consider your hand," she continued. "I, too, yearned for the man who stole my heart three years ago. I've searched for him inside of you a *thousand* times. I gave you every chance to be *that* man, and sometimes, I thought I glimpsed him in your eyes. In your smile. Or in a kind gesture . . ." Her voice broke, and she had to struggle for composure before she said, "I would have revealed myself to *him*." Imogen didn't know which made her angrier, the man in front of her or the tears escaping down her cheeks despite her valiant fight against them. "But now I know that, just like Ginny, he exists no longer."

Cole opened his mouth, but an ominous metallic sound broke their silence.

"Make a move and you die." The impossibly deep voice identified the moment's intruder as imposing, African, and authoritarian even before Inspector Rathbone materialized, a pistol expertly trained on the duke. "Step back," he ordered.

Deadly as a plague, dexterous as a lion, and dusky as a shadow, that was Roman Rathbone. He'd obviously dressed in a hurry, as his shirt draped open, revealing a broad chest of gleaming teak.

His dishabille made Imogen marginally less mortified over her own state of undress, though words eluded her as she realized how close he'd come to catching them doing what they'd done against that trunk only minutes beforehand.

"Your Grace?" Rathbone's swarthy features contorted with indecision as he inched his pistol toward the ground, but not completely. His eyes, a striking gray, quickly assessed the casually dressed duke, the crying countess, the nude portrait, and the trunk in disarray. It was enough for him to keep the gun pointed at the other dangerous man in the room.

Imogen wondered if it was possible to die of humiliation.

"You are to be commended, Inspector." Cole sneered, though he had the presence of mind to turn slowly to face the armed man. "Were I the murderer, I'd only have killed her and everyone else before you deigned to stir yourself from your comfortable suite."

"It was O'Mara's turn to take watch," the inspector explained, bemusement turning into concern.

"Then where *is* he?" Cole bit from between clenched teeth.

The blithe Irishman in question was still in the process of tucking his shirt into his trousers as he all but skidded around the doorway, his brutish features a bit flushed and his expression sheepish.

"Trenwyth?" he sang with delighted recognition. "I was . . . tucking one of the maids in when I thought I heard a crash—" The tableau finally had a chance to register in almost comical degrees of expression. "What in the name of the saints is going on here? Did he hurt you, Lady Anstruther?"

Imogen didn't recognize the bitterness in her caustic sound as her own. Of course she was hurting, and he was the cause, but not in the way O'Mara suspected. She'd let him inside her. Hoped he'd taken her body to lay claim to her, not to shame or castigate her.

She and hope had not often been friends. Especially not when it came to *him*.

"Pull that trigger and make sure you don't miss. Because if you do it'll be the end of you," Cole warned Rathbone, not one to be held or threatened by any means, even by a lawman.

Gathering the vestiges of her strength and the last of her tattered dignity, Imogen stepped forward. "There's no need for violence, Inspectors. He didn't . . . this isn't what it looks like."

Rathbone finally lowered his weapon, his gaze bouncing back and forth with shrewd curiosity. "You want us to . . . leave you two alone?"

Imogen didn't dare look at Cole. Couldn't bring herself to meet whatever terrible censure she'd see in his eyes.

"Perhaps you can escort His Grace out," she whispered, suddenly exhausted.

"Don't bother." Cole's imperious tone froze whatever warmth she had left for him. "I'm already gone."

And in a few furious strides, he was, leaving her alone with two very uncomfortable men.

"Begging your pardon, Countess, but . . . is there someone you'd like me to be fetching for you? Your sister, perhaps, or your ma?" O'Mara asked.

"No, thank you, Inspector. I just . . . need to go to bed. This will all be sorted in the morning."

The two men respectfully averted their eyes as she wrapped her nightgown around her, and marched between them with her chin as high as she'd seen the queen hold hers not long ago. The tears fell faster in the darkness of the stairway as she trudged in the wake of a memory she once treasured. Cole's soporific words spoken in gentle intimacy a lifetime ago.

"You are a rare find, Ginny."

"How's that?"

"A genuine person in a world full of deceit . . . Is Ginny your real name?"

"No,"

"You'll have to tell me what it is."

She had done, after he'd fallen asleep, but that mattered little now. It mattered not at all, in fact. A chill that had nothing to do with her state of undress skittered through her, and for the first time since he'd returned, Imogen felt a true sense of loss and loneliness. Her sumptuous home felt too big and too empty, and her usually swollen heart felt too small and too . . . empty. Emotions battled questions that cried for answers she couldn't summon. It hurt to breathe.

Perhaps he'd been right, and this was inevitable. Out of all the horrific possibilities she'd imagined might arise in the aftermath of the revelation of her deception, there was one consequence she hadn't at all prepared for.

The death of hope.

Since the night they'd met, made love, and separated, she'd carried this strange and feeble hope with her in regard to the Duke of Trenwyth. It sustained her while he'd been missing, and had been whispered in her every prayer for his safety. It had flared when he'd landed in St. Margaret's, miraculously given into her care. *Her,* who cared more than anyone at the time would have guessed.

She'd carried a tiny ember of it with her, she realized in these several months since his return. Tending it gently, giving it fuel with willing breath. Perhaps he'd overcome his antagonism toward her. Maybe, if she was patient enough, if she was kind enough, if she was bright and witty and beautiful enough . . . he'd forget Ginny. He'd forget his imperious arrogance. He'd forget his fury. His pain. His loss and loneliness.

And fall in love with her . . . with Imogen.

Because she'd been in love with him all along. She understood that now. Love had allowed her to be gentle when he was stern. To forgive his cruelty. To understand his pain.

But she'd been a fool to nurse that hope. If a man, especially a man of his birth, wanted a woman, it was for what she could be to him. What she could provide for him while he chased his purposes and passions. A home. An heir. Solace, sex, and sustenance. These were the singular duties of a woman.

But what if a woman had purpose and passions? What if she wanted to reach beyond her dictated place behind her lord and step forward on her own path? History was littered with heroes who had a destiny, who vanquished their foes through means fair or foul.

The man she loved had been determined to be her foe. That was her tragedy. He'd longed for Ginny, but he'd constantly rejected Imogen.

In his arrogance, he'd been certain that offering a place at his side as duchess could only be the culmination of her every desire. That recanting the chance at his hand in marriage was the worst punishment.

It wasn't. Imogen's heart was broken, but she'd meant every word she'd said to him.

She had a purpose. She had passion. She was going to live her life fighting against the vice and villainy that plagued the women and children of her city. That had once taken everything from her. Not in the courts or Parliament as Dorian and Farah did. Not with the law, like Morley.

She'd give the only thing she had. Money, kindness, and care. She'd create the havens that she could and gift those that were searching something they'd lost. Something *she'd* lost.

Hope.

If she believed in anything, it was that everyone deserved a second chance.

And she'd hoped for one with Cole . . . but it was not to be. They'd both become too vastly different. He'd let the injustice he'd suffered turn him into someone hard and angry. She'd been shown benevolent mercy, and had let it take root within her. She'd protected her newfound life with secrets.

And, in doing so, destroyed any chance she had with the man she'd wanted.

It seemed fate would have her choose between her two passions.

She'd made the choice, because in the end she wanted a man who would let her have both. His love, and his support of her chosen path.

Devastation threatened to buckle her knees from beneath her, but she managed to stagger through the open door of her bedroom and leaned heavily upon it after closing it behind her.

Gulping a few desperate breaths of air, she let her nightgown slip to the ground, and padded, naked, to the basin, where she poured water from the pitcher. Numbly, she wet a cloth, found the soap, and washed. First her tear-streaked face, then cooling the skin of her neck and chest heated by mortification. Then she tended to herself intimately, contemplating the possible consequences of what she washed from her thighs. Of what he'd left inside her.

She hadn't the energy to worry about that now, though longing soothed the stab of anxiety clenched in her belly. Discarding the cloth, she turned to face her empty bed, still in disarray from her restless sleep. Her room was so cozy, especially in moonlight and shadow. A delightful shade of pale green, always strewn with fresh flowers in exotic vases perched on delicate white furniture. She'd never dreamed she'd have a place half so lovely or grand. And now . . .

The sobs escaped her then. Burst from her in great, panting gasps.

Now she might sleep here alone forever. All because she fell for a stubborn, haughty, unyielding, irresistible, principled, damaged man.

Bugger it all.

Crying and cursing her own stubbornness, along with

men in general, she stomped to her wardrobe and
wrenched it open, fishing inside for a new nightgown.
Finding one, she closed the doors and began to wrestle
with the tiny buttons, the darkness and her tears impeding her progress. Finally, she lifted it over her head.

"Don't." The voice didn't belong to Cole. Nor to one
of the two men she'd just left downstairs.

The command was gentle, though the intruder smothered her sound of surprise with a strong palm, crushing
the fabric to her lips and nose. "I much prefer you naked."

Imogen's fear turned her mouth to ash as she struggled
and felt herself being smothered, recognizing the pungent,
etherlike odor against her nose and mouth as chloroform.
A powerful anesthesia.

She stilled and held her breath, her head already swimming, unconsciousness both threatening her and beckoning to her.

That voice. It was heartbreakingly familiar. One she'd
thought was a friend. One who'd vowed never to do harm.

"Dry your tears, my love," he whispered as he dragged
her back against his front, much as Cole had mere minutes before. "I'm here. And you're finally mine."

CHAPTER TWENTY-FIVE

Cole broke things, destroyed them, hoping to release the pressure caused by the presence of both extremes. Fire and ice. His skin burned, so much so he wanted to peel it from his body. Fury creating an inferno that threatened to incinerate him.

But for the ice. A bleak and terrifying chill frosted his insides like the panes of a window in January. His chest felt at once brittle and numb, as though one tap could shatter him into sharp and gossamer shards.

He left a path of devastation in his wake as he stormed and thundered through Trenwyth Hall. The corpses of his mother's priceless vases. A splintered antique table Robert had acquired in Sumatra. An upended glass-cased shadow box of rare coins it took his father a lifetime to collect.

Rubbish. All of it. Everything. The trinkets of people who'd left them behind. Who'd left him behind. Who could take nothing with them to the hereafter. The legacy of an empty family built on little else but tradition and held together by insubstantial things. Money. Expectation. A title.

A name.

What's in a name? a star-crossed lover had once inquired. What, indeed?

He reached his study and locked the door, aware that a few of the staff tiptoed up from below stairs to investigate the commotion.

Would a rose by any other name be as sweet? Would a woman by another name remain the same woman?

Apparently not.

American natives had taught him that a name held much power, a belief held by many, including the Catholic Church. If one could exorcise a demon, one must first learn its name.

Leaning against the window, staring out at a garden both foreign and achingly familiar, Cole knew it would take more than even an exorcism to free him of her.

Not of Ginny. Of *Imogen.*

Damn her. He made a fist and raised it, but only rested it gently against the cold pane.

She'd somehow crawled inside of that empty cavern in his chest so many had abandoned. She'd filled it with bright colors. Claimed it with her easily won smiles and infuriatingly stubborn altruism. She'd become a part of him without him even realizing it.

A kind, caring, clever, beautiful woman. A consummate liar.

He worked his jaw over powerful emotion and encroaching indecision. All this time. She'd been right below this window.

A window from which he'd considered her below his notice as well. She'd been right about that.

She'd been right about a lot of things.

Closing his eyes, he leaned his forehead against the window, letting the cool glass temper the heat of his skin. In the darkness behind his lids, he finally conjured Ginny's face. Imogen's face.

She'd been gaunt and pale, all sharp, prominent bones and large, melancholy eyes. He'd thought her an ethereal wraith, a dark-haired, delicate beauty. Was that because he'd not cared to recognize desperation and poverty when confronted with it? He'd not considered that her heavy makeup hadn't been meant to entice, but to conceal. Conceal skin with an exotic hint of color and a touch of freckles.

During every moment he'd spent in that hellish prison, he'd inspected and dissected different parts of their experience together. Of her. The soft hitch of surprise on her breath when he'd pleasured her. The spread of her lashes against her pale cheek when her shyness overcame her. The gleam of her dark hair. The warmth of her body as he sank inside of her. Her delicate shivers of bliss. Her sweet whispers and words.

In that dissection, he'd lost the whole of her. Of course there had been drink, and dimness, and deceit to help muddle things. But had he truly looked at Ginny, he might have actually *seen* her. Furthermore, had he really taken a moment to look at Imogen, at Lady Anstruther, as anything but a collection of labels he'd already given her, he might have found what he was searching for ages ago.

He was *so* angry at her. But no more than he was angry with himself.

He'd thought his hubris would protect him, that he could look down upon the world from this lofty tower and shut out that which threatened his survival and sanity.

But he'd forgotten one very important thing. That whichever room he locked himself into, whichever wall he built around himself, reinforcing it with contempt and cruelty, he'd never been able to escape his worst enemy.

Himself.

His own past, his nightmares, his memories. His prejudices, his upbringing, his title.

Opening his eyes, he gazed down at the garden, *her* garden, and ached.

Imogen was no longer the same woman. She was healthy, vigorous, unashamed. She was the mistress of her own destiny. A destiny that might not include him, because he'd never presented himself to her as an enticement. Only an opponent.

He'd pompously thought the whore he'd fallen for would take him in whatever capacity he offered. That she'd be happy to accept this broken, bitter, barbarous man he'd allowed himself to become.

It had never occurred to him she'd want more. Or that he had no right to her secrets. That he had no claim on her heart.

The cold inside began to lick at his skin now that his ire and ardor had cooled. Now that the warmth he'd found inside of her body faded and the heat of her passion had become frigid rejection.

She'd gently and kindly thrown him out of her home. Out of her life.

Turning to his chair, he reached for his jacket, and paused. Remembering he'd left it on the bench before climbing the trellis to the balcony. He glanced out the window at the empty bench. Then followed the trellis over to the balcony where the door to the master's rooms stood ajar.

In all his years as a spy, he'd learned a rule to entering a house undetected which he'd never broken.

You always leave things as you found them.

He'd shut and locked the balcony door behind him.

What if, in his self-righteous distraction, he'd led a killer right into Imogen's home? What if he was too late?

What if she became a casualty of his pride?

Trenwyth bolted out of his study, almost bowling over his butler. "Send for Inspector Morley," he ordered. "Someone's broken into the Anstruther house."

Unholy dread chased him through his own gardens to the fissure in the wall beneath the tree. The stone and bark abraded his flesh as he forced his way through a space he'd used care to maneuver in the past. He didn't even feel it. Desperation drove him forward.

An arrow of fear pierced his heart, the force of it almost knocking him off his feet as he watched his nightmare become a reality.

The countess suites of the Anstruther manse were not as grand as that of the master's, and did not boast a balcony because of the high, rounded parapetlike structure with a grand window seat. The lady of the house might enjoy the panoramic view from indoors, away from the elements, situated higher than any other room save the attic.

It was from this window that Jeremy Carson was trying to lower Imogen's limp body, secured by nothing but a makeshift hammock of bedclothes tied in what Cole prayed to God were secure knots.

Doused with a fear colder than the Baltic Sea, Cole summoned a burst of speed like he'd never done before, tormented by the knowledge that if Jeremy dropped her now, not even *he* would make it in time.

"She's not dead. But take one more step and she will be."

The threat planted Cole's feet to the ground, his every muscle strung tighter than a crossbow. His temper and desperation pushed the pressure needle to red, heat gathering in his blood with no release. He needed to think. He needed to stay calm.

Imogen's life depended on it.

"I love her. Loved her longer than you, I expect," Jeremy called down casually, and Cole had heard enough lies in his life by now to ascertain the truth. "But I'll send her to heaven before I let you soil her again. See if I don't."

Another truth.

Cole put up both hands, the metal of his prosthetic glinting a little in the moonlight. He hoped it made him seem less threatening somehow. He noticed that, though Jeremy was holding the sheets in both hands, his boot braced against the ledge, he didn't seem to be straining beneath her weight.

"How are you holding her secure?" he asked, fighting to control his voice as terror threatened to steal it from him.

The man's disarmingly young face split into a sneer. "You work the docks long enough, you learn a bit 'bout leverage, don't ya? Though I doubt a toff like you done an honest day's work in his bloody life."

Cole let the taunt go. "Have you harmed her?"

To his astonishment, Jeremy let out a harsh bark of laughter. "That's bloody rich, coming from you." He sneered down at him, his lip curled in disgust. "She was pure as an angel before she met you, before you turned her into a whore."

Cole was well aware of that, and shame needled in beneath his rage and panic. They both loved her. It was something he could use. "Why isn't she moving, Carson? Are you certain she's alive?"

The villain made a derisive noise. "Just dosed her with a bit of chloroform I bribed off of that bitch nurse, Molly, at St. Margaret's before I did her in."

It was difficult to process all the information that sentence contained while simultaneously swallowing the bile churned into his throat by the brick of fear that landed in his belly.

Chloroform was a powerful anesthetic, when used properly. He'd employed it himself, in his tenure as a spy. But in large doses, it would be lethal, especially when mixed with alcohol.

"You murdered Lady Broadmore, and the others." Another bit of knowledge permeated his fear.

Roman Rathbone slid from the garden door, remaining concealed beneath the balcony. He'd removed his shirt and shoes, and was clad in only a pair of dark trousers, shadows, and skin the color of carob.

If Cole could keep Jeremy talking, Rathbone might have a chance to position himself beneath Imogen's body without the madman noticing.

"I did it to save Ginny's life," Jeremy said. "They wanted her, wanted to take her, to watch her suffer, but I wouldn't let them. I gave them substitutes and kept them fed. Flora first, the cheeky whore. That washerwoman in her building. The nanny and the nurse. I didn't want to, you see. But they made me. They were hungry for it."

"Who are they?" Cole asked evenly.

"They. *Them.*" Jeremy hit his temple with his palm repeatedly. "They. They. They." He chanted in time to the strikes.

Cole took an involuntary step forward as the vulnerable bundle that was Imogen swayed precariously now that she wasn't stabilized by both hands.

"I said stay back!" Jeremy looked wild now, his sanity slipping.

Rathbone made progress against the wall, but Cole began to despair that he wouldn't reach her in time. Even if he did, they couldn't be sure the two-story drop wasn't enough to cause them both irreparable damage.

"Jeremy." He stopped. "Mr. Carson, we both love that woman, and want to protect her—"

"You don't love her!" Jeremy produced a gesture of scorn with his free hand, and his grip slipped, dropping Imogen several inches before he grabbed on with both hands again.

Cole died a little in that moment.

"You don't even know what she's been through because of you, do you?" The astonished disgust in Jeremy's voice dishonored him.

Did he? "I never meant to hurt her."

"Empty words, they say." Jeremy squeezed his eyes shut and shook his head, as though trying to clear it. "Empty words from an empty man. Did you know saving your worthless life cost her her position at the hospital? She came to *me* when it happened. Not you. Told me the sad tale, that she worried her family would starve. That night, she was attacked in an alley and she stabbed the man. Almost killed him. But I finished the job, so the blood wasn't on her hands. So she could still go to heaven. So *they* wouldn't take her back to where they are from."

"They?" Cole asked.

"Demons. Demons. Demons Demons . . ." Jeremy said the word faintly at first, then repeated it louder. "They want her. They want her light. But I protect her from them. That's why I'm taking her, don't you see? I'm taking her somewhere they can't find her."

Sweet Christ, he was truly mad. "Who are these demons?" Cole asked, gesturing to Rathbone to hurry. "Where are they? I'll help you fight them."

Jeremy's face fell. He didn't look young anymore.

A cloud crossed the moon, casting the night in pure shadow. Cole dropped his arms while simultaneously unsheathing his hidden blade. He worked to free it from its coil in his prosthesis, his fingers slow with mounting terror. He couldn't see Jeremy any longer as the window had become a black void of shadow.

His eyes tracked where Imogen swayed limply in the white sheet; only a fall of red-gold hair and one delicately arched foot were visible. He'd never been a praying man, but as he carefully and quietly worked on freeing the knife, he prayed to every deity he'd ever heard of in his extensive travels. He bargained. He pleaded. And he vowed.

I would have your forgiveness, God, but I'd side with the devil to save her.

"We all have demons, don't we, Your Grace?" The voice came from the window. It was no longer Jeremy. But someone else. Someone who resided inside of him, a construct of his diseased mind.

Cole knew there was no bargaining with this iteration. "Don't do anything foolish," he ordered, letting the fury seep into his voice. "Whoever you are, it's not worth what I will do to you if any harm comes to her."

"I am one of *them*," the voice confirmed, disappointingly undaunted. "I don't know which I find funnier, the fact that Jeremy thought he could hide her from me, or the fact that you think you can save her from me." The evil laugh that rolled from the darkness twisted the knife in Cole's gut.

She slipped farther down, before stopping with a jerk, her body swinging against the side of the house.

A raw growl escaped Cole, and he rushed forward.

"No you don't," the voice taunted, releasing her once more, and again catching her with a cruel yank.

Barely controlling the tempest inside of him, Cole again planted his feet. "What do you want?" he asked tightly, feeling at once helpless and homicidal.

"I *want* to decide what would be more fun. Making you watch her die like this, or pulling her back up and seeing if you can race up here before I crush her windpipe with my bare hands."

Cole's breath caught, his eyes swinging wildly to the clouds, to Rathbone, to his knife, and back to Imogen.

"You die tonight," he vowed. "But I'll give you one chance to go to the grave with your limbs attached. Let her go. *Now*. Or the consequences will be more painful than you can imagine."

"Let her go, you say?" The clouds shifted, just enough . . .

"You choose." Cole's voice was hard. Violent. Almost as demonic as the man holding her hostage. "Release her, and you die quickly. Do anything else, and you die screaming."

"Very well . . ." Jeremy's voice turned serpentine. Almost gleeful. "You've talked me into it. I'll release her."

And he did.

Cole threw the blade with lethal precision as three things happened with perfect, simultaneous fluidity. Rathbone caught Imogen, rolling them both to the ground to minimize impact. O'Mara splintered open the door to the countess suite with a powerful kick. And Jeremy pitched forward out the window as the knife he'd not seen found purchase in his chest, before he landed in a broken twist of limbs.

Gasping her name, Cole sprang for Imogen, grappling her away from Rathbone and gathering her to his chest.

He checked her in the dark, running hands over her naked body, searching for bumps or breaks before tenderly pulling the sheet tighter around her.

"She didn't fall far," Rathbone confirmed. "He'd lowered her enough while taunting you for me to safely catch her."

Then why wasn't she moving?

"Is she breathing?" Rathbone's voice deepened with anxiety.

Cole put his cheek next to her ear and held it there for longer than he needed before summoning the strength to lift his eyes. "Get a doctor."

CHAPTER TWENTY-SIX

Imogen was tempted never to wake. In dreams she found what bliss had been denied her for so long. What might remain lost forever.

Cole, wrapped around her like a long, sinuous protective shell. Sharing his warmth while whispering soft, longing, unintelligible things in her ear.

Sometimes others would visit her dreams, would tempt her back to consciousness. Her mother, anxious and encouraging. Her sister, shy and tearful. Her friends. Dr. Longhurst with his short, pert directives. Argent's smooth and sinister voice punctuated with Millie's lively alto. Scottish brogues and soft words of support.

But then *his* dark presence would drive them away, and his shadow would settle upon her with a delicious intimacy. She knew it was Cole because even though God painted him with the sheen and strength of alloy, he was a creature of this place. Of the darkness.

And she was not. She wanted sunlight and bright colors and soft comforts.

But she didn't want to leave him in the dark. And so she'd stay a little longer, as long as she could. Stay *here* where he'd say things against her ear. Beautiful, wondrous words she'd always fantasized she'd hear from him.

"I do love you, Imogen. *You.* Not your memory. Not Ginny." A gentle weight would depress her mouth, and she'd feel such intense joy, but only for a moment.

Because that spike of pain would return, and she'd remember this was a dream.

"Wake up," Cole would coax her softly, his hand a gentle demand against her own. "Wake up, Imogen, it's time."

"Must I?" she queried groggily. "Must I wake? Must I leave you in the dark?"

"It's not dark," said the dream voice, a little curtly now. "It's day. And I need you awake so I can examine you. Can you open your eyes? Can you squeeze my hand?"

She did as he asked. Well, that was uncharacteristically sweet of him to offer to—

Imogen slammed into awareness. She'd squeezed his hand. His *left* hand.

Her eyes flew open and met the relaxed, gentle gaze of Dr. Longhurst, who was bent over her, framed by the familiar canopy of her own bed.

Bugger. She blinked away tears of disappointment, staring at the motes of dust dancing in the silver dawn.

"Welcome back," he said, as gently as he ever said anything.

She tried to hide her distress, but she could tell by the twitch of concern on his brow she'd not succeeded.

"How do you feel?" he asked alertly.

She took stock of her body. Wriggling her hands and toes, tensing her muscles, testing her joints. "Other than a touch of queasiness and a very dry mouth, I feel fine. Maybe a little bruised on my shoulder."

"May I?" He held up the stethoscope, and she nodded, submitting to his examination.

Finally, after he'd used almost every instrument in his bag but the sharp ones, he poured her a glass of water from the pitcher someone had thoughtfully perched on her bedside table.

She pushed herself up to sit against her mountain of pillows and accepted the drink. Tears stung her eyelids again, and Imogen wiped at a stabbing itch in her nose.

"Lungs are clear. Reflexes good. Skin shows signs of normal blood flow. Your pulse is steady, if a little slow," Longhurst informed her, his eyes sweeping away from her apparent emotion as though it made him uncomfortable. "It is believed that when chloroform is lethal, it's because it damaged the heart. But I'm confident that yours is strong."

"Are you?" she whispered, trying to breathe through the cavernous pain in her chest. "I'm not so sure." It didn't feel strong. Only broken. Truly damaged. She'd known to expect devastation when all was said and done—when Cole had uncovered her secrets—but not this harrowing desolation.

Someone entered the room so violently, her bedroom door crashed against the wall.

Imogen started, gasped, and clutched a hand to her chest. Her heart certainly worked now, as it was thundering like an entire herd of galloping wildebeests.

And not just because of the startlement. But because Cole stalked to the foot of her bed, looming with a barely leashed, aggressive emotion vibrating in the air around him. He stood over her, dressed in only a rumpled white shirt and dark trousers, scanning her with sparking copper eyes. He reminded her once more of an archangel, possessed of such flawlessly rendered features that only those heavenly warriors dared to demonstrate, as no human deserved them.

He certainly didn't, she thought mulishly.

"What is he doing here?" she breathed, not realizing she addressed Longhurst instead of Cole. She wasn't ready for this . . . She was barely awake, and should like to fall back into a coma any moment now.

The man in question drew cruel brows together in a scowl.

"He hasn't left since he saved your life," Dr. Longhurst informed her with a long-suffering exhale. "Good thing you survived," he muttered, glancing at the duke. "For both our sakes."

"How is she?" Cole demanded, also addressing Dr. Longhurst though his eyes would not leave her, would not stop drinking her in.

He'd saved her life? Jeremy had been in her room when he attacked her which meant . . . Cole had come *back* after he'd left.

"I—I'm fine," she stammered.

He held up a hand to silence her, and Imogen's astonishment turned to something like outrage.

"How is she?" Cole asked again in the voice of a man unused to repeating himself. "Was she injured in the fall? Any permanent damage done?"

"The fall? What fall?" Imogen's question fell on deaf ears.

Dr. Longhurst furrowed his brow. "The chloroform

mixed with the alcohol in her system seemed to intensify the other's effect, resulting in a longer loss of consciousness. Though she was dropped from the window, her lax pliability may have been what saved her life—"

"I was dropped from the window?" she asked, a great deal louder this time.

"How *is* she?" Cole exploded, taking a threatening step toward the doctor.

Longhurst leaped up, obviously glad her bed was in between them. "In a word. She's fine."

"Good. Get out."

Imogen made a few stupefied sounds of disagreement as the doctor gathered his instruments. Finally she found her voice. "I already said I was fine. I want someone to explain to me what happened."

Longhurt froze, forehead creased with indecision.

"Get. *Out*." Cole's teeth no longer separated, and his lips drew back with a snarl. The good doctor abandoned her to Cole's smoldering glare and ticking jaw with undue alacrity.

Imogen closed her eyes to summon strength, but found her reserves depleted. "I know you're still angry." She sighed. "But I simply don't have the strength to listen while you—"

"You *will* listen to me, woman, and you will listen well." His tone brooked no argument, his eyes glinting with a warning to rival the sparks from Hephaestus's hammer as he tempered Zeus's thunderbolts. "You are *going* to marry me, Imogen, and this is why." He ticked the reasons with the touch of his index finger to that of his alloy ones. "Firstly, because I want you to, and I happen to be a very powerful duke who is in the habit of getting what he wants. Secondary, because you will find it easier to attain more of your philanthropic objectives as a duchess rather than merely a countess."

"M-merely a countess?" Had those words ever been spoken before? Had he just . . . proposed marriage? Surely that couldn't be right.

"I'm not finished," he said curtly.

She made an astonished sound somewhere between a squeak and a groan. Was it possible she was still dreaming? That she was having some strange and ill reaction to the chloroform? Surely that had to be the case, as it sounded like he was agreeing to her charity work, offering his title as support.

"Tertiary." He sent her a quelling look. "After the events of last night—no, strike that—due to your terrifying and *infuriating* tendency over the past few years to attract various enemies and obsessed lunatics—not to mention your affinity to find yourself in dangerous situations—it only makes sense that we reside together so I no longer have to rush all the way next door in order to continue to save your life. Which is, apparently, my new vocation and takes up entirely too much of my time. And in conclusion because—"

"Because you love me?" Imogen asked, gasping in a breath tinged with that very thing she'd thought had abandoned her.

Hope.

His lashes lowered over his eyes, as his gaze slid elsewhere to avoid hers. "Of course I love you," he told her bedpost, worrying at something imaginary in the woodwork with distracted, anxious fingers. "I informed you and your entire household of that only a million times last night when I thought . . ." His sentence trailed away as Imogen watched his throat work as though to swallow shards of glass.

"Cole," she murmured gently. "Look at me."

"I can't." He stood staring at her bedpost, waging a silent, desperate struggle with his greatest opponent. Himself. "I can't *fucking* survive something like that again," he finally admitted in a suspiciously husky voice. "I'd return to prison before I ever saw you in danger like that. It was the singular worst experience of my life."

Imogen glanced at his prosthetic, the whole of it visible as his shirtsleeves had been rolled up at some point during his vigil over her. He couldn't mean that.

Although . . . Could it be she'd not dreamt of him lying next to her? That he'd really been there?

"I mean it." His voice allowed no question.

Her breath left her in a rush, half gasp, half sob, as Imogen lifted her arms to beckon him to her.

Suddenly he was there. Her covers were gone and he replaced them, clutching her to him as he took her offered mouth with ferocious gentility. Clinging to him, she relished the heat building inside of her, answering the scorching flames he licked into her mouth with a demanding tongue. She tasted love on him, love and fear and earnest need.

Desire fanned through her, at once tensing and releasing her muscles. She turned into a puddle beneath him, her legs falling open, her body making way for his weight.

"Good sweet God," he groaned. "I'm going to taste you everywhere."

He cradled each side of her face like a monk at prayer, one hand warm flesh, and the other cold steel. So much like the dichotomy of this man.

His lips fanned over hers with skillful, drugging pulls. His tongue made wicked swirls inside of her mouth, exploring with unapologetic languor. The groan was that of a damned soul finding sanctuary. His tongue, a sword of silk, penetrated and retreated in a rhythm that flooded Imogen's loins with passion.

Abruptly, she pulled away. "Where is everyone?"

His brow furrowed with confounded indignation, lips wet and hard above her as he processed her words between panting breaths of mounting lust. "You interrupted what was possibly the best kiss in the history of the empire to ask such a question," he said tightly.

She loved this arrogant, grumpy beast with all her heart. "I'm about to make love to you, Your Grace, and I don't want to be interrupted."

The temperature in his eyes flared from molten to volatile. "Your mother forced everyone to go to church to pray for you." He touched his nose to hers with sweet affection that caused her heart to double in size, simultaneously slipping a hand to wander perilously close to her breasts. "Lovely woman, your mother."

"Bless her pious heart," Imogen agreed, then arched her body against his, silently pleading for him to resume her ravishment.

He lit her blood on fire with his next kiss, then knelt up and over her to grapple with his shirt, his frantic hand less dexterous than it had been before.

"Here, let me." Imogen batted his hand away, unfastening his shirt and pulling it down wide, breathtaking shoulders. "I suppose dressing and undressing you will be one of my many wifely duties," she said, discarding the garment to the floor before spanning her hands over the familiar width of his chest.

"I have a valet," he argued haughtily, then stilled, ceasing to even breathe, though his heart thundered beneath her palm. "Did you say wife?" His voice was laced with a hesitancy she'd never before heard from him.

She nodded, her throat full of emotion. "I love you too," she managed.

Struck similarly mute, his eyes shone with something more powerful than heat, more eternal than lust. More selfless than need.

Gently, slowly, he slid the bodice of her nightgown off her shoulders, and she helped him ease it away from her.

His hot gaze roamed her like an impatient surveyor would an uncharted land, as though he couldn't decide where to explore first. He settled for the arch of her throat, barraging her with an assault of kisses as they both worked to free him of the rest of his garments.

Ripples of warmth sang along her skin when his lips reached her breasts, taking her nipples into his mouth and stroking them into taut and tender peaks. She made a soft sound underscored with desire, her fingers digging into the hard power of his shoulders. She'd not known she'd been pushing him lower until he complied, the tense muscles rippling as he descended her body, marking the journey with his tongue.

Oh Lord, perhaps she wasn't ready for this just yet. To say "I love you" was one thing, to . . . to let him do what he . . . well, that was quite another.

"Oh . . ." She lost her breath as he imprisoned her thighs open, not preparing her at all before the flat of his tongue spread her sex apart.

Imogen gasped, and bucked, knowing the moisture he trailed against her intimate flesh wasn't only from his mouth, but from her body.

An appreciative moan vibrated against her, sending echoes of pleasure to her every extremity. Another unhurried lick cleaved her world in two, though he stopped the moment before he reached the quivering pearl of her clitoris. He circled it instead, stopping to nibble here, to tease there, tormenting her with skillful evasion.

"Cole," she begged, desperately grasping for his hair. "Please."

Another pleased groan caused her feminine muscles to clench against the sensual promise in the sound, and she surged against his mouth. He latched on to her then, his clever tongue flicking and laving, creating sensations of overwhelming delight.

She cried hoarse relief to the canopy as wave after wave of crippling ecstasy crashed over her. Her breath came in sobs and inarticulate words. It felt like bliss flowed from his tongue into her body, bowing it with paralyzing spasms until the fingers she'd used to hold him to her now clutched at him to pull away before she expired from ecstasy.

His glossy lips lifted with wicked masculine delight as he prowled up her body. He wiped his mouth before hunkering over her, his movements impeded slightly as he carefully situated his left arm.

Imogen reached for it, and didn't miss the hesitation that overtook his posture.

"You don't need this," she soothed. "Not with me." He didn't look at her as she unbuckled it and set it aside, though a nearly inaudible gasp escaped him as she smoothed soft fingers over the rounded skin left with similar marks her thighs suffered after she removed her garters at the end of the day.

Then he was pulling her beneath him, his strength absolute, and his alacrity remarkable.

The blunt head of his cock prodded her, finding where desire and release made her wet and open. Locking his eyes with hers, a tenderness there she'd not read before, he rolled his hips forward, feeding her inch by agonizing inch until he filled her completely.

Her body. Her heart.

Retreating, he glided inside once again, aided by her slick desire, sinking a little deeper with each gentle thrust. At last he rested, fully seated, inside of her. Heated steel sheathed by silk and velvet.

The way he looked down at her broke Imogen's heart. It was the astounded, incredulous expression she imagined the family of Lazarus felt once he awoke from the dead. An interruption of pure grief. A revelation of something eternally lost.

A little bit worship, a little bit disbelief. A vulnerable incomprehension of happiness.

"How could I not have known?" he moaned, dropping his head from his powerful shoulders to shower her with light, reverent kisses. "How could I not have recognized you by how badly I wanted you?"

Slowly, he withdrew and pressed forward once more, their breaths mirroring one another's in perfect synchronization. "Wanted this." He lifted and sank with dewy, pulsing friction. "Only you. No one else ever . . ." He trailed away, losing the ability to form words as he became intent upon the growing ferocity of his rhythm.

Imogen relished the sensation of his hard, male body moving against her. The strength in his corded arms. The weight of his chest against her breasts. The defined curl of his abdomen with each thrust. Even the way the coarse hair of his muscled legs tickled the inside of her thighs.

He thrust deeper, ever deeper, and she lifted to meet him, chasing a thrum of sensation coiled around her spine, the promise that if she could angle just . . .

There. In one, long, smooth stroke he stretched her

wider than she thought possible, filled her to glorious effect, and she lost herself over a precipice from which there was no return. She distantly heard him growl her name, and she tried to answer him through pleasure that shattered her into a thousand pieces.

It wasn't until they both melted into an entwined knot of contentment that Imogen returned to herself. Overcome with emotion, she held him to her, one hand stroking over the straining muscles of his back, the other threading through the silk of his hair.

He breathed out in a sigh so long and hollow she wondered if he expelled tension and emotion kept there for three long years.

They remained joined, clinging together, no longer separated by secrets or walls. They let their hearts beat next to one another as rare sunlight broke over the city.

Finally, he stirred, pulling away, his face a mask of sorrow and shame when he gazed down at her.

"Last night . . ."

She pressed soft fingers against his hard lips. "We don't have to speak of the past."

He kissed her hand, and then covered it with his own, moving it from his lips to enlace their fingers. "I was hurt," he conceded. "Wounded that you weren't searching for me. That I was right in front of you for so long, alone and lost in absolute darkness, and you didn't reach for me . . . I don't blame you, understand that, I just . . ."

"I can't tell you how many times I wanted to reach for you," she said. "But I was afraid. I didn't know how to find you. If you were still there. If you'd even want me anymore."

He tucked a tendril of her hair away from her face, true veneration smoothing the regret she read in him. "How could anyone not want the warmth of the sun on their face after so long in the shadows?" He became serious. "You are the only light I've known. And I must warn you, the sun cannot shine so bright for me now that I've lived in darkness. You were right about so many things, but especially that." He held his empty wrist aloft, and she covered it with her hand. "That year changed me. Carved me away from myself, until I barely even recognize the face in the mirror. I have clawed my way back to some semblance of humanity, but I fear—I know—I cannot be the man I was when we met."

Imogen lifted her head and nuzzled at him, melting at the sibilant sound he made deep in his throat. "Then I will love the man you have become. And if you live in the shadows, I'll find you patches of sunlight, and we'll venture into them together when you are able."

He clutched her to him with a desperate strength that almost hurt. "I will love you for your light, if you can love me through the dark times. And that love will be like the clear night sky when the moon is full. Not like the sun . . . but beautiful and bright enough to find our way."

A tear escaped Imogen's eye and slid between them, though this one carried happiness instead of sorrow.

She realized with a little alarm that he hadn't yet released her, that his body remained tense with an emotion other than pleasure.

"What's wrong?" she inquired, soothing a hand over his bunched muscles.

"When I think of the things I said, of how I took you last night . . ." He buried his shame in her hair. "God, I was such a beast."

"You *are* such a beast," she teased, rolling her hips beneath him and smiling when he twitched within her. "To me, you have always been a wolf." She blew across his neck, watching the skin burst into gooseflesh and a ripple chase down the muscles of his spine, making his cock gloriously full once more. "You know the one—from all the cautionary fairy tales—who devours the hapless innocent should she venture into his lair." She wriggled beneath him feeling naughty and happy and ready to play after so much work and fear.

"That I am, my love," he growled, using his teeth to nibble at her ear, her neck, and then closing his lips around the bite to soothe it with his tongue. Heat rushed between her legs, carrying moisture with it.

"I could sup on you for a lifetime and never get enough," he growled.

"Then—" She struggled between hitched breaths as he began to move. "You must devour me one bite at a time."

"Gladly," he breathed. "Every. Delicious. Morsel."

It didn't take a lifetime. Only the span of a few enchanted hours.

Coming soon. . .

*D*on't miss the next novel
in the Victorian Rebels series by
KERRIGAN BYRNE

The S*cot*
B*eds* H*is* W*ife*

Available in October 2017
from St. Martin's Paperbacks